"What do you mea
"I mean, he
The only thing he can b
trust me. It's my fault that you were even in this position. I thought I could protect you myself but I'm failing. You need to go to your Guild, you need to tell them what's going on and ask for their help."

"You see, it's not as simple as that."

"You're going to have to make it simple. We don't have any other choices. I promise you," he reached forward and took her hand, "I will find the Masterson Files and I will end this. Then they won't come after you anymore. You'll finally be safe. And you're right, working for Corinthe...you might not come out of this free and that's what I want. I want you to be free."

He offered her his open hand.

"Come on, I'll take you home."

"Thanks, but I don't think so," Rune said, ignoring him, his hand and his offer. Instead, she stood up and went to the landline sitting on a small side table by the couch. She was flipping a small card in her fingers as she picked up the receiver to start dialing.

"Who are you calling?" he demanded. She turned as she waited for the dial to summon her callee, smiling at him softly. "Hello, Maxamillion. Yes, I slept fine, thank you. Look, I don't want to take up too much of your time..."

"What are you doing?!" St. Benedict demanded, crossing the space to hit the plunger and hang up her call. Quickly, she moved to block him with her body as she continued to talk with a light and airy voice.

"Yes. I have a counter offer for you."

Copyright © 2018 byMegan Mackie
ISBN 978-1-950565-92-4
Cover design by J. Caleb Clark
Edited by Jenna Stanton
Line-edited by Patricia Lee Macomber
All rights reserved. No part of this book may be used or reproduced in any manner whatsoever without written permission except in the case of brief quotations embodied in criticalarticles and reviews
For information address Crossroad Press at 141 Brayden Dr., Hertford, NC 27944
A Mystique Press Production - Mystique Press is an imprint of Crossroad Press.
www.crossroadpress.com

Crossroad Press Trade Edition

THE SAINT OF LIARS

By Megan Mackie

For my teacher, Phyllis

"True love will triumph in the end—which may or may not be a lie, but if it is a lie, then it's the most beautiful lie we have."

- John Green

Prologue

Justin Masterson rushed up his drive, fumbling with the keys. The stupid light over the door didn't kick on as he approached and it made it twice as hard to find the front door key. His trembling, sweating hands didn't help any. He about screamed in frustration when the pile of keys dropped in a jangled mess onto the front stoop.

Checking his voice at the last second, he instead vented his frustration at the doorbell.

"Come on, come on. Fucking hell Anna, answer the goddam door," he growled, before bending to retrieve the keys, scraping his knuckles on the rough concrete and drawing a little blood. The sting seemed to refocus him and he managed to find the right key in time for the light to sputter on. Dressed in an unattractive pair of pajama pants and one of his black undershirts, his stupid wife Anna opened the front door.

"Justin? What's wrong...?" she started to ask, but he shoved passed her.

"Get dressed," he ordered. He made his way to the back office behind the stairway of their two story house. Passing the mirror that hung in the semi-dark hallway, he wouldn't have recognized himself if he had bothered to look long enough. Tall and slender, Justin had always been considered a handsome catch of a man. He had the angular face and lithe, long body of a rock star while his brain was deemed genius level protégé. Coupled with the charm of Don Juan, the fact that he was married was rarely a deterrent for other women.

Instead of doing as she was told, his stupid wife, who would rather stuff her face with chocolate than abide by the strictures laid out in their pre-nup that she remain a certain weight, followed him into the office.

"Justin, what is going on? Where have you been?"

"We need to leave. Tonight. Get whatever you can't live without," he said, taking a direct line for his computers. He needed to erase everything, everything he had ever created, but he wasn't sure there was time. And that might be stupid anyway. If the company caught up with him, he would need a bargaining chip.

"Justin, what do you mean we are leaving?" the stupid wife persisted. She crossed her arms over her ample chest, one of the few parts about her he actually liked. The gesture was more to comfort herself than to display anger or defy him and he checked himself. Screaming at her would slow things down. He needed her to comply.

"Something bad has happened. You need to trust me and do what I say." He didn't look at her as he spoke, typing furiously at the computer. For the moment they still seemed secure, but tick-tock, tick-tock. He simultaneously started uploading and downloading, splitting the program into fragments. That would work. He would be able to find all these pieces again, both in real life and in the digital realm. He had to hurry. Hurry. Think faster. Be cleverer. He could still win this.

"Where is my spare cell phone?" he asked himself, as he plugged the one from his pocket into his system.

It shocked him to turn and see Anna still standing there. She had moved in closer, doing that eerie trick she had to find things without looking for them. She swore she wasn't a Talent but no one had been able to explain to him how she did such a thing without magic. It made his skin crawl every time. The small, black phone emerged from the mess on his desk as she pulled it out from underneath a stack of papers. There was no way she could have simply seen that.

"I said go!" This time he shouted. Goddammit! Why couldn't the stupid woman do what she was told!

"No," she said, jutting her chin out in timid defiance. "Not this time. You will tell me what's going on." A single tear rolled down her cheek and a small part inside Justin ached. He hated it when she cried.

It only provoked his anger further.

"If you don't get upstairs this minute, I will leave your worthless fat ass behind!" He started toward her then and Anna flinched, dropping the phone to shattering the screen on the floor. She backpedaled away from his larger form. He had never hit before, so he had no idea why she was giving him that reaction. He pushed the guilt away, deciding he didn't care enough about her in order to even bother. He didn't have time for this.

"Get upstairs," he growled and began to turn away.

Her hazel eyes darkened and something flashed behind him. Then those same eyes widened. Justin turned toward the light, white and cold, bursting through the windows.

It was too late.

"Justin?! What is happening?"

"I...I did something...." he started, but it was impossible to finish. How could he explain it?

"What did you do?!" she demanded, her voice becoming shrill with fear. The leaves and grass outside swirled malevolently as an oncoming storm kicked up. Shadows cut across the cold light.

Justin rushed to his computers. He had to destroy them, destroy everything. Forget the bargaining chip.

"Most of it is sent," he muttered to himself, as he checked the screen. The audio pulse coder had completed its jobs, transforming his work into transferable sound. The auto dialer had sent those pieces to fill every voicemail box of every contact number he had ever known in that phone. It would have to be enough, but what about the computer itself? With a mighty shove, the computers went off the table.

"Justin!"

"Fire, we need to burn it down!" Some part of him knew he wasn't thinking rationally anymore, but that wasn't the part in charge either.

"Justin, what is happening? Answer me!" Anna grabbed his arm, yanking him back even as he tried to grab the small crafting blowtorch from the desk where he built and soldered his own hardware. It was a tiny blowtorch but needs must....

He didn't realize he had backhanded Anna off of him until he heard her hit the back wall. It was too surreal. The light, the shouting coming from outside, the sight of his young, curvy wife sliding down the wall, her face stunned and hurt. He stood there shocked, holding the lit blowtorch in hands that no longer seemed attached to his body.

What had he done?

"I embezzled money from the company," he heard himself say. He needed to answer her. Needed to answer that face that looked so betrayed and hurt. "They're coming for us."

He hurled the blowtorch. Why did it break so easily? The fire erupted. His notebooks and circuit boards, his entire short life's work. The only thing besides himself that he cared about. He felt nothing as he watched the flames lick it all up. He felt like he was standing in a vacuum of time as he watched it all burn.

"Justin!" Anna screamed. Sight, sound, and heat flooded into sharp relief. Justin turned in time to see three men dressed in black military swat gear double march through the door, weapons drawn. Two of the men went for his wife, hauling her up by her outstretched arms that were meant to repel them. Where had the third man gone? It was all happening too fast.

Disoriented, Justin tried to bolt forward, imagining in his mind that he was going to haul the huge men off of her. Instead, his momentum was arrested backward. More men had entered through the office windows and seized him from behind. Why was this happening?

Someone punched and all Justin saw were stars. When the stars cleared, he was being pressed face down on the ground as cold metal snapped onto his wrists. The weight of the hired muscle holding him down was crushing the air out of him. Through the chaos of fire, smoke and boots he saw Anna.

She was in the same position he was, her head pinned to the side as a man straddled her from behind to handcuff her. Her face was a mess of tears and snot. She was so ugly when she was afraid.

"Ok, let's get these assholes up," a commanding voice said.

"Justin?" Anna's voice pleaded as they locked eyes.

"You stupid bitch," he snarled. "Why didn't you just do as you're told?"

Chapter 1

Six Years Later

Rune Anna Leveau sat in the Lucky Devil's booth staring at the open magic tome before her. Her bar, also called the Lucky Devil after the iconic statue that sat in that booth with her, was empty, closed for a week of renovations. Cleaning supplies were lined up on top of the old well-loved, well-maintained bar. All of the bottles of liquor that usually lined the back wall were gone, stored away in the back while the dust and magic were flying. At least, what little magic they could afford.

Liam was kicking up plenty of dust behind the bar. Her four-armed bartender had been going hard at the wood shelving with polishing oil, bringing back the shine that the metal tin promised was in there somewhere.

In the next room she could hear Alf, both her bar manager and one of the retainers of her Wizard's House, shouting. She ducked her head closer to her book. She was not going to get up to see what was going on. Even if she would intervene, there was a good chance he wouldn't listen to her anyway. For one thing, he simply knew more about the business of running a bar than she did. For another thing, he had barely accepted that Rune was the true Heir of the Magdalene, the Wizard House of her Aunt Maddie that was more or less attached to the bar itself. After her death, Aunt Maddie had left everything to Rune, despite all of Alf's strenuous objections. And even though Alf had sworn his fealty to her, the new official "whatever magic user" of the House of the Magdalene, it was still hard to say for certain some days who was the boss of whom. She was having a hard enough time trying to figure out the magic required to reanimate the bar trashcan.

Normally, the squat awkward trashcan hopped around back and forth behind the bar, catching any refuse that the bartenders swept down to it. Lately, it had been doing a poor job, moving sluggishly and failing to catch the peanut shells and napkins that was its regular diet. Last week it failed all together. Now it stood there, like any other trashcan, completely devoid of magic.

"So how does this work?" Ally, Rune's teenage retainer, asked. The beautiful girl sat across from her in Lucky Devil's booth trying to help. Ally was the newest addition to the House of Magdalene, though she was the first to swear fealty to Rune. Ally's long blonde hair was in her "serious" braid and she wore a t-shirt and jean shorts instead of her usual catholic school uniform. The city of Chicago was in the full swing of summer and school had gotten out a few weeks before. Unlike other teenagers, instead of going to the beach or working a part time job, Ally was attending to her duties as a wizard's, or whatever's, retainer. So far it had mostly involved being Rune's personal assistant.

Even with the windows fully open and the breeze from the outside, the bar was sweltering with Chicago heat, a special kind of heat only those who lived there completely understood and could complain about with authority. The air regulation spell inside the bar, which kept temperatures adjusted appropriately not only during the seasons but based on internal crowd size, went kaput hard last week. Rune had tried to scrounge up some used window units, but they too were not up to the job.

Wiping sweat from her forehead, Rune took a sip of lukewarm water. Ally tugged at the old spell book, but only succeeded in reading the words upside down. Not that it would have done her any good as the book was handwritten and not by someone who had practiced their penmanship.

"I mean, can you really cast this?" Ally asked, squinching her perfect eyebrows at the page. "I mean, you're only a Talent. And your Talent has nothing to do with animating things, right?"

"Nope. Finding things, and occasionally people, has nothing to do with Reanimation magic," Rune said distractedly.

"Then how you gonna cast a Reanimation spell?"

"Very carefully." Rune finally looked up from her tome. "Look, do you have three thousand dollars for a Reanimation crystal?" Ally shook her head glumly. "If I can't make it work then we're only out a hundred." Rune flipped the book back to the first chapter, wondering if her teacher voice sounded anything like Maddie's had. "At its core, all magic, no matter the Talent, is a transfer of energy. This is why if one magic practitioner creates a spell and stores it into a crystal, another magic practitioner with a completely different Talent can activate that spell by feeding it magical energy. That same principle applies to imbuing any object with a continually running spell. It's just really, really, really hard."

"Then why not make up a bunch of Finding crystals, sell those, and buy a Reanimation crystal?" Ally asked.

A look of guilt crossed Rune's face. "I don't actually know how to transfer a Finding spell into a crystal. It's not a very common Talent and every time I've tried, even with Maddie's help, I couldn't pull it off."

"But I thought…." Ally sat back in the booth, chewing on her words as she tried to work it out. "Then what do we do?"

"Come up with three thousand dollars, try it ourselves, or live life without an animated trashcan since there is no tech equivalent to this. I'm trying out option number two."

"But I mean, couldn't you go back to the original person who cast it and get it recast for cheaper or something?" Ally pressed.

"No, she's dead," Rune said, staring hard at the book's writing.

"Oh, that sucks." Then Ally went still as what Rune said connected up for her. "Oh, sorry. You mean, your aunt…."

"All the magic in here was cast by Maddie. She was a real wizard, not some Talent hack," harrumphed Alf as he appeared beside the table. Alf was a little person and that put his chin at about level with Lucky Devil's elevated table top. His size didn't stop him from leaning his knuckles against the edge of the table, becoming an imposing presence all the same. "Maybe you could use your 'Finding' Talent to find the real Heir of the Magdalene."

Rune didn't reply to the jibe, only looked at Alf with an impassive face, waiting. At first he only stared back, challenging her, but then slowly he pursed his lips harder and harder together until a very terse "My Lady," came out. Then Rune smiled a Cheshire cat smile at him.

She knew it was a bit perverse to force him to address her by the honorific when she forbade Ally, her only other retainer, to use it. But, he did try to force the bar out from under her with their mortgage company. She should have at least fired him for that, except he then swore fealty to her as the Head of the House. As punishments for betrayal goes, addressing her as "My Lady" every time he spoke to her, would be very mild if he didn't hate it so much.

"Do you need something, Alf?" Rune asked in a sickly sweet voice. The shorter man worked his jaw, the beard that lined his chin working with it. He dropped the mail on the table in the middle of the spell-casting supplies. Ally picked up a colorful pamphlet that was sitting on top.

"The last of the self-cleaning tubs in the Main Bar finally kicked it," he said, crossing his arms. "One of the new waiters left glasses in there overnight and the whole thing has shorted out. We lost over a dozen glasses."

"How did we lose glasses? They're just sitting in soapy water." Rune asked, furrowing her brows together.

"I have no idea, girl! I don't know how it works. I just know that now several of them are cracked and they all smell like something died in the water and we can't serve death-smelling glasses to customers!" With that, he turned on his very short heel, and stormed back into the Main Bar grumbling to himself.

"We could just get a dishwasher!" Rune yelled after him. He didn't answer, much to Rune's relief. She wasn't in the habit of baiting bears. Instead, she refocused on the task she set herself.

"How's the grinding coming?" she asked, before glancing at the bowl Ally had abandoned when she picked up the pamphlet.

"What's Wizard ConClave?" the teen asked, turning the

pamphlet around to face her boss. Wizard ConClave, with the second "c" in conclave capitalized, was printed in epic lettering one would see on a comic book.

"It's a magic users gathering hosted by the Magic Guild. Mostly it's vendor rooms and celebrities, but I think there are talks, panels, and stuff too. Big meeting of the big wigs, that kind of thing."

"Can we go? It opens tomorrow," Ally said, bouncing in her seat a little. If she was in her little dog form, her tail would be thumping.

"You got $150 each?" Rune asked.

Ally visibly drooped. Her strict Polish mother had rescinded her allowance after Ally's vanishing act a couple months prior, and it was so unfair, as Ally was inclined to inform everybody who did or didn't bring it up. Rune saw it more as a symbol by her mother to let her beloved daughter have the freedom to choose her own life. It had been Ally's choice to become a retainer and embrace her Changeling nature. That allowed her to transform into a little white dog at will.

"Do you regret becoming my Retainer?" Rune asked.

"No, she can keep her money," Ally said sullenly. Taking up the pestle again, Ally renewed her attack on the incense sticks in a metal bowl, releasing their thick scent. It didn't smell bad, both earthy and fresh-green-grassy, but it was overwhelming. "Okay, two pinches of cinnamon, and roll that together some more." Rune pinched up the cinnamon herself from a plastic bottle stolen from her bar's kitchen, sprinkling it over the mix. Ally applied the ceramic pestle she had been using to the bowl again.

"Rune, are we going to be ok?" Ally asked shyly.

"Yeah, kid, we are. Why do you ask?" Rune measured out a fourth cup of distilled water from a jug as the base for the mixture.

"It's just, you keep saying we don't have the money, and the mortgage is due again in a couple of weeks…."

"I've already paid it for this month, that's why we don't have the money. I'm not going to let those corporate bastards get us like that again." Rune shook the small jar of bat wing tips to separate them before tweezing out three.

"Yeah, but what happens when you can't? What happens to you then?" Ally asked.

Rune pursed her eyebrows together. "Ally...where's all this worry coming from?"

"I was just thinking. What if you lose the bar and Kodiak comes and...well they know about your secret right? That you're actually Anna Masterson and actually an unregistered Talent and since that's illegal they can just haul you away."

"Honestly, I don't know what Kodiak knows, but if they were sure about who I once was, I think they would have come already."

"But they aren't because St. Benedict is protecting you?" Ally blinked with wide-eyed innocence at the question, which pretty much gave away how loaded it really was.

"Sure, we can assume so," Rune said. She hadn't heard a word or seen a sight of the mysterious corporate spy who had crashed into her life two months previously and she truly had no expectation that she ever would again. He had promised to protect her from those nefariously seeking her out and so far that seemed to be true. No one else had come looking for Anna Masterson since.

"Okay, but say something goes wrong and they come for you. Are they going to arrest me too?"

Rune double blinked at the question. "What? Why? Why would they do that?"

"I'm a Talent too, right? In the eyes of the corporations, I mean. Even as a Changeling, I'm lumped into the same category as any other magic user, even though I think that's stupid and racist or whatever term you'd say that is like racist."

Rune understood why the kid was scared. It had only been a couple of months since Ally had discovered her power to shift into a small, white dog and suddenly the laws governing magical people applied to her in a big way.

"Yeah, except," Rune cut into Ally's stream of consciousness, "the difference is, your mother registered you with the government. You have a license to practice. They've got nothing to hold against you. They can't do legal squat to you. And if something should happen to me, then you do whatever Alf says, okay?"

"But he hates you. And you hate him right?"

"I don't hate him." Rune sighed. She couldn't say she got along or particularly liked Alf, but just like Lucky Devil or the bar or the devilish kitsch on the walls, Alf was as much a part of the bar. Ingrained. Like tree fungus.

"So what *is* his problem?" Ally wrinkled her nose.

"The problem is, he's right about me. I am lying and breaking the law, and I'm barely magical to boot," Rune said, giving Ally a bit of resigned smile.

"But that's so unfair. You're not really Anna Masterson."

"Legally, I still am."

"No, legally you're Rune Leveau."

"Yeah, and Rune Leveau doesn't have any magic and has said so on many, many legal forms."

"But that's not your fault. *They* made you a criminal." Ally was getting worked up.

"Ally!" Rune admonished, making the hush gesture. "We don't shout about this outside of my office, for obvious reasons. The windows are open."

"But…but…you're one of the good guys." Ally was really struggling.

"Yeah, I'd like to think so. But I am also breaking the law by hiding my true identity and Talent, never mind using that Talent to earn money."

"But you're doing that to protect the bar!"

"Yeah, that's true."

Ally was flummoxed.

"So, if you're the good guy, then Alf's the bad guy! He's going to betray you again someday!"

"You really think it's that easy?" Rune raised an eyebrow.

"Well, why not?"

Rune sighed, "That is one of the eternal questions I think."

"I hate it when other adults say that. It's such a non-answer," Ally said. Rune chose not to laugh at Ally counting herself as one of the adults. In a lot of ways, the kid was right. Claiming a retainership in a wizard house was no small lifetime commitment and Ally took it all very seriously.

"You're right, it is a non-answer." Rune nodded her head toward the Main Bar. "Hurry up, and go see if Alf needs help. Until further notice, he is your superior retainer and you can learn a lot from him."

Ally jumped up that time before swiftly shrinking inside her clothes. Out of the bottom of her long shirt a small white dog emerged.

"Ally," Rune started to admonish, but the little dog shook her tail with a couple of hard flicks and ran off, leaving her clothes on the floor of the bar.

"That was completely unnecessary to go to the next room," Rune called after her, then bent to pick up the abandoned clothes to lay them on the booth seat. Rune didn't want to restrict Ally's use of her power to shift, but the kid was seriously looking for any excuse to do it anymore. It wasn't really a very useful Talent to have in a bar. She also partly suspected that Ally did it because she devilishly wanted Liam to catch her changing into her clothes. Oh, what a scandal!

The door to the front opened and Rune sighed again.

"I'm sorry, but we're closed... What are you doing here?" She double blinked at the sight of Calvin Harrison standing at her front door. "What the hell do you want?"

She was not happy to see the former employee of her mortgage company. Calvin had used that position to basically bully her every chance he got, and worse, he had been part of the conspiracy to steal her bar away from her. The poetic justice of it all was that because of those actions and a series of others, he had become the Oberon, the Faerie King of the lost and defunct Faerie Court.

Looking at him now, Rune concluded that it wasn't going well.

Rune felt sorry for the Faeries. They didn't deserve to have to deal with a low-life like Calvin.

The torn, stained jeans and unzipped old grey sweatshirt was a far cry away from the sharp suits he had worn two months prior. It was odd to be wearing a sweatshirt considering it was sweltering in a tank top, but he kept the hood up in an effort to hide his face. Calvin would have almost been handsome if it wasn't for the veneer of sliminess he always had, that even now wasn't entirely erased from his demeanor. The bags under his eyes were deep and his crystal blue eyes, the only part of him that was beautiful, kept darting around himself like he expected every shadow to attack him. When the darting eyes landed on Rune, he hitched in his step, then came to a complete stop as he stared at her.

For one brief second, a sinister half-smile ghosted up his cheek, probably out of habit from his money-grubbing thug days. It washed out almost instantly to be replaced by fear and weariness.

"Leveau," he croaked out and for a brief moment he swayed, as if he was going to collapse onto her floor right then and there. And she had just swept.

"I need your help," he said desperately, his pale blue eyes nailing Rune as if he was more accusing her than pleading. He moved across the distance left between them with such speed that Rune flinched back a step in surprise.

"Woah...a what?" She threw her hands up, attempting to halt Calvin, but he was heedless of the gesture and grabbed her shoulders in his larger, broken-nailed hands.

"I need your help, Leveau, please," he repeated, his breath and its accompanying halitosis washing over her face.

"Paws off!" Rune shouted and swiped her arms up and out to dislodge him. He did let her go, but his intensity didn't diminish.

"Please, please. You have to save me," Calvin begged, clasping his hands together instead. He started to kneel down to the ground, but Rune halted that by shoving him up and away.

"Oh no. No, you don't and no, I don't! Get out of my place!" Rune shouted angrily.

"I need to get out!"

"Yes, I know. That's what I'm saying."

"No. No, I mean out of this hell. I'm not a king!"

"What are you talking about? Yes you are! You're the Oberon of all Faerie-kind and stuff. That's your bed, man. You did that to yourself, ok? You can't take it back!"

"I didn't know. I didn't know anything about any of this, they...they tricked me! Please. I can't...I can't do it." Despite her effort to keep him on his feet, Calvin collapsed anyway, sobbing the whole way down. "They want me to lead them. And they all keep calling me Father. That's insane. Look at me! I'm no one's father! That's not how it works...oh hell!" He continued to blubber and Rune had to let him go. No way was she getting onto the floor with him. Instead, she set her hands on her hips, rolling her eyes when he started to wail.

"Calvin. Get up. Get off of my floor." He continued to sob. "Look, man. You're a king. Kings don't sob on the floor of bars without buying the place out. Now get up."

"Money? You want money? I have money." He reached into the pockets of the sweatshirt, dropping large gold coins onto the floor with pattering clinks as he rose to give what remained to her.

"Calvin, stop it." He didn't heed her words as he tried to shove the coins into her hands, which made even more of them land on the floor.

"You have to help me. I can't take it anymore."

"After all the intimidation and threats, for months," Rune could practically spit the words, "You stole from me...you punched me in the face..." Her voice rose as the memory became real again in her mind. "You even tried to kill me! The only reason you failed was because of Faerie rules." It was Calvin's turn to back up, backpedaling until his back hit the wall beside Rune's door.

"That wasn't me! That was the thing they made me!"

"Get out!" she shouted.

He whimpered, pulling his chin away from her since he couldn't move backwards any further.

"She's going to kill me," he squeaked.

At that, Rune's rage simmered down. "What?" she asked crisply.

"I...I don't know who she is. But she's trying to kill me. I can hear her voice and no one else can. I'm going insane." He dropped all of the coins left in his hands uncaringly, cupping his face with his hands as he slid down the wall to crouch in front of it. "Things keep happening. I keep having near misses. Near death stuff."

"What do you mean?" Rune asked. It was obvious she was not getting him off her floor any time soon.

"Things….keep happening. I almost got electrocuted by a blender."

Rune double blinked. "Okay…?" She couldn't believe what she was hearing.

"And I got chased by a dog."

"Wait, let me go get my violin," Rune said irritably. Why wouldn't he go away?

"I've almost drowned three times. Once in my bathtub. Random strangers keep attacking me." He started counting on his fingers. "Seven times."

Okay, that did sound suspicious.

"On the way here, a cinder block fell off that building down there, missed me by inches."

Oh, damn.

"Okay, okay. You're right. It sounds like you've been cursed. But Calvin, this isn't my problem and even if it was, I don't know what I would be able to do to help you," she said quickly before he cut her off with more pleas.

"I've got nowhere else to turn," he whined.

"Where is Lady Trella? Or the monochromes? Aren't they supposed to be keeping you safe?"

Calvin opened his mouth, and thought better of it. "They can't help me. They don't want to help me. I want out. I want to go back to being normal again. They don't want that."

"Look Calvin, I can't imagine what you're going through, but you're technically a Changeling now. There's no going back from that."

He furrowed his eyebrows. "A what?"

"Didn't Lady Trella explain any of this to you?"

Looking away like a petulant child, Calvin huffed through nose. "Yes, I guess. I just… I don't understand."

All Rune could do was sigh. "Look, Calvin. I'm going to explain this as simple as I can. You are now a Changeling. You were a hominal, but now you are one of the unlucky idiots who has done the insanely rare thing of actually acquiring magic…"

A squeal piped from the corner of the room. With a glisten of colorful wings, Viola, one of the tiny Faeries Rune was keeping safe for the Faerie Court, was spinning in place. Sparks of lavender light danced off of her.

"Father's here!" she shouted from the top of her tiny lungs. In one great cacophony, a flock of little Fae rushed out of their hiding places throughout the bar to swarm around their pathetic King.

"No. No!" Calvin shouted, throwing his hands up.

It broke Rune's heart to hear the excited squeals and loving praise, while Calvin cowered away, trying to swat at them like they were bugs.

"Stop that! They're just children," Rune admonished, grabbing for his hands. Panicked, he didn't stop, scrambling instead to run away out her front door. The little colorful Fae tried to follow him, but once he crossed the threshold they stopped, drifting down onto the tables and chairs all around the room in a collective wave of sadness and disappointment. Rune looked around the room at the drooping little wings. "Hey! Who wants some ice cream?" she called with forced cheer. A handful of the little Fae rallied at that idea with excitement, rushing off toward the bar's kitchen in the back. Others followed, less enthusiastically. Five little Fae remained, staring after where Calvin had gone. "Come on, everyone to the kitchen."

"Ms. Rune?" one of the remaining Fae lighted onto Rune's shoulder. "Why did Father run away from us?" She wanted to say that he hadn't, but it was so obvious that he had and Rune wasn't going to hurt these little ones more than she had to by lying to them.

"The Oberon is having a rough time adjusting I think," she said instead. She couldn't bring herself to call him their Father since she didn't entirely understand why the Fae called the Oberon "Father" and the Titania "Mother," even if the current leaders of their people weren't their actual parents. She also maintained that these little Fae didn't deserve Calvin in the least. "Come on, let's go get some ice cream."

"Is he afraid of us?" another little one, Gunter, asked, flying by her head. Rune moved toward the kitchen, the remaining four Fae in tow.

"I'm not going to speak for him and his feelings. What I do know is I like each and every one of you." She held out her hand for the four other little Fae to land on and went into the kitchen. It took a half an hour to get all of the little ones set up with ice cream, six of them to one full bowl. Once she got Ally into the kitchen to watch over them all and clean up after, Rune was able to retreat back into her Lounge Bar.

"I need a drink. Let's hope this day doesn't get any worse."

First, she went to pick up all of the coins Calvin had dropped, resolving to give them back to Lady Trella. Taking Faerie gold came with its own rules and taking gold from a piece of slime like Calvin? That was one Fae she had no intention of being beholden to ever again. She'd have to try to send a message the next time one of the monochromes, a Fae that moved through shadows, came to check up on the welfare of the little ones she was fostering.

She started to partially pack up the magic supplies while she eyed the liquor bottles on her bar. Liam had switched them out with the cleaning supplies and had left in the middle of reorganizing them on the display shelf. She tried to decide which she hadn't tasted in a while. Once she had her drink, she was going to move all the magic supplies to the office to finish. It had been really stupid to try to do it out in the Lounge Bar where anyone could simply walk-in. She had scolded Ally but she should have really scolded herself. She was getting too lax with doing magic, or at least attempting to, out in the open sans a license.

Setting the pestle and mortar into the defunct garbage can so she could carry it in one go, she finally went to her bar and sat on one of the well-loved stools. Staring at the bottles of liquor, instead of selecting one, her thoughts drifted unbidden again to delicious memories. Strong arms wrapping around her from behind. Soft, warm breath against her ear sending shivers skittering across her skin. The thoughts invoked an ache inside, an urge to burrow her face into a shoulder and feel safe. She longed for the scent of a man long gone. To feel his warmth pour into her.

Then other thoughts began to embroider the memories, fantasies of things that she wished would happen taking the place of the things that did. She imagined him coming through the door. Skipping the parts where he would tell her where he had been and her shock at seeing him again after she was so sure she would never see him again. Her fantasy went right to the good part, the juicy part. The part where he was too close. The part where his hand slid into her longer hair and he didn't care what size of clothing she wore. The part where he pulled her close against his body to feel how much he didn't care, that he, in fact, wanted her because of it. Because men like women made exactly like her…

Rune growled frustratedly in her throat. This was stupid and these thoughts were just making it worse. She glanced up at the door to verify for her brain that no one would be standing there no matter how much she willed it.

"Excuse me, might I have a word with the proprietor of this fine establishment?"

Chapter 2

He was a tall man, with dark, warm skin that painters would have to use the entire palette to achieve. The stranger was dressed very well, in a fine suit. He wasn't particularly handsome, nor did it seem to bother him. There was an air of self-assuredness about him that felt almost like a magnet as he walked deeper into the bar. But what captivated Rune's attention the most was his hat.

It was a fedora. It wasn't the fedora itself or the man wearing it, but the sight brought back a brief memory of another man who wore a fedora in a time when almost no one wore a hat any more.

"Sorry sir, the bar is closed," Rune said automatically, as it was the protocol in situations like these.

"I'm not here for a drink," he said, smiling a perfect white smile.

"Men who wear hats like that in this place never are," Rune countered, smiling a less-than-perfect white smile back at him.

He blinked a moment and his smile dropped to something more genuine. "Ah, I think you are referring to our mutual associate, St. Benedict."

Rune's eyebrows hit the ceiling and her heart did a double skip before taking off on a sprint.

"St. Benedict…" she said softly. She hadn't said his name out loud in two months and it felt foreign on her tongue.

Casually, the stranger reached into the front inside pocket of his jacket.

"My understanding that this is the place where I can spend this…." From his pocket, captured between two fingers, was a green jade coin.

Rune's eyes went even wider at the sight of it.

"How did you get that?"

"With some difficulty I assure you," the corporate man, who had yet to introduce himself, said.

"Well, if you want to use it, the instructions are here," Rune said, plucking up the spare laminated card about Lucky Devil's booth from behind the bar to hand to the man. He didn't look or take the card.

"I understand that if I put this coin in your carousel figure's glass over there," he indicated the Lucky Devil statue, who was indeed holding a low-ball glass waiting for a drink, "and write my wish on a slip of paper to put into his pocket, that piece of paper will disappear and reappear in your pocket while your carnival trick there swallows my $1,000 coin. A consulting fee, I'm assuming?"

Rune stared at him. It was true that Lucky Devil, the bar's tourist attraction and namesake, was in fact nothing more than an animatronic statue that laughed when people gave him wishes, drinking their coin in exchange for a wish granted. Most tourists kept their wishes to simple things like nachos or another round of beer. Usually the only time someone would get a bigger wish granted was when they dropped a jade coin, of which there were only thirteen made, into his cup. Rune had accounted for eight of the jade coins and those eight could still be obtained from the old-fashioned cigarette vending machine positioned behind the booth. It was an open secret and only those who knew the code could even access the coin through the machine. Even to those people, Lucky Devil's trick was a mystery. There was only one person she was aware of, other than Maddie or Rune's retainers, who knew the secret to the trick. And he wasn't the man standing before her.

"Who are you?" Rune asked, folding her arms in front of her chest.

"Excuse me," the stranger said before clearing his throat, shifting on his feet to re-present himself. "I am Maxamillion Corinthe, CEO of the Corinthe Corporation." Belatedly, he reached into his other inner jacket pocket and produced a business card, which he held out to her. Rune hesitated a moment, because taking the card would mean leaving her bar stool to take a few steps closer and this guy knew way too much about her already. She had to remind herself that she was in *her* House and that it would protect its Lady. After all the decorative devils on the walls weren't only for show.

The card, once she took it, was very fancy, embossed with a dark silvery color on very fine paper and rounded corners. On one side was an image of an old Roman style column with a big crack in it, slantwise left to right. The other side had the usual information. It also contained a whisper of what Rune needed to find him, using her magic instead of a phone or email. Sending a little bit of her magical Talent into the card, a small tendril of light only she could see popped out. It wafted in the air like a filament of gold, then rainbow, and back to gold drifting lazily but strongly in the air between the card and Mr. Corinthe. The intention in the card was for the bearer to find Maxamillion Corinthe and that was who was standing in front of her. Identity verified. Rune smiled to herself. She hadn't realized before that she could use her Talent in this way. She would have to test it further.

"Where is St. Benedict? Why didn't he come with you?" Rune asked, slipping the card in her back jean pocket. The minute she did the magic filament dissipated. Or at least she thought it had, but then something strange happened. Another filament tugged hard, originating from herself outward. Like a string pulled taut, it went straight through the window of the Lounge Bar, directly down the street about a block away. Rune knew, without knowing why, that it led straight to St. Benedict. He was close, and if she looked out her door, she would find him down the street.

She heard Maxamillion say some words. They didn't register as she crossed to her window to look out. She couldn't see anything so she moved to the door.

"Ms. Leveau?" Maxamillion asked, a bit perplexed. "Did you hear me?"

"He's out there, isn't he?" She asked instead of answering.

The corporate man's eyebrows pursed together for a second as he tried to figure out what was happening. "Is that a guess or do you know?"

"I know." Rune tugged on the handle of her door.

"He doesn't want to see you," Maxamillion said before she took a step to go out the door. Mr. CEO crossed to put his own hand on the door, indicating she should shut it instead of leaving. "Said it might complicate things. I'm not sure what he meant by that, but now I'm glad he did. I think it answers any lingering doubts I might have had about your abilities. So how does it work exactly? Precog or psychic power? Can you see through walls?"

"What are you asking me exactly?" Rune crossed her arms, not liking any of this. St. Benedict didn't want to see her? Why? The pit of her stomach twisted a little harder.

"Your magic, Ms. Leveau. How does your Talent work?" Maxamillion looked like he was entitled to an answer and expected to receive it.

"None of your business," Rune said.

"I'm given to understand you need an object to find another object and that was the extent of your magic. I had a little test prepared for you and everything, but just now, you found the location of my subordinate with nothing more than his name."

"I have an emotional connection to him," Rune said before she realized what it would sound like.

"Ah I see. So you fell in love with him too?" Maxamillion asked, simply. Like he was only gathering information. "That's interesting. Don't worry, everybody does. It's what I paid for. There's always a few weeks of adjustment period with new hires as they fall in love and break their hearts over him. You'll be ahead of the curve."

That pulled Rune's attention fully back to the corporate suit. She took a new look at the man standing before her. His suit was finely tailored and fit him well. He was athletically inclined in a way that said he went to a gym to have his workout as tailor-made as his suit. Everything about him felt optimized to Rune, conveying the ideal, haughty image of a corporate elite, the new nobility of this dying democratic world.

"You make it sound like you own him."

"I do." Maxamillion did not look at all bothered by his answer, saying it like it was a simple fact of life. "Every nut and bolt of him."

"He's still a man."

"He's a resource."

Rune cocked her head to the side. "Is that what you want with me? I'm a resource to be acquired?"

Maxamillion blinked and stepped back, as if disengaging from a fencing duel after a few quick passes, reassessing her.

"I don't work with corporations," Rune said firmly. She tried to make it sound like that was the end of the conversation. It had never worked before, but still, she tried to put a button on this dangerous line of questioning. She knew an offer when she heard it. "I'm a free agent."

"Ah but you see. That's what I like about you," Maxamillion said. His placid face broke into one of deep, dark-eyed intensity.

"Really?" She asked as she moved to behind her bar, to a position she felt marginally safer in.

"Yes, despite everything, all the odds against you, you resisted. Resisted corporate influences. Resisted the legal system. Resisted social norms." He laid his hands against the bar to lean his tall frame toward Rune. His energy was tangible, both drawing Rune in and repelling her.

"Social norms? What are you talking about?" Rune was starting to wonder if this corporate elite was actually just a crazy in a nice suit.

"I know who you really are, Ms. Leveau." The placid face tried to reassert itself, which made the vague threat even more effective. Rune felt her breath escape her as the dark gaze bored into her, his chocolate eyes becoming more like twin black holes to lose herself into.

"I don't know what St. Benedict…" she swallowed once, not expecting his name to hitch in her throat like that, "…told you. I only know what he told me, and he said that he wasn't going to involve me in any more dark, secret, evil-corporation shenanigans." Rune didn't exactly tell Maxamillion to leave, but she hoped she was implying it plenty hard.

"I know everything." Something changed in Maxamillion's face and Rune almost did a double take. Immediately, the threat disappeared like smoke in the wind, replaced by the friendly understanding of a preacher man.

"At least what there is left to be known." Maxamillion took off his hat and set it on the bar, his short, tightly-curled hair looking freshly cut and only slightly silvered at the temples, adding to the classic look.

"Then what is it you know? I'm not going to play this twenty questions game or accidentally confirm something you don't actually know. You either tell me straight or get out. On second thought, get out any way. I don't deal with corporates unless they're here to buy drinks and today we're closed."

Rune felt so bad-ass saying that, leaning parallel to him across the bar.

"Your name is Anna Masterson. You were illegally imprisoned six years ago, implicated by your husband Justin Masterson as an accomplice in his embezzlement scheme. You were held by corporate authority, destined to live the rest of your life as a slave to the corporate criminal system. Your aunt, who was a wizard, freed you and you have successfully changed your identity and hidden yourself in plain sight." He emphasized the word a moment before continuing. "You have even hidden your own special magic Talent from any legal or corporate authority."

"Aren't they one and the same?"

"The fact that I am *in* the position I am in, is because I know the difference. Taking away the rights of anybody, takes away the rights of everybody." Again, he stopped himself, forcing the calm veneer to pass over his face to cover some deeper intensity. "Now that I've proved my credentials… We're going to stop this charade of cat and mouse. There's no point to it."

Rune felt like she was standing on cracking ice. This person standing so self-assuredly in front of her had the kind of power to make a small entrepreneur like her suffer if he wanted. In a world where every shop was a subsidiary of some other corporation, independents like herself held on with their nails and what little legal protection she got from the Magic Guild. But she had continued to ignore the summons of the Magic Guild, and that put her in a precarious position either way. Compounding that with, as he put it, "hiding" her true identity and he was correct, he had her dead to rights.

"Very well. What do you want with me?" Rune asked softly, keeping her gaze steady and bracing for the worst.

Noting her iciness, Maxamillion sighed and sat down on the stool, repositioning his hat on the bar. "I have no intention of turning you over to *any* authority, but I do need your help and I can't really afford for you to tell me no, do you understand?"

Rune quirked her eyebrows together, really unsure now what was going on. Needing something to hide her agitation with, she pulled out a low-ball glass from under one of the towels laid over to keep the glasses clean from the flying dust. To her frustration, she remembered too late that the insta-cold boxes were dead from lack of magic. So she filled the glass with water from the small sink and no ice, before flipping one of the cardboard coasters with Lucky Devil's face winking up and setting the glass before her visitor.

"I'll promise to listen. I can't guarantee I can help you."

"You can. I know you can," he said, confidently. He set the jade coin on the bar and slid it toward her, then folded his hands one on top of the other. "I want to do this properly. I'm seeking an audience with the Wizard here."

"It's Wizardress," Rune corrected.

"Excuse me?"

"My aunt went by Wizardress, not Wizard. She was very 1970s that way," Rune explained.

Maxamillion nodded his understanding. "Wizardress then."

"Well no… I'm not a Wizardress. I wouldn't identify that way," she corrected again, shaking her head. She was really complicating this.

"What should I call you then?" Maxamillion asked unsure.

"Nothing. I'm nothing. Sorry. What…what do you want to ask me?" She waved dismissively.

"I want to know, and a lot of people want to know, where is Justin Masterson?"

Even though Rune thought there was a possibility that one question would be the one he asked, it was still a shock to hear it out loud. Having nowhere to sit, Rune drifted back until her bottom was stopped by the counter behind her. Maxamillion watched her reaction, but his face betrayed very little of what he was thinking. He simply waited patiently for her to process it.

"I won't…I don't want to do that," she said softly, with the voice of a small child being asked to face a terrible storm.

Maxamillion nodded once as if to indicate he understood, but it changed nothing.

"Why? Why do you want to find him so badly?" Rune asked, her brain starting up again.

"You know about the Masterson files, correct?"

Rune huffed and took up Maxamillion's untouched water. "I was there when they were created," she said before quaffing the water in one go.

"You were?" Maxamillion's eyebrows rose in genuine surprise.

"I never saw them," she added, "I only saw him try to send them out through the phone and try to burn the rest as the corporate police surrounded our house."

"But you know what they are?"

"A computer program that would allow a computer to cast magic," Rune said simply. "It was never proven he managed to do it."

"I know for a fact that he succeeded in doing it," Maxamillion said.

A different kind of chill slipped down Rune's spine.

"How?"

"My telling you would break several promises that at this time I intend to keep. The point I am trying to convey to you is that if it can happen once, it can and will happen again."

Rune furrowed her eyebrows. "And you want to find Justin first so you can find out how he did it and rule the world?"

Maxamillion sat back abruptly at that suggestion. He looked insulted, and for a moment, the look of the ideal corporate poster boy seemed disconnected from him.

"I want to keep such a powerful and world-altering thing from being controlled by the corporations who seek to dominate and rule us all."

"You talk more like a revolutionary than a CEO," Rune noted, crossing her arms in response to his intensity.

That checked him a moment. He stood, picking up his hat.

"You understand the stakes here, Ms. Leveau. I am not the only person who will come to you about finding your husband."

"St. Benedict said he would protect my secret," Rune countered.

"And how did you think he was going to do that? He's trying, but he can't sustain it forever," Maxamillion said gravely.

Rune felt her connection to this man's corporate spy ping again. She felt the urge to go to him outside, to ask, or rather demand, an explanation. Was that why he didn't want to come in to see her again? He was failing in his promise to her? The whole mess made Rune feel sick.

Maxamillion moved to the door, setting a perfectly manicured hand on the knob. "Someone has to find the Masterson files or Justin Masterson himself, if he's still alive. For now, you have the choice of who that's going to be. We are the best option you're going to find. Make that choice while you still can. I will be back tomorrow."

With that he exited without another word. Rune didn't move a muscle as she focused on the Finding connection with St. Benedict grow thinner and thinner until it was completely gone, the connection too weak from distance to follow anymore.

"Are you going to do it?" Alf appeared at the end of the bar, the small man having gone unnoticed by both Rune and her visitor.

"You heard the whole thing?" Rune asked, not looking at Alf as she stared unseeing at Lucky Devil in his booth.

"Yes, my Lady," Alf answered.

Now she looked at her bar manager, feeling so lost. "What do I do, Alf?" Tears welled up, flooding down her face thickly.

Shifting uncomfortably for a second, Alf plucked up a bar rag and stepped up on one of the boxes installed behind the bar for him. He cleared his throat and thrust the rag out to Rune. His awkwardness in comforting her actually did more to anchor Rune's emotional torrent than the rag.

"I can't believe I'm crying about this," she tried to laugh, wiping her tears away a bit too hard.

"Objects in the rearview mirror may appear closer than they are," Alf responded. It was one of Maddie's favorite quotes. It reminded Rune of how much she missed her. At least she didn't break down every time someone mentioned her anymore.

"Yeah," Rune agreed. "I wish Maddie was still here to talk to."

"But she ain't kid...my Lady. " Alf picked up the used water glass and set it into the wash-up sink.

"Why are you being so nice to me all of a sudden?" Rune asked, refolding her arms. "Is this a duty for a retainer? To offer comfort to their...whatever I am."

"Don't get me wrong, I would like nothing better than to see you cast down from this place and replaced with anybody more suitable. But this thing with your husband...." His face became dark for a moment, his eyes seeing something far off from a past he had never shared with Rune. "That wasn't your fault. And what those people did to you...no one deserves that."

He stood up a little straighter then and met Rune's eye with conviction. "If you wish it, then let them try to come for you. This House and its people will defend you as long as we stand." Something rippled through the walls when he said that. The various little statues of devils that decorated the inside of the bar all seemed to be in attention to what Alf was saying and Rune got a feeling of agreement from them all.

The first time the bar had responded like that had been creepy. Rune still didn't really understand what was happening, but in that moment she felt safe and loved. When Rune had claimed her Wizard's House, the magical construct attached to the bar that a magic user could draw power from, the devils on the walls as well as Lucky Devil himself had come to life and jumped to defend her from the people there to hurt her. She looked around at each of them now, wondering at how she could ever make that magic work again.

Then, there was a burst of light and sparks coming from one of the magically lit orbs that hovered near the bathroom, just before it fell to the ground, cracked and black.

"What good is that if all the magic around here is breaking?" groused Rune.

"Well you better figure it out then before the whole place comes down around our ears!" Alf growled angrily before hopping down from his box to go get a broom.

Chapter 3

It was hours later before Rune gave up on trying to reenchant the garbage can. Everything she tried, no matter how precise she was with the ingredients and the timing or how much magical energy she pushed into the spell, nothing would get that trashcan to do more than sit there.

Throwing the used up ingredients into the said garbage can, Rune left her office with a headache. The light outside the bar had turned to the gold twilight color of oncoming dusk. Even with the sun leaving, the heat still persisted. It was strange to see the evening light arriving and no one in the bar with the windows closed up. The clean-up operations went well at the very least. The bar itself had a slight gleam of fresh polish and the mirror on the back wall was spotless. All her workers seemed to be gone for the day so Rune headed toward the interior door that led up to her apartment on the third floor.

Touching the crystal implanted above the knob of her door, she muttered the word "open" and the lock snapped obediently. She knew it wasn't the safest lock word and if she had wanted to bother she could have used her actual keys, but it was too much work to try to change it. She was glad that this crystal magic still worked. Without the crystals holding spells, she was forced to live no better than any other normal, or hominal, person.

Toeing off her sneakers, Rune beelined through her semi-loft apartment to her bathroom. Both the bedroom and the bathroom were walled off from the rest of the apartment, hence the semi part of the word loft, but it was Rune's favorite place to be, with its dramatically slanted wood ceiling and skylight. She stepped over the pile of towels crowding the door of the bathroom and tried to not look at the other clothes strewn throughout her bedroom. She was going to have to solve her laundry problem soon. All her closets and the wood dresser had lost all of the magic they used to automatically clean her clothing. Which meant either Rune needed to find time to get her clothes to a local laundry mat or buy new clothes when the current ones were too dirty to wear. Both options were expensive.

Sighing, Rune washed her face instead of showering and changed her jeans for her last pair of yoga capri pants. Not feeling very hungry, she pulled out a cold bottle of sparkling water and went out onto her back porch.

The air outside was strangely still, like the heavy silence just before a severe, summer storm. Rune settled herself onto one of the two lounge chairs waiting for her in the corner of her meager porch space. Each chair was made of shaped metal and the seats each had canvas cloth festooned in retro patterns of burnt orange and sage green paisleys over a hot pink background. A large beach umbrella was set up between the two chairs, shading them from the street lamp that had just started to come to life as dusk burned away.

Before she could lean back and relax, something creaked on the porch below her.

"Alf, is that you?" she called down. Her bar manager lived in the apartment below and their back porches were built with wooden staircases that crisscrossed back and forth until it reached the alley below.

She crawled over the second lounger to look over her wood railing, trying to catch a glimpse of whomever was below. Something moved, just faster than she could perceive, ducking back underneath. "Alf?"

Rune got up from her seat and went down the stairs, her bare feet clopping in a gallop rhythm as she took the stairs two at a time. But when she landed on Alf's porch, her bar manager wasn't standing there. The window of his apartment was dark, a clear signal he wasn't home. Then the harsh yowl of a cat made her jump as the creature streaked out from under the single, lonely beach chair, crashing into a trashcan noisily as it went.

"Geez," Rune gasped from the fright, grabbing at her chest.

"That was a horror movie cliché," she called to the cat's back as she headed back up the stairs. Then in a faux Southern accent, "Gave me the vapors."

She went back to her lounger and picked up her bottle of water, still trying to shake the feeling that something was about to pounce on her, when something from her roof pounced on her.

An arm snaked around her shoulders and throat while another hand clamped over her mouth and nose. Dropping the bottle with a sharp crash, her hands flew up to grab the arm and her whole body bucked in terror.

"Stop it! Stop it!" a familiar voice growled in her ear. Rune lost her footing a moment as Calvin levered her up, using massive strength that she knew he wouldn't have normally. She was practically hanging inches off the ground. Some vague thought considered that his becoming the Faerie King had something to do with it, but the idea was drowned out by more urgent matters, like breathing. Rune continued squirming, but already the denied air was taking a toll. Everything was getting brighter, while the edges of her vision were slowly eaten up by pools of black. If she didn't breathe soon, she would pass out. It started to look inevitable.

"Stop fighting me, you bitch," Calvin snapped at her, his voice tinny and far away. "This wouldn't be necessary if you would just help me. It's going to be alright once you listen to me. You're just going to do some magic and make this all go away."

Giving up on the arm, Rune's fingers clawed up at the edge of the hand, trying desperately to pull it up enough to get a breath. Her kicking legs were becoming weaker. She didn't know what to do, she wasn't in a position to think her plans through.

Power.

Like a wave, power erupted from Rune. Her body was fighting back, stabilizing itself. Magic cleared her vision and Rune blinked. She wasn't suffocating any more. No, that was wrong. She was still suffocating, but it was as if her body needed less air to function. Her lungs expanded, pulling air in, even though she knew she shouldn't be able to do that.

She realized Calvin was still talking, muttering about how this was her fault, if she would only help him. So, he was magically strong, and now crazy to boot. Great. He hadn't seemed to notice yet that she had stopped struggling.

Slowly, Rune lifted her legs, trying not to shift her weight too fast. When she was sure he hadn't noticed, she kicked hard against her rail with all the strength in her body, or maybe it was enhanced by her magic. Either way, Calvin stumbled back and slammed hard against the bricks of the wall. Stunned, he let her go and Rune's feet touched blessed ground, dropping her into a crouch.

A shadow moved above her. There was another crack as the shadow punched Calvin across his jaw. Wetness landed onto Rune's neck and hair like a spritz of rain. Rune didn't focus on it. She scrambled away from Calvin and the attacking shadow.

Calvin roared as he tried to wrestle a gun out of his hoodie pocket, waking up all of the dogs in the neighborhood who barked in sharp chorus with him. Instead, he dropped it. The weapon skittered across the wood boards to teeter on the edge, not quite going over, but definitely out of reach.

Bereft of his weapon, the deranged Changeling brought his left hand down on the shadow, but said shadow seemed to side step, snaking away. He redirected the slap harmlessly to the side and landed his own smacking punch again into the side of the lesser man's face.

The second punch seemed to do the trick, as Calvin's neck shot to the side and his whole body went slack. Falling back against the wall, he started to slide down it comically slow. The shadow man stood over him, breathing hard. Then he turned to Rune, extending a hand.

"Come on, we gotta go," he gasped out.

"As in, 'come with me if you want to live?'" Rune quipped.

St. Benedict cracked his infamous smile at the quote. "More or less, but be warned, my Austrian accent sucks."

A bullet stopped any further exchange.

"No!" Calvin squealed covering his head. "Don't hurt me!"

Grabbing her hand, St. Benedict ignored Calvin's pleas as he pulled Rune down the stairs, not that she needed more encouragement to follow him. Her speed down the steps was more agile than his and she overtook him on the second landing, letting go of his hand to pass him as she tightly rounded the post to go down the final set to the street. Her bare feet thumped the wood. Another bullet took a chunk from a post, throwing some wood shards.

"Why is it when you're around, people start shooting at me?!" Rune shouted as she ducked.

"Must be my charming personality!" he shouted back as he grabbed Rune, moving her against the alley wall as if to shield her with his own body. She hit it with her side and covered her head instinctively, the Saint's pressure against her hip holding her there.

"Sniper. He's panicking now that he missed his shot. Not a Saint then," St. Benedict breathed into her ear. She dropped her hands so she could scan the alley. Running barefoot in any street in Chicago was not an ideal situation, with or without the flying bullets.

"What do we do?"

"We have to move quickly," he informed her, his face intense with a smile that was downright predatory. "We're exactly in the midpoint of the block, either way that we run makes the alley a death trap when someone starts firing from above."

"Are you talking to me or someone in your ear?" Rune asked.

St. Benedict glanced at her. "You. I'm running solo on this." He looked away again, calculating. "I'm sorry. I failed you."

"Failed me?"

"I couldn't keep them off you anymore," he said. Though he was being cryptic, Rune had an idea who "they" might be.

"Kodiak Corp," she muttered under her breath.

"Maybe. Possible. But that isn't a Saint out there so…."

"What makes you say that?"

"They wouldn't have missed. We need to move."

"Through the bar," Rune suggested, moving toward the backdoor to the bar itself. It was a few feet beyond the clearance of the wooden porch, and completely exposed.

The second Rune cleared out from under the wood stairs, gunshots came from above making the water puddle beside her jump upwards. St. Benedict pulled her back to safety. Two more shots made the water dance.

"Can you make us a door?" St. Benedict asked urgently, pulling out his own weapon from a holster under his arm. The yellowish street light glinted off the barrel as he lifted it up. "Unlock, user St. Benedict," he muttered to it and a small pinprick of red light on a black bracelet on his wrist flipped to blue. A corresponding blue light flicked on handle of the gun above St. Benedict's fingers. His eyes never left Rune's face as he did this. "Remember, like you did two months ago?"

Rune swallowed. Though she had done it previously, that unusual bit of magic had been unreplicable ever since.

Before she could answer, Calvin's scream echoed off the walls. "No! No! Go away. Don't touch me." Above were shadows of more feet on the boards, but Rune couldn't make out who else was up there with Calvin. There was a shatter of glass as someone broke her back porchlight, leaving only the alley streetlight to give any illumination. With the newly made dark, came silence up above. No feet moving. No pathetic whimpers.

"Switch?" St. Benedict asked softly, his eyes glued to up above. Quietly, they switched places. Abruptly, there was more gunfire, but it didn't seem to be directed down at them anymore. St. Benedict leaned out and Rune saw his eyes flash blue. Normally, they were a hypnotic green, but when his augmentations fired up, blue light blotted out his irises. It was alien to look at.

"Looks like our sniper is more of an amateur than I thought. Should have run once he missed his shot. Either that or they're desperate."

"We need to get out of here," Rune said, wishing she could think of something. A revving sound echoed down the alley. St. Benedict twitched, and turned the gun to lock on the newest threat, his glowing eyes growing hard. Headlights flashed on at the end of the alley, but while Rune had to squint against the light, St. Benedict didn't seemed to be bothered by it.

"Oh crap," St. Benedict muttered, his shoulders dropping a little of their ready-action tension.

"What?! What is it?" Rune asked, her alarm not at all eased.

St. Benedict glanced up checking again for the sniper or any other threats from above.

"Don't worry, just a guy with delusions. When he pulls up, you jump into the car and I'll cover you." St. Benedict's blue-lit eyes moved as if they were seeing things that Rune couldn't.

"Down!" he shouted suddenly, pushing Rune to the ground, his hand on the back of her head. More bullets ripped across the alley above where they were standing, coming from the same direction as the car. Tires screamed on pavement and the car came barreling down.

St. Benedict lifted up his head slightly so he could see past the rim of his hat. From his perspective, faint circles appeared in his vision as targets surrounded the otherwise invisible gunners. St. Benedict raised his own gun, keeping Rune tucked under his arm so he could act as both shield and weapon. Three squeezes sent three shots, each hitting three targets perfectly. New circles took the place of the fading targets. A dozen of them. Things were getting out of hand quickly.

Thankfully, the car squealed to a halt beside them, the stench of burnt rubber wafting bucolically.

"Go!" St. Benedict pushed her toward the car door at the same time it swung open.

"Hurry, hurry!" came the voice inside the backseat of the car.

Rune's eyes widened as she took Maxamillion's hand. He hauled her into the smooth leather-coated backseat. St. Benedict popped off more shots, dodging back toward the wall to cover and distract from her escape. She spun on the seat to turn back to him. He was only five feet away from the door, blocked by a hail of bullets biting pieces of her building's wall as they struck around him. He kept moving about the wall, his eyes flashing, avoiding the bullets with uncanny anticipation.

"Stop right there!" A gruff voice commanded, echoing and modulating off the walls.

"Definitely corporate police," St. Benedict called, and answered with a couple more shots.

"St. Benedict!" Rune cried out for his attention, reaching her hand out to him. The noise was cacophonous as more shots were exchanged all around the car.

"Go!" the Saint shouted.

"Get your ass in here!" Maxamillion answered.

St. Benedict tried to move toward the open door when another bullet cut into his back. More bullets zipped by and Rune yelped as she thought she had felt one whoosh under her hand, but when she clutched it against her, she saw no cuts or blood.

"Go!" St. Benedict repeated, as he began to stumble back against the brick wall of the building.

"No!" Rune shouted, panicked that the car would drive off without him. If only she could do something.

"Leave me, it's fine!"

Like hell it was.

With no understanding of what she was doing, Rune grabbed at St. Benedict. In her fingers was the gold cord she usually saw when she was doing a Finding, only it was real and solid in her hands. This was all she could do, Find him. If only it also allowed her to pull what she wanted toward herself. So she tried it. She pulled.

Like someone had grabbed him with a hook, St. Benedict went sideways toward the door of the car. More bullets whizzed above like angry bees as St. Benedict ducked his head at the last second, landing across Rune's legs.

"He's in!" Rune's fingers scrabbled to shut the door behind him.

Instead of driving though, Maxamillion cracked his door open and stuck an arm out with his own gun, firing a few shots behind them.

"Stop firing you idiot!" St. Benedict growled at the executive. "Car—drive!" That's when Rune realized there was no driver behind the wheel. The tires of the car spun in place a moment, fishtailing slightly as the car took off, barreling down the alley. Circles of cracked glass popped into the windshield, many of them centering around where the driver wasn't.

The living people in the back were having a hard enough time sorting out their limbs in the limited space. Maxamillion was flung against the backs of the front seats, dropping his gun to bounce onto the floor. The back door he had been shooting from swung out madly, banging hard and metallic against a dumpster the car was driving too close to. Still draped over Rune's lap, St. Benedict scrambled to grab his boss before the other man went tumbling out. Rune also leaned that direction, stretching as hard as she could to reach the handle of the free swinging door, but the Saint's weight pinned her just out of reach.

Then fire, bright and fierce, licked around the car, enveloping it in a wave of heat before disappearing as quickly as it had appeared.

"...the hell!" Maxamillion yelled as he jerked away at the same time Rune screeched involuntarily. More fire burst, but this time behind where the car had been.

Just as the car reached the end of the alley, something like a body bounced up onto the hood, adding more cracks to the windshield as whomever it was went up and over the vehicle. As the body fell over the side, the door was slammed shut, banging the ends of Rune's fingers painfully as she was still reaching desperately for the door. The tires of the car squealed as the vehicle turned hard onto an empty night street.

"Drive, drive!" Maxamillion ordered the car, though it hadn't stopped doing that. Everyone stared out of the back window, waiting for more attacks to come, yet there was nothing. Only a normal night street and the frantic pounding of hearts.

"Are you ok?" St. Benedict asked, his voice almost making Rune jump. The car turned another corner at speed and the Saint allowed the centrifugal force to pull him back up to sitting. "Car—resume normal street driving," he ordered.

"The door got my fingers," Rune said clutching them with her other hand.

"Let me see," he said softly, taking her fingers into his hand. Rune couldn't help but study his long, strong fingers as he gently pressed each finger and articulated the joints, slowly checking. She had no memory of it hurting. Part of her couldn't believe he was actually there. They were talking to each other so easily as if no time had passed.

When she started studying the small scars all over his hand, she realized what she was doing and Rune pulled her own away. "I think I just stunned them, they're fine. No big deal." He didn't contradict her, letting her hands go and settling down to sit properly on his seat. He winced when he started to lean against his back.

Rune blinked a moment, then remembered. "Are *you* okay?" Quickly, she began to paw at his back, trying to get him to turn in the cramped space, "You've been shot; let me see!"

Gently, St. Benedict laughed. "I'm fine, I'm fine. Look." He pulled on the collar of the black shirt, stretching it to reveal the bulk of a vinyl-like vest underneath. "I came armored this time," he explained, before letting the collar go and sitting back.

"But…what if you had been shot in the head?" She tried to push that image out of her mind. St. Benedict didn't answer at first, reaching forward to fetch something out from under the driver's side seat. Setting his fedora on his head, his eyes sparkled in the passing streetlight, having returned to their human-like green. He knew how cool he looked. Rune tried not to smile, which only made her grin bloom wider.

Rune was hyper aware of the feeling of his body pressed against her side, since there was no room for the three adults in the back to have a margin. She really had missed the dark, mysteriously sexy corporate spy calling himself a Saint. Maxamillion pressed in on her other side as he too took his proper seat, and she also remembered what the Saint's owner had said about that being a common reaction to St. Benedict. That helped cool the jets a little.

"That was exciting," Maxamillion said, intensely. Adrenaline was still pumping through the man; he was having a hard time sitting still.

"Your gun went out the door," St. Benedict said flatly to Maxamillion. That cooled the other man's jets a little too. Blinking twice, Maxamillion shook out the bracelet from his sleeve. A small blue light was blinking on it and he tried to press a tab that Rune couldn't really pick out. The light continued to blink heedlessly.

"You're out of range of the signal," St. Benedict judged, his lazy tone sounding like that was exactly what he expected.

Then he said to Rune, "The bracelets are synced to our guns. He's attempting to disintegrate it, but they've only got a short range."

"What good is that?" Rune asked, marveling at the technology in spite of herself.

"Only the person with the bracelet on, holding the gun, can fire it. Keeps enemies from claiming your weapon and using it on you. You have to purposely unlock it for general use."

"Or disintegrate it if you really lose it," Rune finished, putting it all together.

"Yeah, provided you're in range of it." St. Benedict gave Maxamillion a pointed look.

"You just said yourself. They cannot fire it, the gun is useless to them," Maxamillion snapped, looking more like a put-out child than the cool, calculating business man from earlier.

"Still traceable," St. Benedict said softly.

Maxamillion took the information in a moment, then his eyebrows furrowed and he rubbed the bridge of his nose. "Crap."

"Very succinctly put, sir." St. Benedict cracked a smile, but it didn't look like it had any mirth in it. Rune was not enjoying being in the middle.

A feral look flashed in St. Benedict's eyes. "You shouldn't be here, sir," he added.

"I gave you resources and you did not use them," Maxamillion replied. "You lost control of the situation."

"The situation lost control before I became involved."

"You should have anticipated this! It's why you exist!" Maxamillion sharply shouted, cutting off the Saint's words. After a heavy moment where St. Benedict stared straight ahead and Rune didn't breath, Maxamillion continued in a lower tone. "Now our time table is in shambles. I don't even know where we stand. Too many…too many lives are on the line here. Too many resources. Too much is at stake."

"I know what's at stake better than you do. That's why I'm still alive, right sir?" St. Benedict asked. The silence became heavy again and all the occupants of the car soaked in it for a long time. The car had resumed normal driving and Rune realized after a few glances out the darkened windows that it was taking itself out onto the highway.

"Where are we going?" Rune asked. St. Benedict jumped the tiniest amount when she spoke as if he had dozed a little. Rune would have missed it if she hadn't been pressed into him. He raised his arm to lay it along the back of the backseat, which gave a little more air for Rune, even if it had a distinct male smell to it. It wasn't entirely unpleasant.

"That depends on you, Ms. Leveau. I have some options I could suggest," Maxamillion stated, though Rune felt like she had really been asking St. Benedict.

"You're not kidnapping me, then?" she asked, trying for levity she didn't really feel. "No need. I think I already know which option you're going to choose," the CEO said self-assuredly.

"Stop playing with her," the Saint muttered under his breath.

Rune blinked at St. Benedict's coldness. Even in the face of danger, he had always had a smile, albeit a wicked one, on his face. His frigidness now was palpable.

St. Benedict's tone was not lost on Maxamillion. He heaved a big sigh, tapping his leg with his manicured fingers like they were picking out a brief tune on his knee, going still when he began to speak again.

"We are headed to my Chicagoland headquarters, Ms. Leveau. Until we determine exactly who attacked you back there, you will be our guest."

"I know who attacked me." She turned back to St. Benedict. "It was Calvin Harrison."

"I thought so," the Saint nodded. "There was also the sniper and then the gunmen at the opposing ends of the alley. I do not think any of them were working together."

"Who is Calvin Harrison?" Maxamillion asked.

"An idiot who used to work for a shell company that holds the mortgage on the Lucky Devil. Or at least he did."

"Did?" Maxamillion asked, very interested.

"About two months ago, he left the company. Family obligations," Rune said, hoping she didn't sound too dodgy.

"He's the new Oberon," St. Benedict added, his eyes far away. "And he was an obvious threat to your target."

"You didn't think to take him in?" Maxamillion growled.

"There was a sniper and then those other gunmen. Something has changed. The asset is compromised."

"Am I supposed to be the asset?" Rune interjected. St. Benedict looked at her but before he could answer, Maxamillion cut in.

"Then what changed?" Maxamillion bit the words, barely suppressing his growing anger.

"You visited her. I can only speculate but as hard as we may try, sir, you're a public figure and it is near impossible to hide your movements when you move publicly. We are playing against opponents who have probably been in the game longer than either of us and with more resources than we have."

"We all agreed to the meeting," Maxamillion countered.

"You wanted to move up to the next level of the game and here it is," St. Benedict continued. "It comes with added risks. Sir. You wanted to meet with her and that has made someone or maybe several someones very panicky. She's in danger now because we moved in. Now we have to deal...."

"You know, I'm still in the car, right?" Rune asked, pushing both men off of her. She was getting very fed up with being talked over. Literally.

Both men settled back, neither having realized they had been leaning increasingly closer and squishing Rune in the process. Rune took a big breath in. After another long moment, Maxamillion regarded Rune again. "The noose is coming around your neck, Ms. Leveau. I had hoped to give you more time to think about my offer to find your husband's work."

"But I told you, he uploaded that into who knows where. My Finding ability doesn't work on things like...abstract concepts or ideas," Rune insisted, though she wasn't entirely sure that was true or not.

St. Benedict snorted a chuckle as he thought about that idea. "I suppose that's one way to think about it. Computer code really is simply a language for abstract ideas made concrete."

"The night Justin and I were arrested...." Rune continued, but her words died away. Again the memory surfaced. Justin's face filled with anger and fear as he madly typed at his computers.

His attempt to burn everything and his screaming at her. The armed men bursting around them, pinning her to the floor as she screamed, heedless of how they were hurting her.

A warm hand cupped over her clenched ones. Her fingers had gone white with the force of them clasping together. St. Benedict didn't squeeze, only rested it there. It was enough to send warmth up her arms. She took a deep breath in and let her shoulders unknot a little.

"It isn't an idea we want you to look for, Ms. Leveau. Your Finding talent may make you the only person who could find what we're all seeking," Maxamillion countered, not noticing the exchange between his travel companions as he had turned his gaze back out his passenger side window.

"The Kodiak company made many mistakes in its early days, before it became the conglomerate powerhouse it is now. My guess? The sub-company who owned the prison that held you for Kodiak, made a mistake in letting you go. The supervisor was more interested in making a quick buck off of your aunt than they were in understanding the long term implications of losing you. And for six years your aunt kept you hidden and safe from them. Now she's gone, and you've more or less come out of hiding."

"Kodiak knew where I was the whole time," Rune countered. "At least the…well-dressed woman made me believe so."

"The well-dressed woman?" Maxamillion was genuinely perplexed.

"I told you, the woman who was most likely demonically possessed," St. Benedict said.

Maxamillion failed to suppress a shiver. Rune didn't blame him.

"She never told me her name," Rune explained, then screwed her eyebrow together as she remembered something Maddie had told her. "Or, maybe she traded her name. If she was demonically possessed, then maybe her name was part of the bargain…."

"Her name?" St. Benedict asked.

"It is possible. It would explain why no one can even mention what it was. She simply became the well-dressed woman to me."

Rune sat forward, acutely finding it harder to breath. "Dammit. Dammit," she murmured under her breath. "I thought I had dealt with this."

"We'll get you something to drink inside," St. Benedict said, rubbing her back firmly. The car came to a stop outside a large building. Through St. Benedict's side window, Rune saw trees and thought they must be near the Forest Preserve; they hadn't driven for long enough to truly be out of the city. Maxamillion opened his own passenger side door and stepped out. Rune shifted to follow him, trying to ignore the fact that she was still dressed in her pajamas and no shoes. St. Benedict exited the car from the other side.

"A drink sounds great…." she started as her bare foot hit the pavement outside the car. Lights glowed up at the building and Rune's heart stopped for a second.

"No…no. Oh god, no!" she heard herself say. Other voices were talking but Rune was already screaming, pushing her way back into the car with senseless animal panic.

A voice shouted, but Rune didn't care. All she could see was the prison where Anna Masterson had been tortured a lifetime ago.

Chapter 4

"Rune! Rune, you're safe! Safe!" The voice continued to shout, but Rune did not care. She continued to kick and push back away from the open door, the prison building looming behind Maxamillion, who looked back into the car, perplexed. Rune's back hit the opposing door, but she didn't stop trying to drive her heels into the leather seats. It was a nightmare. A nightmare made real. They had trapped her, tricked her, taking her back. She wasn't going to go back.

"Rune, calm down!" Maxamillion tried, but she continued to scream, kicking at his hand with her foot. It made contact and he recoiled with a hiss.

"We need to get her out of there!" another gruff voice called.

"No, no, no," Rune repeated, chanting the word like a mantra. She tried to look around herself, figure out an escape. Could she dive for the front and make the car drive again? Should she exit the car and run for the trees?

Before she could get her thoughts together for a coherent plan, the door she pressed up against fell away. Her full weight had been against it and with its absence she fell backwards with a gasp into a set of arms that roughly yanked her out and onto her bare feet.

"No! No!" Rune screamed and twisted for all she was worth, but the arms knew how to hold a person who was trying to fight. Fear fueled by helplessness brought her back to the small room with the grey table and small rounded chairs. Someone was holding her from behind, laughing in her ear and hurting her, while the well-dressed woman sat impatiently waiting for the prisoner to settle down.

"Stop it," a hard voice hissed in her ear, "Rune...Anna look at me." Rune ceased her struggling at the sound of her old name. She was panting hard.

"No, please. Please, don't hurt me," she begged pathetically. The arms let go of her and she almost fell over as they spun her around.

Then a gun hit the palm of her hand.

Rune ceased breathing, staring down at the warm, dark-grey metal. Two male hands covered hers, holding the gun in her hand. They guided the barrel to point straight at his chest. Stunned, Rune looked up into St. Benedict's face. There was no malice there, no judgement. Only a warm, tender smile, filled with peace.

"You're safe, I swear to you," he continued. One of his hands let go of the gun, and he brushed a thumb under her eye, sweeping the tears away. "My life is yours," he whispered softly, intimate as a confession, "I will not let anyone harm you, or hurt you. I swear."

"No, he...." Rune glanced over at the CEO. Maxamillion's face was twisted in anger. "You're lying to me...you're a liar."

Pain passed through St. Benedict's eyes, turning them dark and intensely haunted. He lifted up his wrist so she could see the bracelet. Letting go of the gun, a finger pressed on the bracelet's tab so he could speak into it directly. "Unlock for general use."

The gun buzzed in Rune's hand and her eyes widened as she knew it was live. As soon as the gun buzzed, St. Benedict pulled his shirt over his head. His fedora went with the shirt, getting wrapped up in the fabric. Rune's heart skipped a beat in its rapid tattoo.

"St. Benedict, what are you doing?!" Maxamillion shouted.

Taking his shirt off revealed the bullet resistant vest and with two quick pulls on the Velcro strips, St. Benedict pulled that over his head too and threw it aside.

"Take her! Take her from behind!" A voice called. Rune panicked and partly turned to see a semi-circle of armed people encroaching on her position. Even as she started to turn to face them, St. Benedict seized the gun and retrained it back onto his now vulnerable chest.

"Stay back, she's live!" he called, and pivoted them so his

body was between her and the encroaching semi-circle.

"Sir?" the man who called asked. The line of what had to be building security held their positions, not one of them taking their eyes off of Rune.

"St. Benedict!" Maxamillion gave a warning look from behind the line. Several other security personnel had moved into place, surrounding their CEO, creating a shield of bodies around him.

"Everyone stay back," St. Benedict shouted over his own shoulder at them. As one, the security personnel stopped, some looking at each other in confusion.

"I...I can't...." Rune's hands were shaking and she started to lower the gun.

Immediately, St. Benedict grabbed it and placed it hard against his chest, just over his heart.

"My life is yours," he repeated to Rune. He didn't care who heard it.

"Your life is mine, St. Benedict!" Maxamillion shouted.
"You see? I'm very important to him. He doesn't dare make a move on you while you've got that trained on me. We are going to go inside that building and you *are* going to come out again. As long as I'm your hostage, he has no choice but to let you go free and unharmed." St. Benedict continued to smile reassuringly.

"That...doesn't make sense. There's so much, so much he can do...." Rune struggled to speak but fear was choking her.

"But he won't."
Rune stared at their hands, wrapped together over the weapon.
"I...I can't take your life," she whispered. Her hands were shaking so bad, but she was also afraid to let go of the gun, knowing it *was* the only thing that was keeping the others at bay.

"You won't. Like I said, I'm giving it to you." She stared into his eyes. He was so sincere and so confident.

"You're crazy," she whispered to him, meaning it.

"Oh, yes, very. Now do you think you are ready to go inside?" he asked.

She took a shuddering breath, and looked up at the building again. Nobody was breathing as she faced the unfaceable.

"You won't leave me?"

"Absolutely not."

"What if...what if it's a trap? This is just some elaborate trap?"

"Then you pull the trigger."

She looked down at the weapon. This was against everything she believed about herself. She should let it go. Her hand wouldn't open.

"Rune, look at me."

She did.

His eyes were very serious. "If I betray you, you pull the trigger, you understand me?"

She swallowed.

One small nod was all she could manage. It felt like her neck and back had frozen and she would never be able to turn her head again. "How...how do we do this?"

"You come alongside me, keep the gun trained on me and rest it against my ribs. I'm going to put my arm around your shoulders and we're going to walk in nice and slow. Like it's no big thing." As he talked, he did as he said, stepping around her very slowly until he was facing the same direction as she was. He used his own hand to guide the gun.

"Shooting me here will guarantee that the bullet punctures my heart," he said.

"Don't tell me that!" she squeaked.

"It's alright."

"Stop saying that too!"

"Yes, ma'am." His voice was so mirthful considering the situation.

"This isn't funny," she hissed. "This is life or death!"

"All life and death situations are funny," he countered. "Don't worry. I trust you. We're going to get through this just fine."

Not knowing what else to do, she set her free hand against the bare skin of his back. It felt awkward.

"You just had to take off your shirt," Rune muttered.

St. Benedict chuckled softly. "Needs must when the devil drives." Somehow that made Rune feel better, more normal about all this.

"Everyone, stand down. I don't want any mistakes," St. Benedict called out.

"Absolutely not!" Maxamillion commanded. No one moved.

"It's your call, sir, but I humbly posit that this will be the only way to get her inside and that lost gun isn't going to destroy itself." Though the Saint's face was calm, with the same knowing smile on it, Rune felt his heart beating a hundred miles a minute against the palm of her hand. So he was concerned.

Maxamillion paused a moment, letting go of whatever he had been about to say. His eyes landed on Rune and something seemed to click in his brain. Then he cleared his throat, "Of course, the prison. I miscalculated," he said. Gesturing to the nearest security officer, he turned away to speak to them. It was the one who had been issuing commands, Rune thought.

"Rune, do you mind if I bend down and retrieve my shirt?" St. Benedict asked through the side of his mouth.

"What? Oh, um. Yeah, yeah," she stuttered, sounding like an idiot. "My brain is like a scrambled egg."

"It's my fault. I should have warned you about where we were going," he said, holding his hands out and making sure each agent looking at him saw what he intended. Something in the way one of the agents shifted made him check his move down. "Rune, get behind me again and bend your knees with me," he instructed. The agent he had locked eyes with gritted his teeth in a grimace as Rune did as she was told. St. Benedict narrowed his own at the guy.

"He was going to shoot me, wasn't he?" she asked, meeting the agent's eyes over St. Benedict's shoulder as he lowered exactly enough to pick up the shirt.

"They're just following corporate protocol," St. Benedict assured. It took a few blind seconds to fish the fedora back out, which he handed wordlessly to Rune. Then he slid the shirt back on, his muscles moving smoothly, minimizing the time the neck hole blocked his sight.

"Stand down," the order came from Maxamillion. There was only a half a second before the shoulders dropped and the guns pivoted towards the ground.

"Put them away, folks, and back away now," the leader barked as well.

The security people stepped back and did as they were told, the angry agent being the last to comply.

"Rune, come around again," St. Benedict said, lifting his arm so she could do so. He took the fedora back from her and set it on his head with the authority of a man completely in control of the situation.

Maxamillion still stood where he had, his hands clasped behind his back as he waited for the last of his security team to line up behind him.

"How would you like to proceed, Ms. Leveau?" Maxamillion asked politely, though his eyes were talking to St. Benedict. "You have my best asset at your disposal. You are in control of this situation, so it's your call."

A pang of guilt rippled through her and Rune started to lower the gun, but St. Benedict rumbled, "Don't drop it." He took a breath in to speak, but Rune cut him off.

"I…I want to know what this is all about," she called. "And I want to be free to leave whenever I choose."

"Ms. Leveau," said Maxamillion looking up at the black sky above with its scant stars in a show of exasperation, "I can assure you that…."

"I've had enough assurances to last me a lifetime, Mr. Corinthe. And I've lived two already." Her voice became steadier as she focused on the CEO and not the building behind him. St. Benedict's back shook a little, chuckling breathily.

"Can it, St. Benedict," the CEO ordered. "You've already cost me enough tonight."

St. Benedict stilled his face.

Maxamillion stepped back and gestured to the doors of the building.

"If you follow me inside, Ms. Leveau, I swear I will show you what you ask. I also swear you are free to leave at any time you choose, whether you have a hostage or not. That is all the reassurance I can offer at this time, other than granting you the use of my employee as your collateral. Shall we, Ms. Leveau?"

Rune only considered a second before nodding assent. The

walk inside was the longest of Rune's life.

Security personnel moved around them like antibodies surrounding a foreign body, opening the door ahead and creating a line behind. Maxamillion led the way, moving heedless of the activity, as if this was natural. Rune got the impression that walking through a war zone would seem natural to Maxamillion, as if he was simply too powerful and important to be bothered with the activity of lesser people.

Rune hesitated a moment at the threshold. It was surreal to walk willingly into the building again. It had been years since she was dragged into it, handcuffed and with a throbbing face where someone had hit her. There had been no lawyer, no advocate there to defend her rights. No trial or justice. Things like that had simply not existed in that place, despite what the corporate prison systems insisted was standard protocol.

"I'm surprised you recognized the building from the outside," St. Benedict said softly as Rune forced herself to take the next step inside.

"I remember," Rune started to say, but she had to lick her lips, her eyes going wide as they entered the high foyer. "… Maddie, when she came to take me away from here…." She blinked, the memory overlaying what she was actually seeing. "Have you ever had a moment seared into your mind? Even though you only saw it once, you can never unsee it again? It's etched perfectly in your mind forever."

"Yes." St. Benedict squeezed her shoulder.

Maxamillion slowed a step to turn to Rune. "This building is mine; we acquired it earlier this year," Maxamillion said with casual pride. Rune thought the declaration odd. After all she technically was a hostage taker. Politely, she tried to focus on the space around her.

The foyer was in blank white marble with hints of grey threads throughout it. It was about ten feet long and eight wide, feeling utilitarian, more like a hallway than an entrance. A security desk of black wood as tall as chest height sat the far end. The security personnel who had entered approached the one standing at the desk, speaking softly to her as Maxamillion strolled up. A familiar industrial-looking door with a hatched, bullet proof glass window in the top was closed next to the desk.

"Rune, it's just a door," St. Benedict whispered to her, when she jerked back a half-step.

"I know," she hissed back, but her eyes couldn't leave it.

St. Benedict wished he could take her out of the building that minute. He should have known that coming here would be a problem for her and he didn't blame her for reacting the way she was.

"The first time I walked into this building, I threw up," he admitted to her, and only to her.

Rune blinked twice. Giving her a piece of truth worked; she tore her eyes away from the door to look at him instead.

"You did?" Her voice was small, like a child's looking for a scrap of hope. She nodded knowingly. "They held you here too."

The door opened, security allowing them through. Maxamillion naturally went first. Again gentle pressure on her shoulder helped Rune start her feet forward.

She went, her jaw locked resolutely. She was so brave. St. Benedict kept talking, distracting her as best he could. "We were all brought here, all those on Masterson's team. After the embezzlement scheme was discovered, the whole of us were suspected. They arrested all of us," he said.

"I remember," Rune said, "I mean, what you told me before. About you and your wife."

"Yes," he said absently, losing himself in his own memory.

On the other side of the door was an elevator that they all entered. There were no buttons since it had only one destination. As the door closed, St. Benedict passed one last eye over the contingent of security that remained downstairs by Maxamillion's orders. Each of them eyed him and Rune in return with varying degrees of concealed contempt. The security contingent hated the Saints in Maxamillion's employ, mostly because they didn't know who and what he was or how he ranked in this little world. Such things can chafe and St. Benedict was very aware of the fear and hate the unknown could create. The Saints went against the natural order of things. Very few knew about what the honorific Saint meant. Very few understood the power and effectiveness he had been upgraded with via his augmentations. If he wanted, he could have taken out several of them before the other half had drawn their weapons. He also had no doubt they would have let Rune shoot him if they had a personal choice. Not that she would, and he knew that with every fiber of his being. It wasn't who she was. Yet, she knew what *he* was, about the modifications done to his body to make his sight more accurate, to enhance his endurance, and allow his consciousness to pass through the singularity. And here she was putting her faith in him. It was more than he deserved.

Rune took a large gasp as the elevator doors opened again into the larger room beyond. Where the foyer had been white and stark, the cavernous room was warm, darker and open. The floor was like wood that sprung a little underfoot. There was a soft ambiance to the light, making the place feel safe and comfortable. Throughout the room were computer terminals in little clusters and people working at or around them.

"It's a lot better now that we've renovated," St. Benedict said cheerfully. "Hey Malachi!"

Over to the forward side of the room was a fully decked out kitchen with black marble countertops and stainless steel appliances, including three refrigerators. It would have been perfect in a bachelor executive's loft apartment.

Malachi, a youngish man about the same height as Rune, was exiting the kitchen area looking like he hadn't changed clothes in days again. His brown shaggy hair was sticking out in odd angles and threatening to go full mullet if scissors didn't intercede soon. The pink glasses he wore when doing intense, long term computer work were pushed back into the mess of hair like a headband. In one hand he carried a plate of food and a couple cans of something sugary and caffeinated were tucked under his arm. Malachi stopped mid-stride, raising his plate hand to signal a wave at St. Benedict, but it stopped halfway up when the computer tech's brain caught up with sight of Rune sticking a gun in his friend's ribs.

"Hey, St. Benedict," he said carefully, "What's going on?"

"You remember the Talent, Rune Leveau, right?" St. Benedict

smiling broadly like he was introducing her at a party. "She's holding me up at gunpoint."

"Uh," Malachi raised an eyebrow, "Hi, Rune."

"Hi," she said, feeling really wrong.

"Um, do you mind me asking, why are you holding a gun to my friend's ribs there?" Malachi glanced over at a bank of computers where people were working. At least they had been, but many had stopped and looked up from their terminals at the more exciting events happening only feet away.

"Well…because he told me to," Rune said truthfully, nodding her head a little at St. Benedict.

Malachi nodded once. "Sounds about right. Would you like something to drink, Rune?" He gestured back to the kitchen.

"Uh, no thanks."

"Yeah, sure." Malachi stood awkwardly, looking around for someone to give him some direction. "Oh, St. Ben, uh, St. Rachel said to tell you she's looking for you the minute you get back."

"I will take a Manhattan," Maxamillion said, cutting into the exchange. All eyes shifted to him.

"Oh! Sure boss. Um, are you okay with that?" Malachi asked, nodding once to indicate Rune and St. Benedict, which caused him to lose one of his drinks and initiate a juggling act with the plate of food.

"What the hell?!" a woman's voice shouted and all attention pivoted to a beautiful woman carrying some files. St. Benedict had noticed her crossing the room but before he could call out to her, she had dropped her folders and drawn her gun with the same speed St. Benedict used to put himself between Rune and her shot.

"St. Rachel, stand down!" Maxamillion shouted, though the Saint had already checked herself.

"Oh, for Pete's sake, St. Rach. I can't have another woman holding me at her mercy without you getting all jealous and such," St. Benedict mocked, shaking his head disapprovingly.

St. Rachel's eyes flashed with rage, but she also kept the barrel of her firearm pointed at the industrial ceiling instead of Rune.

"What the hell is going on, St. Benedict?" she demanded like a displeased goddess.

"Rune, this is St. Rachel," St. Benedict said, stepping to the side a little so the women could see each other. "St. Rachel, you remember Rune? You two met a couple of months ago."

"At the coffee house," Rune remembered.

St. Rachel pursed perfect ruby lips together. Apparently, she remembered too.

"For the record," St. Benedict said raising a finger, "her having the gun on me was my idea."

"It is." Maxamillion shot St. Rachel a confirming glance.

"Christ, St. Benedict!" St. Rachel cursed. "Why do you have to keep doing these stupid, asinine…pranks?!"

"Pranks?" St. Benedict laid a hand on his chest in mock offense. "Madam, I have no idea what you might be referring to."

"This is not a joke!" St. Rachel wasn't letting him get another word out. She put her gun away. "You keep doing these stupid…. What is she doing here?"

"Messing up our group dynamics, apparently," Malachi interjected as he walked through the tension with his plate of food and a Manhattan in a triangle shaped glass instead of his sodas.

"She's here at my invitation," Maxamillion said, taking the drink.

"There was an incident at her bar," St. Benedict added. He grabbed Malachi's shoulder as the tech walked past. "We need to get all the nearby cameras up on the screens. We need to see everything that happened."

Malachi nodded, "Got it," and scurried off to give instructions to the other techs.

"If you rescued her, then shouldn't she be more…grateful?" St. Rachel spat the word petulantly, putting her hands on her hips.

"Oh, is this community therapy time? Would you like to air out your issues in front of everyone in the room? Go ahead St. Rachel, you first." St. Benedict's smile went sickly as he challenged the beautiful woman.

She narrowed her eyes even more at him, which made her look even more sultry, the epitome of beautiful-when-angry.

"I purchased the two of you for your skills, not so you can fight on my time. Now, Ms. Leveau, if you will come this way, I wish to settle the matter between us so we can get on to more important work." Maxamillion gestured toward a far wall where an oblong conference table sat with matching chairs, all in dark wood. A large screen bolted to the concrete wall was a blank flat backdrop to the table.

Rune felt the eyes in the room follow the small group as they headed there, St. Benedict's arm still firmly around her shoulders, his gun firmly against his own ribs. St. Rachel still stared sharp, cold daggers at Rune and Rune tried to pretend she didn't see. Without being told, Malachi returned from relaying orders, heading straight to a computer terminal beside the screen, his sandwich hanging from his mouth as he tapped at the keyboard with both hands. The large screen came to life, first flashing the cracked pillar logo in the middle of the white space.

"Bring up all personnel files," Maxamillion ordered before taking another drink from his martini glass.

"A please would be nice," Malachi grumbled.

Images filled the screen, popping up one at a time in order, starting at the top and moving down as each row filled. Rune narrowed her eyes, trying to focus on each image. There were two images per pop, one of the person looking forward and one looking to the side. Names were listed to the side along with stats. Rune's eyes widened as she recognized Malachi's face when he popped up. The face in the image had sunken-in eyes and scraggly hair compared to the man with the bright, alert eyes and a healthy countenance. He waved at her a little when she looked over to him, knowing she was comparing their images. More faces filled the screen until the bottom row, when St. Benedict's and St. Rachel's faces appeared. St. Benedict's image looked hard and cold, a face Rune recognized, the one that laid under the constant smile he otherwise wore. St. Rachel's echoed her counterpart. Then the final image appeared, this one of a dead-eyed, young black man. The screen was finally full.

"Highlight my file," Maxamillion said, then added a belated, terse, "Please."

The bottom-most picture double clicked and then enlarged to fill the screen with the young man's face. The kid looked down at the camera taking his picture with a haughty contempt, despite the slightly swollen eye he bore. His hair was long and tightly braided, wrapping around his shoulders like coils. It was hard to make anything else out from the image.

"As you can see, this is me," Maxamillion said and that was the moment Rune realized it was. Comparing the two men, the living one was older, with more maturity in his bones, his hair was cut shorter and he didn't have any scraggles of facial hair on his chin. One was cultured, the other rough, but they both had fire in their eyes.

"Yes, I can see that," Rune said, looking back and forth between the older face and the younger.

"Everyone you see on this board was a victim of the corporate authority," St. Benedict stated.

"And now they work here?" Rune turned to look at the other people working throughout the room, picking out some of the faces from the screen.

"Everyone you see on this board is part of an underground organization whose sole mission is to undermine and break the hold corporations have over the people of this city," Maxamillion declared, his voice echoing pride and certainty.

"We're the resistance," Malachi piped in.

"We're more than that," St. Rachel said, her gaze far away as she scanned over the faces on the screen. "We may be the last hope for…." she didn't finish the sentence, instead letting it die.

"This, Ms. Leveau, is our secret," Maxamillion answered, stepping in front of the projection screen, his own image warping around his actual form. "I realize that I asked you for your trust without offering any reason to. We are not what we seem. I told you I am the CEO of a corporation but what I didn't tell you is that this corporation is in itself the legitimate mask for our true work."

"You're…an underground resistance posing as a corporation," Rune repeated, not sure she understood what she was hearing.

Malachi chuckled. "Yeah, the outside world thinks we're

primarily a security company." The tech leaned on the desk with crossed arms. "They don't know we're working to bring them all down."

"The Corinthe Corporation is our front, the legitimate face of our secret organization. Our sole mission is to upset the balance and return power to the people. Years ago I was simply an anarchist, unable to do more than start protests and thumb my nose at authority. Now, I have the power to change the course of actual events. To truly make the differences that need to happen to free all of us from this modern serfdom before every shred of our freedom is gone forever." The veneer of the cool corporate business man melted away from Maxamillion. Instead, he stood there in the projected light looking every inch the noble, dashing rebel leader full of fire and inspiration.

"I...I don't understand. What is this?" Rune asked struggling to take it all in. She couldn't imagine it, a world without corporations? Or the Guilds they were replacing? "It's impossible."

"Why?" Maxamillion asked, like a teacher waiting to hear his student's objections before leading them to the answer.

Rune growled in disgust. "Because.... They have too much money and power and influence. They control everything."

"They are a cancer to be sure, but not a terminal one," Maxamillion said confidently, "Especially since the cure is within reach."

"How?" Rune shook her head unconsciously. "How can you bring down a corporation? I mean, even if one files bankruptcy another will buy it out and take its place." Flashes of her social studies and government class in high school told her that was true. It was part of the reason her parents had been so eager for her to marry Justin. His standing, and his family's, in their corporation was the only way her own family could move up in the world. At least, it had been until his fall from grace. The more powerful the corporation one belonged to, the more rights and privileges one had, the more seats they had in every level of government to advocate for you. It was all based off of the old system of representational government that existed decades ago, when people were represented by unions and guilds who would send elected representatives sponsored by each Guild. The larger the Guild, the larger the number of representatives per district. All of it basic civics class.

"This government is invulnerable to change. And that change is based in Magic, at least partly." Maxamillion leaned forward on the table. "Which is why we need you, Ms. Leveau, not just for your Talent but because you can be our connection to the Magic community. If we are to defeat these giants, we're going to have to come together." He gestured at the screen around him. "I show you this only to prove to you who we are and what we intend. We are trying to save the world, Rune Leveau, and we need you to help us. I know you were afraid to come here, afraid to touch us, but I swear to you, you are safe here with us. We are the good guys, and we need you."

Rune stood speechless for a moment while Maxamillion's words rang in her ears. She was honestly stunned. She didn't snap out of it until St. Benedict brought the gun back to his ribs for her. She hadn't noticed it drifting down.

"That's why you want me? But, you could get anyone for that. Someone better connected to the Guild than I am."

"Show her," St. Benedict said, flatly, pinning his boss with intense eyes. Something indiscernible passed between the two men.

"Are you sure?" Maxamillion asked finally.

St. Benedict took a deep breath as if he expected the question but also dreaded it. Then he nodded at Malachi. "Show her what we found."

No one said anything more as the screen changed and Maxamillion moved out of the way.

A video, grainy and grey, filled the screen. Rune's arm holding the gun lost its strength and flopped to her sides, the weapon hitting the ground. She didn't even notice. Her eyes were as wide as they could go as she stared at a face she hadn't seen in ages.

Justin Masterson, looking the same as he had six years ago, sat at a table very much like the one Rune had all those years ago. Both his wrists were locked in manacles fixed to the table in front of him. He was haggard and gaunt with obvious suffering. The sight of it made Rune's heart ache, much to her own surprise.

"State your name," a disembodied male voice demanded.

"Go-Fuck-Yourself McFuckerston of the Give-a-Fucksville McFuckerstons," Justin replied. Before he could chuckle, Justin began to scream as electricity went up his arms with a loud repeating snap through the manacles.

"State your name," the disembodied voice repeated.

"Justin… Masterson," the prisoner panted out.

"And why are you here?" The voice asked.

"Because…." Justin licked his lips. Rune could see the joke he wanted to make flit across his face.

Shaking her head fearfully, her fingers flew to her lips. "No Justin, don't do it," she whispered, lost completely in the video. As if he heard her, he checked himself, his eyes dropping to the manacles on the table.

"Because…I have something you want."

"You have something that belongs to us," the voice corrected, "We want it back."

"It doesn't belong to you. It's mine. It's my idea, it's my code," Justin growled.

"But we own you, Justin. Of course we do. This company has invested quite heavily into you. We expect a return on that investment. You owe us for everything you have. Your wealth, your status, your wife…."

Justin spit across the table. More electricity was the response. Tears filled Rune's eyes, blurring her view.

"Turn it off! Turn it off now!" St. Benedict ordered. She vaguely felt his hands on her shoulders, trying to turn her away, but she refused as the image of her once-husband froze, his face twisted in pain.

"Get off me!" Rune shouted, pushing St. Benedict's hands from her.

She turned on Maxamillion, who stood somberly to the side, waiting.

"Where is he?" she demanded forcefully, a bit surprised by her own reaction.

"We don't know. This is only one of several of the Masterson files we've been able to recover."

"These aren't the true Masterson files," St. Benedict corrected, "We recovered this, and videos like it, from this company when we acquired the building. This prison was a subsidiary of the Kodiak Company."

"Not that they knew that's what they gave up," Malachi chuckled.

"Kodiak tried to recreate his experiments but they were only part and partial. He wasn't able to accomplish it, not before he disappeared," St. Rachel stated. From the darker tone of her voice, Rune felt St. Rachel was of the negative opinion about whether this theoretical program was even possible.

"They've never stopped trying," Maxamillion said, "We have no idea how close or far away they are. There is only speculation."

"Do you know what the Masterson files contain, Ms. Leveau, or Rune?" Malachi asked.

After a moment Rune found her voice to speak, the well of emotions clogging up her throat. "Rune. And yes. Insofar as I know what he was trying to accomplish. Magic cast by a computer. And as far as I know, it never succeeded."

"The rumors say he did succeed," St. Rachel said, her voice edged with accusation. "Once."

"I don't know. I don't know." Rune crossed her arms.

"Do you understand our stakes now?" Maxamillion pointed at the still image of Justin. "If the corporations get a hold of the technology to create magic on a massive scale, it's over. There will be no limit on their power. But if we get our hands on it, *we* remake the world."

Goosebumps rolled over Rune's skin as the implications sank in. A lifetime of not thinking about it was finally catching up with her.

"We don't intend to take this power for ourselves either. Which is why I need to reach out to the Magic Guild. We need to build a coalition. If this tech exists, it needs to belong to all of us," Maxamillion answered before she could ask. "You are the only person who can stand in this juncture and bring us all together."

Rune snorted at the grandiose statement. Maxamillion flinched a little but steeled his expression against her derision.

"Are you trying to tell me I'm some sort of 'chosen one'?" Rune wasn't even aware of her slightly shaking head as she spoke.

"You are one really good option," Maxamillion said levelly. "One we are trying to make work."

"Rune, I understand what you are saying," St. Benedict finally interjected, turning her toward him. "Yes, he is sales pitching you a little bit, and yes we could find someone else and make it work, if that's what you want. But you are unique in one very important regard, you were there that night. You *know* why this is important."

"The night...they came for us...." Rune closed her eyes. Why was this happening? Why couldn't her past stay in the past?

"Rune, you don't have to answer," St. Benedict said softly.

Didn't she?

She forced herself to look at Justin's face again. It had been years since she had seen it. Never once had she wanted to try to Find him, to find out what happened to him. It was easier to be angry at him for what he had done to her, casually wonder, or simply try to heal beyond it. It had taken six years before Rune felt she had gotten anywhere with that, and now this. Now, he was being thrust back into her life. Yet, Maddie had said there may come a time, before she was ready most likely, that she would have to face him again, even if only symbolically.

As her mind whirled with thoughts, her gaze drifted to the gun laying at her feet. Slowly, deliberately, she squatted down and picked up the cooling handle firmly.

"St. Benedict, I don't want to carry this anymore," Rune said softly, holding the weapon out to him to take.

"Are you sure?" St. Benedict asked, his eyes searching her face, trying desperately to interpret the expression there.

She turned the barrel down and held it out to him, offering a small, calm smile. "I believe you." She looked around at all the faces watching her. "I apologize for my overreaction...."

"It wasn't an overreaction," St. Benedict said, cutting off her apology, as he received the gun, slipping off the bracelet from her wrist onto his own.

"Still, thanks for taking the risk for me."

"Story of our lives, sweetheart," Malachi said as he crossed through again to retrieve his sodas.

Chapter 5

Giving up the gun dispelled the tension in the room. While work never fully stopped, attention was returned to the business at hand, leaving the small group around the conference table to continue without a surreptitious audience.

"Does that mean you'll join us?" Maxamillion asked, sliding his hands into his pockets, slipping into his CEO persona like it was his tailored dress coat.

"No, not yet." She regarded him coolly. "You're worse than a car salesman. No matter what you say about your reasons, you're still technically a corporation." She raised an eyebrow.

"And you don't work for corporations," St. Benedict finished, mirth dancing in his eyes and maybe pride.

"I don't make life changing decisions in the moment," Rune responded instead.

"Well, how nice to have that luxury," St. Rachel said with faux politeness, crossing her arms on her judgement.

"You are welcome to leave now if you wish," Maxamillion said to Rune. "I meant what I said about being free to leave at any time." Maxamillion reclaimed his glass, a trace of liquor still swishing in the bottom.

"Even though I know your secret now?"

"Who would you tell?" Maxamillion asked seriously and Rune didn't have an answer for him.

"Camera analysis completed, sir," one of the techs said, approaching the group.

"St. Ben!" Malachi called, getting up from his terminal, gesturing for the Saint to join him.

"We should figure out what happened in that alley before we do anything else," St. Benedict said, nodding toward Malachi.

"Let me know your findings as soon as you have them," Maxamillion confirmed before turning away. "Well Ms. Leveau? Are you staying or going?"

Rune sighed. "I would like to know more about what happened in my alley before I go."

"Fine. Now that, *that* is settled. St. Rachel, I would appreciate an update on the Northside situation," the CEO said, before downing the rest of his drink and handing the other Saint the now empty glass.

St. Rachel pouted her lip as she walked the glass the short distance to the sink, before quickly wiping the expression away into a mask of supreme control and aloofness. Turning elegantly, she claimed her dropped folders before leading the way for Maxamillion. Heading to another cluster of terminals on the far side of the room, she opened her recovered folders to hand things to her boss as they walked. Unable to hear what they were saying to each other, Rune continued to follow them with her eyes. If St. Rachel's figure was "perfect" in her business skirt and cream colored jacket, then Maxamillion's slick appearance matched her equally. And Rune was still standing in yoga pants and bare feet.

Acutely feeling out of her depth, she finally noticed St. Benedict had turned his own attention away to watch what Malachi and a few other techs were doing around a cluster of screens. Feeling the weight of her eyes, he opened a palm toward her in invitation. She offered a small smile and crossed to stand behind Malachi, St. Benedict coming up beside her.

"Is…is that my alley?" Rune asked, her eyebrows shooting to the ceiling. The image on Malachi's screen was of her back alley from a really high angle. It was in sharp color, the images on the screen looking almost liquid, it was so sharp.

"I installed a camera two months ago," St. Benedict said, looking at her askance for her reaction. "Invasion of privacy, I know, but…."

"All a part of your promise?" Rune asked, nodding. "To protect me from…whomever." She waved her hand at the screen.

St. Benedict nodded, watching her watch the screen. A thought occurred to Rune. Over the course of the whole last two months when she had only memories to replay and bastardize into fantasies, he had fresh images of her whenever he wanted.

"Were you stalking me?" she asked, feeling almost shy to ask the question.

"Only in order to check in," he lied.

Holding out his palm, St. Benedict made a quick fist before popping his hand open again. Light burst into the space above his skin as his holographic augmentation came to life, projecting a small globe of dancing lights. Rune's eyes went wide at the sight, the technology still as foreign to her as magic was to him. With his other hand, he fiddled inside the light orb like it was really physical. Images too quick for Rune to pick out passed over the orb's surface. Then he plucked something out of the orb, pulling it out with glowing fingers. To Rune, it looked like a tiny thumbnail picture. Flicking his fingers, St. Benedict directed the image to a screen above Malachi's workstation. A light came on from a little box that seemed to be held on to the corner of the screen with black tape, wires Gerry rigged into it. The monitor turned itself on, filling with the image of the front of Rune's bar.

"Don't be that impressed, he's showing off," Malachi said, rolling his eyes. "I could have done the same thing with this mouse." He held up the said mouse to wiggle it at St. Benedict mockingly.

"Jealous?" St. Benedict asked, smirking.

"Extremely." Malachi turned back to the screens.

Rune leaned toward the monitors beside Malachi, captivated by the images.

"It's amazing, it's…it's as clear as a scrying crystal. I thought all monitor images were kind of fuzzy." she said, a ghost of a smile creeping up on her face.

"Technology, baby. We'll be all caught up to magic in no time," Malachi said, tapping at his keyboard with a flourish.

"Someday, we may even surpass the capabilities of magic," St. Benedict said. Being a magic user, Rune pursed her lips at that sentiment.

"Is this what's happening right now?" Rune leaned in closer to the nighttime footage on the screen which put her closer to Malachi, who jumped a little at her proximity.

"Yes, yes, this is live now. As you can see, all's quiet. Not even a siren in sight." The tech tried and failed not to look in the direction of Rune's too close assets.

"Did anyone even call the corporate police for this area?" St. Benedict asked.

"They wouldn't," Rune said dryly, rolling her stiffening shoulder as she straightened. "This neighborhood is still pretty Magic Guild heavy. We all know better than to call corporate police."

A shadow passed over her face and St. Benedict had to swallow down a flash of rage that flared in his throat. "It doesn't look like the Sheriff's department came either," he said instead.

Rune furrowed her eyebrows, "That's true."

"I'd say it's a complete cleaning," Malachi said, lifting the pink glasses to verify what he was seeing in the picture. "Not very often you see an alley so immaculate."

Indeed, the image on Malachi's screen showed an alley with no trash bags or dirty refuse of any kind. The dumpsters were lined up against the walls, completely whole and unmarked, sitting at regular intervals. Even more disturbing, the camera had a clear view of Rune's back porch.

"My umbrella is gone!" Her chairs were still there, but the umbrella that she used to block either sunlight or streetlight was simply gone.

"But they replaced your lightbulb. Remember? It broke during the struggle above us. Can we use any of the other cameras in the area?" St. Benedict asked, but Malachi was already shaking his head before the Saint finished asking the question.

"Not if we don't want someone to notice."

"We don't," St. Benedict conceded.

"Have we downloaded all of the footage yet from our camera?" Malachi asked, leaning back dangerously in his office chair to talk to a pair of equally disheveled techs a few feet away.

"The download keeps failing," one of them reported, slamming his hands on the keyboard, earning a dirty look from his partner.

"Failing?" St. Benedict asked, tucking his hands across his

chest into his armpits, cocking his head to the side.

"Have you tried turning it off, then turning it on again?" Malachi piped up. That earned him a duo of dirty looks.

"The problem isn't with our equipment, *sir*."

"Malachi, don't tease the help," St. Benedict whispered, lightly kicking the bottom of the tech's rolling desk chair.

"We keep downloading the files from the camera, but when we go to play it, there's only three minutes of footage. Nothing else."

"Nothing else?" St. Benedict held up his bracelet, the one connected to the gun he had given her and mumbled something to it. The light that had been red blinked blue twice and went dark. She marveled at the risk he had taken, giving her his gun like that. Not that she really thought she could have fired it. Rune only hated guns a little less than she hated snakes, because honestly, who can really tell with snakes?

Her former "captive" didn't notice her discomfort as he focused on the computer screens. A window was open, its playback bar sliding forward as the counter ticked up, showing the alley as clean as the live feed showed it now. St. Benedict pulled a keyboard toward himself and began typing, his right hand jumping to the mouse to click without breaking his momentum. Windows opened and closed on the screen, each filling with gibberish before disappearing.

"Dammit, this is slow," St. Benedict muttered derisively under his breath. Rune watched the two techs share flabbergasted looks behind the Saint's back. Apparently, what he was doing to the computer was boggling their minds as much as it did hers. In the time it took them to have those reactions, he straightened, shoving the keyboard away from him in disgust. "You're right. It's corrupted. Deliberately."

He turned away, lifting his fedora to run a hand through his hair in agitation.

"Start running recovery...." Malachi started to say, but St. Benedict slashed his hand in the air to cut him off.

"Don't bother. There won't be anything to recover. The memory's being destroyed. The camera will short out as soon as we disconnect from it," St. Benedict said.

"Hey, even if it's just a ghost, there's always something to recover." Malachi said.

"A Saint's gotten to it. Believe me there will be nothing," St. Benedict added. He stared at the ground, his hands on his hips, thinking.

"But that is impossible. Or at least very unlikely. I mean, to corrupt our camera, they'd have to know where to find it or that it was even there."

"Not to mention, to run a program like that would take a lot of planning ahead of time to set up the necessary software," one of the techs said.

"We've been monitoring the equipment, we would have noticed something, St. Ben," Malachi insisted. Then he stopped, a look passing over his face like he swallowed a bug. "Do...do you think we're compromised?!" Malachi looked panicked and he forced his voice into a harsh whisper. "Do you think we have a mole?" He turned an accusatory eye on the two techs.

Both pairs of eyes went wide and they shook their heads with sotto voce expressions of "no, not me!"

"I actually doubt it. A Saint could do it if fully immersed into the system, wouldn't take a lot of time and if they were good enough, they could get it done without us noticing," St. Benedict said, ignoring the silent inquisition happening beside him.

"That would mean they traced it back to us," said one of the techs.

"No, I got it now. That's why the data is terminating. They're using my track sweeper against the cameras. It won't lead them to us, but it also blocks us from downloading anything. Too many redirects. Capture the flag style, only they create a false flag, and see if we come to fix the cameras."

"So we go get the cameras?" the other tech asked.

"No, they're dead to us," Malachi said dramatically.

St. Benedict smiled. "We need to know who was in that alley," he repeated before leaning back and flipping a switch bolted to the end of Malachi's work desk.

A few feet away, lights snapped on over a ring of monitors revealing something that made Rune immediately think of a dentist's chair, only one from a really terrifying horror movie. It was angled backward at a slant, complete with armrests. Everything was covered in cracked brown vinyl, with pressed dents in it from the repeated pressure of the weight of a body. Around the head rest was an extra layer of black electrical tape shining dully in the overhead light. Wires and cords trailed around the chair, across the floor, and into the various monitors. It all looked dirty and malicious.

"St. Benedict, what are you doing?" Malachi asked in a warning tone, eyeing the circle as monitors started booting on.

"Preparing to dive, obviously. Call Zita up for me," he said, toeing his shoes off to slide them next to Malachi's desk.

"You don't have to dive, we can get the information another way." Malachi's agitation made Rune feel uneasy.

"I'm pretty sure we're dealing with another Saint here, and if that is the case, then we need to use the resources available to us," St. Benedict said, matter-of-factly. The lights of the circle had attracted the attention of the rest of the room.

"What do you mean by that?" Rune asked.

He smiled and unbuckled his holster. He handed that to Malachi, who dropped it into a drawer, automatically locking it and handing St. Benedict the key on a chain. The chain popped over the Saint's head, disappearing into the shirt to join another chain already hanging there. His fedora he dropped onto Rune's own head. It was slightly damp and warm, a bit too large for her head so it wobbled forward over her eyes a bit.

"Bring up the dream recorder," St. Benedict said to Malachi while he disarmed.

"Why?" Malachi challenged, surly now, even as he complied.

"I want to pull a full memory of the alley along with everything I saw." St. Benedict tapped his temple. "I recorded the whole thing with the augs. It's going to be the only way to get a clear picture now," he said to Rune.

"Damn it," Malachi said, murmuring agreement with that swear word.

St. Benedict smirked. Malachi knew he was right. It was easier, and more efficient, than trying to restore the lost data or steal the images from elsewhere. Moving into the circle of lights and equipment, St. Benedict sat on the edge of the scary looking chair, waiting for Zita to come up to check his vitals. Malachi and the two other techs moved around the space, working with the equipment in preparation for the dive. Rune had followed him to the edge of the light, her eyes full of questions and a little concern. St. Benedict had to force himself not to look away uncomfortably. He didn't want her there, watching this process, but there was no good reason he could even give himself to justify sending her away. Unfortunately for her, he was the only person she trusted in the whole building. He couldn't abandon her like that.

"You can cross in," he offered, gesturing for her to join him by the chair.

"What are you about to do?" she repeated her question, the concern highlighted starkly in the colder light.

He swallowed and forced his smile to become easy. Like what he was about to attempt was no big deal.

"You know the trick I do with the hologram projection in my hand?" he asked, popping his example open again. She nodded as she was hypnotized by the soft, blue rectangle floating above his palm. He closed the palm, dispersing the image before gesturing over to the larger rig. "I'm going to do something similar over there. Those computers are going to link to my mind simultaneously and pull out the image of the alley. Then they'll be able to process those images and project them into a larger, more complete hologram."

Her eyebrows furrowed slowly as he explained. He was dumbing the language down so she could understand and even then he was taking big jumps in the logic.

"It's dangerous isn't it?" she asked, acutely.

He shrugged one shoulder. "Yes and no. I've done it lots of times. This technology is still relatively new, hence there is always some risk. Computers themselves used to take up a whole room. Something like this diving rig, someday might be as small as a simple device I can wear in a pair of sunglasses."

"And you're wanting to extract a memory?"

"A recorded one, yeah."

She huffed a breath a moment. "Wouldn't it just be safer to

have a mind Wizard do it for you?"

The question took St. Benedict aback a moment. "You mean let a magic user dig in my brain?"

"Well, yeah, essentially. I think they take the memory and put it into a crystal and then you can relive it over and over."

"And do you know how to do that?" St. Benedict asked, genuinely interested.

"No, of course not. I'm a Talent and not for mind work." It was obvious Rune hated admitting her limitations, but St. Benedict understood that. From what little he had learned over the past couple of months about magic society, being a Talent wasn't anything to really brag about. While the government classified all magic users as Talents for bookkeeping purposes, those who could do more than one kind of spell, like someone who could cast fire and water spells instead of just fire or water, had higher status in her world.

"You haven't come out to your people yet, have you?" he asked. She shifted away this time and he caught her hand to keep her from going.

"You know why I can't," she said.

"I know why the world in general shouldn't know who you used to be, but I don't understand why Rune Leveau couldn't be a Talent?" To be honest, St. Benedict knew very little about the magic community's politics, yet something about her hiding it still felt wrong to him. "Couldn't your Guild help you with that kind of transition with the government?"

Rune started to say something, some practiced excuse he had probably already heard from her, but neither got very far with the topic as Zita slid into the circle of light. St. Benedict felt Rune's hand spasm involuntarily at the sight of the Naga.

Zita smiled as she approached, her lower snake-half coiling around herself as she came to a stop beside the scary dentist chair. She had her long black hair pinned to the top of her head in a bun with chopsticks stabbed through the top. Glasses rested on her nose and she was sporting a very clinical white coat that draped around a soft fall colored dress.

"Feeling adventurous again, St. Ben?" Zita asked, her breath soft and musical as she pulled a small flashlight out of one of the coat pockets. Then she noticed him holding Rune's hand and she paused, tipping her head to the side slightly with curiosity. "Hello?"

"Zita, this is Rune Leveau," St. Benedict jumped in smoothly with the introduction. "You remember her? She helped us out a couple of months ago with our daring rescue from Kodiak."

The smile dropped from Zita's face, replaced with urgency. "You mean…." she started to say but it was like the words were stuck in her throat.

"She was the one who did that magicky thing to find us," Malachi said, stopping his work to hover near his mate apprehensively. The last couple of months had been hard for both of them since the incident. Having a gun shoved against one's head would do that to any sane person. St. Benedict and Malachi exchanged a quick glance. Malachi had told him, her nightmares had only just recently stopped, at least as far as he could tell. St. Benedict was too much of a coward to tell him that was highly unlikely.

"It was you…." Zita started to say again. Before anyone else could react, she sprung forward, grabbing Rune hard. Rune's breath exhaled in a rush as it was crushed out of her.

"Thank you, thank you, thank you," came Zita's muffled tearful voice from against Rune's shoulder. The huggee's arms were trapped by the huggers' and Rune didn't know what to say. Most alarmingly, Zita's lower, scaly half was starting to curl around Rune's feet as well.

"Zita. Zita!" Malachi cried, as he grabbed his mate's arm, afraid of letting her both continue and worried about startling her at the same time. "You need to let her go now."

"You're going full python on her, sweetheart," St. Benedict echoed.

Malachi's face flipped from concern to full on affrontery. "Really?! I can't believe…. Geez, St. Ben, really sensitive of you here."

"No, it's alright, it's alright," Zita said, releasing her hold. Rune tried not to take in a deep, dramatic breath. While she was still able to breathe in that hug, she had unconsciously held it in anyway. The Naga was so grateful, the last thing Rune wanted to do was insult her. And she was a little embarrassed by her heebie jeebies. The only other time Rune had seen Zita was at a distance as she and St. Benedict had chased after them while they were being dragged away by Kodiak security. At the time, she had been more worried about saving their lives to give her other fears much breathing room.

"When...when they put that gun to my head, and demanded that I create magic...I thought for sure I was going to die. If it wasn't for you, they would have killed me," Zita continued, speaking like the words had been dammed up in her heart only to flood over now. Her dark eyes searched Rune's face for understanding. It didn't help that she felt Zita's gratitude was misplaced, as Rune and St. Benedict had split ways before he had caught up with and rescued his team. Yet, saying that would also obviously do more harm than good.

In her mind's eye, Rune saw Maddie, reaching out to a slime troll who had just lost her son and comforting her with a full body hug, while the troll cried and slimed.

"I'm glad we made it," Rune said, using her newly freed hands to reinitiate the hug that Zita still seemed to need. Maybe it was cheating that the Talent counted to a whole five Mississippi's before letting go again. The Naga didn't seem to notice and the tension dropped out of the smaller person's frame.

"Are you alright now, Zita?" Malachi asked tenderly, his love for her blatantly apparent.

She smiled and leaned over to kiss her worried mate with a small, acknowledging peck, her elegance contrasting to his slovenliness.

"Sorry. Sorry everyone," the Naga cleared her throat, then turned to St. Benedict in the chair. "You called me up because you are planning on diving?" Zita slipped on a professional demeanor.

"Yes, we need to pull a memory," St. Benedict confirmed. She nodded once and reset one of her hairpins that had shaken loose. She slithered over to a covered stack of medical equipment at the head of the scary chair.

St. Benedict shot Rune a wink before leaning back into the

smooth, worn vinyl of the chair, settling his body into place. No one said anything more as Malachi turned back to his work and Zita pulled out wires with sticky pads on the ends. Automatically, St. Benedict lifted his shirt so Zita could attach them to his chest, his gaze already far away.

While they prepared, Rune felt very much in the way, dancing back and forth to get out of the techs' or Zita's way.

"Ms. Leveau, would you care to join me?" Maxamillion's voice called, giving Rune an easy exit from the preparations. As she stepped out of the light, however, she saw St. Rachel step in, purposely striding to her counterpart's side. St. Benedict sat up a little as she approached, exchanging words Rune couldn't hear. Then he sat up a little sharper, looking around and becoming more alarmed. Figuring he must not have noticed that she had left, Rune waved and smiled at him, catching his eye to reassure him she was fine. He nodded once and settled back, exchanging more words with St. Rachel.

"Ms. Leveau." Rune turned and saw Maxamillion holding out a green flannel robe, presenting it to help her slip it on. "I took the liberty of having these brought in for you."

Rune couldn't help smiling, partly from his turn of phrase and partly because she was touched by the courtesy. Slipping the robe on was an immediate relief. It was butter soft and instantly she was warmer in the overly air conditioned room. Maxamillion also produced a pair of leather loafer-like slippers bursting with softness inside and hard soles on the bottom.

"Thank you," she said as she also slipped them on, her ice numbed toes wiggling inside to get some blood back into themselves.

"What do you think of your husband's legacy?" he asked with no preamble.

"Excuse me?" Rune looked around trying to puzzle out what exactly he was referring to. "You mean the Masterson Files?"

"I mean the dive set up." The executive gestured towards St. Benedict's rig. "His last project for Kodiak before he disappeared from the face of the known world."

"Justin created this?"

"Yes, and I believe he was one of the first few people to have successfully dived."

Rune saw the set up in a new light. Justin created this. He had continued his work after he had left her life. It was equal parts sad and surreal.

"If this is one of Justin's creations, how is it here?"

"Oh, it's available for anyone who owns a Saint, if you can pay for it."

"It's hard to think of Justin having done anything else after he left me there....or rather here, I guess," Rune said.

Side by side, Maxamillion and Rune watched the activity on the inside of the circle.

"For all of his flaws, Masterson certainly was a genius," Maxamillion finally said, his voice taking on a tone of appreciation. Neither of them looked at the other, continuing to watch as they spoke.

"And what flaws would you say those were?"

"I apologize if I'm speaking out of place."

Rune shook her head. "No, don't be. Justin is long gone from my life and I probably could list more flaws than you ever could. I'm just...interested. I know what I've thought about him, but how do all of you see him?"

Maxamillion took a deep breath and sighed it out as he spoke. "A flawed but brilliant individual, who like so many others of his ilk, was exploited and used all the while being fed delusions of grandeur to keep him compliant until it didn't work anymore and he ceased to be useful." Maxamillion cleared his throat. "Of course, we don't really know what happened to him, do we?"

"Apparently. I've been waiting for him for most of my life. He still hasn't showed up yet," Rune said, not even trying to keep the bitterness out of her voice. Then she too chuckled. "If I saw him now I suppose I wouldn't care too much. Or maybe that's what I'd like to think."

"You on the other hand are not how I expected you to be," Maxamillion continued.

"Oh really? And what did you expect?" Amusement colored Rune's voice.

Maxamillion cleared his throat. "We only have reports to go by, of course."

"And what did they say?" Rune glanced sideways at the CEO and enjoyed the sight of him chewing on his lips while he debated with himself on what to reveal.

Finally, he reached into the inner pocket of his jacket and pulled out a mobile phone, the Kodiak logo stamped in a corner. He flicked it open and tapped a little at the screen. Finally, he cleared his throat, reading from it.

"A woman of lower intelligence. Trophy wife, second rate at best. With a write-in of 'not much going on there.'"

Rune nodded, unoffended. "That sounds about right. So your conclusion is I'm nothing like that?"

"If I didn't have St. Benedict verify it for me, I would never have believed such a smart and talented, or capital 't' Talented person, if you prefer, was the reported wife of Justin Masterson."

Rune's smile turned to something contentedly bitter, like good coffee. "You're right to say Talented with the capital 't.' My greatest accomplishment has been Finding, with a capital 'f,' myself. I may never stop looking."

A bit of commotion in the circle ended the conversation.

"That took longer than usual," Maxamillion commented. The light in the circle changed, going blue. Rune focused on St. Benedict sitting in the chair, wires coming out of him like a statue swamped with mechanical vines. His eyes were glowing an ethereal blue, washing away his natural green. His dark, short hair danced a little as if touched by wind, except there was none in the enclosed space.

Maxamillion leaned toward Rune to speak in her ear. "This is always the exciting part."

Chapter 6

"What, you're not going to ask me if this is entirely necessary?" St. Benedict let his smile touch his eyes. St. Rachel didn't take his bait, she was getting to be less fun that way, and instead held up her hand. Her finger tips glowed slightly. "Do you want me on deck to pull you out if things go south?"

"You mean you want to be on deck in the deck?" St. Benedict quipped.

Finally, she gave a small, indulgent smile back. He lifted his hand up, paralleling hers. His own fingers lit and they touched palms.

"It's a local dive only, little danger involved. Footage has been compromised. We can get a clean copy from my head."

St. Rachel scoffed. "Most days I feel like a human storage container."

"It does make spying a lot easier, plus it's cool," St. Benedict offered.

"Easy for you to say, you love this crap."

"What I loved was the look on your face when we came in with the gun on me."

"And you would have reacted differently?" she challenged.

"Absolutely not," he conceded. The linkup between their hands completed and he could now sense St. Rachel in his mind, like a presence that was just on the edge of one's periphery. Which was especially strange when that presence was actually standing in front of him. He could talk to her through the link if he wanted, a man-made sort of telepathy.

"But I would wonder if you were letting someone keep a gun on you like that while defending and protecting them was because you had somehow developed feelings for them," he said out loud instead, leaning back again into the dents in the cushions of the chair.

"*And you want me to ask you that question,*" she said, the words filtering into his mind like she was speaking through water.

St. Benedict sighed a large breath. "I'm not," he said out loud. "*Very convincing,*" she retorted. "*I understand she's important to your mission. I know you, St. Benedict.*"

"Sinners like us, we don't get happy endings," St. Benedict said softly, his smile didn't leave his face, but it softened into something sad but accepting.

"Maybe together...." St. Rachel started, but St. Benedict pulled his hand abruptly.

"*There is only the mission for me. Nothing else.*"

"*You don't know your wife is dead,*" her inner voice almost a whisper.

"*I do know. She's gone. I'm seeing this through to the end because it is my only reason for continuing.*" He didn't look at her as he thought it, instead staring blankly ahead at a dark future only he could see.

"Malachi, are we ready? What's taking so long?" he asked, out loud.

"We're ready, just waiting for you to stop your one-sided conversation, which is very annoying to the rest of us normals, you know."

St. Rachel stepped back, keeping her eyes on St. Benedict, but he needed to put her and her feelings to the side right then. Gratefully, Maxamillion was distracting Rune and St. Benedict was able to concentrate.

Refocusing his eyes, St. Benedict turned on the monitor directly in his line of sight, code dancing across it, opening the door for him to jump through. Like a whoosh through an air hatch he felt himself connect to the computer. A distance away his body's nervous system reacted, reporting the pain of the connection. He noted it and immediately dismissed it. His ocular implants immediately began adjusting and his body relaxed.

"Someday we'll figure out how to make that a smoother transition," he said to St. Rachel.

"The direct implant into the brain works better," she commented.

"No mass market appeal. Imagine what the marketing team would have to spin in order to get people to consent to have pins shoved into their brains willingly," St. Benedict retorted.

"You'd be surprised."

"Yeah, I would. That's the sad thing."

From his own perspective, he felt like he was floating in a pool of water, only that pool was data. In the contained pool of the Corinthe corporate network, he could simply float forever, letting the numbers and letters flow over him to form the words and pictures that made their corporate enterprise work. If he tried to fight the information, it would most likely result in the system electrical overload that Malachi always worried about. With good reason. Trying to process all of that data at once could fry his brain from the inside out.

The trick was to stay calm and let the information float through until the brain's filters were able to orient and push away what he didn't want invading his being.

"*How are you doing there?*" St. Rachel asked, her voice still in the same place just on the edge of his perception.

"*Fine, I'm entering the recorder now.*" The code of the recorder swamped his being and he had an impression of yellow light that melted into a dreamy white. Outside, he knew the holographic projectors were coming to life, filling the remaining empty twenty foot space next to his chair with light.

And then his vision cleared. Or what took the place of his vision. Looking down at the artificial body of his avatar, constructed from the light of the holograms, he waited as he materialized inside a representation of Rune's alley. To his senses it felt like a less sensitive body, as if it were clad in latex. Still functional, still controllable, but lacking in the fine sensitivity only naturally grown nerves could have. To the outsider, St. Benedict knew his avatar's body would look fit and well dressed in a close-fitting, button-up shirt, suspenders connected to finely tailored trousers and his signature fedora set onto his head. He knew this because he designed the avatar to look that way. He smiled as he surveyed the space that now was filled, down to the last dumpster and the beach umbrella over Rune's back porch. Just on the edge of the light, he saw the back of Rune looking in at his real body.

To most others, seeing their real body was always disconcerting. Gazing at it now, he wondered if this was what it was like to be dead. Was it like this, getting a last chance to gaze down at the worn, tired remains, which his definitely were now? In a distant place in his mind, he felt the bruises starting to form on his back and shoulders from where the bullets had hit the flack vest. Now to his artificial perception, they were far away, distant aches to deal with later. St. Rachel was still standing beside him, looking far more put together than he did, but she was adept that way. He remembered being held up for three days in a bunker beside her and during that whole time, even though they all were covered in blood, sweat and mud, she still looked as alluring as she did right then. Maybe even more so.

"What do you think?" he called out through the avatar, forcing his attention away from St. Rachel, back to Rune. She jumped at the sound of his voice, which was actually coming from a speaker system above the hologram, interpreted from his mind-speak so anyone could hear him while he was jacked in. It made his voice echo a little.

Rune turned to stare at him and he almost laughed at how wide her eyes were. He twirled in place for her, his hands stuck into his fictional pants so the twirl came off like a suave dancer's might.

"St. Benedict?" she asked, before doing what everyone did, turning back to look at him still sitting in the chair, looking unshaven and half-dead.

"Yes, pretty cool, huh?" He looked around at the alley. "Does this look about right to you? You've spent more time in this alley than I have."

Rune made a show of looking about, but she was too stunned to really answer his question. He didn't mind. It was a delight to watch her virgin perception of this whole thing.

"This is amazing," she finally said and he had to agree. She took a step forward into the hologram and immediately it began to disintegrate. She retracted her foot.

"Don't come in here. It's all light and your physical presence will disrupt it," St. Benedict explained too late.

"Sorry," she said, but he waved it off and turned to the end of the alley.

"Malachi, is the upload completed yet?" he asked.

"I think so."

St. Benedict couldn't suppress the groan.

"Hey, dude, lay off. It's not like this is a precise science," Malachi retorted. More things filled in the alley, all draped in the shadows of the night, a few bags of garbage he must have noted and the like. Down at the end, Maxamillion's car light appeared and above St. Benedict saw his mental version of Rune moving.

"Is that me?" Rune asked, pointing up from her vantage point at the top of the alley stairs. "Why am I fuzzy?"

"Because he couldn't see you very well from down below so his memory wouldn't have recorded it properly. This is not an exact thing like a picture. The further away from St. Benedict's perception the fuzzier what he remembers is," Malachi explained, cutting off Maxamillion before he could start speaking.

"Indeed," Maxamillion added, giving Malachi a look.

"Malachi, roll everything back," St. Benedict cut in, looking back down the alley again.

"How far?" Malachi asked.

"Just keep rolling until I say," St. Benedict ordered. Letting go of control, St. Benedict let the recorded memory rewind, moving his avatar for him. Which was back under the steps of the porch. And then he didn't move.

"Okay, I was standing here." The recording stopped and began to move forward. Not much changed. As he remembered it, sounds of the city began to filter through the speakers. He had been standing there for a while, soaking it in, breathing, listening, debating with himself about whether to go upstairs and knock on her door. Then above, her back door opened and shut metallically. His heart pounded loudly at the sound. She was above him; every one of his senses felt her.

"Stop."

Breaking from where he stood, St. Benedict moved into the center of the alley and looked around. Above on the deck he saw Rune, dressed as she was now, looking out. She looked right at him, but of course she didn't see him; he hadn't been standing there to be seen. Instead, he looked above her on the roof edge of her building.

"The assailant appeared there, correct?" St. Benedict asked.

"You mean, the king of mob movie extras, Calvin? Yes, I came out on the porch and then he pounced down on me from above," Rune confirmed.

"Malachi, fill that in with a marker shadow," St. Benedict pointed, while he turned around to look at the other edges.

"Why are you doing that?" Rune asked.

"Because he didn't see him. We can only project what St. Benedict actually saw," Malachi supplied.

"But he didn't see me. If he started under the porch, he couldn't see me up there, and I'm extremely clear."

"He can see you right now," Malachi stated. It wasn't enough of an explanation.

"That's why you're so clear now, my mind is playing tricks, filling you in because I am looking directly at the real you."

Rune nodded as she looked at the representation of herself, who was wearing the robe and slippers she was wearing at that moment in reality. "So that's what you mean, about this memory projection thing not being an exact thing?"

"It is the difference between a memory and fantasy," St. Benedict added, his avatar gesturing to her, "I barely remember the idiot, even after I rushed up there to help you. If I'm not focused enough I can turn him into what I think he looked like or even project a complete fiction over him." For the briefest moment, a different shadow passed over the form representing Calvin, monstrous and disturbing, before becoming the placeholder it had been before. St. Benedict furrowed his brow at the Calvin representative. The avatar began moving, first reverting to its start position then moving forward and up very speedily to match his memory. It all played out again, the grappling, his fear tremoring through him as he saw her being choked to death.

"Stop again," he called. The playback froze in place, St. Benedict in mid-punch against the jaw of the man he now recognized as Calvin. His heart was beating hard as if he was back in that moment and he had to force himself to step out of the incident again to look around. There were more shadows of rooftops, mostly fuzzy since he hadn't been looking at them, but something caught his eye.

"Malachi, emphasize that," he said, pointing at the glint on the opposite roof.

"Yup, I see it. You did see something, got it." The image pulsated for a second and then light filled it in. A shadow person appeared and a long shadow gun.

"They were closer than I would have thought prudent," St. Benedict said wryly.

"Who is that?" Maxamillion asked.

"That would be our wannabe assassin. Can we jump me forward to a moment I might have seen them better?"

"Them?" Rune asked.

"Until we know for sure, I'm not going to assign a gender or race to this gunperson. It can skew the memory." St. Benedict jumped over to the opposite side of the alley as if leaping a small pond. Once there, he squatted down beside the shadow being, lying on its stomach obviously behind the scope of a gun. "Shorter than me for certain."

"Sorry, St. Ben. This is the only time you saw them."

"What do you think, St. Rachel?" St. Benedict asked, looking at the silhouette.

"No clue. Definitely not a Saint."

"Ok, then let's move on." The hologram popped him right back to where he punched Rune's assailant, feeling all the satisfaction he experienced the actual time. The scenario continued to play and during it everyone was silent as the holographic Rune and St. Benedict's avatar rushed down the stairs, halted underneath by bullets.

"Recorded trajectory places the first bunch of bullets coming from the assassin, then those three from above were from Calvin, who we are still considering an independent agent," St. Rachel said.

Rune snorted.

"Are you reading that from the analysis?" St. Benedict asked. "Yes. I can also see it from here. We were shot at by two sources."

At the end of the alley, car lights flooded the space.

"And here comes our daring rescue."

"St. Benedict, do you see that? I mean, do you see what you saw?" asked Malachi, stuttering over himself in his excitement.

St. Benedict narrowed his eyes against the glare of the car lights.

"Yes, yes I do."

On the edge of the car lights, figures in long coats stood highlighted. They were black and white. At first he thought that it was simply the car lights flooding out any color but as he broke from under the porch and moved freely, which he hadn't been able to do before. As he neared, he saw what they really were.

"Monochromes."

"What?" Rune exclaimed, moving along the edge of the hologram to parallel him in order to get a better look.

"Am I right?" he asked Rune, gesturing to the closest figure, half in and half out of the shadow. The monochrome man was about the same height as St. Benedict, his skeletal painted face practically glowing against his ink black skin. It was caught in mid-turn, as if he was swinging in surprise toward the light, his black hair swishing to the side in a way most super models would envy.

"What are monochromes?" Maxamillion asked as he joined Rune to look over her shoulder.

"They are Faerie folk," Rune answered, unable to hide her surprise that they didn't just know that.

"They serve the Orange Lady. I told you about them," St. Benedict added.

"Well, that's not quite right," Rune interjected. "They serve the Faerie Court and Lady Trella, the Orange Lady, is a member, or was depending on how you look at it."

"What were they doing in the alley?" Maxamillion asked.

"Good question," St. Benedict said, flipping back and trying to see what there was to see at the other end of the alley.

"Coming for Calvin obviously. Maybe also to protect me. I would think I'm at least a smaller slice on their priority pie chart," Rune suggested, "After all, I am a Faerie Friend."

There was a sniff from St. Rachel. "Then why didn't they intercede when you were being attacked, if you *are* their friend." While St. Rachel's tone of voice was contemptuous, she made a solid point. They served the Oberon, but Calvin was the Oberon. Speculating to herself, Rune was pretty sure the only reason Calvin could harm her at all was because of his Changeling nature. Or maybe he hadn't been intending to hurt her. Maybe. Intention mattered more with Fae than most other peoples.

"And who are they?" St. Benedict asked, gesturing at the corresponding figures at the other end of the alley.

"Boy, a lot of people showed up for this party," Malachi quipped.

The memory started up again, popping St. Benedict back to his position under the porch. The monochromes disappeared and St. Benedict glanced up to see the extra feet appearing above them.

Malachi paused the simulation. "Wait, wait, what just happened? The monochromes are on the porch now?"

"They move through shadows," St. Benedict said, uninterested.

"Right, because they weren't terrifying before," Malachi said dryly.

With a gesture, St. Benedict started things up again but this time he looked to the left as Maxamillion's car pulled up, the light reaching fully to the end of the alley.

"Who the hell is that?" Malachi asked.

Rune moved closer to the image, again taking a step and disrupting the image a second. "He shoots first, and not at us," she said, peering at it.

St. Benedict stopped the action to turn to look behind. "Always check your hours." While he hadn't really processed seeing the figures to the left at the time, he had caught a clear glance and that was enough for the program to render them.

"Five corporate police," St. Benedict concluded.

"How can you tell?" Rune asked. She squinted at the figures, each wearing goggles and black tactical clothing which created a uniform, dehumanizing effect.

St. Benedict's avatar approached one of the figures. "St. Rachel?" he asked.

"I agree, corporate police. And that is St. Dominic, right up front."

"Confirming." St. Benedict's avatar made a sweeping gesture around the closest one. The new Saint was highlighted and he began to turn him in space, looking at the figure from all three sides. On the parts he hadn't seen, a lattice framework intuited the rest of the figure. He turned the figure back to face him. Stepping up, he focused in on the face. Taking one finger, his avatar traced around the goggles, highlighting them.

"Delete," he commanded and the goggles deleted, leaving lattice work in its place. He double tapped with one finger on the skin of the figure and filled in the lattice work. It wasn't perfect, but now they had a face.

"Why hello, St. Dominic," St. Benedict said to the unresponsive face.

"Definitely Kodiak then," Malachi replied and the highlighting around the figured flashed as Malachi copied the image into his computer.

St. Benedict proceeded to remove the goggles from two other figures that had clear enough faces to be worth the effort. Once he had finished he glanced over to where Rune had taken a seat next to Maxamillion. Someone had placed a small table between them and while Maxamillion was nose deep in a report strewn over most of the table and his lap, Rune was leaning her head on one arm nodding off. St. Benedict did an internal check and realized it was well past midnight. On top of that, she would be feeling the adrenaline crash right about then.

"You don't have to stay," he said to her, his avatar coming as close as it could to the edge of the hologram circle. She jumped a little at the sound of his voice coming closer, though it was the speaker doing that, giving a sense of audible proximity to the avatar. He grinned at her.

"I want to stay, this is fascinating," she said, blinking herself upright. "I'm fine really." She glanced over her should at his still body in the chair. "It's a bit strange."

"What, being in two places at once?"

She nodded. "Maddie tried to get me interested in astral projecting at one point, when we were trying to figure out the extent, or lack thereof, of my Talent. It always seemed insanely dangerous to me."

"Why is that?"

"If you die outside your body, they say you become a ghost." She wiggled her fingers as she affected a haunted sound in her voice on the word ghost.

"Do you?" His grin cracked wider.

She half-shrugged. "No clue. It's one of those things that has always been hard to verify."

"And how does one astro-project?" Maxamillion asked, interjecting into their conversation.

"Uh, meditation mostly," Rune said, fidgeting with her robe belt. "I never really managed to do it but trying did help with… other things."

That same haunted look passed over her face again.

"We have a hit off of one of the faces for sure and three likely possibilities within a 75% index," St. Rachel reported.

"Can you say that out loud, St. Rach, not everyone can here you," St. Benedict said out loud himself, cutting off whatever more Rune was going to say.

"The first figure, we can confirm is St. Dominic. The other face matched up with three possible people, one of which is an employee with the Kodiak Island Correctional Company. The third offered too many possibilities to be useful.

"Kodiak," Maxamillion said, his jaw tightening at the information.

St. Benedict nodded, turning the information over in his mind. He wasn't surprised, but it wasn't ideal. "Alright then, let's see what Kodiak was up to in the alley." The scenario as he remembered it continued to play. He was back at the car, memory-Rune pulling him in...somehow. There was a disturbance then, the whole hologram phased away for a moment.

"What was that?!" Malachi exclaimed.

"The Talent used magic, don't worry about it," St. Benedict said, covering. He wasn't entirely sure what had happened then and considering Rune's perplexed look, she probably wasn't sure either. He decided to ask her about it later in private.

Much of the alley flipped to wireframes once he landed inside the car, since he didn't, in fact, see it. The car revved and began to pull away.

"And that's about it, right?" Malachi asked.

"No," came Rune, "there was a fire."

There was another phase out disturbance and then fire enveloped the simulated car.

"Stop," St. Benedict ordered. "Roll back 1/10th speed." Slowly the fire peeled away, sucked back toward the front of the car.

"Where the heck did fire come from?" St. Rachel asked.

"Someone came and brought a blowtorch to a gunfight?" Malachi asked, wryly.

"Magic. I bet it's magic," Rune became urgently excited. "Can we see what's going on outside the car?"

"I didn't get a good look at it," St. Benedict said regretfully.

"Yes, you did," St. Rachel piped up. "Move the scenario forward." The car bounced, barreling to the end of the alley. "Stop! Focus on the rearview mirror."

"Oh, she's right. You glanced in the mirror. We've got a reflection," Malachi acknowledged. St. Benedict's avatar sat up impossibly on Rune's lap and reached into the front seats pinching his thumb and pointer finger together, before opening them in a reverse pinch motion. The mirror expanded the reflection to twice its size. He outlined the figure in the mirror with a lit finger and double tapped it. "Run that as well."

"On it," Malachi confirmed.

The scenario continued, almost to the end. After the car exited the alley, St. Benedict slashed his hand, dissipating the car around him. "End it here, there is nothing more we can glean from this." St. Benedict closed his avatar's eyes and waited for the scene around him to reset into the wireframes. Keeping his artificial eyes closed helped him not get disoriented from the abrupt shift out of the memory.

"Well, that was productive," Malachi said.

"Indeed." Maxamillion's voice sounded almost warm.

"You should jack out now," St. Rachel said. "Zita isn't liking how your vitals are looking."

"I see you."

"What did you say St. Rachel?"

"I said you should jack out now. We're all tired and Zita…."

St. Rachel's presence disappeared from his periphery.

"Do you mind…?" Rune started to ask, catching Maxamillion's attention, "we are done, correct? With the… memory thing?" She circled her finger towards the holographic set up to help clarify what she meant by "thing."

"Yes, they're done. St. Benedict will pull out of the machine and wake up in a few minutes. If you'll excuse me, I suddenly need to make a few calls I was hoping to avoid." Maxamillion stood and Rune with him, even though she really didn't have anywhere to go.

"Rune, do you want to come sit with me while we wait for the tall drink of water to de-tank?" Malachi asked, waving a hand at Rune.

"Excellent," Maxamillion said and turned to walk off without another word.

"Is he always so…?" Rune asked the tech, her eyes following after the direction Maxamillion went.

"Yeah, that's pretty typical. He's got too many gears spinning in his head and so any extraneous niceties are straight out the window. I'm expecting to start talking to him in only anagrams and abbreviations soon." Malachi pushed a rolling desk chair out for Rune to sit on, which she slid onto gratefully, leaning onto it sideways so she could rest her arms on the back.

"Is he going to be long?" she asked, nodding toward the circle of light where St. Benedict's body continued to stare with blank, blue-lit eyes, still as a statue.

"Yeah, it can take him a few minutes to back out of a dive. While you're waiting, is there anything you'd like to see?"

Rolling that thought in her head, Rune turned her attention back to the multiple screens Malachi was working with. It was all gibberish to her, much like Maddie's magic books, only even more incomprehensible.

"Actually...could I see Justin again?" Tremors rolled up her arms into her chest to her stomach as she spoke.

"Are you cold?" Malachi asked, sidestepping her original question.

"It is freezing in here. It's gotta be eighty-five degrees outside right now, isn't this a little excessive for late summer?"

"It's all the tech. We have a lot of processing power but that generates a lot of heat, hence continual cooling. One of a dozen things we do to keep all this running as smooth as a baby's bottom."

"A cold crystal could have taken care of that with minimal energy needed," Rune said.

"Cold crystal?" Malachi looked at her perplexed, like he had never heard the term before. "Well, magic doesn't interact well with tech, so that would be a different challenge to overcome."

"Another reason to get ahold of the Masterson Files?" Rune asked, giving Malachi a knowing eye.

He took a breath in to say something, then thought better of it and blew it out. "Yeah, probably." Turning one of the screens toward Rune, he tapped quickly on his keyboard.

"You said you wanted to see a bit of the Masterson Files?"

"You do actually have them?"

"We have some of them, not enough to recreate what Justin Masterson created. There's whole pieces of the program missing. If we could find them, we would be able to finish reverse engineering what he did. It's the mysterious puzzle of our age," Malachi said reverently, before snapping back to attention. "What we showed you earlier, that came with the building. Maxamillion dropped an insane amount of cash to acquire this place, so that he could get his hands on those files we showed you earlier."

"Then you know what happened to him? To Justin?" Rune asked, trying to ignore the beating of her heart as it pounded in her ears.

"No. We only have footage from between certain dates, but St. Benedict found accounts of him after the dates we have. Our spy extraordinaire over there believes Kodiak has the rest stashed somewhere, possibly with the rest of the program."

"Can I see him? Please?"

Malachi's fingers stilled on the keyboard. "St. Ben wouldn't like it. He didn't want you to see anything more about Justin."

"Well…that's not up to him."

"Most of the footage we have isn't pleasant. What you saw…."

"I know. I was there." Rune's voice was steady and calm. Malachi took that in, warring with himself. Then, before he could talk himself out of it, he tapped a few things and a still image of Justin Masterson reappeared on one of the screens.

Rune stared long and hard at the image of her ex-husband. He was exactly as she remembered him. Handsome, with long, dark hair that framed his angular face. He was a bit on the angular side all over, with long legs and arms, but when dressed in black skinny jeans, he looked like a rock star. Shirt optional. His mouth was a hard line as he stared at his interrogator. The camera didn't capture the hypnotic color of his hazel eyes, or the shading on his lips that made him so easy to kiss. There was no way she could smell the scent of his neck or feel the weight of his arms, it was only a recording. She wanted to see him laugh and smile as he told a story about something interesting he had learned that day. It was always a random fact, unconnected to anything else, but that had tickled his fancy and wonder. She missed the way that wonder would sweep her along and she would see the world in a way she hadn't before and how she would go off to research it later, to know more, while he had already drifted off to another interest. The recollections soured, as she recalled that his wonderings didn't apply only to interesting trivia.

"You've been burning bridges, while I've been building homes," Rune sang softly under her breath.

"Sorry, what?" Malachi asked, pausing in his work.

"Oh, nothing. It's a song lyric. I listened to it a lot after my divorce," Rune explained, wondering where it had come from.

She hadn't heard the song in years.

"What song is that?" Malachi asked, oblivious to how it might affect her.

"Irrelevant by.... Oh damn. I can't remember. I'm always bad with names of things." Rune looked off in the distance for a moment, quirking her brow as she tried to conjure the artist's name.

"How did it go? Maybe I'll know it." Malachi paused in his typing to look at Rune expectantly. Rune shook her head and the tech left it there.

"Do you still love him?" Malachi asked, or maybe it was Rune's own voice asking the question. She wasn't sure.

"I think.... I do want to find him," Rune whispered the thought, barely mouthing it.

There was a snap feeling inside Rune, followed by a cascading sensation that rolled down Rune from the top of her head to the bottoms of her feet.

"Ms. Leveau? Rune...are you alright?" Malachi asked, but his voice sounded distant and tinny to Rune's ears.

"I...." She blinked. "I feel weird."

"Do you want Zita to look at you?"

"No, I...."

"Maybe you hit your head and have a concussion or something." His voice was starting to panic.

"No, that's not it." Rune closed her eyes and when she opened them again she allowed her secondary sight to flood in. She saw everything at once. The past, present and future splitting and reverberating in every inch of the world. Yet, something was different this time. Usually, using her second sight was insanely overwhelming. This time, it felt natural to see so much at once. The tinny sound in her ears crystallized. "I want to find...." she hesitated again. She knew once she said the words she had avoided for so long, there would be no taking them back. "I want to find Justin Masterson." There was a ping sound. A single ring that was felt and seen as much as it was heard. Strings of light exploded out of Rune's heart, streaking throughout the space.

"Woah! What's happening?" Malachi asked, lifting his

fingers from the computer as mini electrical arcs popped out between the keys. The strings of light zipped in and out, weaving not only into Malachi's computer, but one string ended in Malachi himself.

"Do you feel that?" Rune asked, fascinated as she stared at the red light leading to him. The light had never been red before.

"Feel what? What is happening?"

Rune stood up and turned to look throughout the cavernous room. The lights went on in all directions, each one red as an arc of blood. There were dozens of them moving forward and back in time and space. More threads broke off of thicker main ones, some threads reconnected together.

"It's a web," Rune breathed as she spun slowly in a circle, taking it all in. When she had completed the circle she found herself looking directly at St. Benedict in his chair. A string of light connected the two of them as well, this one the strongest of them all. "He will lead me to Justin," she said with the certainty of knowing, a feeling she had only experienced once before, knowledge that she had no way of explaining, yet knowing it was true all the same.

"Malachi! What's going on?" Someone shouted.

"I have no idea!" Malachi's voice was now far away. "She's all...prophesying or something."

She turned back to Malachi. "Malachi...."

"Your voice. Holy crap, your eyes!" Malachi said, is saying, will say. The effect of the second sight made him echo forward and backward in time and space.

"What are you seeing, Malachi?" she asked, looking back at the red line that connected her to the tech.

"Your eyes are bright white! Zita! Zita come over here. You have to see this!"

"They're connections, but I don't understand. I don't understand where they all lead." Rune started spinning again, trying to count the red lines, but they continued to shift and morph, uncountable as each decision she looked at varied where they went. What was happening? Then there was a shimmery feeling along the one that connected her to St. Benedict. It wasn't simply red; a gold line wrapped around it, twisting together as their magics merged. She stepped along the line watching the magic weave into itself. Her sight followed it until she stood next to him. Gazing down at his face she felt the buzz of being so close to him, but there was more. Darkness swirled behind him, curling over him like smoke.

"St. Benedict!"

St. Rachel shoved Rune to the side, disturbing her sight. "Malachi! Get over here! He's crashing!"

A shiver rolled down St. Benedict's spine, which was strange since an avatar wouldn't shiver and any reactions his body was having should have been distant and indistinct. St. Benedict turned in place, realizing that outside the hologram's circle of wireframes and light…was nothing. Endless blackness. The rest of the room was completely gone.

"I see you, deceitful man. Betrayer of wives. You bare his mark."

The voice was cold, the hard consonants taking on sharp edges as it spoke. St. Benedict tried to turn in place, to pinpoint where it was coming from, but the voice stayed just behind him. He could feel the pressure of it on the back of the avatar's neck. Or was it actually his real neck?

St. Benedict imitated the concept of a deep breath, bringing his mind back into focus. He closed off all other thoughts and attempted to release the program around him, to fall back into the ocean of code and drift toward the exit. But there was no sensation of movement, no buzz as the code washed over his consciousness, no heaviness that came with returning to his body to wake up.

Slowly, he opened his representational eyes. Only darkness. He tried to look to see if he still he had a holographic body, but he couldn't move, or if he moved, he couldn't feel it and certainly couldn't manage the concept of looking downward.

"*Relax*," the terrifying voice said. "*You have his mark. It'll all be over soon.*"

"*I don't think so*," he said and was relieved to hear himself in the black space. At least there was that. Then there was a sensation of a hand sliding up his leg. Ignoring how disturbing that felt, he told himself that at least he still had a leg to molest.

"*I'm only trapped in some bug in the system. Some hole we never knew was there. I only have to initiate force command."*

"A bug am I? Creepy crawlies up your skin?" The voice teased, obviously enjoying the control they seemed to have over him.

He hated to send out the command to forcefully log out, kicking himself for the hundredth time for not making Malachi change the emergency exit codes. What the tech had picked was just stupid. St. Benedict also didn't relish being shocked out of the system, it often made him vomit and increased the risk of electrical backwash to the brain, but it was always better than dying trapped in the system, in this darkness. He assumed; he had never been a vegetable before, so maybe it wasn't better. St. Benedict mentally refocused in preparation for the shock.

"Dorothy."

Nothing happened; not a response, or error message.

"Ha, ha. There's no place like home." The neuro-spike shot through St. Benedict and off in the distance of the dark, he felt his body let go.

"You are not going anywhere. You're going to stay here with me, at least until it's all over." The voice giggled, tripping up and down the chords like musical bells or desperate screams, it was hard to tell. *"Stay with me. Don't leave! Don't leave me, please. I love you…."*

"Where is it?!" Zita dumped the box onto the table, frantically sifting through the jumbled medical equipment. The medical devices St. Benedict was connected to were screaming a pitched beat, no lines moving on its screen.

"Zita! He's dying!" St. Rachel shouted. "His consciousness is slipping away! I can feel him dying!"

"St. Rachel, jack out now or you'll go with him!" Maxamillion barked.

"Oh god." Malachi crouched to the ground, his hands clasped over his head, unable to do anything helpful.

"Malachi, you can forcefully jack him out, right?!" St. Rachel shoved the smaller man over, fire and fury blazing down on him.

"If I do, he's dead any way. The brain shock will kill him."

"You!" St. Rachel wheeled to Rune. "You can use your magic. You can heal him!"

Rune shook her head frantically. "No, I can't! I'm not healer!"

"Liar! He told me! You've done it before!"

"That's not how it works! I'd need a crystal or something preloaded with the spell…." Rune didn't see the slap until it connected with her cheek.

"He's going to die! Do something!"

"St. Rachel, log out! Now!"

"Who moved them?" Zita screeched, dashing the useless equipment to the ground.

"What do you need?!" Rune shouted, grabbing Zita's arm to get her attention.

"Adrenaline! He needs a syringe of adrenaline to his heart!"

Instantly, a string of gold light burst from where Rune held Zita's arm, shooting across the space to another box just outside the circle of monitors. Then Rune, in her desperation, thrust her other hand out toward the dart of light…and she grabbed it, just like she had in the alley. It was solid and as real in her hands as actual rope. She yanked hard on the line and a package, wrapped in plastic and paper, shot along it into Rune's open hands. It all happened in the span of a second.

Rune stared at what she done, her eyes wide as shooter marbles. But there was no time to contemplate what had happened. She had missed it in the alley and she was going to miss it now too. Spinning in place, she thrust the package to an equally wide-eyed Zita. "Is this it?"

Zita snapped out of her awe and seized the package, tearing it open with her teeth. In the same motion she released a lever to drop St. Benedict's chair back flat. Inside the package, she yanked out the syringe with an impossibly long needle.

"Someone cut his shirt open!" the doctor ordered. Without hesitation, St. Rachel whipped out a knife from who-knows-where, snapping it open in one smooth, practiced motion. She started a cut at the top of his shirt, before grabbing the fabric in both hands, tearing hard to rip the shirt open, exposing his unmoving chest. From under the shirt, the two chains clinked together. One was the key to the gun drawer and the other was weighed down by the small, carved metal box that hung at its end. It fell in such a way that it blocked Zita's ability to administer the shot. Without being asked, Rune snatched the chains, pulling them clear. Whatever was inside clinked.

With a thrusting force, Zita slammed the shot into St. Benedict's heart. The moment it hit, Rune yelped at the violence of it.

St. Benedict shot straight up to sitting. He gasped in hard, as if he was trying to take in all the air in the room at once. Hands grabbed him from all around, stabilizing him so he remained sitting.

"Take it slow! Slow down!" Zita instructed. St. Benedict continued to breathe hard and his eyes were open, but he didn't respond to anyone's voice.

"He's not there," St. Rachel said, grabbing at him to force the blank face to look at her.

"What?" Maxamillion barked.

"His body is working," Zita tried to say, but St. Rachel cut her off.

"His consciousness, it isn't there." St. Rachel's face went ashen and for the first time since Rune had met her, the Saint looked ugly as death.

"I don't understand, his vitals all say...." Zita stared hard at a monitor. "This is impossible. It says...there isn't any brain activity. That can't be...."

"Do something!" St. Rachel screamed. "Somebody do something. Please!"

"I can't!" Zita cried, distraught. She slithered back into Malachi's arms, who pulled her to hold and be held as shock was giving way to grief.

"St. Benedict," Rune whispered, barely giving the name voice. Moving entirely on instinct, Rune took the metal box around his neck in her hand, wrapping her fingers around it.

"Leave that alone!" St. Rachel screeched, but Rune ignored her, and whomever stopped St. Rachel from tearing the small box from her hand. Keeping her eyes focused on St. Benedict's glossed over green ones, Rune felt a surge of magic pour out of her, into the box, connecting her to St. Benedict. Then, the magic went through him. Prickles rushed over Rune's skin and the gooseflesh that rose up was almost painful.

"St. Benedict, come back," Rune whispered again. She

could feel him on the other end of the line.

"*St. Benedict, come back.*"

St. Rachel's eyes went wide.

"*What...what are you doing?*" Rune thought she heard St. Rachel say in her mind. It was strange, but she realized they were connected, the three of them. Those two through their tech and Rune through her own magic recognizing St. Benedict as friend. How very strange.

The world around Rune went dark, but she still felt the connection to her body and to him on the other end of the line. To counter the encroaching darkness, Rune opened her secondary sight. Like someone snapped their fingers on either side of her ears, the world rushed at her in color and motion and sound all at once. Things moved, moving, will move from the past, into the present to pass on to the future and all the futures and all the pasts. Rune relaxed into it, not letting the overflow of information overwhelm her spirit.

"*Who are you?*" A fourth, harsh voice demanded. The voice in the darkness.

"*I am Rune,*" she declared.

"*Rune?*" The voice asked, almost child-like. Then it screeched. "*Leave here!*"

"*No.*" Instead, Rune focused her attention onto the warm metal box in her hand.

"*What do you seek here?*" The voice returned, a little confused.

"*My friend.*"

"*You're lying.*"

"*St. Benedict, come back,*" Rune called again into the everything, ignoring the senseless voice.

"*He's a liar, traitor, deceiver,*" the voice tried to shout over her. Rune continued to ignore it.

"*Rune?*" She heard him. He was so far away.

"*I'm here. Come back.*" Rune felt the magic had pulled, pulling, will pull her forward, or was she moving at all?

"*Rune?*" His hand met hers, his larger one stretching to interlock with her fingers.

"*I'm here.*"

"I'm here," she said out loud, the darkness abating around them. She was doing it! She was bringing him back.

"*No, he's mine!*" the harsh voice whined in the distance, becoming more distant in the dark.

"*Go away,*" Rune said firmly, casting the darkness aside. "You are not welcome here."

"*He who has hurt you, will set you free,*" the voice said, barely a whisper in Rune's consciousness, then the voice was completely gone.

Rune closed the secondary sight, her real eyes remaining open, letting the world reset back into the present. Back into the real world.

"St. Benedict," Zita asked tentatively.

Rune blinked twice. St. Benedict's hand was heavy around her own, making the corners of the box dig into her palm. Her friend's green eyes were still staring straight forward, but the machines around them had calmed to regular beeps.

Then he blinked, his eyes brightening with that spot of life that could not be imitated.

"You there, man?" Malachi asked, tentatively.

Rune thought to remove her hand from him, to give him space to finish coming back to himself, but when she tried to pull away, he grasped harder. Slowly, he raised his head and looked deeply into Rune's eyes.

"Two women walk into a bar," he whispered. Those around him double blinked, looking at each other for an explanation. Rune burst out laughing and St. Benedict's blank face eased into a mischievous side smile.

Chapter 7

"Is this your room?" Rune asked, staring wide-eyed around her.

"It's the one I'm using," St. Benedict said, through a clenched smile. He had been trying to be cavalier about almost dying from the moment Malachi helped him off the diving rig all the way up to the apartment's door.

It looked like an apartment taken straight from a chic metrosexual magazine. A combination of fine wood and steel permeated the fixtures of the room. The contrasts complimented each other and screamed of money. Modern light sconces along the walls gave the room soft lighting. The floor plan was open like her own apartment, but the different rooms were indicated by raised or lowered sections of flooring. The dining room with its long oblong table was set up a step and the sitting room with its square grey armchairs and sofa around an antique wood coffee table were down a step. The kitchen was like the one in the tech room they had just come from, steel appliances and marble counters.

St. Benedict would rather have walked the last few feet to his bed under his own power and originally, the Saint had said he was fine. Yet, jelly legs, and Malachi being more determined than St. Benedict, yielded them the compromise of Malachi supporting St. Benedict to his rooms.

After the second flight of stairs, St. Benedict's arm was leaning hard on Malachi's shoulders. Rune followed behind the two men, carrying St. Benedict's fedora and his shoes. Malachi, his mouth in a determined line, his own arm wrapped around the Saint's back to stabilize him, walked through the apartment space to another doorway, passing into an equally refined bedroom. There was something poignantly noble about the two friends, one helping the other walk. It made Rune think of a war movie, like they were two soldiers determined to survive together.

"Alright, take it slow," Malachi said, as they reached the bed and he began to lower St. Benedict down to it.

"Yes, nurse," St. Benedict tried to quip, but it was almost too hard for him to hold up his smile much longer. Zita slithered behind, struggling to get up the two steps into the bedroom while wrangling a saline bag and line.

"Do you need help?" Rune tried to offer, but Zita waved her away.

"I've got. I've got it," she said dismissively before moving to the side of the bed and pulling out a collapsed metal stand that was tucked between the bed frame and night stand. She telescoped the stand to its full height, snapping out a metal hook perpendicular to itself at the top. From that she hung the saline bag. She took the end of the attached line and unclipped the cover to reveal a needle point. Within moments, she had the patient's arm swabbed and the needle inserted. "Now you're going to stay here and sleep."

"I doubt it," St. Benedict muttered, laying back and covering his eyes with his arm.

"Is the light painful?" Zita asked.

"No leave it on," he said.

Rune felt useless at the end of the bed. The bed itself had four posts at the corners about mid-height and she set his fedora on the end of one, then deposited his shoes on the floor beneath it.

"Ms. Leveau, you wanna come with me?" Malachi asked, touching her shoulder with a whisper of his finger. Rune felt torn, not wanting to leave St. Benedict, but not having a good reason to stay. These were his friends, or at least his people. They knew him better and had more invested in him than she did.

"He's going to sleep now," Zita confirmed, looking over her shoulder at Rune, her hands in the pockets of her white coat.

"No, I'm not," St. Benedict said, his words a little slurred.

"With the amount of drugs I put into your drip, you better," Zita chided. St. Benedict groaned but it was all he could do as his head lulled to the side, dropping into unconsciousness.

Zita looked up and smiled smugly.

Rune returned it to be polite and turned to follow Malachi out of the room.

Malachi led the way down and up across the space to another door on the opposite wall. Without waiting he pushed it open.

"These two rooms are suites, so you can stay in here if you want," he said as he passed through the door and slapped up the mid-range lighting. Inside was a parallel apartment to St. Benedict's, except the color scheme was more warm, cherry-wood and sage green paint. Malachi passed into the opposing bedroom, flipping lights until he reached the bathroom. "There is a shower here and lots of those super fluffy towels. Use as many as you like. We've got laundry service. That closet and dresser have clothes of various sizes. You should be able to find something that works for you. If not, let one of us know and we can have something brought in."

He turned back to look at Rune and she nodded. Running a hand through his shaggy hair, he looked down at the ground before saying, "I hate it when he does that."

"What?" Rune asked, since it seemed to be the question Malachi was waiting for.

"Puts himself in danger like that. I mean come on, I'm not a coward or anything, but I'm not an adrenaline-junkie-idiot either!"

"He does that a lot?" Rune asked, wrapping her arms around herself. She looked back the way they had come. She could still see him lying on his own bed, long, socked feet framing his head. Zita checked his pulse, nodding in time with her counting. Another shiver invaded Rune's spine.

"Look, I know it's confusing," Malachi continued, pulling Rune's attention back to himself, "but jacking in, we call it jacking in, is technology that's only a few years old and it's already advanced so quickly. They say it's the way of the future; where we're all going to be able to jack in to this augmented reality and interact with each other, but right now, I feel like freakin' Wilbur Wright and my brother just crashed the first plane really badly. I mean, how many more crashes do we got to have before he stops walking away from them?!" Malachi had started pacing back and forth during his rant, gesturing with each emphasis.

"You need to calm down, dear," Zita said gently, but firmly, her words passing through the door before she did. "Everyone from here to Lake Michigan can hear you."

Malachi ran his hands through his floppy hair again. "I just can't keep doing this, Zita, I can't keep watching my best friend almost die and sit on my ass and do nothing." He punched the wall in a show of emotion, not enough to damage it or himself, but enough to make Rune and Zita both jump. Zita approached him to take his face in her hands. He stilled at her touch, closing his eyes as his own hands dropped to his sides. He let her guide his forehead to hers.

"We're all going to talk about this when he wakes up," she said softly after he had been calm a moment.

Rune felt a little awkward standing there, watching something so intimate. She remembered St. Benedict saying something about Malachi and Zita being a couple, but what exactly he said she couldn't remember. Even if she could gracefully exit, she was in a strange place and didn't really feel like she had anywhere else to go.

The bedroom was nice and the bed looked inviting with its high-end hotel quality down comforter and pillows. Rune looked down at her clasped hands, realizing they were streaked in blood and dirt. No way she was getting into a bed that nice without a shower.

"Do you mind if I examine you a moment, now that we have a chance?" Zita asked, interrupting her thoughts. The Naga turned away from a now quiet Malachi, to face Rune, her eyes roving over her body in a detached, clinically assessing way.

"Um, I…are you a doctor?" Rune asked. She really didn't want to say yes or let Zita near her if she could help it. It took all of her willpower to not look at the twitching end of Zita's scaly tail.

"Yes. In India," Zita said. "Here in America, I am not allowed to practice legally."

"Why?" Rune asked, truly surprised.

"Corporate ban. They want me to go to school again before I can be recertified here," Zita replied gesturing to the bed for Rune to sit. "And my heritage may be part of it."

"Xenophobic bastards," Malachi muttered.

"Please don't," Zita said cutting him off with the sigh of an old argument. She turned back to Rune. "I assure you I know what I am doing. I trained in hominal medicine. Does anything hurt?"

"I...feel fine," Rune answered but she wasn't sure, going still as she tried to determine if what she was saying was true. Little aches and pains began to bleed through her awareness.

"I understand, but you may be having a delayed reaction from all of the adrenaline. The last thing we want is for you to experience more shock," Zita said, firmly patting the bed again. Screwing up her courage, Rune made herself sit down, even if it was a bit stiff. She hesitated for a second, not sure if she was expected to take off the robe.

"Even I can see that she's starting to get a shiner," Malachi commented, pointing at his own eye to indicate where.

Rune probed her upper cheek gently. It was indeed on fire, her mind bringing it to the forefront now that she realized it was there.

"Right. St. Rachel slapped me," Rune stated, remembering.

Zita tilted Rune's chin towards the light with gentle fingers. "I saw that," she muttered.

"We all saw that," Malachi said darkly. "I'm sorry Rune...I mean Anna Mas...err, Ms. Leveau...." he made a face and huffed. "We should have said something at the time."

"Call me Rune," she assured. "And as for St. Rachel...." She looked away a moment, trying to decide what to say. "I guess I am not shocked that she did that. I get the impression she cares a lot for St. Benedict."

Malachi snorted.

"They are very close," Zita said, though she was giving Malachi a side eye. "Still doesn't excuse what she did. Malachi, could you go find something for our guest to eat?" Zita asked smoothly.

"Yeah, sure. What would you like?" he asked.

"Get her some soup, something easy on her stomach," Zita replied for Rune, "and go use the Praetorium kitchen. I'm pretty sure this kitchen isn't even stocked."

"I could use St. Benedict's." Malachi suggested.

It was met with a hooded look. "He doesn't have anything worth eating in there, come on," Zita huffed. That's when Rune was sure the Naga was trying to subtly get rid of him and he wasn't realizing it.

"I would like a drink, if that's ok?" Rune added. "Nothing sounds better than a whiskey sour right now."

Malachi and Zita exchanged a glance and the not-doctor nodded with a half shrug. "By the time you come back with it, we should know for sure if she can have it or not. If not, you can score some more points with Maxamillion."

"Rocks or no rocks?" Malachi asked.

"I'd prefer ice."

Malachi erupted into a smile, getting the joke. "I like you," he said and turned to head out of the door.

Zita regarded Rune and sighed as she rolled her eyes.

"Oh, one more thing," Malachi said, doubling back.

"My goddess! You're like a cat that won't get a clue!" Zita cried, throwing her hands as she reared up a little. Rune would have equated the move with a stomped foot if the Naga had feet.

"I was just wondering," Malachi started, catching himself on the doorframe. "What was that thing you and St. Ben were laughing at so hard? I mean what was the joke?"

"Oh," Rune's eyebrows shot up as she remembered. "It was a couple of months ago. He, um…actually, I cast a healing spell from a crystal that sort of went crazy and turned him to a ravaging monster. We got some help from some Faeries but first they wanted proof that he was still human. So he cracked a joke. 'Two women walk into a bar' was all he got out, but it was enough to…." Rune started to chuckle again, but it died quickly as Zita and Malachi continued to stare at her blankly. "It was enough to convince them of his humanity."

"Huh. So that's how it starts, right? Your best friend gets a girlfriend and suddenly you're on the outside of the inside jokes," Malachi said dramatically, then tragically turned and exited stage left.

"Finally," Zita said, "do you want to wait a moment to make sure he actually left?"

The door to the apartment audibly shut.

"I think we're ok. Um, what exactly do you want me to do?" Rune asked, resetting herself on the bed.

"First off, I'm just going to do the usual things, blood pressure, temperature, and so on." She began pulling equipment out of her pockets to lay on the bed beside Rune. Then the not-doctor opened the nightstand to reveal a blood pressure unit hidden within. "After vitals, we'll take a look and make sure you're not bleeding anywhere you can't feel. Do you feel faint or dizzy at all?" Zita asked and they proceeded with the examination from there, removing clothing as needed. Rune had to admit, it had been a couple of years since she had gotten a physical. Zita was very gentle with her touches and talked the whole time about what she was doing so nothing was a surprise.

"Now is there a need for a pelvic examination?" Zita asked gently, pulling the stethoscope from her ears.

Rune pulled up the robe again, forgoing her original pajamas since she was going to need to take a shower anyway. "No, I don't think so. I mean, I'm sure I need a pap smear or something."

"Nothing else happened when you were attacked?" Zita continued to ask.

Rune finally got what Zita was hinting at. "No, nothing like that. Calvin just tried to choke me out." Her stomach turned at the thought. "It's…it's not the first time he's tried to assault me like that."

"I'd say you're going to have some minor bruising, but so far you look fine," Zita concluded, rehanging her stethoscope around her neck and putting her hands back in her pockets. "I would recommend getting that pap done when you next see your regular physician or healer. Do you want to talk further about what happened?"

"No, if that's alright." Rune didn't want to be rude or dodgy. She just wanted to be done with the whole thing and go to sleep, hopefully.

"Of course. You can go ahead and shower now if you are ready. I would recommend using the rosehip shampoo. It's really expensive so you know it's good."

"You've asked me a lot of personal questions today, do you mind if I ask you one?" Rune watched as Zita moved away, pocketing the few tools she had laid out on the bed.

"Go ahead."

"You and Malachi, St. Benedict told me you two are dating?" Rune felt her ears burning, but after the exchange she had witnessed and her sitting there thinking about it during the examination, her curiosity was getting overpowering.

"I would say it's more than dating," Zita answered, sounding put out.

"Oh, I'm sorry. So you're married?"

"No, that's going too far. We're mated. My people don't really marry as you understand the term."

"Yeah, but how does that work...?" But Rune stopped herself, realizing too late that the question was rude. Now she was blushing harder, wishing she could take the question back.

"It works," Zita said as if she hadn't noticed. Then very clinically she added, "Would you like me to loan you some books on the subject?"

"No. No. Thank you." Rune stopped, knowing that every word coming out of her mouth would only make things worse.

Zita's tense face finally relaxed as she took in Rune's fluster. "Please don't worry about it. I know you're only curious. I have had far worse questions and at least you didn't ask to see my cloaca."

"Someone asked to see your cloaca?!" Rune was genuinely shocked. Even she knew that was beyond the line.

"Some people have a hard time seeing other peoples as anything more than animals," Zita said, knowingly. The Naga moved back into the bathroom and Rune heard the sound of a shower starting up. "There is something about me being a

Naga that seems to make people think they can ask me about the most personal stuff."

"I'm so sorry, I shouldn't have said anything." Rune felt terrible.

"No, no, please. If you're feeling guilty, you shouldn't." Then she said very sincerely, "I don't mind you asking about me and Malachi. We are all trying to get a handle on you, too."

"On me?"

"Yes. For the past year, you've just been a name on a page. A part of the mission, but now here you are, living and breathing. St. Benedict has been real mysterious about you, which hasn't helped the rumors." Now Zita was smiling a knowing smile.

"What kind of rumors?" Rune asked, though she had a good idea.

"The sexy kind."

"Are you going to ask me about my cloaca now?"

Zita laughed and the tension between them finally dissolved. The atmosphere shifted and for a moment, Rune felt like she did when she went to visit her friend Taki, the mermaid dog groomer. All ease and friendship.

"I hate to say it with so much expectation on us, but nothing happened. I mean, between St. Benedict and me, that is." Unbidden her eyes drew themselves to his sleeping form, far, far away. "He said we couldn't even be friends."

Lowering herself to the ground so an arm leaned on the edge of the bed, Zita propped her chin on the palm of that same arm. "But you like him don't you?"

Rune gave a half-shrug. "I don't know. I haven't dated too much after my divorce. It took a while to even try." Staring at him across the way, something quivered inside her stomach in a way that hadn't in a long time. The last person to make it quiver like that was Justin. While most people would take that as a good sign, to Rune it was more like a red flag.

"Look, Rune, there is something you need to know about St. Benedict," Zita started to say, her voice taking on a little extra gravity. "We all like to joke about all the females around here that are secretly in love with him, but we all learn sooner or later to leave him alone. So many around here keep hoping they'll be the special one to open up his cold heart. He's charming and I like him as my lover's friend, but he's also frozen inside. Which makes him very dangerous. St. Rachel is the only one who can be considered close to him and even she knows to keep herself to herself. It's a Saint thing. They have their true feelings trained out of them or something. The hell the Saints go through to become…it connects them in a way only they understand, even when they fight each other."

"I think I know what you mean," Rune said, thinking about St. Augustina, the Saint she had encountered two months previously.

"St. Rachel may be closer to him than anybody."

"What about Malachi? Isn't he St. Benedict's best friend?"

"It's not the same. There is this darkness inside the Saints, and especially St. Benedict, that drives them. It is probably one of the reasons they were chosen to become Saints."

"I know something of darkness," Rune said, though it had been more like a thought that had snuck out of her mouth.

"I don't doubt you do," Zita conceded. "I hope you don't mind. I read the medical file on you, from after you were released from Kodiak's corporate prison."

"You…how? Maddie always took me to a private healer."

"A simple thing for someone like St. Benedict to acquire once he knew what to look for," Zita answered cryptically.

Rune nodded, believing it, even if it was a violation of privacy. Maybe she was simply too tired and sore to really care. They watched St. Benedict together, silently musing their own thoughts for a few moments. Rune contemplated the darkness that drove this man who had forced himself into her life. The last time she had seen him, after she had revealed the truth about herself, that she was actually Anna Masterson, she remembered the look he had given her. It hadn't been a look she liked, yet at the same time it had been mesmerizing it had been so intense.

"So what has he told you all about Anne?" she asked.

Zita stopped, her eyes widening. "Anne?"

Rune opened her mouth to speak again, but a realization made her close it. Zita understood any way.

"He told you her name?" she breathed. "The name of his wife?"

"But not you guys?"

The Naga shook her head, still a bit in shock. "We know he had a wife, but he never spoke her name to anyone." More puzzle pieces began clicking into place. "And your real name is Anna." Zita looked between Rune and St. Benedict as her mind worked. "It makes some sense now."

"I hope I didn't spoil the mystery. Two months ago, he thought I might have been his missing wife, but it just turned out we had very similar names."

"That explains...."

"What?" Rune asked, urging her on.

"There has been a change in him, that we can't put a finger on. Malachi noticed it first and I have been starting to agree with him about it." Zita was quiet for a moment longer, thinking, then she turned away and rose up on her coils, breaking the tension. "I'm sorry, I'm keeping you from your shower. I'll get out of your way."

"Thank you for this," Rune responded. She hated to admit it, but it was a relief that Zita was going, even if she had enjoyed talking with the Naga. With a smile and nod, Zita slithered out of the door.

Her absence allowed Rune to feel the weight of everything that had happened over the past few hours, or lifetime, whatever. It took every speck of willpower she had to push herself off the bed.

The shower was exquisite.

The shower itself wasn't anything special, having ordinary tile and a hotel-styled shower head, but the hot water was everything it needed to be and more. Rune wished she could use the scalding water to burn away the thoughts of Justin. They had intruded slowly, first as the water hit her half numb body, bringing it to life. Simply standing in it, letting the water cascade like molten rainfall over her head, she wished closing her eyes would make the room dark enough for her to pretend she was somewhere secret and safe. Memories of his face, of his touch, things he said both kind and cruel, awoke the familiar hunger for him she had thought she had long ago suppressed.

"I don't want to see him again," she said to herself out loud as she poured too much of the rosehip shampoo into her hair. Yet, her thoughts drifted over to the footage of him being tortured, screaming and defiant. Her heart beat quickened and no amount of rubbing her scalp could soothe her.

An old memory of him, embroidered with fantasy, tread unbidden yet welcome in her mind. It was one she had used too often in the early days after her divorce, when she was still hopelessly in love with him despite all that he had done to her. In her mind's eye, he would come into the shower to wrap his arms around her from behind. The smooth skin of his long, lanky arms would come around her, cupping her torso, creating a tingle of anticipation up and down her spine before his chest would meet her back, wrapping her up warmly. His nose would nuzzle into her neck. Exactly on the edge her periphery, she would see black, wet tendrils of his long hair. His long, strong hands would start exploring her skin, making every part of her feel alive. His breath would dust her skin as he slowly turned her around to face him.

And he would never be there.

The familiar, painful ache clenched her stomach and Rune shut the water off, frustrated. Why were these old feelings coming back again? She hated them, the insatiable ache that could never be fulfilled because the one who could fulfill it never came through her door. Never called, never even thought of her.

"I've moved on," Rune tried to insist to herself, stepping out of the shower and snatching up one of the reportedly luxurious towels. She didn't really note its qualities as she toweled off and wrapped up her dripping hair. Since she couldn't exactly put her old dirty, bloody clothes back on, she left them abandoned on the floor. She was still alone in the bedroom, but it had changed since she went into the shower. Fresh clothes were laid out on the bed, a butter soft shirt and matching pajama pants the color of merlot. On top of the night stand, a tray with a cover on it waited for her as well as a familiar brown drink, ice already half melted in the glass. The door had been discretely closed so she was truly secure to walk out with only a towel turban.

Rune dressed, sat on the bed, ate the barley and beef soup that awaited her and drank her whiskey all while eying her door, her thoughts far on the other side.

What did moving on really look like? Obviously, she hadn't actually been doing it, because here she was, dredging up emotions that were never based in logic or sense. The few other males she had dated never went anywhere past a few dates and most of her time had been spent being with Maddie. What if she replaced the man in the shower with someone else?

"He doesn't think of me that way," she answered.

Rune gave a passing thought to sleep, then got up to go to her door. It seemed like the better, more responsible idea, to go see how St. Benedict was doing. Then she could put herself to sleep. She promised.

The suite she had been given was empty as well, with the door between the two apartments having been shut. She stalled for a moment before it, trying to decide if she should knock or if that was being silly. Instead, she cracked it open and peeked through. The last thing she wanted was to wake him up.

Across the space, still gently lit by the sconce lighting, Rune could see his bedroom door still open. He lay there peacefully, one hand on his stomach, his other arm lying open, receiving needed help from the IV line. Encouraged, Rune started through the door, when a blanket drifted out and over him in a smooth fluid motion. St. Rachel came into view, carefully tucking the blanket around him, making sure it covered his feet. Then the beautiful woman sat next to him on the bed, her back toward Rune in a perfect outline of feminine curve and grace. Timidly, the goddess reached out a single finger and brushed his hair to the side on his forehead, not because he needed it cleared, but as a tender gesture of affection.

Rune withdrew behind the safety of the door. Shutting it quietly, she leaned back against it and sighed. "See. I knew it."

"Knew what?" Rune jumped as Maxamillion entered the suite from its main door, his suit jacket hanging from his fingers, over his left shoulder. "Excuse me for simply entering without knocking." He shook his head, rubbing at his temple. "It's been a long night already."

"I'm still waiting to feel sleepy," Rune agreed, moving away from the connecting door.

"I wanted to chat with you quick before retiring for the night," Maxamillion said, entering the rest of the way into the main room, shutting the door behind him with a soft click.

"Do you want some coffee?" Rune looked around the foreign space. "Or is that something you should be offering me?"

He barked a laugh. "Would you like some coffee?"

"Actually, I hate coffee. Do you have some tea?" Rune moved into the kitchen area, spotting a silver electric kettle on the counter. She plucked it up and went to fill it from the sink.

Joining her in the kitchen, Maxamillion dropped his suit coat over the counter and began foraging in the cupboards. "We should have a whole stock of tea. Ah, here we are." He pulled out a small wooden box with no top and a row of multi-colored little packets, presenting it to Rune like it was a prize. He then found two cups and waited while she selected her color packet.

"What did you want to chat about?" Rune asked, having decided that a Chamomile Plus sounded good.

"I wanted to ask you," he started carefully, "what do you think about my operation here?"

"I will admit, it is very impressive." She looked around the well-appointed room. "How do you afford all this?"

"Part of what Corinthe Corporation publicly offers is security services for other corporations."

Rune laughed. "Wait, wait. You mean to tell me that the secret vigilante underground resistance is also the security guards for the very people they are trying to bring down?"

He joined her laughing, "With a very good reputation." He leaned against the counter, crossing his arms and legs casually while he continued to giggle. "To be perfectly honest, I'm not sure how we got here either. I just remember it being a diabolical idea originally. It was a risk, but it's paid off. I'm now on the brink of being able to invoke real change. Which is why I need you."

The water bubbled loudly and Rune poured her tea. "Smooth segue."

"What do you think? Now that you know I'm on the up and up?"

"And what exactly do you need someone like me for? You're up to your ears in technology."

"For one thing, your connection to the Magic Guild would be very helpful."

Rune narrowed her eyes. "You see, this is why I don't have much interest in working for a corporation. Even a secret one. You want more. Corporations are all about owning people entirely. I'm sorry, but it's against everything I stand for."

"You're surprisingly defensive." Maxamillion arched an eyebrow at her.

She checked herself. "What do you mean?"

"You know who we are, what we're about. Yet, you are still dead set against us because of the mask we wear."

Rune took a deep breath. "Your mask looks a lot like the real thing."

"It wouldn't be effective otherwise." He leaned forward a little, his voice becoming more intense and soft. "You could do a lot with us to further our mission. Get back at those who wronged you and using their own weapons against them."

"You mean revenge against Kodiak?" A shiver spilled down Rune's spine. Maxamillion took up the water pot and started pouring his own cup of tea. The break in tension gave Rune a moment to look around the suite and its opulence. There was definitely a temptation to "join the cause." Why didn't it feel right?

"I'm not interested in revenge," she said.

Maxamillion paused in his dipping of his teabag. "What are you interested in?"

"I'm not sure yet. And until I am, I'm pretty sure I shouldn't be making any long term commitments." She nodded. That sounded like a good, fortune-cookie thing to say.

"Is that your final decision?"

Rune laughed. "Nothing's final until you're dead. But for now, I'm going to say no thanks again."

Maxamillion nodded, pushing his teacup away undrunk. He plucked up his coat and slid it back on, taking something from the pocket. "I know I've already given you one of these, but in case you change your mind, call me and we'll discuss details."

Rune took the new business card, nodding.

"Thank you for all your help, Mr. Corinthe," she said.

"May I ask you one more thing?" He stood there with his hands in his pockets, the top of his dress shirt open, the tie long gone. "If you wanted to find Justin, you could do it, right?"

"I don't."

"Why not? If I was in your position, with the world coming at me with problems he created, I would want to know 'what the hell man,'" he said, letting a little slang cut through the business-perfect speech.

Rune furrowed her eyebrows, acknowledging to herself that he had a point. "Yeah, but would you sell your soul for answers?"

Maxamillion shrugged. "What else is it good for?"

Chapter 8

Nightmares plagued St. Benedict throughout his sleep. Even though Zita always promised the drugs would keep him from dreaming at all, it was never the case. Hands grabbed him in the dark. Running up and down his body, weighing him down, putting themselves in places they didn't belong. He didn't fight them though. As much as they terrified him, he felt he deserved this. He had earned this hell and it was only just and right that he should suffer. The hands began to tear into his flesh, little pinches at first, but when he didn't scream, they became bolder, taking bite after bite out of him. Then they invaded his body, entering orifices that in turn became burning, tearing fire. After a moment, the fire would become so hot he would be engulfed, only his beating heart existing in the middle, his teeth grinding together as he went numb. The absence of pain was more terrifying, because he knew it meant he was dead. But he still existed. Forever would exist. Alone. In the dark. Numb. Ash. And then he would scream.

"I'm here," a voice said, cutting through the darkness. "You're safe. You're safe," it repeated. The darkness still held him and he tried to thrash away. There was a crashing sound and a yelp.

"St. Benedict! It's alright. I'm here! You're not alone, you're safe!"

Finally, his eyes snapped open. He was panting, staring around wildly trying to piece together where he was. He had a body, and it ached. He was alive.

St. Rachel was holding his arm, trying to rub her fingers soothingly down it, but she had no idea how much worse she was actually making it. He pushed her hand away, licking his lips as he tried to get his breathing under control.

"Oh no, you're bleeding," St. Rachel said. Instead of being disturbed by his rejection, true to form, she got to work on the most urgent problems. Taking up a hand towel from the nightstand, she seized his left arm. This time he let her have it and she pressed the white towel, dabbing at the inner part of the elbow.

"You tore yourself," she clucked, "when you jerked, you pulled your IV straight out. Zita's not going to be happy."

"I've got it," he said, taking over the towel. She relinquished it and turned to setting the IV stand back up. "How many bags?"

"I'm sorry what?" she asked, as she rehung the IV bag on the stand.

He gestured at it. "How many bags of solution have I had?"

"Three. It's about 9am now. You actually slept through the night."

"No, I didn't," he grumbled. He threw his legs over the side of the bed. Staring at his socked feet, he ripped them off, letting his bare feet hit the cold wood floor. "I wish I was in my own bed."

"You are in your own bed," she replied, not understanding that he meant the bed that existed in his secret place. "Malachi and that Talent dragged you in here while I had to clean up your mess. I was able to salvage your memory record, but having to 'Dorothy' you out of the system gummed everything up. I wasn't sure I was going to manage it."

St. Benedict said nothing to that. Instead, he got to his feet and made his way to the bathroom. After he had peed out three bags of fluid, the bleeding on his arm had slowed. A quick bandage would allow him to forget about it.

"I look like shit," he muttered to his reflection with its day-old stubble and sickly bags under his eyes. The Saint box rolled back and forth across his chest as he moved, never letting him forget, even if he wanted to. He touched it with two fingers, lifting it to kiss with thoughtless practice, before dropping it to let gravity tug on his chain.

"Do you want help?" St. Rachel asked, appearing at the door as he was stripping off his shirt.

"No," he answered, dropping his pants in front of her with zero consideration for the delicacy he knew she didn't have. He couldn't care less if she saw him naked or what she thought about it. Whatever she did think, not a wisp of it was betrayed on her face. Besides, they had seen every inch of each other's' bodies before in darker contexts. There was nothing new to see. At least that was what he thought.

"Those bruises on your back are not insignificant," St. Rachel said archly.

"I'm fine."

"You're inhibiting your peak function if you only intend to ignore them."

"Did Zita look at them?"

"I have no idea," St. Rachel said dismissively.

He stepped into his shower, turning on the water after he was in. He punished himself with the ice-cold water, and began washing before it even got warm. "Any updates?" he asked, as he pulled out his razor and proceeded to shave in the mirror he kept in the stall.

"Yes, we've got a 63% confirmation on the image recovered in the car mirror. It's not bad, but it's not great either. Doesn't help that the database we got it from is incomplete at best."

"Clarify."

Her blurry image looked away, crossing her arms as she leaned against the door in her killer femme fatale look, coming off more artistic now with the pebbly glass between them.

"Magic Guild," she said, darkly.

St. Benedict took that in. "Makes more sense than someone showing up with a flamethrower."

"The problem is, it's not an exact match, but the clothing and partial insignia we caught is enough to be very confident it's Magic Guild."

"Do you have the specs with you?" he asked, now finally getting intrigued.

She slid open the door on his shower and popped her hand in, the hologram already running above her palm. The image from the reflection stared back at him and he rinsed his face before looking at it. Lighting his own finger, he swiped to the side and the reflection was replaced by the matched file. A face very much like the first one appeared along with a very empty stats column beside it. He flipped between the two faces a couple more times, before retrieving his shampoo/conditioner bottle.

"You only got a 63% match?" he asked, dropping the bare minimum amount into his hand.

"I know. Eyeballing it, they seem a closer match than that."

"They're twins," he said before ducking under the water stream.

"What?" St. Rachel asked incredulously.

"Look at them again. Male and female faces. The one in the mirror is male for sure, the one in the picture is female." St. Rachel's hand disappeared and he cranked off his water.

When he opened the stall the whole way, he saw she had retreated out of the room, focusing on her hand. He grabbed a towel and roughed his hair before deciding at the last minute to wrap it around his waist. He always felt like less of an ass after he showered.

"It could be a sex change," St. Rachel said, sitting on his bed while he went into his closet.

"Then the percentage would be higher. Sex changes don't usually alter that much. I suppose you could be right, if they had surgery to change their identity, why not go all the way to flipping gender as well. But then why make your face close enough to what you used to really look like? Besides these are magic users we're talking about. I'm sure there is magic enough that could alter your appearance far smoother than surgery could."

"Maybe we should ask our new pet Talent." St. Rachel didn't even bother keeping the dryness from her voice.

"Where is our guest anyway?"

"Sleeping still, in the suite next door. I'm surprised she didn't try to crawl into bed with you."

He came out of the closet, now dressed in soft grey slacks and a button up shirt, his short dark hair combed back.

"Now, how could she do that when I had a guard dog watching over me all night?" he asked, planting a brazen kiss on St. Rachel's cheek before sitting on the edge of his bed to slip on new socks and then shoes.

"Did you just call me a bitch?" St. Rachel asked, narrowing her eyes at him.

St. Benedict chuckled, "You know all my tricks."

"Best you remember that. I may have your back but I will not be made a fool of."

"You have nothing to worry, my dear. She is one of the only women I have ever met who was able to resist my charms." He stood, taking his hat from the end of the bed to set it on his head with his usual cool flourish.

If she was impressed by his transformation from near death to smooth, cool super spy, St. Rachel didn't show it. "Corinthe wants to talk to you as soon as you are on your feet."

"Thank you for letting me shower first." St. Benedict stuck a hand in his pocket and moved toward the door of the bedroom. "Is he in the Praetorium?"

"He left an hour ago for his meeting. He wants you to call him." St. Benedict slid past her to go into the main room of the apartment. Instead of leaving though, he dropped down the step to the living room and took one of the chairs there.

"Is there coffee?" he asked, popping his hand open. The holograms came to life and quickly he tapped a few things to make the call.

"No," St. Rachel answered as she took the other seat in the space, gracefully placing her legs crossed to one side, her hands resting on her knee. "And I'm not your mother."

A bubble hologram appeared around his head, like a collar with a single marble of light sweeping in a circle around him. As the call began to ring, the marble danced in its sweep. He could have kept the call private, but having it open would keep him from having to repeat anything to St. Rachel.

"So then, how much would it cost me to get you to make some coffee?"

A light pricked her eye at that. She said nothing, but got up to go make the coffee much to St. Benedict's surprise. He thought he'd get either a metaphorical or literal smackdown for his obviously chauvinistic request. That sobered him a bit. It must have been a closer call than he was acknowledging.

"Yes," Maxamillion's voice barked as the call picked up, interrupting his thoughts.

"Guess what, I'm alive," St. Benedict said in return. "So are traditional greetings for people who lead conventional lives?"

"Pretty much, but I'm glad you're still with us. Replacing you would greatly jeopardize our mission."

"Oh, I feel all warm and tingly inside," St. Benedict quipped.

"This is not Malachi you're talking to," Maxamillion said dryly.

St. Benedict changed posture.

"Sorry, sir. Close encounters with death always make me a little giddy."

"What happened in there, St. Benedict?"

"I can't really say for sure, sir."

"I need to know if it was a system malfunction."

St. Benedict furrowed his eyebrows. "I don't think that would be accurate. What happened was more.... It was something new. If I was to guess I would say it felt more organic."

There was a pause of silence while Maxamillion processed the information. "What does St. Rachel say?"

"She's right here." St. Benedict turned to look at St. Rachel, who was snapping the coffeemaker shut to start it.

"I did a full sweep of the system. As far as that is concerned, everything was functioning normally. The only error report we got was that the user simply failed to live."

"Failed to live? Is that even a thing?" Maxamillion asked.

"Technically, yes," St. Benedict conceded. "But it's rarely a message to be sent by itself. Usually it's coupled with a few other alerts, like neuro-spike, or heart failure or blood poisoning. More biodata like that."

"It was the only error message," St. Rachel confirmed firmly. "You simply started dying."

"That...is not reassuring," St. Benedict said. He thought about the voice and the sensations he had felt. They were vague at best, his memory about what happened was somewhat limited, but it was very clear that there had been an intelligence behind the encounter. "I wonder if this is a new kind of attack?"

St. Rachel's face actually displayed surprise. "You mean, another Saint?"

"The technology is new. What if someone figured out a way to kill me without spiking me?"

"Alright. We need to minimize risks at this point," Maxamillion said, taking charge. "I want a full diagnostic run of our system. We need to know if we've been compromised. How much is that going to set us back?"

"There are two operations that are in process, but we can tell the one we're going blind, they should be fine. The other is the one you are on right now. You will have zero support for at least three but more likely five hours," St. Rachel said.

"Needs must...." Maxamillion started.

"When the devil drives," St. Benedict and St. Rachel finished. There was a pause for a moment as the creed reverberated amongst them.

"As for the magic user," Maxamillion began after the moment had passed.

"Yes, I think I'm going to...." St. Benedict started.

"You're going to send her home. We are going to pull all resources from her protection."

St. Benedict was on his feet. "What?!"

"We gave her a chance to join us, but we don't have the resources to be doing even this much, especially if she isn't going to join us."

"Sir, we've barely given her time to...."

"We don't have the time to give. I know that you have something invested in her, but..."

"It's not that simple, she could be the key to getting you the rest of the Masterson Files."

"I frankly don't see that. At this point in time, she is costing us too much and has given very little in return."

"We can still force her compliance," St. Rachel interjected.

"We don't have the expertise in this. We saw the effects of her power last night. I think we should all count ourselves lucky that she didn't use that power to kill you on the spot, St.

Rachel, after you slapped her."

"You slapped her?" St. Benedict's thoughts went black for a second.

"I did what I had to," St. Rachel defended, sticking out her chin in defiance. "I got her to save your life. She was just standing there, doing nothing while you were dying!"

"Cut her loose," Maxamillion commanded. "Focus on the leads generated from the attack in the alley. It's a likely bet that the other pieces of the Masterson Files we seek are held by them and that's where we need to put our limited resources. This is our big push and we aren't taking in any more money at this time, so we have to use what we already have where it will be most effective. Maybe if things get hot enough for her out there, she'll come back around."

St. Benedict didn't answer, only locked his jaw as he stared at St. Rachel. She noticed, but affected her ice cold defense as she stared back.

"Am I understood?" Maxamillion asked, when no one answered him.

"Yes, sir," St. Rachel barked back, clearly and defiantly.

"Yes, sir," St. Benedict said quietly and deadly.

"Contact me when you've returned her to her bar." Then Maxamillion was gone.

The holograms around St. Benedict's head faded as the call minimized to his hand only, which he then snapped shut into a fist.

"You said she's in the next suite over?" St. Benedict asked, his voice rumbled in his chest.

"Yes."

He cocked his head and smiled. He saw the shiver involuntarily run down St. Rachel's spine. She certainly did like her men slightly evil looking.

"Let's go rouse her and see what today brings."

St. Rachel stepped backward out of the living room area, navigating up the stairs easily without uncrossing her arms or breaking eye contact with him. It was an impressive display of control and agility. She let him pass her, heading for the in-between suite door.

To both their surprises, a breakfast party was happening next door. At the suite's long dining table, Rune, Zita, and several other operatives were talking and laughing, all enjoying stacks of pancakes. Malachi, wearing a long striped apron, approached the table with a platter covered in more fluffy pancakes, which received jovial cheers and raised cups of coffee or juice.

"More bacon coming," Malachi announced to even more cheers, hamming it up.

"Hey tavern keeper, where can a soul get a cup of coffee around here," St. Benedict called out. The room turned to look at them and more cheers went up, even some applause.

"He lives!" Malachi shouted, throwing his hands up into the air. The two men approached, hands mirroring each other until they met and mock-kissed each other's cheeks to the laughter and hoots of the crowd. "For you sir, your money; it's-a no good here. Sit down, sit down," Malachi continued in a bad faux Italian accent. "I bring-a you some-a coffee in a minute-a."

Seats emptied out at the table as people who had finished started to report for their work shifts.

"Tell people there are more pancakes if anyone hasn't eaten yet," Zita called after them, before helping herself to another stack of three. Rune herself hesitated, her own syrup coated plate a testament to how much she had already consumed.

Taking the seat across from Rune, he was grateful when she glanced up. She looked very well for having had such a rough night. She was wearing new clothes, a soft, dark-colored raspberry shirt that pooled over her thighs and a pair of jeans that hugged her hips, tucked into a new pair of knee-high boots. He was glad someone had shown her the closet-of-many-clothes. His mind danced over images of what she would look like in some of the cocktail dresses he knew were in there. Her hair was French braided sideways along her crown and tied behind her head. Even though she didn't have a spot of makeup on her face, she looked fresh and bright in a way that only natural could, despite the blooming bruises on her face.

"You sleep okay?" he asked, helping himself to two empty plates. He set the first one down in front of himself and the other in front of the empty seat next to him for St. Rachel.

"Eventually. How are *you* doing?" Rune asked, pointedly looking away to stab some pancakes with her fork. She deposited them onto his plate, not looking at him while she did it.

"Every day I wake up is another day," he said, accepting the butter, raspberry jelly and syrup as it was slid toward him by Zita.

"Is that supposed to be deep?" Rune asked, arching her eyebrow at him.

She only got a smile for an answer.

"St. Rachel, are you going to sit down and eat?" he asked the shadow still standing over his shoulder. That's when he saw the glance Rune gave her. It was quick, barely noticeable, but very informative.

"No, I've eaten," St. Rachel said coldly as she turned away. "I will see you in the Praetorium when you've finished." She exited a little too dramatically.

Rune busied herself with prepping her fresh pancakes. The laughter in the room had died and was replaced with a tension. St. Benedict chose to pretend he didn't know why. Tactically, about when Malachi approached the table with the much needed cup of coffee, St. Benedict asked, "What did St. Rachel do?"

The question surprised everyone so much they stopped whatever they were doing to look at him, then at each other.

Finally, Rune spoke. "She slapped me, while you were dying."

"Why would she slap you?" he asked, forcing his voice to stay neutral.

"She believed I was holding out on using magic to save you," Rune answered, equally as neutrally, chopping up her pancake in layered forkfuls.

"I see." He let those words sit in the air for a moment. "What do you want to do about it?"

Rune blinked twice, then gave him a questioning look. St. Benedict set the coffee down and dumped a spoonful of raspberry jam into it. "I promised you that no harm would come to you while you were here and harm came to you. I am obligated to see that made right. What would you like me to do to her?"

"I don't know, what is exactly on the table?" Rune asked, with cautious wryness, like she was preparing to laugh if he was kidding.

He was glad to see that the events from the previous night hadn't sent her spinning back into the dark place it would have two months ago. Of course she could be putting on a brave front or it hadn't really caught up to her yet. "Anything you'd like. If you want an apology, I will get one from her, though I can't guarantee the sincerity. I can also threaten her, make it very clear that laying a hand on you again will force me take steps she won't like. I can simply take those steps, if you would prefer." Several possibilities flitted through his mind. In alphabetical order.

"Isn't she someone you care about?"

"She is someone I work with, someone I have history with. She's also someone who knows what I do when my word is broken."

"I doubt that she would have hit me like that if you didn't matter a great deal to her."

"She still shouldn't have done it," Malachi opined as he set the plate of bacon in front of himself while he took a seat.

Rune lifted her eyebrows as she nodded, conceding the point. "It's not that I don't think that too. I'm simply trying to be diplomatic."

St. Benedict looked at her, shaking his head a little and giving a shadow of an enigmatic grin.

"What?" she asked.

The Saint's heart stopped a second, realizing she had caught him thinking what he had been thinking.

Malachi cut in, "So...Everything we've ever heard and seen about you, you know from the Masterson Files that we have, you don't really resemble what we all thought of as 'Anna.' You know?"

"Do you want to try explaining that again? I don't think you worded it awkwardly enough," St. Benedict said.

"I'm still her," Rune said, her voice taking on a memory quality and another bite of pancake. "I'm just a woman now." Zita snorted her juice as she laughed. A few more women at the table giggled and saluted with their drinks as well.

"Speaking of footage," Rune said, obviously seizing an opportunity that had opened for her. "I would like to see all the footage you have on Justin." She jutted her chin a little, conveying that she intended to be stubborn about this.

Getting up from the table, St. Benedict moved to the coffee pot to refill his only half empty cup. "My instinct is to say no," he chose to say.

Rune cocked her head at him, her eyes assessing. "You just said you owed me for St. Rachel's slight toward me. I think I would be most compensated by you giving me what I asked of you."

St. Benedict growled low into his coffee. Damn he hated the taste of it, but Zita would have thrown a fit if he went back to caffeine pills.

"Most of the footage is not easy to see," he challenged as he leaned back against the kitchen counter, crossing one arm under his coffee arm.

Malachi cleared his throat. "I could check through and pull out the stuff that's less with the torture…."

"No," Rune stated firmly. "I want to see all of it. I have a right to see all of it. I can handle it. And if I can't, that's my problem."

Everyone still sitting at the table stared hard at their plates, the mood plummeting back into uncomfortable again. Only Zita dared to give St. Benedict a sidelong glance. St. Benedict and Rune stared off across the space from the kitchen to the dining table. Rune looked so resolute. Something had changed overnight while he had been asleep. Something he wouldn't be able to control.

"I need to know," Rune continued to argue.

The Saint pushed off the counter of the kitchen. "I know everyone isn't finished with breakfast, but would you mind giving us the room?"

Most of the people at the table were all too eager to escape, a few taking their plates with them.

"Me too?" Malachi asked, pulling the bacon platter toward himself with its remaining dozen strips.

"If you don't mind," St. Benedict nodded as he moved back to reclaim his seat, plucking two pieces of bacon from the tech's platter. Before making his exit, Malachi dropped another two strips each onto Rune and St. Benedict's plates and took the rest with him.

"St. Benedict." Zita stopped a half beat too long. He guessed she meant to say something else, then changed her mind. "I need to record your vitals this morning, when you're done."

He nodded and she left too. Once the room was finally cleared, he leaned across the table toward Rune.

"Maxamillion has rescinded the deal," he said carefully. He was going to have to handle this delicately.

"Deal? What deal? We never agreed on anything." She set her fork down, her voice edged with anger.

"I made a deal. It hinged on my being able to persuade you to work for us. I used Corinthe resources to keep you safe, but Maxamillion feels we've given you enough chances to agree and now he's cutting us loose."

"Us?"

St. Benedict flinched. Crap. He hadn't meant to say it that way. "I mean, he's yanking me off of protecting you, essentially." Dammit, why were words not coming out right?

Rune blew out a sigh. "I guess I can't say I'm surprised, can I? But that is ok. I have a plan."

"Oh really?"

She nodded, swirling her last bit of pancake in her dregs of syrup. "I've decided to find out what happened to my deadbeat husband." St. Benedict took a measured drink from his coffee cup, so Rune continued. "You help me find him, I'll help you get your hands on his work."

"And how is this different from working for Maxamillion?"

"Because it's you and me. I can trust you."

St. Benedict barked a laugh. "No, you can't."

Rune waved her hand dismissing his words. "Yeah, yeah, I know, because you are such a bad man, yadda yadda yadda. And then you go and hand me a gun and offer me your own life in order to keep me safe." She tried to meet his eyes, but he wouldn't look at her.

"You don't owe me anything," he said instead, straining to sound bemused.

"You're right. I agree." That surprised him enough to get him to look at her. She smiled. "I owe it to myself to know what happened. The whole story. Not just what I remember. Not just what I tried to forget. But I also know you won't help me for free, so I'm offering to help you, *you* St. Benedict, help you to find the missing pieces from your past too."

"You don't know anything about my past." He forced his face to stay still, to stay smiling. He held his breath, since he wouldn't be able to disguise the panic any other way. Her eyes cut through him, earnest and mystifying at the same time. She was showing him everything and yet he couldn't read what she was thinking.

"You told me yourself, that you worked with Justin on that master program to make computers cast magic spells en masse."

He double blinked. "I did," he nodded, remembering.

"I imagine that the reason you're looking for it is because it haunts you too. Something you created destroyed your life and took away...." she hesitated on saying his wife's name.

Steeling herself, she stretched out her fingers and touched his hand. She wanted to grip it, to feel his fingers lace around hers but she didn't completely dare, settling instead to pat the top in a gentle, friend-zone way. The fear of him pulling away from her was more painful than resisting the desire she had.

"The only reason you and I met was because of the one letter difference between your wife's name and mine. You are a good man. You came for her, even if she wasn't me. Now, I want to look my own husband in the eye and find out why the hell it isn't him sitting there across from me instead of you."

He captured her fingers and squeezed a little in acknowledgement, pulling away smoothly, signaling he was releasing, but not rejecting. Then he said very carefully, "I can't help you. I've been ordered to stop. And Rune, you are unprotected. You need to concern yourself with that. We both know that the people who know anything about Justin are dangerous."

Rune's face faltered. "No. No, that is the wrong answer.

Your line is, 'Yes Rune, I think that is an excellent idea, forget Maxamillion, let's work together.'"

"It would be an excellent idea, if I thought…." he checked himself. His instincts told him to attack her plan, undermine her psychologically. If he could make her doubt herself then she might give it up. But he didn't want to do that again.

"If you thought what?"

He gently smiled. "Look, Rune. I don't want to offend you, but I'm not going to do this with you."

"Do what?"

"Be your partner. Be something more than what we are now."

"Ha. I'm not asking you out on a date," she laughed, hoping her nonchalance was convincing. The urge to ask what exactly he thought "they were now" passed through her mind, but as fast as she thought it, the moment to ask it had passed.

"I have my own agenda, and you know that. I can't fulfill that agenda by playing bodyguard for you all the time. This is not personal."

She rolled her eyes. "Nobody says that unless they think it *is* personal."

He shifted away. "Look, you're not the first person to try to tie me down as a partner. It's not how I work. Ask anyone here. The people here are tools, and so am I. We use each other and then move on to the next task. Unfortunately for you, that's not how you work, is it?"

"Care to explain better than that?" It was getting harder to resist getting upset. Rune knew there was a chance he would say no and she thought she had prepared for it.

"You make relationships that last," he said pointing at her. "You have retainers. You're part of the old system of mageocracy. Ally and Alf have to serve you for life, don't they?"

Rune shifted in her seat. There was an uncomfortable truth slapping her in the face. "By their choice," she said. That was entirely true, they had both made their vows to her before she even understood what they were doing. For Alf, it had been a matter of course, insofar as he had been Maddie's retainer and he had no desire to be anything else. He certainly had desire to serve anyone else, but not to not serve. On the other hand, Ally wasn't even out of high school yet. She had her whole life ahead of her. Rune knew too well what a mistake it could be to make a lifelong choice too early.

"Don't worry so much about it. They belong to you and I belong to Maxamillion. If you want me, you have to deal with Maxamillion, but you don't want to do that." He sat leaning back in his chair, projecting ease.

"That's not funny," Rune's mirthful smile melted off her face.

"I'm not trying to be funny."

"You're always trying to be funny." She was quiet for a pregnant moment. "Should I have taken Maxamillion's deal?"

"No! No, you shouldn't have. You did the right thing," St. Benedict said swiftly. There was no condemnation or alarm on his face. "You do not want a piece of this, Rune." He got up from his seat, casually pacing while swirling the dregs of his coffee in the cup. "This is a war we are fighting. A real war, with pain and death right under the streets of Chicago. A cold, silent civil war for the heart of everything I ever hoped to believe in. You can live beyond this. I can't, but I can damn well die to see it come true."

"A Saint's death wish?" she asked. "That's very lone action-star of you." She tried to chuckle at her joke, but when he didn't laugh it died in her throat. Instead, his green eyes looked through her as he stalked up to the sink.

"Think Rune. Where can you go that you will be safe? If you were a part of a corporation, I would tell you to go to your private security force." He stopped as his mind pulled up the magical equivalent: The Magic Guild. "Right, there might be something in that," he said too softly to himself.

"What?" Rune asked, but St. Benedict was already putting the ideas together.

"You need to go to your Guild for help!" he said, finally feeling some relief.

"The Magic Guild, huh," she said. There was something off about the way she had said that, like it was the answer to a different question than the one he was trying to answer. She seemed to be staring at something in front of her nose. He saw nothing but air. Then, curiously, she stretched out a finger and plucked at the air. For the briefest of moments, he saw a shimmer, then it was gone. Or maybe he was seeing things.

"I may not be able to help you, but they're obligated to," he continued as if she hadn't spoken.

"My Guild...." She took a big breath and blew it out. "I haven't exactly been the best member."

"You need to go to them anyway."

"And the Masterson Files? I mean...you need me, right?"

Truth be told, the analytical side of him said that they did. A part of him wanted to capitalize on her offer, turn her to working for Maxamillion. Yet that made him angry. Before, when it had been the only option to keep her safe, he was willing to sell her out like that. Now, there was another way. A safer way. He slashed the air with his hand.

"Don't worry about the Masterson Files. I promised you I wouldn't bring Justin back into your life, didn't I?"

"So what? I'm bringing him back into my life."

Oh, why was she always fighting him!

"Rune! Justin is dead!" he shouted, then checked himself. *Don't shout at her. She hasn't done anything wrong. Force a smile. Be a friend.*

"What do you mean, he's dead?" Rune demanded.

"I mean, he's probably dead. Forget about Justin. The only thing he can bring you is more pain, dead or alive, trust me. It's my fault that you were even in this position. I thought I could protect you myself but I'm failing. You need to go to your Guild, you need to tell them what's going on and ask for their help."

"You see, it's not as simple as that."

"You're going to have to make it simple. We don't have any other choices. I promise you," he reached forward and took her hand, "I will find the Masterson Files and I will end this. Then they won't come after you anymore. You'll finally be safe, but I can't do both. And you're right, working for Corinthe...you might not come out of this free and that's what I want. I want you to be free."

He meant it, every word. The truth was coming out of him so easily he almost giggled with the relief of it. He offered her his open hand.

"Come on, I'll take you home."

"Thanks, but I don't think so," Rune said, ignoring him, his hand and his offer. Instead, she stood up and went to the landline sitting on a small side table by the couch. She was flipping a small card in her fingers as she picked up the receiver to start dialing.

"Who are you calling?" he demanded. She turned as she waited for the dial to summon her callee, smiling at him softly.

"Hello, Maxamillion. Yes, I slept fine, thank you. Look, I don't want to take up too much of your time…"

"What are you doing?!" St. Benedict demanded, crossing the space to hit the plunger and hang up her call. Quickly, she moved to block him with her body as she continued to talk with a light and airy voice.

"Yes. I have a counter offer for you."

Chapter 9

"Smile," Malachi said, demonstrating for her as he pushed the button on the digital camera. She complied as the flash washed her face.

"How does it look?"

The techie nodded as he returned to his seat at his computer. "Looks good." He began tapping away at the keyboard. She watched him replace her last OmniSin renewal picture on his screen. He filled some more fields then picked up what would be her new OmniSin, the card that contained all her legal information, and stuck it into a card reading machine. "And you are all credentialed. That card will let you in and out of the building, the Praetorium, and suite twenty-seven, which is the suite you were in last night. That is now your private suite to use and abuse while you work with Corinthe. I also refilled your bus pass and connected a business credit card for you. Try to only use it for business expenses, it has a $10,000 limit."

Rune stared at her new OmniSin as he handed it to her. "Wow. Okay. Thank you. And a computer?" Rune asked as she slipped it back into its pouch on her belt.

"I have set up a computer in that side room there so you can watch at your leisure. It has open access to our entire archive of the Masterson Files." The techie stroked a finger along a list of files on his own screen. "These are video files, these are technical aspects, and these are transcripts of the videos. If you have any questions, I'll be here the rest of the day." She nodded, glancing over at the small room, no bigger than a study cubicle. It was hard to not look across the main room where St. Benedict worked. They were pointedly ignoring each other anyway.

"Thank you, Malachi," she said.

"You are very welcome," he replied. "I'm just impressed that you decided to stick around."

"I decided six years was long enough not to ask for alimony," she quipped, turning to go into her little side room. It felt strange that no one else in the Praetorium said anything or even glanced at her as she went into that room. If they were gossiping about her, they were keeping it very under wraps. The warm reception from breakfast was all but gone, and Rune thought over St. Benedict's words about how this company worked together, making and breaking alliances as the situation required. Not exactly a way of operating she understood. But everything about this still felt right. She was going to find Justin and for the first time the idea was exciting.

Sitting down in front of the computer, she took a deep breath. She didn't want to spend too much time thinking about what she was doing, so she seized the mouse and clicked.

It was the same room as before. The same table, the same clothes, the same expression of defiance on Justin's face. The only markers of time passing were the several days' growth on his chin and the slight lengthening of his hair. There were pictures strewn across the table in no particular order.

"And then there's this woman, the secretary that works or rather worked with Samsing." A new photo appeared at the bottom of the screen.

Justin looked down at it with bored contempt. "Fucked," he said and looked away.

The picture turned back as the interrogator she couldn't see regarded the photo again. "Really? You simply fucked her? Such a strategically placed person."

"I had no idea who she was, she was just up for it, okay?"

"I'm starting to have more and more sympathy for your wife. Did you at least get tested regularly?"

Justin didn't respond, he simply continued to look away. The photo dropped to the table in an attitude of disgust.

"Okay, well, I'm not feeling like we're getting anywhere here so let us check in on little wifey-poo."

There was a distortion sound and then as if through a

speaker, Rune heard her own voice. "But I don't know anything. Please, ask Justin."

"We have asked Justin," the well-dressed woman's cultured voice replied. For a moment, actual Rune thought she was going to throw up, but everything stayed down.

"Ah, she's asking for you again. You sure you don't want to talk to her?" Justin's interrogator asked.

"I got nothing to say to that worthless piece of trash. I told you, you can't get to me through her. I don't really get why you're even trying. I mean you're the one who keeps bringing me all these photos, does it look like I give a damn about her? Look at all this!" Justin rose up to shove the photos hard at his interrogator with his handcuffed hands, though they were halted by the short length of chain binding him to the table.

"Oh, Justin, don't do that," Rune whispered to herself fearfully.

"Okay, well, better to learn this lesson sooner rather than later." A male hand appeared at the edge of the screen, holding a remote. Dramatically, it pressed one of the buttons and Justin began to convulse. It was impossible to see on the screen, but Rune knew there was electricity arcing up the chain into his cuffs. Justin stumbled and fell back into his chair. The interrogator let up on the button.

"Don't worry about the smell, I've smelled it before. It's very common to lose control of your bladder."

She clicked the video off. Her hand shook as she lifted it from the mouse. It took a lot of focused will to breathe in deeply, then force it out. She had to do this. She had to stiffen her spine and do this.

She clicked the next file.

It started with screaming.

Rune endured the rest of the day, watching as much of the footage as she could. It wasn't all torture. It was mostly filled with talking, half of which was technical and she barely understood the majority of the techno-babble. What was clear to her was Justin was holding out against his interrogators. When she couldn't do it any more, she left her little room and made her way back to the suite, only hesitating outside her door for a moment, since it didn't really feel like *her* door. She hadn't seen St. Benedict the rest of the day and she wondered if he was on the other side of the inner suite door.

Instead of knocking to find out, she went to the landline phone and dialed out.

"Yes?" came Alf's terse greeting after only two rings.

"Hey, it's me," she said bracing for a tongue-lashing from her bar manager about disappearing again when there was work to be done.

"Yes, my Lady?"

Well, now, that was odd. "Alf...is everything okay?"

"Everything is fine. We've finished the deep cleaning in the Main and Lounge Bars, but the paint is less than acceptable in the Back Bar. We're going to need to do something."

"Right. Go ahead and order new," Rune said.

There was a heavy pause on the other side of the line. "With what money?"

"With the money I'm earning on this job."

There was another meaty pause. "Good, we need it."

"Thanks for being worried about me," Rune said, dryly.

"You are my Lady. You are free to come and go as you please," he said, dismissively.

Rune couldn't help feeling kind of hurt by that. "So you weren't worried at all?"

"Why would I be worried?"

"Because I was attacked last night in the alley. Didn't you hear it?"

"I was picking someone up from the airport last night."

Rune blinked. "Who?"

"An old friend. None of your business," he snapped.

"Was it a female friend?" she asked mischievously.

"None of your business!" he snapped even louder and Rune couldn't suppress the giggles. They were short-lived relief. Too quickly the echoes of the screaming in her thoughts flooded out other feelings, and she went silent. "Are you okay, my Lady?"

"Yeah. Yeah, I'm fine." She shook her head and pressed a hand against her forehead so she could massage both temples simultaneously.

"Who attacked you? Did you call the Sheriff?" Alf asked, finally showing some concern.

"No. No, I was rescued. St. Benedict is back."

"Ah. I see." More heavy silence. "Are you with him?"

"More or less. I've made a deal to get us some help."

"Wait, wait, where are you? Do you need me to come get you?"

"I am somewhere safe. I wanted to know if you were all safe."

"We're fine. The House protects its own, which is why I am confused about how you could have been attacked if you were here?"

"I was on my back porch."

"And St. Benedict attacked you?"

"No, no. It was Calvin."

"The Oberon?!"

"Look, Alf, are the baby Fae okay?"

"They are fine. Everyone here is fine."

"Okay. Keep them that way. I don't know what is going on, but keep an eye out for Calvin. I don't think he's safe right now."

Alf harrumphed, "Then we should be calling the Magic Guild at the very least."

"Just don't do anything until I get home." Rune was losing her patience with this. While everything he was saying was sensible, it also was the last thing she wanted to do, for personal reasons.

"And when will that be?" his voice had gone quiet, almost calculating.

"When I finish up with what I'm working on. Probably tomorrow, okay?"

"I should still come to where you are. You need a retainer by your side," he insisted.

"I don't need you, Alf," she said. It came out too harsh and she winced.

"As you wish, my Lady," was all the reply she got back and then he hung up.

She set the receiver in its cradle, continuing to stare at it while weariness settled over her like a confining blanket.

She didn't see or really talk to anyone the rest of the evening, except the attendant who brought her dinner. Truthfully, that was just fine with her.

Later she heard voices in St. Benedict's suite next door, but she ignored them, choosing a long, long shower instead. There was something soothing about simply letting the water pound down on her, like each patter would knock away the sadness and emotional soreness within. It seemed to work, because after she crawled into bed, she fell asleep and did not dream.

When she woke in the morning, it was to the scent of breakfast. In her little kitchenette, a tray waited with a note from Zita apologizing for not being able to eat with her that morning. That was fine as well. Rune just wanted to get back to work. Or at least, she wanted to want to.

She ate, dressed, and proceeded to head down to the Praetorium, noting on the clock in her workroom that it was 9:05 in the morning. A shout from Malachi caught her attention, but he only waved good morning. She waved back and closed her little workroom's door.

Sitting down in front of the monitor, she took a deep breath and started again.

After a couple hours, Malachi came in carrying two plates with a couple of hoagie sandwiches each. "I forgot to tell you, you have free access to everything in the kitchen."

Rune jumped at the intrusion. If Malachi noticed her reaction, he didn't show it, giving her an understanding smile and her plate. Rune sat back and tried to return the smile as she received the food. Her body felt like one large cramp. She had probably been clenching every muscle she had while she watched her ex-husband be tortured and interrogated. Today though, she had figured out how to fast forward. It had made things a little easier. Unfortunately, she learned painfully little from the interrogations.

"How's it going?" Malachi asked.

"I hate this," Rune said through her pained smile.

"Are you having flashbacks?" The tech asked, taking the extra chair on the other side of the desk. "If you want, you can talk to Zita."

"I might, thanks." She bit into the sandwich gratefully. "I'm a lot more okay than I thought I would be. But I don't know… I've dealt with a lot, so maybe…except whenever I think that, it rears its ugly head again."

"What does?"

"The trauma, the nightmares. My aunt Maddie did a lot of magic to help me rewrite some of the memories, process the worst of it, but there's still a lot I didn't want to face, until now."

Malachi blew out a breath. "You got more guts than me."

"Thanks for your help, by the way. I do appreciate it."

"Oh here, I was instructed to hand this over to you as well for analysis." From under his plate, Malachi handed over a small stack of papers to Rune. "Did St. Benedict mention at all that we've identified the other magic user in the alley?"

"Magic user?" Rune flipped open the cover sheet of the report and stared down at an info spreadsheet complete with a slightly blurry black and white photo.

"Yeah, he was identified as someone with affiliations within the Magic Guild, though we don't have a name. Does he look familiar?"

She shook her head. "Can't say so." She flipped the next page and started reading out loud, "Possible Talent. Wields fire." She knitted her eyebrows together and flipped through the rest of the report. While she read, Malachi slid her own notebook around to glance at it.

"What's that?" he asked. The page had a crudely drawn stickman surrounded by writing.

"Um, when I try to do a Finding for someone, I often create a diagram to help me focus on, well, Finding them. It works about half the time when they're strangers."

"And if you know them really well?"

"I often can just find them. My abilities have been getting stronger recently too."

"But you're looking for Masterson. Your ex-husband…."

"Yes, I know who he is," Rune said, trying not sound too annoyed.

Malachi hesitated at her tone, but pushed through it any way. "Doesn't that mean you should be able to simply find him?

I mean, I don't mean to act like I know what I'm talking about when it comes to magic, you know what I mean?" Malachi gave a nervous giggle.

"I do. I do know what you *mean*." She decided not to point out how many times he said the word "mean." "I wish it was that easy, but I'm encountering something new. I've never had to Find someone who's been missing for more than two-three days, never mind over six years. My power is acting all screwy so I'm trying to focus using that."

"Is it helping?"

"No." She looked down again at the pages Malachi had brought her. "So why do you think the Magic Guild was in my alley?"

"We don't know conclusively. This is the stage of things where we are speculating. The Saints are in agreement that they believe the Magic Guild knows something about the Masterson Files."

"So, someone at the Guild may know about my secret?"

Malachi shrugged. "Maybe? That is the question of the hour. Can you see anything more there that would help us confirm it?"

She set the file down and stood up to stretch. "No, but I have an idea how I'm going to find out."

"You're starting to sound like St. Benedict. All innuendo and I'm left playing the 'what do you mean' question games."

Rune smiled and left the side room, scanning the main room for the Saint in question. She spotted him talking with St. Rachel over at the conference table covered with pictures. Her heart leapt a little.

"I need a ride back to my bar," she said, interrupting them abruptly as she approached. She didn't want to lose her momentum.

"Why?" St. Benedict demanded harshly. Apparently, a day of not seeing each other hadn't cooled his anger at her.

"I think I have a lead. I want to follow it. But I need to get some things from my bar first."

"What lead?"

"A lead," Rune repeated. "All I need is a ride back to the bar."

St. Benedict stared her down, working his jaw a little in the most painful smile she had ever seen.

She shrugged a shoulder. "Okay, fine. Malachi! Is there a train or something that can take me back to the city?" She spun to head back to the techie, but St. Benedict caught her arm.

"Fine, fine. I'll give you a ride," St. Benedict stood up, shoving the table away as he did so. St. Rachel looked back and forth between Rune and him, her ice-like eyes assessing but giving nothing away. Rune didn't offer her any answers, instead she turned to follow St. Benedict out of the Praetorium.

He didn't say a word to her as he stopped at Malachi's desk, fishing the key for the gun drawer from around his neck. He also pulled out what looked like a wallet and mobile phone, stuffing both into side pockets on his pants. No one stopped them as they left the building. Rune didn't even see a single security guard anywhere. It was almost surreal after being out of the world for a whole day. She was glad to be getting out of there.

A nice, metallic-blue car waited for them outside the building.

"I think Justin is alive," Rune suddenly said, as if now that they were out of the building, she could speak more freely.

Her words stopped him in his tracks.

"What?" he snapped. It actually surprised Rune to hear him talk sharply to her. There was no smile on his face now. This was what the Saint looked like truly, seething angry.

"I'm going to find him."

"No, you're not," he said dismissively, turning away again to head to the car. "Whoever killed him will kill you too. Now get in the car."

"What convinces you he's dead?" Rune challenged.

"I can't find any trace of him and I've really looked, Rune, believe me. If he isn't dead I'm going to be really shocked. Get in my car."

The car opened for him automatically and turned itself on in that way that seemed like magic, but Rune knew from experience that it was only something technical to do with St. Benedict and his augmentations.

"He's not dead." Rune did not move a muscle from the top of the steps. She was starting to get angry as well.

"You sound like you're just telling yourself that so you can justify inserting yourself here. This isn't where you want to be."

"Okay. You don't get to tell me what I want," Rune crossed her arms. "I gave you a chance to work with me on this!"

St. Benedict slammed the car door shut, before turning to beeline straight for her. "Yes, I do. In this case, Rune, I need to decide this for you. You were attacked barely two nights ago! You were almost killed and now you want to…you need to have control over something and you keep undoing everything I am doing to keep you safe!"

"Bullshit!" Rune held up a hand, but it didn't slow either of their momentum. "Are you seriously pulling the knight in shining armor card here?"

"What?" He growled with disbelief.

"You know. You get to decide things for me, because you're my hero and, obviously, I'm the stupid damsel in distress who needs you to save me!? Well guess what, pretty boy, I don't need you!"

He kept coming, halting only when he was too close, one step below, meeting her eye to eye.

The shock of the close proximity stopped both their words, only their dueling breaths continued to battle for the little bit of space between them. What was happening? She was so angry a moment before. She was still angry. It felt like his eyes were penetrating her, seeing deeply into her soul. It wasn't just anger she saw in his own eyes. A pleading fear was also there. Rune found herself taking in his face, the contours of his cheeks and lips, the single lock of hair peeking out of the brim of his fedora, all within the span of a second. His proximity made Rune feel both afraid and desirous.

No, it wasn't that. Truly! She was just so mad at him! There was something he wasn't telling her. Something he was badly trying to hide. She could see the negative space around it, but not the thing itself. Why wouldn't he simply tell her the whole truth?

He licked his lips and for a moment, she wondered if she

was going to lean the rest of the way to kiss him.

Then breaking the spell, St. Benedict took a deliberate, careful step back. Rune almost felt the tension snap between them and dissolve. He turned back to the car a third time, throwing a useless hand into the air. "Just get into the car. I'm taking you back to your bar." This time he didn't stop, but got in, slamming the door behind him.

Rune was seething, but the bar was where she wanted to go. Still she got into the car at her own pace before slamming her own door just as hard.

She managed to get on her seat belt before St. Benedict threw the car into drive and peeled out of park.

"You should buckle up," Rune muttered as he shifted the manual car into the next gear.

"Just...don't talk to me right now," he said and he turned out of the gated drive onto a street. She tried to make a note of where they were coming from. That proved impossible as St. Benedict took many turns and twists before he got onto a highway.

Rune would have conscientiously objected to his aggressive driving except she had to brace herself as the car tore through a half dozen streets and she lost the ability to retort. Before she could bark at him to drive the opposite of a maniac, he had already done so, pulling onto traffic on the unfamiliar highway, and slowing down to an acceptable speed. Finally letting go of the panic handle, she settled back into her seat and they seethed together in silence.

While they drove back into the city, she kicked herself for not taking something from the building that would help her Find it again, though whether that would give her enough of a connection to lead her back was hard to define. She'd never needed to find a whole building before. The distance from the city alone would make it difficult to maintain a strong enough connection with the limited amount of magic she had available to her. When it came to her own Talent, she wished she was better at using it.

To literally clear the air, Rune rolled down her window, letting the lovely late summer air roll over her. It was still hot but after the chilliness of the too cold building, Rune needed heat to warm her bones. In the fresh light of day, the nightmares she had faced on those tapes seemed as far away as a balloon floating over Lake Michigan. She had faced those horrible videos of Justin and had not crumpled to a useless pile. She could do this.

In fact, she was itching to talk to St. Benedict about what she had learned and hash it all out, but St. Benedict's locked jaw advertised he was still storming. And frankly, she felt she had every right to be mad too. He was the one who had crashed into *her* life two months ago. If he didn't want her involved, he should have taken her first *no* then. Instead, he did everything in his power to force her to help *him* find Justin. She thought about saying exactly that to him, but just as she opened her mouth to speak, he yawned. At first Rune wanted to take offense, but he swallowed and cleared his throat awkwardly enough for Rune to realize it had been an involuntary reaction versus any kind of commentary.

"Are you sure you're alright to drive?" Rune asked when he yawned a second time.

"Can you drive a stick shift?" he asked back.

"Nope."

"Then I'm fine to drive," he answered. He merged back into the middle lane.

"The car's a stick shift? But the doors open automatically and it turns on by your mere presence." Rune stated more than asked.

"I like stick shifts," St. Benedict glancing at her sidelong, then shifted again. "They're more fun."

Silence threatened to refill the space between them, but Rune wasn't going to let it. "I wanted to learn stick shift. A while ago. It seemed like a neat thing to know how to do."

No answer. Not even a grunt. So, Rune continued on. "Justin knew how to drive stick shift. I tried to get him to teach me, but he wasn't interested, I guess, in teaching me anything. I mean he never said no, he just never acknowledged I had even asked."

St. Benedict shifted the car again roughly, but something stalled and the car started jumping like it needed to sneeze.

After a few more panicked yanks on the stick, he seemed to get it in a better place.

"Do you really think he isn't still alive?" she asked softly as the view of the Chicago skyline began to grow larger in the distance.

"No, I really don't. And if he is, I'll make sure he isn't," St. Benedict said, speaking as softly as she was.

"Do you mean that?"

"You don't want to see him dead too for what he did to you?"

Rune chewed her lip. "I don't want revenge. I want to know why. I want to understand what happened. There has to be more to the story."

"What if we don't find those answers?"

"Then you'll still have your Masterson Files."

"Over my dead body," St. Benedict grumbled so low Rune could almost not hear the statement.

"What?"

He didn't repeat himself.

"St. Benedict, I don't understand this attitude of yours. Really, it's between me and Justin anyway, and I am going to look for him no matter what you say or do."

"Do you still love him?"

The question came at her like a slap.

She double blinked. "He…left me for dead six years ago. I haven't heard anything from him or about him until you showed up." Rune shook her head. "No, it's not like that. I think…." She nibbled a little on her bottom lip.

"So you do love him." St. Benedict shifted the car again as he prepared to exit the highway. "That's a problem."

"I don't," Rune said, unconvincingly. "Look, I think I still love the idea of him. The thought that he's going to come and save me. It's a story I've been telling myself for so long, but I think I'm finally ready to let it go. Which would be a lot easier if you would stop giving me a hard time about it."

She leaned her head back against the headrest and let her gaze fall out to the sprawling residential landscape without really seeing it. "Don't you do that? About Anne? Get obsessed with the stories of how things might have been?"

"I try not to think about anything at all," he said dismissively at first, then, "Yes. Sometimes. When it is quiet, I remember the smell of her hair, even though I can't really smell it, I just think I do."

"See this is how you're different from Justin. You did whatever it took to find her. What was it, two months ago? If you found another clue as to where she might be now, I'm pretty sure you would drop everything to follow it," Rune said, the words ringing true.

Then a thought struck her. "Hey, do you...you still love her, right?" she asked, leaning forward to look at him.

His body shifted away a little. "Yes."

"I could try to Find her for you." She reached out to touch his arm, but he shoved her hand away.

"No," he said firmly. "Leave it alone."

"St. Benedict?" She was perplexed. What was the problem? "It's worth a try, isn't it? If you focus on her, that might allow me a strong enough connection to detect her, I mean if she's close enough. I mean, I can't guarantee it will work at all..."

"I said, leave it alone. Don't touch me."

Feeling hurt, but unable to really say anything more, Rune settled back in her seat and returned to her sullen window gazing. Why was he being so stupid? She thought back to what Zita had said two nights before. St. Benedict had changed over the last couple of months. Two months ago he had learned Rune's secret, that she was Anna Masterson, and it had been the end of his personal mission. His reaction upon learning that Rune was not his missing wife Anne, misplaced because of a typo, was etched into her mind. Therefore, did he believe that Anne was dead?

They didn't talk much more in the car. By the time they had both lapsed into contemplative silence, the surroundings had become familiar. Rune only looked up from her thoughts when they pulled up in front of the painted wood front of her bar. She turned to say good-bye to St. Benedict, but he was already exiting the car.

"I thought you were just dropping me off?" she questioned as she got out of her side. He stepped up onto the sidewalk, looking around.

"I'll leave you once you're safely at your Guild," he said.

Rune gave a start as she stepped up onto the sidewalk. "What makes you think I'm still heading over to the Magic Guild?" Dammit. Said that too fast.

"Your reaction just now," he said, his usual smile finally ghosting across his face.

She scrunched up her own. "You just did a spy mind trick on me, didn't you?"

"That's your lead, isn't it? You recognized the operative from the Magic Guild."

"I'm not telling you anything." Rune crossed her arms. They stood in front of her bar door, but she blocked his way, trying to make it clear she wasn't letting him come in.

"What do you know?" he asked, leaning closer to her.

"Nope, nope." She put her hand blatantly on his face and pushed him back. "That sexy, intense questioning trick isn't going to work on me anymore. Out of my bubble now."

He smiled against her hand and complied, tucking his hands more comfortably into his armpits.

"You should still probably tell me if you know something."

"So are you saying you are changing your mind about working with me?"

"No."

"Yup, well, then later, gator," she said cheerfully and turned to open her bar door.

The door was unlocked, which was good because that would have destroyed her smooth exit. Inside, her staff moved around the space, resetting the tables or restocking behind the bar. Sitting at the bar itself, a still spot amidst the chaos, was a beautiful young man. His shoulder length black hair framed his face as he propped a sculpted cheek onto the palm of his hand. Dressed simply in a plain black shirt and dark washed jeans with square toed shoes, he looked like someone out of a teenage dream magazine ad.

Rune's teenage retainer, Ally, was talking to him. Or, more like gushing at him, from the tender's side of the bar. They both looked up as Rune entered, trailed by St. Benedict who hadn't taken her send-off for an answer.

"My lady!" Ally squeaked, her cheeks going super red as if she had been caught making out with him instead of simply talking. Rune barely noted it though. Her eyes were all on the beautiful young man.

"Elias?" she asked, breathlessly.

The young man she called Elias stood up and turned to her with an angelic smile, opening his arms wide for a hug. Rune wasted no time crossing the space to wrap her arms around his trim, perfect waist. His long arms went around her and squeezed hard, shaking her from side to side, his extra foot of height on her, allowing him the space to lift her off the ground easily. It was almost impossible to speak, she was laughing so hard.

"What are you doing here? Where the hell have you been?" she finally asked when they broke apart enough to look at each other.

"Rune...." he said with a voice that was deeper than his frame would have suggested.

Before Elias could say anything more, Alf burst into the room. Rune could never remember Alf looking so happy.
"At last! Now you see! At last! The true Heir of the Magdalene has come. You're going to get your just desserts now, you fraud! I have waited so long for you to return home, Master Elias. Now a *real* Wizard will be the head of this House." That was all Alf got out before Elias took both of Rune's hands in his own as he dropped to one knee before her.

"I, Elias Fitzgerald Leveau, do recognize you as my Lady and Mistress of the House of Magdalene. I swear my fealty and power is yours to command, to call me when you are in need and dismiss me when I can no longer serve you. I will defend you until the day I die."

A thunderclap of power made everyone in the room jump and Rune stumbled a step back as it hit her. Elias didn't let go of her hands, but held her steady as the House reacted. Without choosing to, Rune's second sight blinked on and she saw a tendril of power connect herself to Elias as well as tendrils going to Ally and Alf. All of the kitschy devils on the walls shifted on their posts and stands, turning to look at Rune and Elias still kneeling before her. Even her other employees had stopped in mid-cleaning to stare in amazement. Then the wave of magic calmed and settled. Blinking water out of her eyes, Rune dropped the second sight.

"No-o-o-o! No, how could...how could you...?" Alf stood there his hands open and pleading as his face became the epitome of devastation and despair.

Elias grinned up at Rune with angelic enjoyment as Alf continued to express his grief. Then her newest retainer's blue eyes shifted to something over her shoulder. Without Rune realizing it, someone had leapt up behind her, and had caught her when she had been staggered by the magic hitting her.

"Who are you?" Elias asked, rising, but still holding Rune's hands.

"Just. A friend," St. Benedict answered, giving his professionally mischievous smile. "Who the hell are you?"

"Her cousin." Elias nodded at Rune.

"You said 'Leveau.'"

Elias blinked. "Excuse me?"

St. Benedict smiled so hard it looked more like he was baring his teeth. "You said Leveau, with an 'O' sound. She says Leveau with an 'oo' sound," he repeated with careful biting consonants.

"Yes, in America, it's so unheard of for families to have divergent pronunciations of the same name," Elias answered, his smile mockingly relaxed.

"Uh, St. Benedict, this *is* my cousin, Elias," Rune answered, not liking that she was in the middle of the obvious machismo match. "And apparently my retainer now."

"How could you do this?!" Alf wailed from behind. "You're a full blooded Wizard. You were Maddie's apprentice. Why? Why won't you take your rightful place as the Lord of the House Magdalene?"

"I am not the chosen Heir," Elias said as if it was that simple, not taking his eyes from St. Benedict.

"But Elias, what are you doing here? You haven't been back in three years, almost four," Rune asked.

"I would say I made a promise to Maddie, but even if I hadn't I would have come for your sake. You need my help and I'm here," Elias answered, completely unperturbed by Alf's continued meltdown behind him. Instead, he turned an eye on St. Benedict, and specifically, the Saint's hands still on Rune's shoulders.

"But why now?" Rune pressed.

"Look, kid, I would have been here sooner, but I was held up. I tried to come when Maddie died…. That's a bad excuse, because I should have called," he conceded, bowing his head. "I am so sorry I didn't get here sooner."

There was a bang. They all turned to find Alf gone and Ally looking uncomfortable.

"He stormed off into the back room," Ally reported, gesturing with her thumb over her shoulder while looking down guiltily, as if she was the one responsible for Alf's rage.

"I take it he has not handled the transition well," Elias said wryly.

"It's been a tough few months for all of us," Rune said.

"His grief for Maddie is quite extreme. I'm not surprised, but I had hoped he would be holding things together until I could get to you."

"He has!" Ally defended, which surprised Rune since it was only two days ago Ally was calling her bar manager a bad guy. But she supposed to Ally, Elias seemed like the outsider. No one likes it when outsiders attack your own family.

"Ally, and everyone," Rune said pitching her voice up so that all her employees could hear. "Thank you all for your work today. I know, we're not finished, but go ahead and mark your time cards for all your hours and head out early." There was very little argument from anyone and soon the bar emptied out after things were shut down and cleared. Only Ally persisted, rushing over closer to Rune.

"But something's going on isn't it? That's what Alf keeps talking to Elias about all secretive and stuff. And now St. Benedict's come back," the teenager waved a little at him still standing behind Rune, but it didn't slow her talking, "I should stay here. I serve you too!"

"Look, it's a bit dangerous around here right now, again, and I promised your mother I would make sure you stayed safe," Rune argued.

"That's all the more the reason I should stay here! It's my duty to protect you and protect our House!" Ally whined, her voice hitting notes that would hurt a dog's ears. Which Rune thought was ironic, but there was no way she could begin to share the thought in the sincere face of her teenage retainer.

"Your duty is to obey your Lady," Rune said, forcing her face into seriousness and crossing her arms.

The kid screwed up her sincere face, mad that she couldn't find a counter to that argument. Rune arched her eyebrow at Ally, daring her to talk back.

"Don't worry, Ally, it's not just you," Elias said. He turned to look at St. Benedict pointedly. "You too. Out."

St. Benedict's eyebrows shot up. "Oh really?"

"Elias...." Rune started, but her newest retainer didn't heed her.

Instead, he crossed his arms. "Yeah, really." He waved his fingers at St. Benedict. "Run along now."

"St. Benedict, you do not have to leave. Elias...?"

"You heard your *mistress*," St. Benedict said, his smile sharpening as his eyes narrowed. "I don't have to go anywhere."

"We can take care of her now, friend," Elias grabbed Rune's arm, her surprise allowing him to pull her behind him as the two men faced off. The sudden move made St. Benedict react, stretching out a hand toward Rune, too late to catch her. He stopped his reaction to follow after her, sensing the impending waves of danger rolling off of Elias.

"Like I said, I'm a friend," St. Benedict said evenly.

"And I am family. Can you make a similar claim?" Elias asked, cocking his head pointedly to the side. A wariness sank into St. Benedict's eyes, before he blinked them, the blue light igniting in them.

"Elias, what are you doing? He's my friend, I told you," Rune said, shoving past her cousin, turning about to face him. "He's *not* your friend," Elias stressed, before gesturing with both hands in the air. Wind, wild and without a clear source, spun up with such strength that St. Benedict actually slid backwards a step as he brought up his arms to block it. "I said leave!"

"Elias!" Rune tried to shout, but the wind sucked her words

away. Turning to the side, she saw Ally standing nearby, her mouth hanging open. While Rune was buffeted, but not moved by the wind, the gale wasn't touching Ally at all.

"Rune!" St. Benedict shouted, reaching a hand out to pull her toward him, but missing as the wind pushed him back again.

"Protect your Mistress! Remove the interloper!" Elias's voice boomed out clearly, echoing with the telltale thrum of power. All around the room, the devils of the Lucky Devil came to life, summoned by Elias's magic. Several winged devils alighted from their perches, flying through the gale as if it wasn't there, toward St. Benedict with claws outstretched. Before they could touch him, thunder clapped and they screeched, scattering away. St. Benedict raised his gun and shot twice more, his blue-lit eyes flashing with each shot. Pieces of the demons cracked and fell as they screeched in pain, swooping away like startled birds.

"No! Don't!" Rune shouted, though even she wasn't entirely sure which side of the conflict she was directing that towards. She stepped forward to place herself between her devils and her friend, but her timing was bad.

"Rune!" St. Benedict shouted, this time surging forward as his feet found purchase on the floor. Some small part of his mind told him that the most logical, tactical thing he could do at that moment, would be to fall back or leave the bar entirely. He was obviously out of his depth and there was a good chance this Wizard asshole wouldn't send reinforcements after him if he did just that. The look on Elias's face basically said all of that with his smug smile. All the Saint would have to do is leave Rune behind. Unfortunately for the rational side of his brain, he had already acted.

Unheeding of the claws that dug painfully into his arm, the Saint had jumped forward to wrap his free arm around Rune's head, pressing it against his shoulder. Bringing up the gun, he fired, blasting the small devil that was accidentally bearing down on her into pieces. Looking through the falling shards, St. Benedict's augmented sight targeted on his true opponent. Encircled with a ring of red that only the Saint could see, he raised his gun, aiming true at the wizard and fired.

A wall of bright yellow light appeared around Elias, the bullet stopping in mid-air. At the same time, devils renewed their attack to grab St. Benedict's arms. He fought back, but there were too many of them and within moments they had him pinned.

"St. Benedict!" Rune tried to grab him as he rose up, but other devils came between them to push them apart.

"Run Rune!" St. Benedict shouted, as he fought to free himself. The devils began to lift him into the air, his motions slowing as he became more and more constrained by their many little hands. Then there was a flash of bright light as St. Benedict's augmented hand popped open. The devils squealed, many of them pulling away or dropping whatever they were gripping onto to shield their eyes. Those that remained weren't strong enough to lift a grown man on their own, which caused St. Benedict to fall to the ground.

"Stop it right now! Stop trying to kill each other!" Rune's voice took on the echo of power Elias's had. Finally, the devils did exactly as she commanded, stopping in mid-fight, many of them returning to their perches. Elias's yellow shield shattered and the bullet clinked onto the ground.

"I don't need you to protect me!" she shouted in the now too-quiet room.

"What the hell's going on in here?!" Alf shouted as he re-entered the room brandishing a garden trowel, which was odd since the bar had no use for a garden trowel.

No one responded to him as Elias took a knee before Rune. "As you wish my Lady, but I will not excuse defending you or this House."

Rune stood there looking down at Elias, panting. Not knowing what to say to her errant retainer, she turned instead to St. Benedict lying on his back near her feet. "Are you alright?"

"Rune, we need to get away from him," St. Benedict continued to argue, rolling into a crouch, preparing to fight again. She glanced at the arm that had protected her, the sleeve having slid up in the fight. She expected to see blood, but there was only reddened skin. Not that St. Benedict even noticed, his focus was entirely on his opponents. One of the devils approached her, holding out the Saint's gun to her. She made herself take the vile thing. St. Benedict was sweating and looking crazy with fear as his unaugmented eyes followed the movements of the devil.

"No one touches this man in my House!" she said instead, laying a hand on the Saint's shoulder, shooting a dark eye at all her minions. The devils on the wall had the self-awareness to look away in various degrees of shame. "He's my *friend*," she reiterated, landing her final eye on Elias. The wizard looked up, shifting the same suspicious gaze to St. Benedict. She felt her friend tense under her hand and she gripped down tighter to keep him still.

"I would die for her," St. Benedict growled, both as a threat and a promise.

"You hear that? He would die for me," Rune repeated.

Elias sighed. "If you wish him to stay then I will concede." He stood then. "You heard your Mistress. Back to bed with you lot," he ordered before making a strange hand gesture in the air by his head.

Immediately, the remaining devils returned to their positions, going still again. The ones shot to pieces reformed instantly, chirping irritatedly in St. Benedict's direction before alighting back to their posts. For his part, Elias jumped up and over the bar, ignoring Alf's half-formed protestations at such sacrilege. The wizard set a bottle onto the bar with authority. With a cheeky smile, he poured a row of four shots, then retrieved a root beer from the fridge under the bar.

That's when Rune noticed Lucky Devil in his booth. The animatronic creation was out of its normal posture, leaning its acrylic cheek on its red fist, like it had been watching in amusement the events playing out in front of him. Once the shots were poured, the Wizard and the Lucky Devil turned to each other and in perfect sync, lifted their real and fake glasses to each other in salute. After going through the motion of drinking from his glass, the Lucky Devil smirked and returned to his original position.

Rune was flabbergasted.

"How did you…?" she started as she pointed at Lucky Devil.

"You've never seen him move before?" Elias asked, refilling his shot glass.

Rune was about to say *no*, but then remembered. "Only once before," she admitted, "and that was when I first claimed the House and I was under attack."

Elias nodded at that. "Yes. That is the other of the reason I am here, to finish your training as a Wizardress of this House. There is a lot Maddie wished for you to learn."

"Then why didn't she teach her?" St. Benedict challenged. He had stood up, taking the same position as before right behind Rune's shoulder.

"She wasn't ready," Elias answered, unperturbed now. "Magic can only be wielded by those willing to do so. When Rune first came here, she was as far separated from her magic as I am from the Great Wall of China."

"Which is why she is unsuited to be the Lady of this House," Alf said sullenly, returning attention to himself. "She doesn't want it and hasn't shown any real ability to learn."

"And you said you would never betray me again," Rune shot back.

Tears, honest to god tears, were pricking at the tough barman's eyes.

"My Lady's life is in constant danger and she is unequipped to face it. I will not lose another Mistress." The tear slipped from his eye and Rune was flabbergasted again. "He is more able to protect this place and protect you. He is a full-fledged Wizard."

The full-fledged wizard in question glanced at the Lucky Devil again. "Has Uncle Lucas come back?"

Rune shook her head. "He left about a week after the funeral."

"Lousy drunk," Alf grumbled.

Rune gave Alf a harsh look, but Elias nodded, "He would be, after her death."

"Who's Uncle Lucas?" Ally piped up, reminding everyone she was still there.

"Aunt Maddie's once and future husband," Elias said as he offered the opened root beer bottle to the teenager.

"Huh?" Ally asked, cocking her head to the side.

"Stories for later." Elias smiled in a way that seemed to indicate he wasn't going to explain, but was enjoying being enigmatic. "You work here, right? I thought teenagers couldn't serve alcohol in the state of Illinois?"

"She/I only serve food," Rune, Alf and Ally all said in perfect unison.

"And you should go home!" Rune crossed her arms.

"Ally needs to stay," Elias countered.

The teen's face lit up with excitement. "Really?!" she said, talking over Rune's consternated. "What?!"

Very deliberately, Elias began to divide the shots he had poured out, sliding one to both Alf and Rune as he spoke. "You are going to need all the backup you can muster, which leads me to the final reason I am here." He looked at St. Benedict as he set the last shot with a purposeful click on the bar in his direction. The two men eyed it in a renewed contest of wills. Rune lifted hers to her lips before St. Benedict moved to halt her hand. "You going to take that shot for her too, big guy?" Elias asked, raising an eyebrow.

"St. Ben, it's fine," Rune said, lowering her voice. He removed his hand and picked up his own shot.

"You have been summoned by the Magic Guild Inner Council," Elias continued as if he hadn't been interrupted.

"Yes, I know. I've been ignoring it." Rune's danger sense was tingling.

"They've called a Wizards Conclave." Elias picked up his own shot, holding it out before him.

"Yeah, I know," Rune said, making a face.

Alf groaned. "Oh, Lords of Hades."

"What? I thought it was a fun Con? Like Comicon? Is that bad?" Ally asked, echoing Rune's exact thoughts.

"Yes, girl. It's bad," Alf snapped, "now that the only viable wizard has foolishly thrown away his claim to our House!"

"A Wizard Conclave is a gathering of the heads of the Great Houses within the auspices of the Magic Guild. Gatherings are often for policy exchanges, political issues, planning, yes there is a vendor room and festivities...." Elias adopted a teacherly voice as he spoke.

"And is the perfect setup for contesting Heads of Houses," Alf finished.

Those words sank in for a moment.

"That sounds bad," Rune said. Alf almost exploded on the spot.

"Bad! Bad my Lady! You think that might sound simply bad? You are chum in the water! It means any wizard who thinks they can, will offer up a challenge to you and if you can't hold up against them, which you can't because you have about as much magic as a caterpillar's fart, we lose this House!"

"We're not losing the House," Elias inserted as Rune whirled on her bar manager.

"Isn't that exactly what you wanted? To see me un-Ladied?" Rune arched an eyebrow as she snapped back.

"To him, of course!" Alf gestured vehemently at Elias. "He's a proper Heir, but to a pissant stranger who would dare call themselves Lord of the House of the Magdalene?! I would sooner die than let this great House fall into another grubby so-called-wizard's hands or to have these sacred halls polluted...."

"Take your shot," Elias ordered, cutting Alf's rant up short. "We're not going to let that happen."

"How?! How?! For Maddie's sake, how?!" cried Alf, desperately.

"By doing what a retainer is supposed to do: protect our Lady. Now let's drink these shots, my arm is getting tired," he said, his arm having stayed up the whole time during Alf's rant. Each adult finally took up their glass, Ally stopped drinking her root beer sheepishly and held the half a bottle up with the rest.

"To our Lady. We can get through this together, as a Household," Elias declared, then he tossed back. Rune was next followed by Ally. Alf held his shot, growling at it for a moment, but drank it, slamming his upside down glass onto the counter. It was a small miracle it didn't break.

Rune turned to St. Benedict, who still held his shot, his intense eyes watching her. She opened her mouth to speak but before she could, he downed it and followed Alf's suit, by setting the empty glass upside down on the bar.

The front door opened with a jingle, followed by a series of clopping sounds.

"Franklin?" Rune questioned as the centaur trotted in. Dressed in his business coat and formal apron, he looked more put together than usual. That changed the second he cleared the door. With a quick tug he pulled out the tie that held his dreadlocks back before yanking out the knot on the sage green tie around his neck.

"I need a drink," he said heavily, sidling up to the corner of the bar to stand next to St. Benedict. He dropped the ties onto the wood surface and groaned as he braced his hands with all of his weight. The bar gave a little groan but held against the massive centaur's despair.

"We're not exactly open right now," Rune said to her regular.

"I just got fired," Franklin said to the bar.

"Oh. Franklin," Rune breathed, immediately sympathetic.

"They said I wasn't pulling my weight. I'm a god damn actuary. I graduated suma cum laude. I'm thirty-two years old. No mate. No foals." He folded over even more onto the bar. "What am I doing with my life, Rune?"

"I'm sorry, Franklin." She moved closer and patted the centaur's back. Everyone shared sympathetic glances. "Do you want a drink, Franklin?"

"Yes please."

Elias went to pour Franklin a shot, but Alf hurried around the bar to push him to the side. "Out of the way, pretty boy," he said before climbing up on one of his boxes designed to raise the little man up to serving height. "We don't serve the crap stuff to friends." With a deft hand, Alf poured out a series of shots from different colored bottles into a shaker with ice, shaking it with the vigor of a mariachi. Then he poured a measure from a dark bottle into a half ball glass followed by the mix in the shaker. Two stirs with a stick apparently finished the drink because he slid it over to Franklin, who had looked up at the noise of the ice.

"Remember friend, you can always find help at the Lucky Devil," Alf pronounced solemnly.

Chapter 10

"I've secured a way into the Magic Guild, St. Rachel," St. Benedict thought. He was sitting alone at the bar. More or less alone. Franklin, the newly unemployed centaur, was drinking his third whatever-concoction Alf had put together for him and staring into the abyss. Rune's other retainers, Alf and Ally, had disappeared while Rune went upstairs to change into something more Wizard-Conclave appropriate. Elias had followed her against St. Benedict's objections, but there was very little he could do about this new invasion into Rune's life.

"*Your little Talent is proving useful?*" St. Rachel thought back, disturbing his other thoughts, forcing him to concentrate on the near-telepathic communication. It was hard to hear her clearly. Her voice sounded tinny in his head. He wondered if it was because of all the magic in the bar, interfering with the signals that they were piggybacking their conversation through. Any camera he had tried to have installed inside the bar would work for a short while before frying out, so it didn't surprise him that his transmission was having some difficulty.

"*I'm convinced now, more than ever, that they have a piece of the Masterson Files.*" He continued.

"*The Magic Guild? You're that confident?*"

"*Yes. They're calling Rune in for some kind of Wizard Conclave. This is apparently unusual.*"

"*So you're thinking they know she is actually the long, lost Anna Masterson.*"

"*Or at least suspect. They can use the threat of their Inner Council to take away her bar as leverage to get to what she knows.*"

"*What would they want with her bar?*"

St. Benedict checked his annoyance. It was amazing how sometimes St. Rachel, who could beat him in 3D chess, could become fixed on irrelevant details. *"It wouldn't matter what the leverage was as long as it was important to Rune."*

"This Inner Council? So you're going to help her save her bar now?"

"No. Never mind. The Inner Council's goals here are irrelevant to the mission. But these summons, united with their involvement with the attack last night, leads me to conclude that they must have a piece of the Masterson Files."

"And they want the Talent to give them the rest. Only we've still got her. Typical St. Benedict. Finding a use for Maxamillion's trash."

"It's the only reason he still hasn't sold me off yet."

"He wouldn't do that. Give him more credit than that."

"Never." He put humor into his thoughts, but he doubted St. Rachel missed the dark undercurrent in them. The greatest risk of letting someone into one's mind, it took a lot of discipline to continue to hide one's secrets.

"When do we inform our illustrious patron of our little plan?" St. Rachel thought with genuine mirth. She was enjoying their naughty deception. He knew she would. He also knew that she would be eager to reaffirm their connection after the standoff that morning. It had been very lucky that St. Rachel had jacked in right away that morning, as he had been able to then discuss this possible plan with her on the way over. Carrying on the dual conversation with Rune in the car had been serious mental parkour.

"We don't until we have something to show for our excursion."

"And how do you suggest pulling that off? You have work you're supposed to be doing."

"I'm doing it." Or at least he was trying, using his hologram augs was slower for him than if he was at a computer with a real keyboard.

There was a tick of silence. *"That's very unsecure."*

"Needs must when…."

*"Oh shut up. If I hear that phrase one more time I'm going to kill

something. Just know that if this goes south, I will be dumping your ass and walking away." He knew there was a fifty-fifty shot that was true, but he could deal with those odds.

"I wouldn't respect you otherwise." He sensed her satisfaction.

"And your little Finder. Does she know the plan?"

"She's a means to get in, but that is all. At the first opportunity, I'll be ditching her. Maxamillion's right, we don't need her liability."

"Ah, you two are still having your little lovers quarrel?"

"Aren't you going to be late for cheerleading practice? Don't forget your pom-poms."

"How long do I wait to hear from you?"

"We're dealing with magic and its people here. Time can get funny, so trust that if you don't hear from me, it's a good thing. I hope the next thing you hear is I've got something."

"Confirm. Running silent."

Then she was gone from his head. She was never one for the formality of goodbyes. Neither was he, if he was honest with himself. There was always a risk of not going through with goodbyes. The opposite problem was also true. Without a goodbye, there was a risk of coming back. And there he sat at her bar, next to a drunk horseman, having done exactly that.

"It's not exactly like that. Don't get me wrong Elias, it's wonderful to see you, but I can't wrap my head around you being here." Rune pulled the clean shirt over her head as she changed clothes for the fifteenth time. After setting Franklin up at the bar, Rune had retreated to her apartment to get changed to go to the Magic Guild.

"Well, I am like a cat. Oh, the cat came back, the very next day," Elias sang out the old lyrics as he jived a step, acting the kid he looked like.

"What do you think of this one?" she asked, holding up another more conservative black dress.

"I think it's not a funeral."

"Oh, shut up." Rune dove back into her closet, which was getting a bit thin since most of the clothing usually contained inside was on her floor or in the piles of dirty laundry occupying the same space. This left her with the options that were more

Maddie's personal style that lived unworn in Rune's closet, mostly because she couldn't bear to purge them out. They were things Maddie had given her, but there was no way in hell she was ever going to wear them.

"You need to wear what defines you as a Wizard," Elias declared, unhelpfully.

"Oh, great. Then I should wear nothing because I'm not one."

"Are you following in Maddie's footsteps with that too, calling yourself a 'Wizardress'?" he asked, throwing up the air quotes.

"I'm not anything, Eli. I'm barely a Talent." Rune slammed her closet door closed, which caused it to not. Huffily, she dropped onto her bed, knocking several items of unapproved clothing to the ground.

Elias ignored her frustration and morphed into dancing a one sided samba, using his words to establish a beat. "Then. What are. You?"

"A lost cause. A hopeless dreamer. A House owner who can't even re-enchant the trash can."

"Oh," Elias stopped his dancing as he pouted. "I liked that trash can."

"Yeah. It's not the only enchantment to go around here. They're all starting to go."

"Don't worry. I'll teach you how to do that kind of magic later. Here. I dated a clothing designer for a little while. Let's see if anything about him rubbed off on me," Elias said as he lifted up a load of clothes onto the bed.

"I can't do re-animation magic without a cryst…."

"I said later." Elias held up a lacy, black bra to his own chest, waggling his eyebrows suggestively.

Rune smiled as he worked. She really had missed him. He had been the first person she had seen after Maddie had brought her home from her time in the corporate prison. He had looked exactly the same then too, except with more of a punk bend to his style, which included messy, spikey hair. At the time, Rune had been so fragile. Walking into Maddie's house, Rune simply let Maddie lead her by the hand like she was a little child. She remembered being aware of Maddie talking to another person, a young man, but Rune never looked up past the deliberate tears in his jeans. Maddie said something and the legs dashed off quickly, bringing back whatever Maddie asked several times. Her great aunt installed her onto the floral couch and proceeded to mix things in bowls or pull out crystals of various colors and hues to use on Rune's battered body and soul.

It wasn't until she had sat on Maddie's couch for a while and traced every pattern in reach with a grubby, broken fingernail that a large goose down comforter landed around her shoulders. She looked up finally to see the face of the most beautiful man she had ever seen, even more stunning than Justin had ever been. He smiled at her then, but Rune simply couldn't react even though she knew that she should return what he was offering her.

After that first day, or maybe it was the second because Rune vaguely remembered sleeping for a long, long time, he was there. Every day he was there, rotating with Maddie, and eventually Uncle Lucas, as they took care of her. Coaxing her to eat. Brushing her hair. Enticing her to come out onto Maddie's back porch to feel the breeze. There were times he simply sat beside her and read to her all the books she used to like or told her all about who he was, how he was her cousin several times removed and how happy he was to meet other family.

The first time he showed her his magic she had freaked out terribly. Magic was still something she detested then. She had been taught to hate that part of herself. Her parents and their friends believed that magic was something dirty and wrong. Poor Elias was only trying to show her a simple wind spell that made a tiny cyclone that hovered in his hand. He made it spin over some colored sand, which it would suck up and use to shift colors. He thought she would get a kick out of it. Instead, she had screamed at him in disgust and charged off to her room to hide there for the rest of the day, ignoring his apologies and pleas to come out. When she eventually did, full of shame and regret at having hurt his feelings like that, he only smiled and asked her if she wanted to get ice cream.

Because of his, Uncle Lucas, and Maddie's care and love,

Rune's wounds, inside and out, healed, setting her on the path to being the person she was now. Which was why it had been a deep shock when he had left three years prior.

Rune contemplated all this as she watched him sort through her clothes, as if he hadn't been gone a day.

"Three years ago, when you left...was it because of me?" she asked with zero preamble.

"You personally? No. I love you and I like you," he answered, as if the question didn't surprise him in the slightest.

"I was the biggest mess in the history of messes. All the things I said to you, crying every other minute, making all that trouble for you...."

"I wouldn't trade being there for you for a yacht full of supermodels and champagne. For one thing, the supermodels would be paid to be there and I don't share company with people who have to be coerced into it." He waggled his eyebrows at her as he held up a satiny blue dress that Rune had worn to a wedding once and never again.

"Right. Well, personal ethics aside, what I mean is: did you leave because Maddie made me her Heir? I saw the will, it's dated from around when you left."

The blue dress was hung back in the closet. "You were always going to be her Heir, and you are her Heir."

"And you resented it and you left," Rune said, since he wasn't going to say it.

"Rune, listen to me. The reasons I left have nothing to do with you. And nothing to do with Maddie. My leaving was only ever about me, can only be about me. I know you weren't ready for me to go and I am sorry for the pain that caused you." More clothes were gathered and matched with hangars.

"But *Alf* said, you were originally meant to be her Heir." Rune picked up one top that she had loved two summers ago but had been thinking about getting rid of. He had rehung three more outfits before she had gotten that one on its own hanger.

"What Alf wishes to be true doesn't make it true. Alf will get over it and come to respect you as much as he respected Maddie."

"I'm sorry, but I can't see Alf talking about me, or anyone, like he talks about her."

"Oh, no, he won't worship you like he worshipped her. That is a different issue…" Elias's eyes flared a second, "…entirely. But he will respect you, tremendously. He's already starting to which is why he's behaving like he is. It'll probably come together about the time you are able to respect yourself."

"I respect myself," Rune said defensively. She turned to the closet to hang up the shirt.

"Then why are we having this conversation?"

"Because I'm not trying to avoid the real danger here of losing the House. I've fought too long to keep this place safe without having it ripped out from under me because I really can't hack it in a magical boxing match." Elias went over to her dresser and started methodically opening them to take a visual inventory of the contents.

Rune huffed out more air and resumed her place on her bed. "And I can't help thinking that Alf is right. *You* should be the Heir of the Magdalene, instead of me."

"I don't. Maddie never offered me the House and I never asked."

"But why? You were her student, a lot longer than I was."

Elias's eyebrows quirked. "Because this is your place. Your home. You love it. Of course it should be yours to keep," he said as if it was that simple.

Rune deflated, flopping back onto her bed. "And that is going to be enough to convince the Inner Council to let me keep my House."

"Probably not."

"Great. Great, glad we're on the same page here."

"It is not about the destination, it is about the journey."

"Oh. My. God. You are infuriating. You're like a freaking fortune cookie in hot pants." Rune screwed up her face, her almost childlike anger crumbling under the pressure of how much she had really missed him.

Her cousin started laughing before tugging her up to sitting and enveloping her in a hug. "I have missed you too."

"You're mean," she chided, yet she hugged him back just as fiercely.

"Yes. I am. And I'm not sorry for it. Neither should you be. But Rune, I want you to know you are more powerful than you think."

Rune took that in for a moment.

"What, you mean in a magic sense or in a personal-power, tree-hugging sense?"

Elias double blinked and hesitated a moment. "Both? I think?"

"Okay." She did break the hug then and rubbed away the rest of her tears. "Okay. I'm more powerful than I think. Fine."

"Have you noticed, probably recently, your being able to do magic that wasn't within the purview of your Finding Talent?" That caught Rune's attention and Elias smiled wider. "You have. That's wonderful. What did you do?"

Rune half shrugged. "I don't know exactly, but the first time…about a couple of months ago…I created a door."

His eyebrows jetted up to his hairline. "You did?!"

"Yeah, but I haven't been able to do it again."

"Were there other things?"

She squinched her face. "Maybe. I cast a healing spell using a crystal, but what was weird about it was the spell just kept going for days. Turned St. Benedict into a raving monster."

"The guy downstairs?" Elias asked, lifting his eyebrows.

"He got over it."

"Anything else?"

Rune's mind danced over the memory of two nights before and her sudden ability to make objects jump to her.

"Yeah, a few other things, I guess."

"Perfect." A pair of skinny jeans hit the bed. Followed by Rune's wrap around white shirt that had miraculously come back from the dry cleaners rewhitened. On top of the clothes landed her knee high, heavy leather brown boots.

"These felt right, don't ask me why," he said and took a spot against her door frame, folding his arms.

"These were the clothes I wore before. The last time…I mean two month ago when I…."

"When you cast your first true spell? Sure, that explains it. Go ahead and get changed."

Rune nodded and spun her own finger in the air in front of him. He rolled his eyes and turned away to face out into her living room so she could get dressed.

She had to agree, pulling the clothes on felt very right. Once she had yanked on the boots, she realized the outfit wasn't complete. Going into the topmost drawer of her dresser, she found her most precious item, her leather belt. Made with three pieces of leather united with two metal rings, it buckled around Rune's hips snuggly. Pouches lined the leather, waiting for Rune to fill them with useful things, mostly crystals, business cards, and snacks.

"What do you think?" she asked, once it was secured around her waist.

Elias turned back and nodded. "Where did you get that?"

"Maddie made it for me. Or she had the Faeries make it for me."

"It's covered in Maddie's magic," he said, his voice becoming hushed as he focused on it. Rune realized he was looking at it with his secondary sight, his eyes going completely white for a moment. "Wow. Even I can't puzzle all that out." His eyes returned to normal. "Guess that's something we'll have to explore together. Now where is your shield crystal?"

That surprised Rune. "My shield crystal? Why would I need that?" Even though she was questioning it, she retrieved it from its pouch in the same drawer the belt had been in.

"You never know," Elias said.

"You think someone is going to try to assassinate me at the Magic Guild?" Rune joked as she slipped the yellow shield crystal's cord over her head, the mineral setting perfectly in the V-neck of the shirt, resting against her sternum. "I don't know how many charges it has left."

"Maddie made that, so enough," he pronounced and turned to go into her bathroom. "Do you want me to braid your hair?"

He actually did her hair out in the main room of her apartment, sitting at her dining room table, which was covered in bills and papers that desperately needed to be organized and shredded, but probably never would be. While he brushed and plaited a wrap-around French braid he swore he learned from a girlfriend he once had, Rune told him about the events of the last few days.

"And now you have Justin crashing back into your life," Elias said.

"I know!"

"How long has this been going on?"

"Two months ago, St. Benedict appeared in my bar looking for Anna Masterson so he could find Justin and his precious program that everyone's dying for. He knows by the way. St. Benedict I mean. St. Benedict knows who I used to be. He's been trying to protect me since then."

"He has? Interesting."

"He feels guilty."

"Why would he feel guilty?"

Rune went still a moment, biting her lip as she debated with herself if this was a secret she could really tell. "Because…he thinks it's his fault that he lost his wife and I think, even though he had hoped she would be me, and he knows I'm not, obviously, I don't know…I guess I remind him of her, or he's protecting me in her place? I don't know but…."

"Do you trust him?"

Rune paused as she considered that. "I do. At least, I trust him enough with my life. That's the more fair answer. I know he isn't always telling me the truth, but I do believe he thinks he has good reason."

"Hmm," Elias commented.

"Why did you attack him like that?"

"It was presumptuous of me, my Lady. I perceived him as a threat."

"How?!"

"You like him. That much is clear. And he's too corporate slick for you. Plastic. Artificial." Elias finished off the braid with a black hair tie and passed a hand over her face before giving her a hand mirror.

"Wait, wait…you were pulling a big brother you're-not-good-enough-for-my-sister routine?"

"He's not good enough for you. You said yourself, he's not entirely truthful with you."

"What is this, a Lifetime movie? Not every relationship has

to be a romance." Rune set the mirror down without looking at it.

"Ha. So says every Hollywood heroine trapped in a rom com throughout the history of ever," he said. "Ready to go?" Rune nodded and he backpedaled toward the inner door and the stairs that led from her apartment to the bar below.

"Yes, then. Yes, it is like that. I like him a lot. More than I've liked anyone since he-who-ruined-my-life." Rune couldn't help but start smiling foolishly.

"Now, that's interesting," Elias said, teasingly, as he flipped around right before his back crashed into the door, opening it instead.

"Why? Because I have the dating history of a middle-aged spinster with too many cats?"

"Can I reiterate again, how much I have missed you?" he laughed as they clomped down the stairs.

"You haven't found anyone interesting to talk to in your travels?"

"Never the way you do. You are singularly unique. Your speech is an eloquence found only in the most special of company," he added with a faux high society flair.

"Stop that. Stop...complimenting me like that. It was the one thing you always did that was so annoying."

"I'll stop if you truly want me to, my Lady."

"Don't do that either. Only Alf has to call me 'my Lady.'"

"He must love that daily reminder."

"I haven't told you the whole story yet."

"You can later. We needs must get going," he said as he followed her into the Main Bar. At the bottom of the stairs, St. Benedict waited, his hands in his pockets and fedora tilted a bit over his eyes. He looked like he had been talking to Alf, but both men stopped when they appeared.

Rune couldn't define the look in St. Benedict's eyes, but they nailed her unblinkingly, like someone had frozen him in time.

"I think your knight approves," Elias commented.

Alf harrumphed. "What the hell is she wearing?"

"What the hell are *you* wearing?" Elias asked instead of answering.

"A suit. What's it look like?" He was, indeed, wearing a suit.

The first one Rune had ever seen her bar manager wear. Except at Maddie's funeral. That sobering realization passed between the both of them before Alf turned away to harrumph at the nearest stool.

Ally, now in her little fluffy, white dog form, trotted up to the group and sat smartly down, wagging her brush tail.

"Why are you a dog?" Rune asked, surprised.

"She said she didn't have any change of clothes to wear that were nice enough and she didn't want to risk going home to change and having us all leave her," St. Benedict explained.

Ally barked once sharply for her universal "yes," looking very proud of herself.

"I guess that means we're off to see the Wizard. Conclave," Rune quipped as she knelt down to pick Ally up. Elias laughed and immediately began singing the refrain.

"Still can't carry a tune in a bucket," Alf groused.

"We could always carry you in a bucket, if you don't suck it up." Elias stuck his tongue out at Alf. Alf's response was to stick up his nose a bit more.

Of course, Elias didn't care. He strolled over to the double doors that led to the Back Bar. Framing these double doors were two devils with especially long arms. Holding up a hand to the door, Elias spat out something that sounded like what one would get if Latin and Bantu had a love child. In perfect unison, the devils stretched their long arms toward the handles of the door and opened them. Light filled the doorways and a quick gust of air blew inward from the air pressure shift. The minute the doors were completely open, Elias strolled through, engulfed by the light. Alf marched in after him like he was off to war. Rune started to go through but realized St. Benedict wasn't following.

"Are you coming then?" she asked. She dropped Ally to the ground. "You go ahead." The dog-girl whined a second, then yapped a yes and trotted through. Returning to St. Benedict, she took his hand and was surprised to find it shaking.

He pulled it away to stuff into his pocket, offering her a smile instead. "You're wearing makeup," he observed.

"I am?" Rune touched her face. "It must have been Elias.

He does this quickie illusion spell that makes it look like you're wearing make-up. It'll wear away in a couple of hours."

"It looks nice," St. Benedict said, meaning it.

"You *are* coming with me then?" she asked, "I thought you were going to head back to...work."

"Only until I see you safe." He nodded at the doorway. "Is this another one of your secret ways through Chicago?"

She blinked as she looked at it. "Oh yeah, kind of. It's Maddie's more direct route to the Magic Guild. We'll cut through a few places first, but you can't beat being downtown in ten minutes." Rune peered through the door. She had seen Alf open those specific ones like that once before, but then it had opened into an entirely different room. Now they opened into a hallway. "I don't entirely understand it myself, but Elias will help me get a grip on a multi-destination door like that."

"I'm sorry...about earlier. In the car," he said, stopping her a moment as she started to exit. "I shouldn't have...yelled like that."

Rune smiled and nodded, "Thank you. Just don't do it again, okay?"

He nodded and something in his shoulders let go a little bit.

"Okay. Lead the way," he said, holding out his now steady hand for her to take.

Inside, Rune's chest warmed. "Yeah, okay."

Together they walked through the door, which the devils shut smartly behind them.

"Good luck," Franklin called from the Lounge Bar.

Chapter 11

"A Wizard's Conclave used to be a meeting of the great minds of magic, now it's a damn circus," Alf grumbled as they walked down a long stone tunnel and into a huge atrium. It had been a while since Rune had walked through one of the pathways that existed in the in-between places of Chicago. From her bar they had passed through a service tunnel, an abandoned overgrown garden into the stone tunnel. Finally, they emerged through a crisscross of fern leaves into a huge rush of people moving everywhere and nowhere.

It was chaos. The elaborate relief carvings inside the Magic Guild building were blocked by countless banners all touting the latest and greatest. Some banners had arrows and labels such as: Vendor Room, Cafeteria, Restrooms, Lecture Hall, Gaming Room, etc.

The main atrium that served as the hub of activity was shaped like a blocky eight pointed star, with halls leading off of each point. The space inside went up three stories, creating a feeling of openness even if there was barely an inch of space on the ground to move through.

"Please, have your tickets ready and facing out!" an authoritative voice called out as more people manifested behind the House Magdalene, and friend. Several people with wands stood on either side of the ferns holding their hands out to take peoples' tickets. The closest one was a friendly, smiling young woman, who held her hand out to Rune for the ticket she definitely did not have.

Smoothly, Elias intercepted her, pulling a crystal out of nowhere and holding it out to the ticket taker. Her eyebrows quirked a second, then she passed her silver wand over it. The crystal came to life flickering gold and aquamarine, the official colors of the Magic Guild. The ticket taker double blinked at that. An emblem appeared on the surface of the crystal, an eye with a cross in the middle.

"Uh, I...I don't understand..." the ticket taker said, looking around for someone to help her. A cheerful-looking Tigerwoman appeared, smiling brightly.

"Yes, let them in. They're a House," she said, offering her smile with a nod to Rune and Elias.

"Oh, I see," the ticket taker said and backed away so they could pass

"Welcome to this year's Wizards ConClave," the Tigerwoman said, gesturing into the overcrowded space. "Usually Houses come through their own entrance, but this is fine. Enjoy."

Rune nodded, sparing a glance at St. Benedict over her shoulder, and their group passed into the atrium. The ticket takers turned back to their work.

The crowd was overwhelming and colorful. Peoples of all kinds passed each other, several dressed in elaborate cosplay. Rune only recognized a few of the costumes from the most recent movies, but the more sophisticated creations were constantly stopped by their fellow con goers who snapped pictures. The constant stopping and blocking of other people's progress made moving through the large space an exercise in claustrophobia emersion therapy. Rune had to resist the urge to grab St. Benedict's hand again, deciding instead to fall back in parallel with him in order to not get separated in the crowd. Grabbing his hand might send off the wrong signals.

There was a crackling energy in the space. Even in her little dog form, Ally danced on her feet with excitement, tail going like it was attached to a motor.

"Elias, where do we go?" Rune asked, gripping her cousin's hand, which was more natural to her, before she lost him amongst a group of scantily dressed little people streaking past.

"There should be a place here to put in a petition to see the Inner Council," he said as he tried to scan over the crowd.

"Where did Alf go?" Rune asked, realizing they were one short. Pun not intended.

"Information desk," Alf said, appearing out of the crowd from nowhere. His appearance was so jarring, a couple of women who were making eyes at Elias tripped over Alf.

"Watch where you're going!" Alf roared, shoving one of the women off of him. She fell on her butt with a yelp of surprise, and a little hurt. Alf ignored her cries and stomped right up to Rune while Elias made the woman's day and helped her to her feet gallantly.

Alf continued to sneer as he jerked a thumb to a kiosk that indeed had an overlarge banner that declared the word 'Information' in bold, blocky letters. "You're going to have to fill out an appointment request form with the Inner Council or something." Alf crossed his arms in front of his chest, making his nice formal, out-of-place suit pucker in the back. "My Lady," he added belatedly.

"This doesn't make sense. Did you tell them we've been summoned?" Elias asked, joining the group again sans the two women.

"No, I went over there and told them I wanted to join the Lollipop Guild. Of course I told them!" Alf barked. "It's a new system. Supposed to be more efficient or something."

Ally barked once and the group turned toward where she pointed with her nose.

"Ah. I'm pretty sure that's the line for the appointment crystal." Elias indicated a massive queue line that seemed to be the source of much of the crowding in their area. Five kiosks with message crystals glowed teal then yellow as they took messages. They were lined up along one wall and there were five snaking lines leading up to them. Amongst that, people flowed in, out and through like water through a sieve, which created more conflict as those in line worried that they were going to lose their spots.

"You better get over there, or we're going to be here forever." Alf shifted out of Rune's way.

"You're still the Steward of the House Magdalene, aren't you?" Elias asked, though he sounded like he knew the answer. "Maybe you should go stand in line for your Lady?"

Alf ground his teeth together, which made a painful sound,

then turned and stalked off to join one of the lines.

"While we wait for him, what would you like to do, my Lady?" Elias asked. He opened a glossy brochure handed to him by one of the people at the door. "There, of course, is the vendor room, but yes, here, there are also several talks and lectures. Looks like they've got a spell exchange room." Elias's voice slowly drifted away to nothing, getting lost in reading the brochure.

"How about we go into the vendor room?" Rune started to say, but was cut off by a bulky voice attached to a bulky body.

"Dogs aren't allowed in here," one of the security guards said, cutting through people who obligingly drifted out of his way, respecting the uniform more than the man himself. He approached the Magdalene enclave. Ally darted behind Rune's legs, the teenage dog trying to make herself as small as possible.

"She's not a dog, she's a Changeling," Rune informed the guard, who could have passed for an orc if he had tusk implants. His uniform was teal colored and had the Magic Guild emblem over the left-side pocket. Much like the corporations it imitated, the Magic Guild employed guards who had the same jurisdiction as any other corporate police, so despite the color of his shirt, the guard's authority was very real. The only difference between this officer and any other corporate grunt was the Magic Guild's governing districts had shrunk to pretty much the Magic Guild building itself, which had created a lot of chips on a lot of shoulders. Another reason Rune still called the Sheriff's Department over her own Magic Guild authority. This guy looked like he had enough chips for both shoulders.

"All Changelings need to be in human form while on the premises," the security guard reported stiffly, like he was reading the whole statement word for word out of a book of rules and regulations.

"Since when?" Elias asked incredulously, interposing himself between Rune and the guard.

"Since last year." The guard sized up Elias, and apparently wasn't impressed by what he saw.

"We didn't know," Rune cut in. "She can't change into human form though, she didn't bring any clothes. Unless it's permissible to walk around naked? She's also only seventeen, so technically she is still a child and not subject to Guild rules as of yet." She knew it wasn't entirely true, but Rune was playing dumb in the hope that maybe that would help them get away with breaking one tiny, brand-new regulation.

The security guard shifted uncomfortably on his feet. "No, she can't stay. She's going to have to leave the premises."

"Are you discriminating against Changelings?" Elias challenged.

"No pets are allowed on the premises," the guard repeated.

"She is not a pet, she's a person. She is a retainer accompanying her Lady." Elias indicated Rune and she started to wish she had chosen to wear the blue dress.

"You're a Lady of a House?" The security guard sniffed, looking down his nose at her. Rune had to resist grinding her teeth like Alf had. Getting the long eye like that was never going to not be annoying.

"We have been officially summoned by the Magic Guild Inner Council and her retainers are required to be present by official orders," Elias stated. He produced the crystal from his pocket that shimmered the Magic Guild colors of gold and aquamarine. The guard double blinked at that, then plucked up the crystal. He activated it with a tiny push of magic and the emblem appeared on the surface of the crystal, the eye with a cross in the middle.

"I think this trumps your regulation," Elias said with finality.

That elicited a sigh of defeat from the guard.

"She'll have to come with me and get officially registered. What was your name again? My Lady?" he added, belatedly to Rune.

Rune stepped forward. "Rune Leveau of the House Magdalene." The guard's left eye twitched once, but whatever he was thinking, he kept to himself.

"I will deal with this, my Lady. Please proceed to the vendor room and enjoy yourself." Elias gave a slight bow to Rune, who had to suppress scoffing or laughing at his extremely formal behavior. "I trust you will keep our beloved Lady safe, whilst I attend to this matter on her behalf," he then said, directing his words to St. Benedict who had stood silently behind Rune the entire time.

"Better than you can," St. Benedict agreed, smiling back as he imitated Elias's slight bow.

Rune rolled her eyes. "Boys, boys, you're both pretty, can we get going?"

Her cousin gave a polite nod before he turned and picked up Ally, who whined a tiny bit with worry. The guard turned and led them both away through the crowd, leaving Rune with nothing left to do, but turn back to her last companion.

"Well...this is not an auspicious start," Rune quipped, trying to shake off her feelings of unease.

"Seems you have some pull around here though." The Saint turned toward the vendor room and offered Rune his arm to escort her in. "My Lady."

"Why sir Corporate Spy, I do believe you are making fun of me," she said, affecting a cartoonish, breathy lady's voice.

"Yes, absolutely," her escort confirmed.

She slipped her hand in through the crook of his arm and together they entered the hallway toward the vendor room with the flow of the crowd. At the end of the hall, a pair of double doors stood open, allowing people to stream through into a larger room just beyond.

"Oh. That makes sense," Rune said as they approached and passed through.

"What makes sense?" St. Benedict asked, shivering a bit as the feel of magic wafted over his skin.

"They've connected this door to another room somewhere else." Rune stepped to the side of the entrance, out of the push of the crowd and turned back. Sure enough, at each corner was a series of five large crystal, glowing rhythmically. "Wow. That's a lot of power to keep the doorway open," Rune noted.

"This is like the door to your office?" St. Benedict asked, lining up behind her. Rune could feel the heat of his presence burning into her back.

"Yes, but it only expends the power when the door is open. To keep it open like this..." she shook her head marveling, "...

that's a big power drain. See those two have already burned out." She pointed at two crystals that had indeed gone dark.

"Then if this isn't the Magic Guild, where are we?" St. Benedict asked, turning to look into the room again. It was huge, with enough space to easily encompass a couple of football fields. Signs were everywhere, giving directions or advertising over tables with people moving up, down, and around them. Before Rune could answer St. Benedict's question with "I'm not sure," he nodded his head. "Ah gotcha. We're at Stephens Convention Center."

"How do you know?" Rune asked. She had never been to the Convention Center before and there were no signs declaring that's where they were.

St. Benedict tapped his temple. "My own brand of magic." He offered his arm again and they joined the rest of the Con participants. The large room was full of tables, people, and so many exotic things Rune's eyes were popping out at first glance. The tables were laid out in a grid and every manner of buyable item seemed to be laid out on them. Figurines on one table were next to costume pieces on another with a book seller on the other side of an artist focusing on watercolor renditions of famous video game characters.

Side by side, they walked between the other attendees and cosplayers, taking it all in. Rune slowed next to a table covered with crystals of different colors, cheap ones they were selling by the scoop.

"What do you think?" Rune asked, as she dug through a discount bin also filled with crystals, but most of the spells were small things like quick cleaning that wouldn't even do a whole table or a pocket sized light crystal that people used for parties or raves.

"Nothing like I expected," he answered. He turned away from a shelf of curvy growing bamboo plants and crossed to a booth that sold hats of different kinds and styles.

Rune's eyes followed him as he stopped in front of a new black fedora, shaped much like his battered grey one. Automatically, her brain noted the shape of his shoulders and how they tapered into his waist. Secretly she admitted to herself that she was loving this. Rune hadn't been on many dates, though walking around like this wasn't really a date. She simply enjoyed the feeling of him being near her. Really. Yet the high schooler in her squealed that this was exactly like a date. An accidental date was still a date. Realizing that she better do something because standing there staring at him while her mind continued its irrational party was how one got caught in the act. So, she came over and picked up a stylized top hat to try on.

"Are you disappointed?" Good. That sounded nonchalant enough.

He gave a half shrug. "When you say something like Magic Guild Headquarters or Wizard's Conclave, I guess I pictured something more fantastical. You know, people flying back and forth on broomsticks or talking plants, sparkles everywhere. This is all pretty...mundane."

"I'm sure we can find the table with some talking plants if you want. They don't usually say much, maybe two or three phrases. Like parrots."

St. Benedict arched an eyebrow at her. "Seriously?"

"Hey, magic folk have their gag gifts too. We are people."

"Like those people?" he asked, nodding toward a pair of green humanoids wearing superhero t-shirts. They seemed to be in the midst of a lively debate as they passed.

"Scientific magic? That makes zero sense," said one as she tried to open a box of candy.

"What else would you call it?" her more androgynous looking, tree-like friend asked.

"Super powers are not magic. They are two very distinctive things."

"Flying and laser vision and super strength caused by fake radiation that turns you colors. Sure, that's not magic," the other's voice dripped with sarcasm.

Rune nodded. "Dryads."

"Are they?" St. Benedict squinted at the couple as they moved away. "They don't look so much like trees as tree huggers. I mean the green hair could be dyed."

"But it isn't, their hair is actually a filament that allows for photosynthesis, much like other plants," Rune said, replacing the tri-cone hat she had been messing with on the stand. She moved away to go to the next table.

"Do they change color in the fall?" he asked. He may have been going for mirth, but it came off a little sarcastic.

"Yes," Rune said carefully. She studied his body language again. He had stuffed his hands into his pockets as he followed her, and seemed to hunch in, trying to make himself as compact as possible as people passed him. It gave him a veneer of cool hostility.

"Who are you supposed to be?" A kid asked the Saint before they had taken a few more steps.

"Excuse me?" St. Benedict blinked at the kid.

"He's from *Werewolves of Chicago*," the kid's probably older sister said as she herded them both away. "Come on, Mom's looking for you."

"Werewolves of Chicago?" St. Benedict asked, turning back to Rune.

"You've never heard of that show?" Rune asked.

"It's a show?"

"Yes, it's a thing that you watch on this other thing called TV. Many, many people have them." Rune's voice adopted a sing-song quality frequently heard on children's shows.

He narrowed his eyes at her, an amused smirk creeping on his face. "Isn't TV a technology thing?"

"Oh! So you have heard of it?" Rune asked, cocking her head to the side, keeping her voice light and airy. "Well, you see, people have this thing called money and whether they are magical, hominal, or otherwise, they can exchange that money for goods or services. And since TVs are easy to make and almost anyone can use them, they tend to sell a little better."

They continued strolling side by side.

"I see, so you're saying magic can't do everything better after all?" he nodded as if he was having an epiphany.

Stopping by a wand table, where several wands were displayed in racks under a glass counter, Rune's face became more somber. Dropping the sing-song voice she said more seriously, "There is a very real danger that technology will replace magic completely, like Malachi said, isn't there? You get the rest of Justin's work and all this will dwindle into nothing. Be obsolete. And you'll all be rich and laughing."

They stood silently, looking at the various woods and inlays of the wands.

"I'm going to destroy it."

Rune blinked and looked up at St. Benedict.

"Maxamillion thinks this technology is something that can be used for good. I'm going to see it destroyed."

"Is that really possible?" She looked down at his hand, thin scars crisscrossing over the surface in no particular pattern, simply the sign of the price he paid for his life. "Once a knowledge is discovered, isn't it only a matter of time before someone else figures it out as well?"

He didn't know what to say to that, so he nodded at the glass case. "I thought all your magic was done with crystals?"

"Crystals are only one way to do magic. Wands work too, or silver or gold or skulls or whatever. Different schools of magic use different tools. Crystals are a universal constant. So they became the most economical way to store spells for everyone to use, our attempt at streamlining, but there are lots of magic users who are better at using wands to do magic outside of their Talent."

"Would you like one?" he asked.

"A wand? No, no thank you," Rune giggled at the thought. "I'm more likely to poke my eye out than actually get it to work.

"Is there anything here that you would like?" he asked, turning out toward the sea of booths. Rune followed his gaze. There were many things she would want, but it felt uncomfortable to say it out loud seriously.

"All of it," she tried to quip, and they both giggled politely. "I don't know…what is the price limit?"

His grin would have made a Cheshire cat jealous. "Maybe keep it under $1000."

"Ha!" Rune was floored, but that was probably the idea. "I…I…why?"

St. Benedict half shrugged. "Because I feel like it."

"Wait. Are you…are you secretly rich?" Rune asked, looking at St. Benedict in a new light. She had always assumed he had money, but she had never really seen him use it either.

"I have some, but I don't usually get to spend it since I never need to," he conceded.

"Because your company gives everything to you?" Rune gave 'company' a nice varnish of contempt.

"Yes. And also there is nothing that I want." They rounded the corner at the end of the row of tables and continued around to the next row.

"That must be nice. Having all your everythings met. I can barely keep my bar afloat and in my possession. If I buy a designer coffee, I feel wasteful." Rune couldn't help thinking about the state of her bar and all the things falling apart there. Several of the booths here had the more expensive crystals available and with an unlimited credit account, a bag full would go a long way to fixing everything quickly and easily. Her thoughts danced over the business card associated with her OmniSin, but buying these things wasn't exactly a Corinthe business expense. She imagined she'd have to validate her purchases later. She would have to wait until she fulfilled her agreement with Maxamillion if she wanted extra cash.

"Then what would you like? On me, I promise, don't even worry about the price tag. Anything on this whole floor."

Rune shook her head. "Thank you, no."

The Saint bounced on his feet. "Oh come on. Please."

She laughed at his little boy antics. "I said no. Thank you."

"Why?" He genuinely looked a little crushed by her refusal.

"It's just...Justin used to do that all the time." She ran her fingers through a bin full of polished wood pieces, focusing on the sensory feeling rather than the familiar pain accompanied the memories. "I mean, I'm sure you mean it differently than he did, but whenever he wanted to show off or he was feeling bad about himself, one of his tricks was to flash money around to impress me. Or whomever. He would take me to stores and tell me to buy whatever I want, go to fancy dinners, spontaneous trips. And it worked too. I'd eat it up. I don't like the person it made me, nor how it made me feel. Because...in the end, he never gave me what I really wanted."

Rune stared down into the wooden pieces, looking gently

sad yet sweet, as if she could divine a better world in the chaotic wooden patterns.

"What was that?" St. Benedict asked softly, barely able to breathe to ask the question.

"I don't want to sound like a sappy cliché." She withdrew her hand from the bin to walk away and shut the dark thoughts away, but she made the mistake of meeting his haunted eyes. They stopped her, requiring her to answer.

"I wanted him to love me. But he didn't." She shrugged and smiled, having paid her toll. She walked around and away from St. Benedict so she didn't have to keep meeting his eyes. She didn't want to know what he thought about what she said. It was her pain and none of his business.

"Hey, before," she said, following a thought she had earlier, "you said you had worked with my ex on the 'Masterson Files?' Why do you need them then? Couldn't *you* simply remember the formulas yourself?"

The Saint smiled, or rather he tried to smile, his teeth forming more of grimace than a grin. "Yeah. You see…I, uh, ha…I have brain damage."

Rune stopped in her tracks, blinking. He noticed and turned to face her, still smiling unfazed.

"What do you mean you have brain damage?" she asked. After glancing over his shoulder at nothing, St. Benedict tapped the side of his face. "When they took us…they weren't gentle about it. I took several blows to the head and some memories were…damaged. I can't remember any of the formulas or what happened exactly. At least, it's really fuzzy and partial at best. It was why we tried to develop the memory scanner, using the implants they put in here to try to fish out the memories. Didn't work."

"St. Benedict. I'm so sorry," Rune said, and tried to touch his face, yet he shifted to let another patron behind him get past, effectively dodging away.

"I'm fine. Better than fine most of the time. The implants help regulate things and I can read at an incredible speed now." He winked at her, turning to keep walking by her side.

"Excuse me. That is beautiful work," a voice interrupted, as they passed a leather crafting table. A large, buxom woman in a top hat emerged from her booth with a kind smile and genuine interest. She indicated Rune's leather belt with two fingers.

"Oh! Yes. Thank you," Rune said surprised.

"It's Faerie-work, correct?" The woman wiggled her fingers at the scrolling on one of Rune's pouches as if she desperately wanted to run them over the surface. "Would you mind...and it's fine if you do, but could I take a look at the maker's mark?"

"Um," Rune set her fingers on her belt, strangely loathed to take it off, but there didn't seem to be a good reason not to. "I guess...."

"Why do you want to see it?" St. Benedict interceded, edging closer to Rune.

The woman blinked at him, only then noticing the Saint standing next to Rune.

"Oh, yes. Faerie Masterworks are very rare. I've never seen one walking around in the wild before," she added, smiling wide, like a small predator. It put Rune in mind of a dog's smile, or actually...a fox seemed more accurate.

"I suppose it would be nice to know more about it." Rune unbuckled the belt and held it out. Delighted, the woman turned back into her booth, flicking a clear fox-tail back and forth that emerged from under the edge of her bright red tunic. She ducked under the overhang she had erected for displaying her goods, her black leather top hat barely clearing. The booth smelled strongly of leather and the oils used on them as Rune and St. Benedict followed her inside. There were so many items that the few people perusing made the space feel tight. There was an array of colors from common brown and black to bright reds, blues, greens and purples.

The foxy woman went to a work table she had set up near the back. A portable, adjustable magnifying glass sat there with a light shining down on the surface and her leather-working tools. It looked like she was in the middle of crafting something, but she cleared the piece out of her way and laid Rune's belt under the light. The fox woman started having a fit of giggles.

"Oh my goodness and gracious," she tittered, running her fingers over the leather as if reading its history in every tooled whirl and sewn pocket. "This is beautiful."

After removing her hat, which revealed a pair of large foxy ears, she readjusted the magnifying glass over the belt and pushed another orange lens in place. A spark made everyone jump, except the foxy woman. She leaned in even more, studying what she saw with intense concentration, then softly started counting under her breath.

"Your belt here has got over a dozen or so spells on it," she declared. Now Rune leaned in with interest.

"I mean, it is Faerie made..." Rune started to explain.

"Yes, yes. I see all the typical spells," the foxy woman gave a dry chuckle. "I mean as typical as leather-working goes. This is incredible work. The blending of magic and leather. I'll never be this good." She continued to study, not even waiting for a response to her comments. It was more like she was only talking to herself.

"What are the 'typical' spells?" St. Benedict asked, since Rune wasn't going to.

"Oh you know, protection against wet and heat. Ward against tearing. Doesn't prevent it, mind you, but it usually lessens the small stuff. Especially when you have a minor self-heal worked in, which you do. Anything beyond that, I usually need to inlay crystals or something, but there are spells here...."

Then she became somber again as she stared harder through the lens. "You...you also have spells worked into the leather that I don't outright recognize...." She sat up straight, her eyebrows pinched in worry, before she looked into a bag that rested at the back of her booth.

"Is everything alright?" Rune asked, stretching her own neck out to try to get a glimpse of whatever the fox woman saw on the other side of her lens. Through the amber lens, Rune saw strings of different colored magic floating over the belt, as if it had its own energy field.

"Yeah, yeah. I just want to look something up. You've got at least four, maybe five different spells woven in here, that I can't really identify." She flipped open a worn spell book that looked like it had been printed in the '70s. After checking a few pages, she stopped to read silently for a couple of tense moments.

"Hey, how much are these gauntlets?" a customer who had been perusing asked, interrupting her.

"$35," she said, looking up.

"Oh, then never mind," the customer said and dropped the black and blue leather gauntlets back on the table.

The foxy woman rolled her eyes and sighed. "Everyone wants it for free. It's not like I'm asking for their eternal souls," she muttered. "As for your belt, someone has really messed with it." The foxy woman slid to the side a little and gestured for Rune and St. Benedict to have a look. "You have a slew of spells here, but they aren't typical leather working spells and I would say aren't Fae ones either. On top of that, they've been broken."

Rune gazed down through the lens, but other than the fact that she could see magic present, she might as well have been looking at an x-ray for all the sense she could make out of it. As if reading her mind, the foxy woman telescoped out a pointer and started indicating whirls on the surface of the belt. "Do you see this line here? Someone deliberately slashed it."

"Yes, I do see it," Rune said, reaching out a finger to touch the mar in the design. The edges of the leather puckered a little, much like a wound, breaking through three whirls. Through the lens Rune could see that the magic lines mirroring the whirls didn't move like the other spells did. Instead they were still.

"Wouldn't the self-healing spell fix this?" St. Benedict asked.

"Not something like this. It's too deep, for one, and had to have been done with cold iron. Cold iron can act as a cauterizer for spells if someone knows how to do it right. That and the fact that it neatly interrupts these extra spells without completely dispelling them tells me that this was done deliberately and by someone who knew what they were doing." The foxy woman started looking at her book again, her face scrunched and puzzled by the mystery.

"Could these be Wizard spells?" Rune asked.

"What are you thinking, Rune?" St. Benedict laid a hand on Rune's shoulder.

"I'm thinking Maddie," she said, realizing he was concerned about her bursting into tears at the mention of her beloved, deceased great aunt. While Rune's throat felt a little tight, she was in no danger of falling into grief. "Maddie was the one who gave this to me." Good. Her voice was steady.

The foxy woman paused and regarded her.

"Sorry, who did you say you were?" she asked.

"We didn't. You invited us in," St. Benedict said in that stiff, polite way that came off as a little menacing.

The foxy woman, cocked an eyebrow, but accepted that, nodding.

"Is it possible to repair this?" Rune asked.

"Oh, yes, easily. Would take me maybe ten minutes?" The foxy woman immediately picked up a squeeze bottle and began shaking it, before biting the cap off.

"Wait. I was only asking. I can't pay for…I mean I was just asking for future reference." Rune hated this part, the part involved in explaining why she didn't have the money to just drop on a simple repair.

"How about I make you a deal, it'll only be a hundred even for this repair, just to cover my material costs?" Rune tried not to groan. It was a really good deal.

"Do you take OmniSins?" St. Benedict asked.

"No. No, don't pay for it," Rune admonished. The idea of him spending money on her was making her skin crawl.

"I…do," the foxy woman said, unsure about Rune's reaction, but already reaching for her Omni-reader.

"Great, ignore her, and hold out your reader. She and I can fight about it later," St. Benedict said with a reassuring smile, then popped his augmented hand open. Blue light glowed over his palm. Wide-eyed and mouth slightly dropped open, the foxy woman flicked her tail with swift, sharp flicks as she held out the Omni-card reader. He passed his hand under the scanner and the light on the machine blinked blue twice. The foxy woman's large eyes managed to get even wider.

"Uh…yes…sir. Thank you. Sir. I'll have this ready for you in a few minutes," and she turned away quickly, dropping the reader clumsily as she tried to reach for all her tools at once.

"Oh dear," Rune said quietly and glanced out at the rest of the shop. The other patrons were staring at them as well with wide eyes ranging from frightened to hostile. An older mother quickly ushered her teenage daughter out of the booth. Two monochromes continued to browse but moved as far away from them as possible.

At the very least, St. Benedict stuck his offending hand into his pocket. "I guess I shouldn't have done that," he said softly to Rune.

"You think?" she hissed back. "I thought you were a good spy?!" She batted him on the shoulder and he took it without removing his hands from his pockets.

"I have a bad habit of being prideful."

"Well, now everyone is freaking out because they all think you're an executive."

"It's not a big deal." St. Benedict turned his head every which way, noting every pair of eyes glancing at him. Obviously, it was a big deal.

"It is to us!" Rune whispered so hard she was spitting and defeating the point of whispering.

"Well, I'm sorry!" he said, finally turning to her, lowering his head so they were eye to eye. They held that close distance for long seconds as their wills battled each other, daring the other to look away. After a full minute of the staring contest, Rune felt the smile creep up her face. St. Benedict's eyes twinkled brightly and then it was too late.

"Fine," Rune said looking away, still trying to sound mad even if her face betrayed her.

"'I'll wait outside until your belt's done," St. Benedict said, moving to exit the booth.

Standing there for several minutes, he stared off into the churning hypnosis of the crowd battling himself in his head. What the hell was he doing? He was so deep in contemplation that he almost missed a single familiar figure cutting through the Con goers. Straightening, St. Benedict double blinked. A red circle appeared in his vision around the figure as his augmented sight began outlining its body. Three times his eyesight flashed and three images appeared in the lower corner of his vision. With his hands at his side, his finger twitched, moving so that the image in his vision was the one that had gotten the cleanest shot of the figure's face. The image enlarged and St. Benedict's heartbeat accelerated.

Chapter 12

When Rune emerged from the booth with her newly repaired belt, St. Benedict was gone. She looked up and down the aisle, assuming he had wandered a little to check out other tables while he waited, but there was no sign of his fedora or him in either direction. Blinking she tried to stamp down the thought that he had ditched her and opened up her Talent instead. Her magic snaked out of her heart, a gold line dodging out and around the people close by. It went on longer and longer all the while getting thinner and thinner. When it got to the width of a piece of fine thread it dissipated.

"That son of a bitch *is* ditching me," she muttered, then shook her head. Maybe he was going to the bathroom. But then why hadn't he told her that or just waited?

The Masterson Files. Rune shook her head as she started to line up some pieces.

He had come with her to the Magic Guild because he had wanted access to the inside of the building. Why not buy a ticket then? The Con was open to ticket holders. No time, Rune decided. By the time he knew he needed to come, he needed in now and using her to gain it and navigate the place saved him time. It had been *convenient.* That was probably why he had insisted on buying her a present, to apologize for using her like that, then taking the moment of distraction to slip away.

Sighing, Rune followed the direction her gold line had indicated. As she walked, weaving her way through the crowd of people, she started to wonder if the Magic Guild did have a piece of her *ex*-husband's work. What would have made St. Benedict sure enough to try to James Bond his way in? She thought back to the picture of the flame-throwing enthusiast.

She hadn't recognized him on sight, but she had recognized the Conclave pin he wore. Her plan was to come to the Con and try to see if she could meet him here. If he knew something about the Masterson Files, then she wanted to talk to him. Yet again, her life pulling her in too many directions was tripping her up.

While her thoughts drifted away from finding St. Benedict, something odd began to happen to her magic string. It strengthened back into existence as it came into range of the errant Saint, then frayed and almost too late, Rune realized that she wasn't keeping her focus on what she meant to Find. Often what would happen was that her magic would fail and she would have to try to do a new Finding all over again. This time, though, her thoughts about finding the Masterson Files dominated her attention and the Finding spell warped like it had at the Corinthe headquarters. The strengthening gold thread connecting her to St. Benedict split, with various other threads peeling off of it, all red colors. Stopping in the middle of the aisle, Rune stared at the new threads. Most were thin and weak, a couple she wasn't even sure she could see clearly, but two were most dominant. The gold one she associated with St. Benedict and a ruby red as blood one running parallel beside it.

Gently, Rune touched the blood ruby one and it sparked. Images shot through her mind: a room, with grooves carved into the ground. Then, a table and a computer. The back of a slight man dressed all in black, with long dark hair, looking like a rock star. Rune's heart began to thunder in her chest. No. It couldn't be.

St. Benedict couldn't believe his luck, which was why he kept a good ten feet back from the target. Twice the target looked back, but they never focused on St. Benedict. The hooded figure seemed to be trying to cut a rough diagonal through the vendor room, making their end goal a bit hard to predict. After the second glance back, the Saint ducked into a stall with very colorful medieval-influenced clothing. Like the leather stall, this one had a plastic-coated metal awning that clothing hung from, so St. Benedict was able to keep an eye on the target without being seen.

The target was a slim youngish woman. She wore a black,

long-sleeved shirt with a deep hood up over her black straight hair even though it was the heart of August. The air conditioning in the room fought to keep up against the crush of humanity heating up the place. Yet, the young woman had chosen to wear a dramatic shirt and skinny black jeans.

The woman was stopped by an over-clogged booth, waiting for the patrons to move out of her way. As if sensing him watching her, she turned back, her eyes roving back and forth. The image of the woman's brother enlarged in St. Benedict's vision and he expressed a satisfied, predatory smile as he compared it to her real face. She was definitely like the magic user from the alley. Still unable to detect what was following her, the young woman furrowed her brow and turned away to continuing the slog to her destination.

As soon as the prey turned away, St. Benedict spun back out into the crowd. He stuck his hands in his pockets, slipping into his cool guy persona as easily as a Faerie slips on ice. Heading over to where the target stood, he continued to focus his gaze past her, so that the weight of his spying didn't attract her attention.

'Saint of Liars, I see you there...'

Fingers ran up St. Benedict's spine. Startled, he turned to confront whoever had done that behind him, but no one was close enough to have reached him at that moment. When he turned back to where he last saw his target, the young woman was gone. Cussing under his breath, St. Benedict sped up to get to the end of the row. Luckily, he caught a glimpse of the young woman as he joined another column of people heading out of the vendor room.

St. Benedict passed through the holes in the groups to slide his way closer, until he was coming right up behind his target. Then the young woman turned away from the main artery of traffic toward a shorter hallway with a door at the end. Another young woman dressed like the ticket takers waited beside it. A sign stood next to her reading 'Houses and Special Guests Only' in authoritative letters. A quick glance at the crystals in the corners told St. Benedict it was another magical doorway to elsewhere. Realizing he was about to lose his target, St. Benedict quickened his step.

The slight woman approached, already flipping open her hand and presenting a crystal like the one Elias had earlier. The young woman nodded and she passed through without slowing. The young ticket taker turned her attention to St. Benedict then, her eyes widening a little above her professional smile. Her cheeks turned a little pinker and her fingers involuntarily captured the end of her long, red hair. Oh, he was definitely getting through that door.

"Can I help you, sir?" she asked.

"I think this is the door I'm supposed to pass through," St. Benedict said, indicating the direction his target had just gone.

"Do you have your badge?" she asked, holding out her hand for it.

"Sorry, my badge?" St. Benedict readjusted his hat so she could see his eyes better. He looked straight into her face, and she pinked a little more, looking away shyly. He never understood what about his eyes made women and girls do that, but then, he didn't necessarily need to know how a gun was made in order to fire it.

"I'm sorry sir, this doorway is for House members and their special guests."

"Yes, that's me. I am a special guest," St. Benedict replied, giving her a charming smile as if nothing was wrong and he expected her to let him through any moment. Service people couldn't help wanting to fulfill expectations.

Her eyebrows pinched a little. "Well, no one is supposed to go through here without a badge. Or invitation crystal? Do you have one of those?"

He sucked air in through his teeth. "No I don't. One of the retainers of the House I'm with has it." The Saint glanced over his shoulder like he was looking for the lost companions he had ditched. "We got separated in the vendor room. I guess I'm the first to make it here."

"What House are you with?"

"Magdalene," he answered confidently.

She double blinked at that.

"Oh. Ok." Then she nibbled on her lower lip a little as she thought about that information. Maybe it had been too soon to ditch Rune? She might have been able to get him past this door, but then he was already losing his target. How much time had passed since his target had gone through? How far could an emo Talent like her get in that time?

"Alright, so I'm supposed to have a badge. Where was I supposed to pick that up?" he asked, seeing if he could help her solve the problem.

"Inside, when you first arrived," she gestured to the door behind her.

St. Benedict snapped his fingers. "Ah! That's it. We came in through the public door. The retainer in charge didn't seem to know where he was going and now we're all stuck on the outside." The furrow deepened in the woman's brow as she looked harder at him. St. Benedict didn't let himself become unnerved. "So can I cut in there and get our badges?"

"Well, I suppose so," the woman said, shifting uncomfortably, "I mean, you are telling the truth." She chewed her lip some more.

"Excuse me?" St. Benedict asked, caught a little off guard by what she was saying.

"Oh, I'm a Truth Talent." She shrugged her shoulders as she blushed as red as her hair, "Just third class. You know, good enough to watch a door."

"Wow, that's impressive." St. Benedict nodded. He had no idea if that was impressive.

She giggled despite herself. "No, it's not. I basically can only tell when people think they're lying. But I am working on distinguishing kinds of Truth. Sorry if that doesn't make sense. It's really technical."

"I bet it is. So you don't think I'm telling the whole truth?" he asked.

The woman started to look through him again. "No that's not it...." A shimmer appeared over her shoulder, something wavering between water and shadow. It was only there for a second and before St. Benedict could focus on it, the shimmer was gone. A feeling of dread gripped his chest. Was that part of her Talent working?

The young woman waved at the door. "Any way, go ahead

and go in. If you go straight then take a right for a little ways, you should find the badge table. If not, ask for Marcia, she can help you."

"Marcia. Got it. Thank you for this," St. Benedict said, moving past, hoping he'd be able to figure out where his target had gone.

The same eerie tingle danced over his skin as he passed through the door. He stamped down the wish that Rune was still with him.

"It's only magic, you idiot. Nothing to be afraid of," he whispered to himself.

The new hallway he found himself in was decorated with maroon wallpaper and gilded gold fixtures. It had the air of a hotel about it and that was confirmed by the plaques at the end with arrows indicating room numbers one way and front desk, pool, and vending machines going the other. Another young woman stood in front of the sign, reading some papers in her hands. She was beautiful, with golden brown hair that waved around her face. Dressed in a simple, curve-hugging skirt and wrap around blouse, she was practically leaning against a decorative side table that was also trying to support a vase with a green plant.

St. Benedict approached her, shining his charming smile. "Excuse me, ma'am, did you see a woman pass through here, all dressed in black with her hood up?"

The green eyes that pinned him were sharp as emeralds. He had heard eyes described as brilliant as gemstones, but this was the first time he had ever seen anyone's eyes come close to that description. They made his own green eyes seem muddy by comparison.

"Yes, I did," she answered, her voice soft and smoky as bourbon.

The Saint experienced a new sensation, one of being tongue-tied. Some distant part of his mind was laughing at him. Another part noted that though the woman was beautiful, he didn't really find her attractive. He never found any woman truly attractive, so what was going on here? Why was he reacting like a love-struck teenager?

"Um...uh...great," he said, trying to force something more sensible out of his mouth.

The woman looked down her pert nose at him as she folded her hands under her arms. She was in no hurry for him to answer. Her gaze appraised him up and down, lingering as sensually as if she had been touching him with her perfect, manicured hand. Every part of St. Benedict's body tingled with the journey of her eyes. Bile gathered up at the back of his throat.

"Interesting," the woman finally pronounced.

"What is?" *There we go. A complete sentence.* It was a start.

"You are. You're very interesting. It's too bad really."

"What is?" Still a complete sentence even if he was only repeating.

"That you belong to someone else. I can see it all over you. You belong to someone else and you've tainted yourself with another. No, several others. Why did you do that?" Her eyes nailed his with the question. Slamming her real nails into them would have hurt less as her too-accurate appraisal of him knifed his insides.

"I...." Several lies flitted through his mind. All the old favorites that he would use over and over, hoping one day they would become truths. Before he could say any of them, the woman's eyes narrowed to slits.

Then she crooked a finger at him. "Come here."

He moved, stepping closer. Closer and closer, until he was a couple of inches from her. It took longer than he expected. Was he dragging his feet? His hands were shaking and he jammed them into his pockets.

"What will you give me to tell you where your prey went?" She whispered her question and shivers ran up his spine again. His breath quickened in and out of his chest.

"How about a kiss?" She cupped his chin with the crook of her finger. She leaned in through the small amount of space between them. "Really, it's a small thing for a wife to ask from her husband."

No. This was wrong. She wasn't his wife. Right? Like a band had snapped, St. Benedict bucked his head away, breaking her spell. "Stop it," he said, biting the words. Except even as he backpedaled away from her, the woman was gone.

Breathing hard, one of his hands tore from his pocket to grip the corner of the hall. The sharp edge pained his palm, feeling reassuringly real.

"To the left, Saint of Liars." The woman's voice echoed in his mind. It was the same voice that had spoken to him before. Every cell in his body wanted to run.

Instead, he straightened and took in his surroundings. They had changed. He was no longer in a T-junction of hallway with the way back to the vendor room behind him. Rather, he was in a four-way hallway juncture. Not a soul was in sight, only more maroon wallpaper and gold-gilded light fixtures. Not even a housekeeping cart. He turned back, checking for the strange woman one last time. Instead of the woman or the blank wall that had been there moments before, he came face to face with himself, reflected in a gilded mirror.

Clearing his throat, the Saint straightened, looking away from his own questioning eyes, before turning to walk to the left. What else could he do? Maybe if he walked fast enough he could outpace the sense of dread that followed him. Something was coming for him, hunting him. Something magical he wouldn't be able to fight or resist. Something that clearly wanted him very, very dead. Or worse.

A stray thought danced to Rune.

He charged around the next corner at the end of the hallway. To his surprise, the slight young woman in black was walking into one of the rooms. St. Benedict slowed his steps and approached at a casual walk. The hallway was otherwise empty. Like a good little spy, he walked past the door, glancing inside nonchalantly in case anyone was watching for intruders. This doorway had the telltale signs of the crystals at the corners. Another hallway was beyond it, this one made of stone. It also contained the disappearing back of his target. There were no guards or other prying eyes. Doubling back, he picked up his pace, pushing his walking into a jog as he continued the chase. The minute he crossed the threshold, the space around him sounded different, more echoey with cooler air.

He didn't let it slow him. Reaching a turn in the stone

hallway, he slid up beside the corner without going around it and listened. Hearing nothing but the hard tattoo of his heart, he took a chance glancing around the corner.

"St. Benedict, do you know how to pick door locks? Is that a skill you have?"

Rune stood in front of a closed door, running her hands over its surface as if she was looking for a secret latch. When he didn't answer her, she looked at him, cocking an eyebrow.

"How did you get here?!" he exclaimed.

Rune couldn't keep it back any longer and started a fit of uncontrollable laughter.

"I'm the Finder. Did you really think you could ditch me so easily?" She turned back to the door. "Actually, I wasn't Finding you, though I knew you were close." She touched the door again. "I found it."

He didn't have to ask her what she meant by 'it.' Closing the distance between them he looked at the door she was standing before.

"I think we need to go through this door," she said, laying a finger on the pebbled glass. Then in a softer voice he almost didn't hear, "He's just on the other side."

St. Benedict examined the door, but there was nothing uniquely special about it, simply a standard wooden door, with pebbled glass in the top half. No plaques or letters stated what kind of room it was or who it might belong to. He tested the knob. It didn't shift, but it did have a slot for an old-fashioned, metal key.

"Do you know where we are?" he asked. Checking the hall again, he unbuckled his leather belt.

Rune's eyes shifted away, her cheeks flashing hot. "This is in the Magic Guild proper."

"How did you get here?" he asked, pulling two dull silver tools from one of the ends.

"Well, not the way you came, I can tell you that. After you ditched me, I went my own way, out of the vendor room, back to the atrium and then to here."

"How do you know what way I came?" He knelt in front of the door and added, "Keep an eye out. We gotta run if I can't get this open."

Rune rolled her eyes. "No, I thought it would be more fun to let them catch us."

He grinned as he focused on the lock. "Probably serves me right."

"Anyway, I think I figured out some new things about my magic, or maybe I'm just getting stronger or something. I was trying to Find you and then I got to thinking about the 'Masterson Files' as you all keep calling them, which is still weird to me, by the way, and I don't know…. Instead of one Finding spell, there were two."

"I thought you needed an object to connect you to the thing you're trying to find, or Find, whichever." The lock was simple and would only take a couple of minutes.

"I guess I'm evolving. It's not like there are any other Finders in the world. As far as I know I'm the only one, so how would I know what the rules are if I don't stumble upon them? There are Trackers, but they don't do things the way I do, so their techniques aren't very helpful. My magic does its own thing."

Click, click, click, slide click and the lock easily turned.

"And your Finding spells led you here?" St. Benedict stood up again and tucked the picks back into his belt.

"Yeah." She continued to stare at the threads that floated all around her. What she wasn't telling him was there were more than the two threads. Overlaying everything around her were threads, pulsing, all different reds. She had no idea what it meant and more unsettlingly, they weren't dissipating. Since she couldn't explain it to herself, how was she going to explain it to anyone else? It was like her second sight was on, but she knew it wasn't. Using her Talent had automatically spawned them, but Rune had no idea why.

"Rune? Rune?"

Double blinking, the Talent looked up, realizing she had been staring hard at what to her companion appeared to be nothing. So no change there.

She grasped at the blood red thread.

"Could the red mean…." she muttered softly to herself. Thought and magic ignited. Images flashed in her mind, like the string was pulling memories she had long forgotten.

Justin's computer was running code, flipping through lines of gibberish she barely understood. Then the screen flipped to something familiar. A standard pentagram, filled in with glyphs that she recognized from a book Maddie had given her once. She had hidden that book under her bed, studying it after her parents had retired for the night, though she only comprehended a fourth of it, and then none of it after her mother had found it. It was the first time her mother had slapped her.

Seeing it on Justin's computer screen surprised her. "What are you doing with the pentagram?" she asked, trying to engage her distant husband.

"You're too stupid to understand it," he said instead, giving her a little push out of the way. "Get out of my office. I told you, you're not allowed in here while I'm working!"

"I just thought maybe we could...."

"Dammit, Anna, don't you understand that what I'm doing is important? Now get out!"

Rune dropped the string, stumbling back a couple of steps as her knees buckled underneath her.

"What's wrong?!" St. Benedict cried, getting up alarmed.

Rune shook her head, trying to clear it, but there was nothing to clear. Had she really let him talk to her like that? Now she didn't let anyone speak to her the way Justin had. She could still see his face, popping up around her like a ghost. She thrashed from side to side trying to swat it away.

"Rune, Rune!" St. Benedict pulled her into his arms, flipping her around quick so her back was against his front and thumped her in the solar plexus with his fisted hands. At once, she inhaled, her panic having made her stop breathing entirely. While she gulped breaths, he supported her from behind. "Keep breathing, please," he whispered soothingly from behind her, rocking a little back and forth to comfort himself as much as her. She pulled away embarrassed.

"I'm alright. Just...."

"Panic attack?"

She looked up into his concerned face. Slowly, he brushed his thumb under her cheek, wiping away a tear she hadn't even felt fall.

"I'm sorry. I'm sorry," she repeated as she wiped any other tears from her face, then chuffed a laugh. "I don't know what is going on here, but I think I am going to…." she sniffed once, "I don't know. I'm sorry. I don't know." There wasn't enough gold in a dragon's horde to make her meet his eyes again right then. Instead, she gestured at the door. "Let's keep moving. I need to know what's in there."

St. Benedict stayed where he was for a moment longer, but she wouldn't look at him. Finally, he seemed to accept that because he stepped back and turned the knob. There was an air pressure shift as it swung inward.

Stepping inside sent the hairs on St. Benedict's arms to rising.

"A ritual room," Rune said, her voice becoming breathy. "Maddie had one at her house."

The room was eight by ten, made of stacked stone and as they stepped inside, light crystals rose out of their sconces and cast a soft yellow light that made the place still seem candlelit. Another door was on the opposite side. To one side of the room was a wooden table coated in the rubbery substance that St. Benedict remembered seeing on his college science tables. The table was a mess with vials, tubes, books, and strangely enough, electronic equipment. Even a soldering rod.

"A computer?" St. Benedict said as he softly clicked the first door shut and approached a small tan and grey box screen in the corner that sat on top of a box CPU. He pushed at the mouse on a worn mousepad that had a cartoon wizard on it giving a thumbs up. The screen blinked awake. Beside it, a large crystal the size of a pair of bowling balls came to life. The light coming from the crystals changed the feeling in the room from warm to something more cold and sinister.

"They're using energy crystals to power it," Rune noted. "I didn't know this was possible."

"It…shouldn't be?" St. Benedict asked, warily. He continued to examine the set up. "How the hell are they regulating the power output?"

Then Rune turned back to the floor. Like most standard ritual rooms, this one had the circle carved into the solid stone floor. But someone was adding to it. A partial pentagram was in the middle of being carved through the circle. A chisel, chalked string, and hammer were abandoned where the carving had been paused.

"What do you think they're doing?" St. Benedict asked.

"I suppose it makes sense. There would be a magic component, right? If you want a computer to cast magic spells, then you'd need something like this, at least to start." Rune had walked part way around the circle and now they faced each other opposite it. "Ruined a perfectly good ritual circle," she derided.

She studied it harder, trying to fill in the rest of the lines in her head. "It reminds me of...something I've seen before...." Rune knelt down beside the bastardized circle and touched it.

"I think you're right about this being part of the Masterson Files," St. Benedict said, mirroring her crouch as he watched her. "I'm going to start taking pictures."

"Wouldn't you just pull images out of your brain?" Rune asked. His eyes flashed to blue, which made him look so ethereal and inhuman.

"That's assuming I don't get a bullet in there too," he said, giving her a wink before looking down at the diagram. "Pictures can be easily sent out for others to use without diving." He flexed his hand and a holographic camera appeared. Manipulating it with his lighted fingers, he began taking pictures as if it was a normal camera, adjusting the theoretical lens to take clearer pictures than the quickie, on-the-fly camera in his ocular implants could provide.

Rune watched, marveling for a while, but when nothing more interesting happened she glanced up at the computer. A diagram full of code was appearing on the screen. "Oh!"

When she said nothing more, St. Benedict raised an eyebrow. "You want to elaborate on that 'oh'?"

"I know where I've seen this. It was on Justin's computer." Following her gaze, St. Benedict jumped to his feet, going back to the computer screen. Even as he moved, the red thread Rune had been trying to ignore ignited. Like it was lined with gunpowder, the circle and pentagram filled with fire, forcing

Rune to jump back away from the wave of heat. Painfully, her magic was pulled from her through the line, fueling it.

"Dammit!"

"Rune! Are you alright?!" She heard St. Benedict shout, but she couldn't respond as the flames grew as tall as she was. Then they jumped out of the etching in the floor, leaving the precut lines to fill in not just the pentagram but beyond the circle, slashing every inch of the room into more geometric shapes. It also cut the two occupants off from any viable exit, and each other.

"What's happening?!" St. Benedict shouted. Rune looked across the wall of flames at him, but he seemed to shimmer and change. The red string wrapped around him, layering a different man over him. That man was skinnier, an inch or two shorter, with long, black hair and angular limbs.

"Justin!?" Rune couldn't believe her eyes.

"What the hell did you do, Anna?" The mirage of Justin was angry, gesturing at the bank of computers behind him that hadn't been there a moment before.

"What's happening?" The question echoed as two voices, one deeper than the other, asked it in unison. The fire was making the air unbreathable and Rune started coughing. It surrounded her on all sides and she backpedaled until her back was against the wall. Sigils of fire wrote themselves in the air over each portion of the newly created ritual circle. Thrums of magic seemed to make the room shake and vibrate to the core of Rune's bones.

Even as the air around her burned, Rune's body began to feel cold. Whimpering, she slid to the ground. Was she burning? Somewhere in the back of her mind she remembered someone telling her that when you burned alive, you would actually go numb after a while as the nerves died, tricking the mind into thinking it was freezing. So it couldn't be true because there was supposed to be excruciating pain first. Instead she felt simply numb, like the life force was being drained out of her and soon she would only be a pile of ash.

"Rune!"

St. Benedict emerged from the flame, his legs curled up

underneath him as he leapt through, using only his arms to shield his vulnerable head. Having to jump blind, he overshot the last line of fire, almost landing on top of Rune. The small kick to her side seemed to wake her up, even as he braced his hands against the hot stone to keep from completely crushing her. Then she was in his arms and squeezing him back as tightly.

"We're going to die!" she cried.

"I've got you," he said, pulling her close. Then he hissed as if something burned him. Pulling away, he grabbed her right hand. It was still holding the red thread.

"Let it go!" he shouted.

Rune double blinked. "You can see that?!" She hadn't realized she had still been holding it.

She let it go.

Immediately, the fire died down. The red string that had started it all had become thin, before shattering into tiny red particles that floated into the air. There were still flames low in the grooves of the newly created ritual not-a-circle. Rune's fingers were stretched out nervelessly before her, her arms feeling like blocks of heavy ice. Slowly she began to lower her hand, but St. Benedict caught it, lacing his fingers in-between her own. The warmth of his hand burned much like the fire had, but it was the good kind of burn. The kind that told her she was still alive and real.

"I saw Justin," she said, though she hadn't realized she was going to say it.

"I'm here," he said, his voice so close, she could have turned and kissed him. "I saw him too."

"So he was real?" she asked, but she knew he hadn't been.

"Not possible. He disappeared into thin air," St. Benedict confirmed. "You're ice cold. What happened to your hair?"

He grasped at a loosened strand of her hair, pulling it forward so Rune could see. It was snow white. Even more horrifying, the skin of her hands had sunken so her bones were clearly seen underneath. She felt weak, and as she tried to move, places inside her ached fiercely.

"What…? What I…." her voice came out croaked, which panicked her more.

She began to thrash in panic, but both of his larger hands wrapped around her withered ones, warm and vibrant. "Rune, Rune!" The voice was comforting, like he was trying to sooth a frantic animal.

"I'm dying! My body is dying all around me, I'm...I'm old!" she cried and his hands slid up her arms to pull her now slighter body against him.

"You're going to be alright. I'm here," he lied.

She breathed in St. Benedict's shoulder, his smell very real. His breath rose and fell and she could feel his heartbeat. Over his shoulder, floating ghost-like over the ritual space, she could still see a visage of Justin, looking at her with contempt and revulsion. How could she ever have thought his face the most handsome she had ever seen? Ignoring him, denying him, she tucked her eyes away. After a few moments she was calmer. She wasn't dying. She was still alive.

"We've got to stop doing this," Rune said once she felt she could sit up on her own.

"Stop doing what?" he asked.

"Hugging all the time. You're going to give a girl ideas."

"I like hugging you. You're a better hugger than Malachi." She chuckled at that. "I'm serious, ever since he started dating Zita, he squeezes like an anaconda."

"You're saying you're a big hugger?"

"No, Malachi is. I've had to learn." He took one of her hands and held it up to look at the skin closer. "What's happening Rune? How can I help you?"

"I don't know." She lifted her opposite hand up to compare. "It felt like my magic was being pulled out of my soul. You know, everything that makes me, me. Maybe the circle was booby trapped?"

She forced herself to give him a reassuring smile. Instead, his green eyes cut through her, stripping away any lies she wanted to say, looking into her all the way to her ravaged soul. Tears budded in her eyes.

"Do I look...?"

He smiled instead, kissing her cheek tenderly. "You're beautiful still."

She swallowed. "You're literally just saying that."

"It's literally my answer."

"Wait. You mean independently of whatever this is," Rune waved her hand over her aged face "you think I'm beautiful?"

Now it was his face that was going red. His widening eyes made it comical. To cover, he got to his feet, pulling her up after him.

"At least you did it," he said, switching subjects fast. "You found a piece of the Masterson Files. This has to be what he used to...."

"What the hell!" A voice shouted from the opposite inner door. A young man dressed all in black stood there, hands braced against the door jamb. His face was awash with anger and shock at the mess before him. Over his shoulder the young woman St. Benedict had been following, obviously the young man's twin, peered inside, her mouth in a perfect 'o' of shock.

"You!" St. Benedict shouted. He bounded across the still smoldering space in a flash to grab the young man by his collar before the other had time to react. "What did you do to her?!"

"Get your hands off me!" the young man in black shouted, trying to bat away St. Benedict's hands. St. Benedict countered easily, but before he could pin the guy's face into the wall, a flare of fire burst up between them. St. Benedict dodged backward, avoiding the sudden flame, yielding a five foot space. The young man in black held both his hands out in front of him, both hands engulfed in blue flame.

"Get Mathus!" the young man shouted to his sister, who turned away in an instant, presumably to do just that. "You're them, aren't you? You're that guy that took Leveau the other night," the young man said, recognizing him. He glanced over at Rune, who had stood up, using the wall to support herself. "Who the hell are you, grandma?"

Across the room, from the door they had come in through, someone started banging.

"Yeah, they're in here!" the young man shouted.

The door banged open and security guards poured in through.

St. Benedict attempted to move toward Rune, but fire hands

attacked, swinging his fists to make arcs of light in the air. The Saint dodged and wove out of the way, but all it did was push him back toward the guards who stood waiting for orders by the door. Rune saw what was happening, but was unable to do anything about it.

Except she wasn't unable. Clear as day, she saw the gold thread connecting her heart to St. Benedict's. She grasped it with both hands and hauled. Unlike when she pulled the adrenaline shot, which was very light comparably, when she hauled this time, all she managed to do was pull St. Benedict sideways a few steps. He stumbled and regained his feet, looking surprised at his sudden leap to the right.

"Grab him quick!" the young man in black screamed, trying to pivot toward his frogging opponent.

"No!" Rune yelled, and she pumped more magic into the line. It swelled and strengthened. This time when she pulled, all the force she had exerted was amplified through it and St. Benedict sailed through the air as easily as the adrenaline shot had. He landed against her, slamming her back against the wall behind her. The air predictably burst out from her lungs and Rune swore she felt something snap in her chest. But he was there next to her.

Grasping her protection crystal in one hand, she whipped out her other palm and coughed out, "Salutem." Energy burst forth as a yellow wall, doming in front of Rune and St. Benedict, sealing them against the walls and floor. The group on the other side stared in silence as they took in Rune's last ditch effort.

"Break it," one of the guards said, but the young man in black slashed his hand.

"No. It's unbreakable. The Wizardress who created the crystal was more powerful than all of us combined. As long as she..." he indicated Rune, "...can supply it magic, it will hold against the apocalypse."

"Then what do we do?" another guard asked.

"The only thing we can do. Wait them out," the young man in black sneered.

"Why didn't you do that earlier?" St. Benedict asked in a low voice to Rune. Regaining his feet, he marveled at the display of magic. "I wouldn't have had to lose my eyebrows."

"I...f-f-f-forgot," Rune stammered under the strain. Casting this spell had never been hard before, the crystal did most of the heavy lifting, but right then, Rune was shaking hard as she focused on keeping the shield up.

"She's going to lose that shield soon. Be ready to converge on them the second it fails," the slight young man ordered, smiling cruelly as she struggled.

Rune licked her lips. "We're...going to....walk out...of... here," she gasped out. Why was it so hard to breathe?

"You can barely stand," the young man snarled back.

"Rune what's happening?" St. Benedict sounded panicked but Rune didn't dare look away. She was using all of her will to hold the barrier in place. She had to hold it. She didn't see the hanks of her hair falling out of her head to the ground. Her breathing rattled her chest and each breath sounded more painful and desperate than the last. Yet, the wall held fast.

"The minute the shield falls, you're dead, Talentless," the young man in black promised.

St. Benedict narrowed his eyes at the slur. He felt useless, standing behind the shield with no weapon and no way to truly fight a room full of deadly magic. Even if he had a gun, he wondered how much use it would have been. Left with no other options, he closed his eyes and reached out to see if he could link a connection with St. Rachel. To his surprise, a connection appeared immediately. Not with St. Rachel, but it was close and familiar and probably a lot more helpful than she would have been.

Smiling a wicked smile, he made the call, his holographic interface appearing around him. It was satisfying to watch several of the magic users in the room take a shocked step back at the sight of his foreign tech. The slight young man frowned hard.

Twiddling his fingers as he interacted with the hologram, St. Benedict felt the disruption from the magic around him and he prayed what little he could do to boost his signal would be enough. His smile deepened when it started to ring and weakened when it was dismissed. Rune groaned a little bit under the strain.

"Just hold on Rune, I'm calling for help," he said, setting his hand on her shoulder wishing he could give her more than his words.

"Alright, change of plans, throw everything you've got at the shield," the slight man ordered, reigniting his hands

"Come on you bastard, pick up," St. Benedict growled. He counted the rings as magic bombarded the shield. Fire, ice, water, wind, stone…other things he really couldn't name pummeled the yellow glowing wall. Mostly the other magic was repelled around its surface, but Rune's hair had gone completely white and looked so thin. "Pick up!"

"This better be really important!" Maxamillion's voice was a harsh gravel growl, almost barely audible through the torrent of magical static.

"I found it. The Masterson Files. You wanna see?" St. Benedict asked, barely taking a breath between his words. The attacks began to slow as the slight young man raised his hand for them to cease, eyeing St. Benedict.

"What do you mean you found it?" Maxamillion asked carefully, followed by the more relevant question. "Where exactly are you?"

"A ritual room inside the Magic Guild. Which must be where you are since our call signal is so strong. How *is* your secret meeting going?"

"Unproductive." There was Maxamillion's typical thoughtful pause, then he asked in an even softer voice. "Are you sure that you have found the Masterson Files?"

"Deadly."

"Hold one moment."

"Sure, we got the rest of our lives," St. Benedict said dryly, but Maxamillion's call degraded into pure static.

Rune tried not to let another whimper escape her, holding the shield. She wanted so very much to let go of the spell. Never in her life had she had to maintain one for so long and never had it been so difficult.

"Keep up the pressure, that shield is coming down!" the slight man yelled.

"No!" Rune croaked out, pushing harder. She had to hold it.

St. Benedict's arm snaked around her middle, holding her close.

"Help's coming," he said in her ear. The weight of him behind her grounded her. She had to hold the shield, or they would both be dead. The look in the slight man's eyes was crazed with his power; he wanted to burn her alive and wouldn't be satisfied until he had accomplished it.

The world began to waver in and out in front of Rune. She realized she was moments away from losing consciousness and then that would be the end of them both. The slight man's harsh grin sharpened as he recognized he was about to win.

And Maddie's legacy would die with Rune.

Like hell it would.

The pulse of magic from within Rune was beyond intense, the next one was like a hurricane. As it hit, thrumming off of Rune's shield, those outside of it were knocked back, their feet kicking up almost comically in unison. All other magic was ended as the casters lost their concentration. The slight young man spun sideways, his fire magic whirling out and away in a small cyclone of flame.

Rune pictured Maddie in her mind. How strong she was, how powerful. Maddie had held shields like this before, defending those who couldn't protect themselves. Picturing her gave Rune strength, and Rune steadied, feeding her magic into the crystal around her neck. She could do this; just like Maddie, she could hold.

And then it ended all at once.

Rune's magic dissipated as she collapsed like a house of cards to the ground. If St. Benedict hadn't been holding her, she would have thumped nerveless as a mannequin. Instead, he stumbled back as he redirected her weight toward him, letting himself hit the wall to slide to the ground as he cradled his body around hers.

"I've got you. I've got you," he whispered soothingly, as he petted his hand over her fine, white hair.

"Does someone want to explain to me what is happening in here?" a cultured voice asked, cutting over the groans from the fallen attackers.

Chapter 13

The woman at the door was beautiful, with skin the color of warm sepia and hair twisting outward in a wave of midnight. She looked older, but no less beautiful for it. Her eyes flashed like chips of amber as she entered the room escorted with a hand draped like a queen over Maxamillion's. While her robes were bright orange and yellow, Maxamillion was dressed in conservative grey with no tie and the top button on his dress shirt popped open in a sophisticated, casual way. Yet they still looked perfect together, a prince escorting a goddess.

The scent of spices wafted over St. Benedict and somehow he felt a little calmer.

Their attackers, realizing the woman had entered, scrambled up to their feet, bowing their heads once they got there. Her gaze passed over them one by one until they landed on the slight man in black, who could barely contain his frustration.

"Abraxas," the woman stated, leveling her gaze at him as she named the slight man in black.

"I caught these intruders in my work space."

"This space belongs to the Guild, Abraxas. Are you in the habit of attacking those that enter it?" The woman's amber eyes waited for an answer unblinking.

Abraxas's face enflamed at the assertion. "As you know, Councilwoman, my work is of the highest secrecy and urgency to the Guild. I caught these spies trying to steal my hard work! At least one of them is corporation!" He jabbed a finger at St. Benedict and Rune.

"My spies, actually," Maxamillion said calmly. The woman's gaze slid to Maxamillion's.

"I must say Max, when I invited you to join us and make

your petition to the Inner Council, I did it in good faith. This is a violation of the trust I put in you."

He bowed his head to her in acknowledgement. "I cannot argue that my people have invaded, but I cannot agree that I violated your trust. In fact I think I have done the opposite, Wizardress Ursula."

The beautiful woman, Wizardress Ursula, hooded her eyes at Maxamillion. She was most definitely not amused.

"Thank you, everyone, for responding to this threat. You have all executed your duty faithfully to this House. You are all dismissed," she said to the guards. There were exchanged glances and worried looks, but one by one, each of the magical muscle left.

"What are you doing?" Abraxas demanded, pitching his voice down so the guards wouldn't really hear as they were leaving, but it simply made his words come out in a hiss.

"Defusing a situation, obviously," Ursula stated, not unkindly, but with the calm authority of a confident and benevolent woman.

"You are handing the hope of our people to the enemy!"

Ursula did not respond to that, holding her look of unwavering serenity. In the face of it, Abraxas took a couple of retreating steps back, lowering his gaze respectfully. Frustrated he clenched his fists hard. "I will inform the Inner Council of this," he threatened.

"Do whatever you feel you must do," was the only response he got. Smoke followed after him as the Fire Talent stormed out.

As soon as he was gone, Ursula approached St. Benedict holding Rune. He was cradling her so that the side of her withered cheek rested on his chest. Both of his arms wrapped around her shoulders, his legs bowled to make a comfortable place for her to sit. While the stance seemed relaxed, his eyes flashed blue at the approaching Wizardress. She heeded the warning and knelt down before him a comfortable space away. She regarded Rune, her eyes roving over the slight youngold woman as if the answers she sought were etched into her weathered skin.

"Who are you?" Lady Ursula asked Rune.

To St. Benedict's relief, she stirred and licked her dry, strange lips. "Rune Leveau," she croaked out, her voice reedier and more strained than he had ever heard it.

Blinking, Ursula shook her head slightly. "Rune Leveau is a young woman."

"She was, until your lackey booby-trapped the room," St. Benedict growled. Again the Wizardress regarded him with her serene amber-colored eyes.

"There is no magic that I know of that can hasten time on an individual. That is science fiction. Manipulation of the fundamentals of time and space are violations of this world's rules."

"All magic is a violation of the world's rules, don't give me that." St. Benedict brushed his fingers over Rune's hair again, sweeping it back.

"It is obvious you care very deeply for her, but may I help?" Ursula asked, stretching a hand out to touch Rune.

"Who are you?" St. Benedict demanded.

"A friend," Maxamillion answered for her, the warning in his voice very clear to St. Benedict.

St. Benedict slid his eyes over to his master. "*Your* friend maybe. Sir."

"I am the Lady Ursula of House Oxum and senior member of the Inner Council of the Guild that she…" the Wizardress indicated Rune, "…is a member. It is not only my duty to safeguard her life, it is also my earnest wish." The professional demeanor slipped into something softer and sad. "She is the apprentice of my dearest friend who is lost to us. I promise you, I only wish to help."

"Ursula?" Rune croaked, realizing it was indeed Maddie's friend. The world kept drifting in and out for the Talent; she was having a difficult time managing. It took a lot of effort to lift her own hand to meet Ursula's offered one, but gently the older woman caught it. Rune's flesh was pale as cream and just as cold, even more so when it met the smooth nutty warmth of the other woman's hand. The older Wizardress turned Rune's hand over in hers as she contemplated something. Then she set it between both of her own. Rune's eyes locked with hers as they began to glow yellow as sunlight.

"Nipa igbẹkẹhin ati aṣẹ ti Magdalene," Ursula said.

Like coils of rope, threads of silver burst and wafted from around Rune's belt. Everyone jumped as the threads spun out in a circle from Rune's body. St. Benedict felt them slink through his own body with odd, unsettling tingles, but there was no way in heaven or hell he was letting Rune go. Spinning like a top, the circle shifted from Rune at its center to a space five feet beside her. There was a crack sound as the circle split into several rings. Spinning ever upwards, the rings released more shards of magic, growing taller until they were about five and half feet from the ground, a single column of silvery light, before crumpling inward in a final burst of fractals. In the column's place stood a very familiar woman.

There was no color to her, made entirely of the silver light, yet she was dressed in a half cape, blouse, and skirt with smart little ankle boots. Her hair was short and feathered upward like a bird's, only tamed by a flat cap sitting smartly on her head. The woman adjusted her glasses and turned to look at the figures around her.

"Ah, I see. I'm dead," the ghost of the Magdalene, Maddie, said.

"Maddie?" Rune asked, barely believing what she was seeing.

Concern flashed on the silver woman's face and she turned to quickly come to her niece's side. As she moved, a thread that had been barely visible flashed, floating like a hair. The glint it made traced all the way back to Rune's belt.

Everyone in the room stared with open mouths at the apparition. The ghost seemed to not notice as she knelt beside Rune.

"Oh, my. Oh no. My baby girl," she cooed at Rune, as her fingers traced over Rune's face without ever truly touching.

"How can you be here?" Rune asked. It was so hard to keep her eyes open that Rune could believe that she had in fact died and Maddie had come to take her to whatever was on the other side.

"I'm not here, sweetie. I've transitioned." She paused in

assessment. "You do know that don't you? I haven't just died?"

"No, you died earlier this year," Rune said somberly. "You're like the simulacrum at the bar, aren't you?"

"No, I am the simulacrum at the bar," ghost Maddie said.

"How is that possible?" Ursula asked, her voice as shocked as Rune felt. "Maddie, what have you done?"

"Your belt. I had it specially made for you so that you would be able to access the power of your House wherever you go. One of my cleverer ideas for sure. It looks like you got it unlocked too. Look at this." The apparition looked down at herself in appreciation. "Though I have no idea what the heck I am wearing. So this means you have claimed the House as yours?" Maddie asked.

"You know I have." Rune scrunched her face. It was so hard to think.

"Not necessarily. I'm sorry if you've told me before."

"What is going on here?" St. Benedict demanded. Rune only then noticed that he was breathing panicked, hard breaths.

"It's alright," Rune said, laying a hand on his cheek. "Before she died, my Aunt Maddie made me this sort of copy of herself to help me, answer questions, that sort thing."

"Like a recorded testimonial?" Maxamillion asked, fascinated.

"Something like that but better," ghost Maddie said, smugly. "I am the sum total of her memories and knowledge, at least up to the moment she made me. I am not alive so I will not grow or change or remember between times that I am activated. The fact that I am here means it worked out."

Rune had more questions, everyone did, but the world became bright and sparkly.

"Oh dear, we must hurry, Rune." The ghost snapped her ethereal fingers next to Rune's ear to gain her focus. Rune lulled her head towards the snap but her eyes didn't focus.

"Touch the belt, Rune. Grab the power from your House and pull it into yourself. Just like it's a crystal. Only backwards. Feed the magic into yourself."

Rune's hands were insensate as she tried to comply.

"Like this?" St. Benedict asked as his hand moved over

her numbed fingers to place them on her belt. At first nothing happened. Rune's head continued to lull as she faded.

"It's not working. What's happening to her?" St. Benedict asked, panic rising in his voice.

"She has nearly depleted her entire life force; she needs to draw more in," Maddie's ghost said, her focus intense on Rune. "Come on child, just like it's a crystal. Pull it in."

"Maddie, what you are talking about makes no sense. Magic is not life force," Ursula said, concerned.

"For her it is," the ghost said with sureness.

Then Ursula laid her own hand over Rune's, nudging St. Benedict's aside. Green light rose from the Wizardress while her eyes went gold again. A sound, like a soft chorus of voices, began to emanate from nowhere.

"What is she doing?" St. Benedict asked.

"She's trying to jumpstart Rune," Maddie's ghost replied. "Ursula's natural Talent is in healing." Breathlessly, the group watched as the Wizardress worked, setting her other hand to a pin shaped like a golden rose fastened to her clothing. More green sparks danced away from the connection.

"It's not working!" St. Benedict said desperately when there was no change in Rune after an eternal minute.

"It is!" Maddie's ghost lifted a hand into his face to stop him from rising and disturbing Rune.

"How do you know?" Maxamillion asked, in a calm voice that also took charge of the conversation.

"Because I would cease to exist if she was dead."

As if on cue, Rune took a deep breath in that seemed to fill her whole being. The aging began to reverse itself. Her face filled in with muscle and blood as the skin tightened again. Skin over her hands smoothed out and the slight body returned to the fuller female shape she normally had. Even her hair thickened, the silver dripping away and melanin replacing itself as quickly. Rune blinked her eyes as she sat up, which glowed white as the magic filled her. She lifted her hands to look at them, moving again under her own power. The moment she let go of her belt, the power faded, her eyes returning to hazel.

She turned to look at St. Benedict. "Am I back to normal?"

"Almost. I'd say you look about twenty years older." He threaded a finger through a cluster of white hair at her temple.

"Way to flatter a lady," Rune chided and turned back to the rest of the group, who were looking at her expectantly. "I'm ok. I'm ok now." She regarded Ursula. "Thank you for showing me how to do it."

The older woman, or at least the actually older woman nodded with a kind smile as she rose. "You are the Heir of the Magdalene. That much I think has been proved."

"Why did Rune age?" St. Benedict asked Ursula. Since Rune had shifted mostly off his lap, he chose to stand, then offered his hand to help her up to her feet.

"I do not know," Ursula answered, before looking at Maddie's ghost.

"That is a family secret and I'm not telling. Even if you threaten me with torture and death." Maddie grinned like a Cheshire cat.

"Maddie?" Rune tried to touch the ghost, but her hand passed right through.

The ghost instead turned back to her still-living niece. "Elias should have returned to explain all this to you."

"He has," Rune nodded. "He…he swore retainership to me."

"Did he?" Maddie's ghost smiled in genuine delight. "Well I never would have guessed that. Where is he?"

"I…I'm not sure, somewhere…."

"Summon him, Rune. He will be able to help you. And don't worry about the rest of the grays. They will fade given more time, a hot meal and good sleep. Also, as long as you stay off of magic for a little while."

"I don't understand," Rune said, but the ghost shrugged.

"I know. I'm sorry. That's all I have for you right now. To continue to generate me outside of the bar would take away from your recovery and may even reverse what we've done. Find Elias, he will have more answers for you." Lovingly, the ghost raised a silvery hand to cup, or appear to cup Rune's face. Rune did and did not feel it. "I'm so proud of you, my heart."

Before Rune could respond, the ghost collapsed into spinning wheels of silver light again, then wrapped themselves around her belt once more.

"I do not understand what just happened," Rune stated as she stared at her belt, trying to visibly detect some sign that explained the magic she had witnessed.

"Your belt is your talisman or fetish. It is a tool that connects you to your House and allows you to draw on its power like mine here does," Ursula explained touching her own golden rose pin.

"What, then, did she mean by summon Elias?"

Ursula pursed her lips at that question, before answering. "One of the abilities of all Heads of Households is to summon retainers and sometimes speak to them directly through the magic of their House. Unfortunately, that will not be possible for you."

"Because I'm a Talent, instead of a proper Wizard," Rune stated.

"Because they are being detained."

"What!?" Rune was shocked, breaking out in a cold sweat.

"Your Guild's turned on you," St. Benedict stated flatly.

"Only corporations do that," Rune bit the words, her neck flashing hot as she said them to Ursula. The older Wizardress's face became blank as stone again.

"Rune, did Malachi show you what we discovered in your alley the other night?" Maxamillion asked. "Your Guild was there. Everyone who was there in that alley two nights ago was coming for one thing. Isn't that right, Lady Ursula?"

"I would not play any more games with me, Mr. Corinthe," Ursula warned.

"And yet I stand in a room containing a significant piece of the Masterson Files. A piece of which you have denied existing so adamantly that if it wasn't for me taking matters into my own hands to discover, we would still be dealing with your obfuscations, instead of the real matter at hand."

"So, you acknowledge that this invasion is your handy work?"

"I am the head of a corporation, madam. Do you truly think there is anything my people do without my knowledge or permission? I do not think you can say the same about your own members."

"The issues within the Magic Guild are none of your concern."

"Yes, but they are mine!" Rune cut in, planting her fists on her hips. "May *I* ask for an explanation? What is all this! Why do you have my husband's work?"

"Rune, you will come with me now," Ursula said, the edge of a reprimanding school teacher in her voice. "You need to understand how many problems have been allowed to fester and grow while you avoided our summons. And as for you, Mr. Corinthe, I think it best you leave...."

"The Masterson Files," Rune said very precisely, effectively cutting Lady Ursula off in spite of the words being soft. Lady Ursula's eyebrows quirked ever so slightly, the first sign of emotion cracking her mask of aloofness.

"The Masterson Files are Inner Council business, and not something you need to concern yourself with."

"My name is Masterson!" The words shot out of Rune's mouth so fast that she even surprised herself. Ursula responded by taking a sudden step back. Rune wondered if she had accidentally imbued a bit of magical force behind her declaration. "Everything about this concerns me."

"Rune." Ursula closed her eyes, before taking a deep breath in. "I am not your enemy. I am trying to help you."

"I'm trying to help myself." Rune wasn't giving her an inch.

"I had no part in whatever attack was made against you by a member of our Guild," Wizardress Ursula said very carefully.

"Be that as it may," St. Benedict said from where he had been leaning against the wall. "Given her own people attacked her, I think it is very understandable that she would have come to us for help. This isn't a question of her loyalty as it is her survival."

"This is a question of all our survivals," Wizardress Ursula agreed. "The corporate world has chipped away at us piece by piece and tries to take the best of us, using it to destroy us."

Ursula indicated the bastardized circle. "We acquired this portion of the Masterson Files, as you call them, a few years ago. We have indeed held this for years. The majority of the Inner Council, led by Maddie, chose to repress this knowledge and keep it secret. But now Maddie is gone. Several seats on our Council have changed hands in the last few years. As such, the Council came to a decision to try to develop this magic into technology we can control. Some feel it is the only way we can continue to compete with the corporate world."

"But you don't?" Rune asked, shivering at the thought of that kind of world.

"They are right," Maxamillion replied instead. "This discovery has been made. Now that the knowledge of how to make magic castable by a computer is out there, it makes it only a matter of time before someone else discovers the secret as well," Maxamillion said, pressing his advantage. "We beat that clock by combining what knowledges we have."

"I do not actually want to see this magical abomination come to being," Ursula said.

"But if it is inevitable, it would be better to be the ones in control of it," said Maxamillion.

Wizardress Ursula sighed. "You follow the logic of most of the Inner Council."

"I am proposing a joint venture, an equal partnership, my company and your Guild." Maxamillion offered his hand to her. "Do you see why I needed to know that you had this?" He indicated the circle. "My company has the technological components you are missing. We can help each other, if only you will agree to it."

"I may be the Chair of the Council, but I do not have the authority to unilaterally decide such a thing. You forget we are a democratic Guild, not an autocratic corporation."

"Then let me make my case. I will lay it all out for your entire council. Everything up front and open, as friends. Not enemies."

The Wizardress Ursula smiled reluctantly, before shaking her head. "I can't help feeling no matter which way I choose, I will come to regret this."

"Lady Ursula," a terse voice cut in from the doorway. If arrogance and condescension could be personified, it was well represented in Abraxas, smirking triumphantly at the door. "The Inner Council summons you." His smugness wavered however when his eyes darted to Rune and her more restored state. "The...Heir of the Magdalene is ordered there too."

"Thank you for letting me know, Abraxas. It was very kind of you to come personally tell us," Lady Ursula said as if his tone didn't bother her at all. Maybe it didn't. With supreme ease, the Wizardress turned to Maxamillion. "Would you escort me to the Council Chamber?"

"The corporate scum aren't invited," Abraxas sneered.

"They are, at my invitation," Ursula answered, smiling gently.

Abraxas's pale face began to splotch redder. "You can't!"

"Oh. And you have the power to stop me?" The Wizardress waited for an answer but it didn't come. Instead, the Fire Talent bowed his head to his superior and stepped back.

"Thank you, Abraxas. You have come far in controlling your passions," Lady Ursula stated.

"Wizardress," Maxamillion offered his arm, which she took easily.

"Oh, I meant to say earlier, you may simply refer to me as Lady Ursula," she said chattily, turning toward the door.

Abraxas swept out of the room ahead of her, just short of running down the hall.

"I'm surprised," Maxamillion commented. "I would think as Chair of the Inner Council, being summoned by it would be a faux pas?"

"My position is tenuous, made more so by my public association with you," she said as she passed through the doorway, Maxamillion keeping perfect step with her. Rune fell in behind, which was what felt natural to her.

In the hall, a group of guards, maybe they were the same group, waited silently. Two took point in front of Lady Ursula and Maxamillion. The rest eyed Rune with stone faces as she hesitated on the threshold. Then St. Benedict appeared next to her, offering her his own arm. She almost giggled at the sight of the gesture.

"Really?" she asked softly. "Like this is a garden party soiree?"

"You almost died five minutes ago. I feel it's the least I can do," he said, matching her softness. Feeling a wave of light-headedness, she took his arm, slipping her hand through the hole his elbow created, gripping it like it was a life preserver.

"Besides, I'm a classy guy," he added, louder as he guided her out into the hallway.

"Classy?" Rune glanced at him poignantly sideways as they trailed after their respective leaders. The guards predictably fell in behind them.

Ignoring the entourage, Rune made a show at looking at St. Benedict up and down appraisingly. His clothes were rumpled from the fight, never mind the black smudges of soot across his skin and slightly singed eyebrows. Despite all that, he was right. He was still pulling it off. "Classy indeed. I don't suppose I look much better?"

"You look like a warrior Wizard," he reported to her. "And you are a Lady of a House. Seems appropriate to me that I should escort you." He readjusted her hand on his elbow. Without breaking stride, she angled herself closer to the Saint, feeling his shoulder press a little more into hers. It was familiar and strange at the same time.

"St. Benedict, would I have known you before?"

"Before what?"

She readjusted her hand, laying it angled down his forearm properly, like she had been taught to do when being escorted by a man, instead of gripping the crook like a handle. "Before you became a Saint and I became an undercover Talent. You know, when we were pretending to be average hominals. Did we meet at a company soiree or social networking party? Did Justin ever introduce me to you?"

"I don't know. Probably." That answer didn't invite more conversation and Rune lapsed into the natural quiet of the hallways of the Magic Guild. Her thoughts kept going at full pitch.

"Do you think things would have been different? If we had met each other first?"

"What do you mean first?"

"My first soiree party was where I was introduced to Justin. What if we had met first and I don't know, you asked me to dance or something. Would I have been a girl you'd have asked to dance?"

At first she thought he wasn't going to answer.

"Sure," he grumbled out.

"Thanks." She smiled, "Saved my pride there." St. Benedict continued to stare straight ahead, his eyes far away.

"Though, I suppose you were already...." She tried to stop short. Would he want to talk about his lost wife?

"Already what?" he asked.

"Well, you and Anne. I don't know anything about you two. When you met or...." She felt so sick in her heart, she couldn't finish speaking. It felt wrong to talk about her. The set of his jaw told her it hurt him for her to even mention Anne. But Rune couldn't help wondering, if she had met St. Benedict first, before Justin, would her life have been different?

She knew it couldn't have been. Her parents had stayed with her every moment of that first soiree. Rune remembered the party well. Her parents had been invited to a conglomeration event, several companies, all affiliates to the larger corporation that would become Kodiak. They came together to intermingle, network, and in her case, matchmake.

Rune, then Anna, had been excited, dressed in an expensive, beautiful pink and cream dress that flowed around her like the petals of a rose. She had gone to the beauty salon with her mother, transforming her into a perfect doll. Lights festooned the walls of the hotel venue and it felt like she had stepped out of the real world into a Jane Austen novel, updated for modern times. Her mother had zeroed her in on Justin, slickly dressed in a fashionable three piece suit like her father had been wearing, his hair back in a low, princely ponytail. Later he showed her the suspenders he had been wearing underneath his jacket and she was in love from that moment on. He had danced with her, talked to her, enchanted her. Justin had only eyes for her that first night and she was swept away by the magic of it.

It had all been lies. He had apparently ducked away a few times during the evening to corner two different waitresses in the coat closet, or to hit a joint with some of his office buddies. Rune had been completely oblivious to it. Their marriage was arranged to smooth over connections between her father's smaller company and Justin's important position as the hot-shot, rising star computer programmer. Rune hadn't had eyes for anyone else at the time. Looking at St. Benedict now, could she have missed something so much better than Justin then?

"I'm trying to imagine what you would have looked like six years ago. Much the same right?"

"I don't know. I don't pay much attention to my appearance," St. Benedict said stiffly.

"Oh, okay," Rune scoffed. "So what are you officially? The Saint of lying?"

"What did you call me?" he asked.

"Oh, come on. Don't stiffen up. I was only teasing." But it was too late, the small bit of fun in an otherwise strenuous couple of days, was gone.

Ahead of them, Maxamillion said something that Ursula quietly laughed at. They were walking down one of the hallways in the Magic Guild Headquarters, this one a little more like what St. Benedict expected. Made of gray stone with occasional tapestries lining the walls. The lighting was more subdued from the floating orbs over carved hands. It gave the place the solemnity of a spiritual temple.

"St. Benedict?" Rune asked when he didn't respond. Even with her voice low, he swore the wide, expansive hallway made it echo slightly. "Come on, I didn't mean anything by it."

"Don't you have anything better to be thinking about right now?" St. Benedict asked.

"Yes. You're right. We're walking toward the heads of my guild, who I have been ignoring for months. Which is no big deal except that there is a very good chance that I'm going to be challenged for control of the House I've inherited in some sort of Wizard's duel I am drastically unprepared to undertake. So, yeah. Isn't it great I just went and pissed all of them off by possibly betraying them to a corporation? Unless that's irrelevant by the fact that they might already know who I really am and I'm about to be imprisoned anyway based on whatever they think I know about Justin. Any and all of that could be true and I could be walking toward my doom with every step. How could I possibly want to talk about anything else?"

Without her noticing, St. Benedict had slowed their steps, letting Lady Ursula and Maxamillion move well ahead of them. The guards behind them also stopped, but kept their distance.

"Do you want to run for it?" St. Benedict whispered intensely. Tearing her eyes away from the unknown middle distance, Rune looked into the wicked glint in the Saint's eye.

"Gods yes." Rune sighed in relief.

"Okay, give me a second to find an exit. You're getting pretty good at rolling with me when I improvise…."

"But we're not going to. Run, I mean." She squeezed his arm gently. "I've been running for six years. To quote every action movie I can think of: I'm done running." She smiled. "Thank you for being here, though. Being my friend through all this."

"I'm not your friend," St. Benedict said, his tongue feeling thick in his mouth.

"No, of course not. You'd only die for me out of professional courtesy."

A pained look crossed his face. "I am only here now because it is optimal to my mission."

"Yeah, that's true," she conceded lightly.

"See, not a hero after all," he agreed. "If I was a hero, I would grab you right now and escape. Or kept you safe in the first place so that you wouldn't even have to be here."

"That's very chauvinistically brave of you."

St. Benedict sighed. "I know, but it makes me feel better."

Down the way, Lady Ursula and Maxamillion had stopped in front of a set of white, French-style double doors. A pair of gray-clad guards stood on either side.

"What my Guild has in store for me is irrelevant. I am going to find Justin, no matter what it takes. It'll be the biggest Finding of my life. I'll ask you again, will you help me do that?"

"No." Why wouldn't she stop asking?

"Fine," Rune muttered, noting the doors, taking them in. "Why are all the biggest moments in my life always behind double doors?"

"Are they?"

"I don't know, maybe?"

A guard behind them cleared his throat suggestively. Together the semi-prisoners turned.

"So I'm on my own here then?" Was she asking him or herself?

"Yes."

"Okay. I can work with that," she said.

Chapter 14

"This is amazing!" Rune breathed, truly awestruck.

"I am so glad you said that," St. Benedict said, as awed as she was.

Rune started to laugh. "When I said garden party…I didn't know." St. Benedict looked at her from under his hat and she lifted her hands up in surrender. "No, seriously. This is a coincidence."

"It's like the Mad Hatter and Madame Pompadour booked the same venue," St. Benedict said. They both stood on the threshold of the door simply staring back and forth trying to take the space in.

It was indeed a garden party. Night had fallen, making the world above the trees dark as ink, heightened by the twinkling of floating jars filled with different colors of dancing light. The double doors opened out onto a stone terrace stolen off of some Ye Olde English manor house. Elegant people of all types and races were dressed in clothes that probably cost the same as one month of Rune's mortgage. They chatted in clusters, all having conversations they were genuinely enjoying. Waiters floated in and amongst them also dressed smartly in matching maroon vests and black slacks that gave uniformity to otherwise un-uniformed people. A few tables were set up along the railing of the terrace, highlighted by more warm lights coming from the garden beyond.

At the head of the stairs leading down into the garden, Lady Ursula and Maxamillion stopped. Everyone around them turned to salute and greet the Wizardress, which she returned with the grace and ease of a beloved politician. More cheers seemed to come from down below in the garden. That was enough to draw Rune forward, her eyes growing wider at the sight.

"It's like the in-between places," she said.

Sprawled out beneath the terrace was a mishmash of settings crammed next to each other, like someone had taken out all of the rooms of a dollhouse and set them out in no particular order on the ground. There was a grassy section, one side of it lapped by the edge of a pond that disappeared into a fountain where a variety of children were splashing and sailing small paper boats. One patch of space was an actual drawing room with cherry wood floors and light green, diamond patterned wallpaper on the only visible wall on one side and it was crowded with antique furniture. Immediately next to that was a group lounging around a large fire brazier while perched on carved log benches. There was a space piled with pillows and satin drapery straight out of the Arabian Nights, another space had various couches of different shapes and sizes, neon signs hanging from a tree above them.

There were many more pseudo-rooms, but at that point Rune became overwhelmed by the grandeur of it all. The different spaces seemed to go on for an acre, an uneven checkerboard of otherwheres all placed together. It didn't make sense to her mind, but the people moving back and forth through the spaces didn't even seem to note it as they passed through shimmering, translucent walls that only appeared when crossed.

For that matter, the people in attendance were all as varied as the rooms. Cat People of different tribes, a centaur or two, hominals, or at least hominal looking people moving amongst dryads and nyads. There were even a few Nagas as well as several more Rune couldn't quickly name. It was very much a similar mix of peoples that had been in the vendor room, only these folks obviously had money and power, displayed clearly for each other to see as they mingled.

Then Rune saw an area that made everything else fall away. "Is that the Lucky Devil?"

Nestled between a space-age styled bar serving glowing drinks and a grove of trees was the familiar worn, red, vinyl-covered booth and the acrylic statue of the Lucky Devil.

Lady Ursula and Maxamillion had descended the stairway, so Rune rushed down it as well, making a beeline for the booth.

"Ah, look who decided to show up," Alf groused predictably as she approached. He was sitting across from Lucky Devil, nursing some blue glowing drink in a really high flute.

"He's had three of those," Ally reported. She was sitting across from him next to Lucky Devil, no longer in her dog form, but dressed in a peach blouse that looked like it should have been worn by someone fifty years older.

"Best damn stuff on the planet," Alf muttered, his voice echoing a little as he stuck his nose into the flute to suck down the little bit at the bottom.

"Fae Moonshine," Rune recognized, taking an abandoned flute and sniffing it.

"Potent stuff?" St. Benedict asked, having followed her down.

"Anything with the word Fae in it is potent stuff. *Especially* on an empty stomach," she agreed, pulling the small, red, plastic basket with an untouched burger toward herself. There appeared to be a half dozen on the table. "I see they found you some clothes," Rune said before taking a huge, delicious bite.

"Hurray for me," Ally said, with all the dryness a teenager could muster.

Rune smiled. The kid's dampened enthusiasm was actually uplifting. Might also have been the burger. "I thought you all were being held prisoner or something?" She nudged another burger basket toward St. Benedict, who obliged himself.

Ally and Alf exchanged a look. "Well, we were told not to go anywhere until you showed up, so I guess kind of." Ally supplied with a shrug.

"Where is Elias?" Rune asked, feeling drunk with relief. Maybe things weren't as bad as she thought.

"He's over talking with the Inner Council, trying to pull your absentee ass out of the fire." Alf was practically slurring.

"Maybe you should lay off," Rune chided.

"Maybe you should shove your…self….up your own ass. My Lady," Alf said, his head swimming side to side before flumping down onto the table.

"Alf!" Ally exclaimed. A few people glanced over at the distinct flump sound. A few small, token cheers went up but nothing else happened. Rune slid the glass away from her bar manager's limp hand as if that would destroy the evidence of how he had shamed himself.

"You haven't had any, correct?" she asked her youngest retainer.

"No, thanks. I know better than to get stupid like that," the kid said indignantly.

St. Benedict chuffed a laugh as he took up the bottle on the table and swallowed back a taste. "Hmm, not bad." Then pointedly offered it to Rune, before turning to look out across the strange crowd, crossing his arms and leaning against the table.

"What?" Ally asked, very concerned by the exchange of smiles Rune and St. Benedict traded.

"Nothing. You're wiser than all of us grown-ups, Ally," Rune said but she didn't even attempt to suppress the indulgent smile before she took her sip of the cool, refreshing Fae spirit, leaving a trailing feeling of sunshine in her chest.

Ally crossed her arms. "I don't like it when you make fun of me."

"Keep an eye on him. If he wakes up, make him drink a gallon of water. Do not let anyone try to sell you a hangover charm."

"Feeling fortified there, big stuff?" St. Benedict asked.

"Oh, yes. I'm ready to go tell all the big wigs where they can stick it." Rune drawled her words a little and even followed her declaration with a tiny burp. "Sorry, that was pathetic. I was hoping for something a lot more robust."

St. Benedict's eyes twinkled.

Rune turned back to the party, scanning around. "Where is Elias and this Inner Council?"

"Over there, by the big tree." Ally pointed with a finger.

Across the way was the widest tree Rune had ever seen. It was a singular fat cylinder, like the tree had forgotten to grow up and instead invested all of its growing outward. Beneath the lowest branches, which were only maybe eight feet off the ground, was an oval table. A dozen people sat around it, but Rune had a difficult time making out any faces.

Moving closer didn't help either. It was like her mind was simply unable to recognize or register the faces beyond. Rune realized as she stopped in front of it, that the barrier floating around the table was stronger than the others, wavering like the shimmer of a heat wave.

"You need to wait with the other Houses until you're summoned." A voice stopped her before she could cross into the barrier.

She turned into the glaring face of Abraxas. The younger man sat on an old, rustic barrel, snapping his fingers to make a flame burn on the end, then putting it out by crushing it in his palm, before repeating the process.

"Actually, I've already been summoned. Remember? You were the one who summoned me," Rune replied.

"You've been summoned, but not this Talentless dreg."

"You kiss your mother with that mouth?" the Saint asked, then widened his smile. "Your sister?"

The fire between Abraxas's fingertips flared higher before the young man could cover his emotions. St. Benedict smiled and Rune rolled her eyes.

"Did you see that? You just made this lovely Lady roll her equally lovely eyes at me," St. Benedict said, directing his chide at Abraxas.

"I think you have earned your equal share of the eye roll," Rune muttered.

"How have I offended you, my Lady?" St. Benedict asked with a faux-Old English air.

"Abraxas may be a jerk, but a male measuring contest is always eye-roll worthy."

"Hmm, indeed," the Saint agreed with a chuckle.

She regarded the squiggly barrier once more. "I think we just walk in," she said. When he didn't respond she glanced over at her not-partner. He was staring at the barrier as if he expected it to eat him, trying to keep his nonchalant mask in place.

"Fine. Go in then. The sooner you crash and burn, the

sooner I get your House." Abraxas snarled as he snapped a final time and stood up.

"Indeed, Rune, please enter," Lady Ursula's voice called, distorted by the magical barrier. "You too, Abraxas."

Rune was already stepping through when she remembered at the last second to grab St. Benedict's hand to pull him with her. Once she had entered, it was very likely he would have been rejected by the barrier otherwise.

Rune was met with a line of eyes, all staring and appraising her at once, making the hair on the back of her neck stand on end. The urge to retreat into something small and unobtrusive was powerful. Rune knew exactly how a small mouse felt when confronted with a room full of cats. In fact, that was the strangest part. She stood in the hollowed out middle of the table but wasn't sure how she had passed through as there seemed no way in or out of the wooden circle. Of course, that was obviously the point. A magical being could be easily contained within a magic circle by magic users such as these, especially if the inner edge of the table was already inscribed like this one was.

"So this is her?" a male voice asked, so old and gruff that Rune assumed it came from the wizard with a short, sharp, white beard, his beady blue eyes contemptuous of her as he leaned back in his chair in that way older men did that was really gross but they didn't care.

"Her?" Another woman dressed in green sneered. The female Pantherwoman next to her rolled a high pitch snarl and laid her ears back as she took notes on a pad on the table.

Feeling desperately alone, Rune realized she had let St. Benedict's hand go. She checked over her should to assure herself St. Benedict was still standing there beside her, but he wasn't. Just on the periphery, she saw he was standing next to Maxamillion, his face stony, impassive and cold, his hands clasped behind his back. Maxamillion had an equally impassive face as he sat at his own small table with a serving of wine and a chair a short way from the circle. The CEO's legs were crossed in that elegant way well-dressed men had, appearing both noble and completely at ease. Like a Roman senator waiting to watch her be torn apart by lions.

"State your name girl," an accented voice ordered, snapping Rune's attention back to the aforementioned lions.

"Rune Leveau," then added, "Heir to the Magdalene," for good measure.

There were more scoffs.

"And you are only a Talent, is that correct?" the accented voice asked, and Rune realized it was coming from the Pantherwoman.

A Toad-like being piped up from across the table. "I cannot believe we are even entertaining this."

Lady Ursula slammed a metal ball hard onto the table top to cut off the growing discontented noise that was coming from all around. "I understand your concerns, Mathus, but we must follow procedures before we can address them."

"It is not simply a matter of procedures. Nothing is going according to procedures!" the Toad-like person called Mathus said. Flanking him was a young woman, who looked and dressed very similarly to Abraxas. "It's the same…crap, excuse my language, that Maddie always pulled. And you let her. This," he gestured a hand at Rune and she decided the speaker was human. "This is the Heir to one of our most crucial Houses. We barely have a standing as it is in this city and one of our greatest Wizards leaves us with this as her replacement?"

"Greatest Wizards? I've never heard you talk about Maddie in anything even close to complimentary, Mathus," a witch, guessing from her owl familiar sitting on the back of her chair, said, her voice laughing.

That's when the name rang a bell with Rune. Mathus. She had met the shaman a few times. The Toad-like appearance was caused by burns from a bombing attack he had survived years ago. It had been a horrific hate crime that had been caused by a racist group of three hominal men. Mathus and his wife had been the only survivors, and Mathus only barely. The scarring had burned not only his face, but also his soul, a testament to his sacrifice to protect his beloved, who had escaped completely unharmed. Even now, healing magic or plastic surgery would do very little to rebuild more of his face than it already had. As much as he had been a rival and critic of Maddie's, Rune could never bring herself to truly dislike him.

Didn't mean she really liked him either.

"There is a great difference between wanting to protect the practical, ancient rules of our Guild from those amongst us seeking to further their personal agenda and not having any respect for those individuals. Maddie was a brilliant Wizardress. Brilliant." He stabbed his stubbed, nailless finger onto the table as if he was pinning the word to it. "And yet for all her brilliance, she takes a Talentless nobody as her Heir?"

"My Talent...." Rune started to say, but Mathus cut her off as if she hadn't even tried.

"The fact that we even allowed it was a disgrace to our institution. The corporations out there are laughing at us. They are laughing and yet we've even invited one of them into our midst! Into our Inner Council!" He gestured emphatically at Maxamillion, who calmly nodded in acknowledgement to the rest of the Council, but said nothing. "This is the legacy of the Magdalene. Chaos left in her wake! And a simple non-Talent hominal child left in her stead. It all feels like a practical joke."

Lady Ursula crashed the ball onto the table again. Twice. It started to crackle with small forks of electricity within. "I believe Madame Pooka had the floor." She nodded to the Pantherwoman and Mathus sat back in his chair.

"My apologies for breaking order, Madame Pooka," he said, indicating with his hand for her to proceed.

Madame Pooka sat upright and stretched down her spine in a cat-like show of indifference common among her people, before repeating her question to Rune.

"My Talent is in Finding things," Rune answered.

"Excuse me?" Madame Pooka asked, squinting down at Rune. Mathus made a disgusted noise.

"Mathus, please. You've been warned," Lady Ursula chided. He flapped a hand at Lady Ursula in acknowledgement.

"Rune," Lady Ursula began before anyone else could speak, "please describe to us what a Finding Talent is."

"There is no such thing!" A Naga male growled, his body whipping back and forth in place as he spoke, forcing him to adjust his square glasses.

"It is not unheard of for new Talents to arise!" Madame

Pooka growled, the fur on the back of her neck half-rising. "Will you please allow me to document these proceedings without further interruption?" All around the circle nodded and sat back in their chairs. "Now." Madame Pooka flexed the claws of her hands twice, which seemed to settle her down. "Now. Please state the Circle under which your Talent falls. Elemental, Mental, Body, or Soul."

Silence stretched out. Slowly, menacingly, Madame Pooka raised her green-yellow eyes to stare down at Rune.

"I...don't really know." It was the only answer Rune could give.

At that Madame Pooka broke her pen and the room erupted as the entire Inner Council began speaking at once. Rune stood trapped in the middle of it. She tried to look over at St. Benedict but he wouldn't make eye contact with her. Instead he was focusing on the chaos, assessing it. Maxamillion was impassive as ever. It was Abraxas who met her eye. He smiled a Cheshire Cat smile ear to ear and then slowly, with hooded eyes, slid a finger across his throat in the universal gesture for 'you're dead.' His master, Mathus, was also not participating in the hullabaloo. *He* was sitting back and letting it play out while he sipped something green from a glass.

"I see you're bringing down the house already," a voice spoke to Rune over her shoulder.

"Elias, at last!" Mathus declared, now standing, his booming voice cutting off all conversation where Ursula's crashing electrical ball had failed. He held out a hand to the beautiful young man and Elias stepped forward to shake it gladly.

"Nice to see you, Mathus. You're looking well."

The shaman waved off Elias's words. "I'm getting old and you are as young as ever. I am relieved to see you, boy. I think we all are." He smiled and gestured to the circle where several heads were bobbing. It was a like a cloud had been lifted at the sight of the Wizard. "Now we can set this whole matter to rest." Cold eyes returned to Rune, and she bit the inside of her cheek to keep from looking away. "We can all assume you've come to challenge this insolent child for the Head of your family's House."

"Nope."

Elias said the words so cheerfully, Mathus nodded at first in delight until he finally processed them.

"Excuse me?" the shaman finally asked.

"I am sorry to disappoint the Inner Council." Elias began to walk around the inside of the circle, throwing his words out so all could hear him. "I have already sworn retainership to my Lady here and she has accepted. Rune is the Head of the House of the Magdalene." He practically had to shout the last part as the roar of the table was trying to drown him out.

Bang, bang, bang, went Ursula's sphere.

"Are you mad?!" Mathus croaked.

"Not at all." Elias smiled. "At least not in ways that matter to this noble Council."

"She is a Talentless girl!" Mathus shouted, stabbing a finger at Rune. "Do you even know what a House is?"

Rune felt the blood drain out of her face. She wasn't a hundred percent sure. "It's a place…of power."

"Magic. It is a place of great magic. Enough magical power to burn a city or build it. The cracks of our world where the magic pours in must be guarded and managed for the sake of all of us. Would you have a toddler running a nuclear plant?" Mathus continued to stab his finger with every point he made, while he preached to the members of the Inner Council. "And worse than that even, she has no legitimate Talent. No true magic!"

Abruptly, a wind kicked up in front of Mathus, billowing his tan robes like he was in a mini-cyclone. Sputtering, he didn't see Elias until the young wizard grasped Mathus's pointing finger with his own long, beautiful digits.

"Please do not point at my Lady," Elias said very politely. A grimace of fear flitted across Mathus's eyes before he narrowed them into hardness again. His poor burned face revealed nothing, nor could it. He withdrew his finger.

Elias stepped away, replacing his hands behind his back. "Also, do not refer to her as a girl, Mathus. It's the twenty-first century. We call twenty-six year old females, women." Her retainer turned toward Rune and gave her a wink.

"You expect us to accept this...woman as an equal to this Council of Houses?" The pointy bearded man beside Mathus asked, while his colleague resumed his seat.

"Yes, I do," Elias said. His walk around the circle completed with him taking up the space behind Rune's left shoulder.

"She is Talentless," the woman in green said.

"Oh, is *that* the problem?" Elias started to laugh. "Because you all think she's Talentless?"

"Elias, please. If what you have told me is true, then would you reveal to all of us why you have so much confidence in your Lady," Lady Ursula encouraged, sounding a little tired.

"My apologies, Madame Chair. And my apologies to you, my Lady Rune. I had hoped we would be able to discuss this privately and I am truly kicking myself right now that I didn't explain it earlier today, but I am not very good with revealing secrets when there are such important summons from the Magic Guild." He cleared his throat. "You are right. Rune is not a Talent. She is a Magi."

There was a small, stunned silence.

"There are no Magi," a new small, stereotypically cute voice said from somewhere behind Rune.

"Of course there are you idiot," a harsher voice said.

"Indeed, there are Magi in the world. I happen to be one as well, as some on this council already know," Elias confirmed.

"Ah, I see. Of course." Mathus leaned back and rubbed his stubby hand over his face.

"How?" the woman in green asked.

"Her name *is* Leveau," someone else stated.

"Isn't she only an adopted daughter of Maddie? That does not make her a blood relative of the family," the woman in green argued.

"My name is Anna Masterson," Rune stated, the first words she was able to get in finally. Without meaning to, her voice thrummed with power, forcing all eyes back on her, but it had actually been worse when everyone was talking about her instead of to her. "My name is Anna Masterson," she said again. She turned to Mathus and more specifically Abraxas. "And you knew that when you cast fire at me the other night."

"What is the significance of her name?" another small, squeakier voice asked.

"Abraxas' special project," a hushed voice beside the squeaky voice answered.

"Oh!"

"You are, in front of this entire Council, confirming that you are the wife of Justin Masterson," Mathus asked very carefully.

"Yes," Rune said, lifting her head up high.

"What does this have to do with her being a Magi?"

"Nothing. Anna Masterson had no relationship with the Magdalene or the Leveau family," Abraxas piped up a little too quickly and very much out of turn. Mathus hushed at him.

"My mother's last name was Leveau before her marriage. I am Maddie's great niece. Elias is my cousin." It felt so good to claim it, to say it out loud. Mathus nodded, while the rest of the Council chattered.

"I have seen one of the signs that what is being stated here is true," Lady Ursula said.

"And were you going to share this with us?" Mathus asked.

"I was as soon as order of procedure was completed," Lady Ursula said pointedly. "That proved to be more difficult than usual."

Mathus's face went more toad-like. "Then by all means, let us finish proper order."

"Madame Pooka, I believe we can list Lady Rune as a Magi for now and forgo any specifics beyond that." The Pantherwoman nodded, and they exchanged a few more technical points that Rune couldn't follow.

Instead, she leaned back to whisper to her cousin. "I don't know what a Magi is! Do they all know what a Magi is?"

"Mathus does. Madame Pooka of course, but her Talent is encyclopedic knowledge-based, so there is very little she doesn't know. Lady Verde, probably. The rest might have heard rumors of a Magi but I would highly doubt any of them really know what one is. It's supposed to be a secret, but every few decades it gets 'revealed,'" he said using air quotes, "and then slips back into mystery again."

"And I am this special, chosen one thing?"

"More like a chosen five thousandth one, but that's still mathematically special."

"Ok, so...when are you going to tell me what a Magi is?!"

"Are you freaking out?"

"Just a skosh, yeah." He chuckled at that, which was getting a bit annoying considering the blender of emotions Rune was feeling. "To explain it properly will take too much time."

"Then explain it improperly." She was really getting tired of his dodginess.

Elias heaved a sigh as he scanned the room. "Okay, here's a frame of reference I guess. Do you see these remaining Inner Council members? Each of them is considered one of the most magically powered beings in the world."

"Yeah," Rune said, letting her eyes drift over her Guild's leaders.

"You alone blow them all collectively out of the water."

Rune's eyes went wide.

"No, this is crap!" Abraxas voice cawed, bringing all attention to the slight man standing beside Mathus. The two men had been talking softly as well, but the younger man was now shouting instead. "She's not worthy! You said so."

"There is a procedure we must follow, Abraxas," Mathus tried to say but the younger man waved him off.

"I challenge you!" Abraxas declared, pointing a finger at Rune like he was going to blast her with fire right then and there. "If none of you lazy, old farts are going to do something about this, then I will. Rune whatever your name is. I challenge you for your House."

"Abraxas stand down," Mathus tried to order.

Instead, Elias step forward and bowed gentlemanly from the waist. "We accept your challenge, sir."

The slight man seemed surprised, but he screwed up his chin and nodded. Mathus stood and gripped Abraxas's upper arm hard, stiffly shifting the younger man to the side.

Lady Ursula cracked her orb on the table in finality. "The challenge is witnessed."

"What!?" Rune asked.

Elias turned around, leaning in to whisper, "It's fine. Don't worry about it right now. We'll talk later."

"Oh great. We'll talk later, so reassuring," Rune snarked. "This is all happening rather fast and I am not even sure what is happening."

"That concludes the business of the Magdalene House for now. Lady Rune, if you would be so kind as to give Madame Pooka a few more minutes to finish taking your information for Guild records, we would greatly appreciate it."

"If it's not too much trouble!" Madame Pooka growled, which seemed more for the rest of the Council.

The circle's mood shifted again. Papers were rustling and aides moved forward to refresh drinks, or in Madame Pooka's case, pens.

"Is that it? Are we done?" Rune asked. Elias nodded.

An aide appeared beside them. "If you would come this way, Lady Rune." A space in the table that hadn't been there before opened up and to Rune's surprise she watched another person walk past the gap, appearing on the other side instantaneously as if the space didn't really exist.

"But what about the Masterson Files?" Rune turned back.

"Rune, our audience is done for now…." Elias tried to say, but Rune took several steps back into the circle.

"What about the Masterson Files?" She repeated loudly. "What about attacking my home in the middle of the night?! What about the fact that you have my husband's research, which I spent six months of my life being tortured over, in your basement? Where the hell is Justin?!"

Chapter 15

The room was dead silent as everyone stared at Rune, who was panting hard having just screamed her voice out.

"Mathus, Pooka, Verde. Everyone else, please leave," Lady Ursula ordered.

"Lady Chair, is this not a matter for the entire Inner Council?" The pointy bearded old man started to say, but Shaman Mathus laid a hand on his shoulder.

"The fewer voices in this conversation, the better. The Tradition faction will be represented by my voice."

"Lady Ursula, I would like to request to stay as well. This pertains to my petition," Maxamillion piped in, standing by his little table.

"Lady Chair, I object. If this is not going to be in front of the full Council...." the pointy bearded man started again. Lady Ursula raised her hand. A wisp of smoke emitted from it, swirling into an orb shape. Rune marveled at her ability to create a recording spell without needing a crystal to anchor it.

"I will make this meeting observable to the full Council. It has been established that we must set these matters pertaining to the Magdalene House and the special project to a smaller committee. Nothing will be decided without the full Council's vote. Do I have a second?"

"Second," Mathus declared and that was mostly the end of it. The rest of the Council filed out with their aides and Rune was left with Elias beside her.

"Where were you? I came over here because Ally said you were here, and then you weren't," she hastily whispered the minute it seemed safe to do so, amidst the hubbub of the Council leaving.

Elias gave a strained laugh. "I ran into someone just outside and I saw you go past too late to catch you. Sorry."

"Who?"

"It was an ex. And not the good kind. I disengaged as fast as possible to get to you, my Lady."

"Don't call me my Lady, I am freaking out right now. This is all going by too fast and I am reacting, not acting, which is usually how people get into trouble!" she hissed.

Maxamillion sauntered up to Rune, his hands in his suit pants pockets, St. Benedict trailing behind him looking odd without a smile on his face.

"You do know how to move things along," Maxamillion said, appreciatively. "I have been trying to talk Lady Ursula into even granting me this meeting for months and not only did your little stunt downstairs get me the meeting...."

"My name is Elias Leveau, by the way. Nice to meet you." Her cousin held out his hand to Maxamillion to be shook, which the elegant man obliged, serenely unperturbed.

"Maxamillion Corinthe, CEO of the Corinthe Corporation."

"Ah, and he belongs to you?" Elias indicated St. Benedict standing behind him.

Maxamillion double blinked. "Excuse me?"

"We all belong to someone," Elias said.

"Are you all right?" St. Benedict asked Rune while Elias distracted Maxamillion, the Saint's voice rumbling softly as he tried to be discrete with the question.

"I am as all right as I was before walking into this room. So...kind of?"

"Remember, you don't need them." His eyes intensified slightly as he let those words sink in. "They need you."

She could barely breathe. What he said made no sense. They needed her? How?

"Please come and join us," Lady Ursula called. Before Rune could utter more than an incomprehensible peep, St. Benedict walked past her, his shoulder brushing against her arm, to rejoin a stiff faced Maxamillion.

The space had been changed. The large, circular table was gone and in its place were couches of three different varieties placed in a horseshoe shape around an oval coffee table that Rune's mother would have stolen if it would have fit into her purse. All of it happened without anyone in the small group noticing.

Three aides remained in the space, but Abraxas was not one of them and was nowhere to be seen. Instead, his sister was serving a large steaming mug to Mathus. Before he sipped it, she added a vial of some red liquid that made the top billow smoke like a dirty campfire. The other aide set a tray of cookies and vegetables on the table while the third set three chairs at the end of the horseshoe. Ursula sat in the middle of the inner most couch, like a butterfly perched on the velvety blue covered, well-stuffed cushions. She indicated with a hand toward the chairs.

"They couldn't spring for a fourth couch?" St. Benedict muttered under his breath. He and Maxamillion exchanged glances and headed over to the new configuration.

"You're doing really well, keep it up," Elias whispered to Rune as he led her to the far right couch.

"Shouldn't I sit on one of the chairs?" she asked, laying a hand on the one she meant to take next to St. Benedict, when Elias had begun pushing her toward the crimson couch.

"You're the Head of a House. Sit on the damn couch," he said as he placed her upon it. "Would you like some tea, my Lady?"

"Yes, please," Rune answered in mock primness, feeling like she had just been forcibly enrolled into a magic charm school and her cousin had been possessed by the ghost of butlers past.

"First off, Lady Rune. I would like to apologize for my apprentice's part on the attack on your House. I only became aware of it after the fact and am prepared to compensate you in tribute after the challenge is settled," Mathus said.

"Oh. Thank you," Rune said, nodding. Then, "Why after the challenge is settled?"

"Well, it's a moot point if Abraxas becomes the Head of your House, isn't it?" Mathus said to his mug.

Rune double blinked at that. "I suppose you have a point. But then tell me, why did he come to my alley in the first place?"

"Let's get to business," Lady Ursula said, cutting off any further back and forth. Lady Verde sat next to Mathus, while Madame Pooka curled up on the end of Lady Ursula's couch, furthest from Rune.

Tea appeared under Rune's nose. She took it, but was surprised when her obliging cousin took up the space behind her instead of on the couch next to her. Lady Ursula seemed surprised as well, but chose not to say anything as she set her orb onto the coffee table.

"Thank you for allowing me to have this opportunity to finally meet with you," Maxamillion said, starting the conversation.

"Yes, a grand privilege isn't it?" Mathus hooded his eyes. "You not only get to destroy us from the inside, you get a front row seat to watch it happen."

"I hope that isn't the case," Maxamillion said, then thanked the aide that brought him a brown drink in a low-ball glass.

"Why are we entertaining this Prince of Finance?" Lady Verde asked.

"We need to discuss again the project Abraxas is currently running," Lady Ursula said.

"Yes and you've invited them," Mathus indicated Maxamillion and St. Benedict. "Since it's clear our little secret is out of the bag, I would like to answer Lady Rune's question."

Lady Ursula nodded.

"As to what Abraxas wanted in your alley two nights ago, from what he has told me, he has come to a standstill in his research. He had heard the rumors, as many of us have, that you, Lady Rune, would have the answers. After your confession to the Inner Council, I can now see why he thought that."

"He didn't tell you my secret?" Rune asked, genuinely surprised.

"Abraxas has difficulty opening up, even to me, his mentor."

"My question is, why didn't you come to the Magic Guild for help when the incident happened, but instead allied yourself with this corporation for aid and succor?" Lady Verde asked. "You certainly had plenty of time."

Rune looked up at the witch over her tea, finishing her

current sip before answering. "When I was attacked the other night, I had little choice in allies. Fortunately for me, St. Benedict," she nodded at the Saint, "owed me a debt and pulled me out of there before I was killed."

Raising a hand, Maxamillion added, "I helped too."

"It's because of both of them I'm still alive," Rune agreed.

"But you didn't contact your Guild for assistance after the fact?" Mathus questioned, steepling his stubby fingers.

Rune thought about throwing Abraxas back in Mathus's face, but she also didn't think it was in her best interests to keep using that as her go-to weapon. She needed allies right now, not enemies. "This is after the fact. The attack happened two nights ago and I'm here now! I came as soon as I was able, to ask you for assistance. Right now. This is me doing it." It wasn't exactly the truth, but it wasn't a lie either.

"You are a very bold young woman to speak to us this way," Lady Verde said. She did not mean it as a compliment.

"Are you unaware how precarious your position is?" Madame Pooka agreed.

Rune knew. Of course she did. Hence why she hadn't come to them for help.

"Bravery isn't the absence of fear, only the belief that something else is more important," Rune said.

"And what is that something else?" Mathus asked bemusedly.

Rune's mind went blank at the question. Or rather it flooded with so many possible answers that it was essentially blank. What was the most important reason she was doing this? She thought of the magic circle down the hallway and its implications for her entire people. She thought of Justin and her desire to find him. That had nothing to do with her Guild and they probably wouldn't accept that answer. She thought about her bar and Maddie's legacy. It was all of them. All those reasons and probably others she hadn't paused long enough to unpack yet. What could she clearly say in this moment?

She glanced over at Maxamillion, who noted it. "The Masterson Files..." she started to say, stabbing at the shape of the idea in her head, "...and who controls them." All four Council people sat in gluttonous silence with severe faces.

"Yes, I believe that is my cue," Maxamillion said. The elegant man scooted forward on his chair, taking the stage as it were. Not really minding, Rune leaned back against the couch and squeezed the cushions with her hands on either side of her legs. She wanted this to be over.

"The Masterson Files," Maxamillion began. "I believe it is very safe to say that everyone present knows what they are and what they mean to all of our futures." The uncomfortable silence stretched, but it didn't deter Maxamillion at all.

"St. Benedict," Maxamillion gestured at his subordinate.

With a flash, St. Benedict's augmentations flared to life, bluing out his eyes. Opening his palm, a holographic replica of the ritual room's floor floated, miniaturized above his hand. He gestured and expanded it to cover the top of the coffee table.

"It appears you have acquired the magical component. We at the Corinthe Corporation have a portion of the technical code Masterson used to combine these two things. Now, from where we stand, we can simply combine this piece with what we already possess. This leaves you out of any discoveries we make. Essentially you'd get nothing."

"*This* is your proposal!?" Mathus declared, his face splotching in the places it still could get red.

"No. My proposal is…."

"What makes you think that we would ever let you leave this room alive with that?" Lady Verde interrupted, her voice flat and dark.

Maxamillion smiled. Without breaking eye contact with the witch, he asked, "St. Benedict?"

"Transmission is complete," the Saint reported. "All files have been uploaded to our servers."

Rune double blinked. He was lying. She knew it, though she couldn't put a finger on why she thought that. As if feeling the weight of her eyes, his own seemed to shift to her for a second, though it was hard to tell for sure without his irises, before returning to the game of chess the others seemed to be playing.

In fact, the four other magic users became very visibly agitated, except Lady Ursula.

"How dare you sit there and…." Mathus began, but Lady

Ursula leaned forward and set a beautiful hand on his stubby knee.

"Let him finish, please," Lady Ursula requested gently.

"How can you be so calm about this?" Lady Verde asked, whipping her fingers about her person, adjusting creases and ribbons on her robe in a sequence only she understood.

"Oh, I see. Maddie's madness didn't die with her." Mathus was practically spitting the words. "Seems our Chair is willing to sell us out to the corporations."

"Would it be better to say I want to sell out to you?" Maxamillion leaned back in his chair, now that his die had been cast. "I want us, the Corinthe Corporation and the Magic Guild, to officially merge." There was more stunned silence. Rune could practically hear the thoughts of the older magic users. She was sure they felt the same sense of recoil at the idea as she did.

"For what sort of benefit?" Madame Pooka asked, narrowing her cat eyes to the tiniest of slits, her large triangular ears dipping backward toward flattening. Still, the question seemed to be the crack of opening Maxamillion needed.

"How many Alderman seats on the City Council does the Magic Guild still hold in the city?" he asked instead of answered.

"Three," Lady Verde answered, her tongue rolling the *r*.

"And poised to lose all three in the next round of city elections." Maxamillion held up a hand to silence any expected argument, but it didn't come, at least if you didn't count the looks of death he was getting. "Corinthe Corporation is in a unique position in the politics of the corporate world. As a young company, we hold no seats on the City Council, but we also are not affiliated with any larger conglomerate, so we have no representation there either. And you have three seats."

"Three seats, yes. Three seats out of fifty to represent over three hundred thousand magic users, magic supporters, and their families in a city of over three million and no coalition since most of our past allies have been absorbed to become corporate citizens. Never mind the state or the federal governments," Mathus concluded dryly.

"All of that can change. Ally with us, and we can change everything," Maxamillion promised. "Admit it, the Magic

Guild can no longer compete with the corporations in this city. They have poached too many of your own for their 'magic departments' and now have started replacing magical services entirely with technological ones and soon—no, in fact, it's already happened hasn't it? The revolution of automated magic is dawning, ladies and gentleman. The question is who is in control of it when it happens. The Kodiak Corporation," he paused a moment to let the name sink in, "…they are willing to do anything, destroy anything, hurt anyone to achieve that end. How many Aldermen have you lost to Kodiak alone? There was a time when this city was the capital of the magical world. Now it might as well be Detroit."

"You leave Detroit out of this!" Mathus barked. Rune quirked an eyebrow, wondering what that outburst was about. What about Detroit? It seemed to hit a target for Mathus and she made a mental note, that she promptly forgot, to check it out later.

"This is what you are willing to sell us all out for, Ursula?" Mathus turned to address the Chair.

"Mathus, when you forced the vote to begin researching the magical anomaly instead of leaving it buried and safe in our archives, I warned you then that you were opening us up to dangers that we as an organization were not strong enough to face."

"So you invited those dangers right through our front door?!"

Lady Ursula stood, gesturing a hand at Rune. "One of our own has been attacked, not once, but twice. And she did not feel safe enough or confident enough in our resources to come to us for help. That is a failure on our parts that I think we all need to acknowledge. Regardless of how you feel about her or her questionable status in our organization, she is very much one of us. Maddie was one of us." Lady Ursula's voice went up another pitch. "We lost Maddie. We almost lost Rune while you let your apprentices play mad scientist. We stand on the brink of losing everything to the corporate wolves with no more backup plans. Mr. Corinthe here is the only one willing to throw us a rope. We have a choice right now, in this moment, we can grab it or we can drown, but please do not imagine that there is a third option."

"There is a third option," Mathus growled.

"You said yourself, your apprentices are at a standstill. The corporations, they are coming for us. They are coming to take away what little we have left. We are standing on the surface sand of an hourglass that is pouring out faster than we can see and the second we see proof of it, it will be too late, we'll already be sucked down the hole." Lady Ursula paused a moment and gestured to Rune again. "If you would like another analogy, we already have our canary. Rune…Anna Masterson," she swallowed, "six years ago, was dragged out of her bed in the middle of the night, incarcerated without legal protections, tortured for the information you have down in that ritual room. Maddie's kin. It's only because she *was* Maddie's kin that she is even sitting here right now, alive and whole. We did nothing. You of all people should be the first to understand the significance of that."

Rune didn't realize her hands were shaking until Elias laid his own on her shoulder. He didn't look at her but the gesture was enough to steady her. She looked back and caught Mathus tracking over her face. Understanding haunted his eyes. It was a kind of understanding that only those who have survived could ever articulate because there were no words that would ever paint a clear enough picture. The older shaman stood up and began pacing behind his chair.

"So Lady Ursula, you have become our own personal Oberon!" Lady Verde growled, again dwelling on the *r* of the fallen Faerie King's title. "Selling us out to benefit yourself, because frankly that is what it looks like to me." The witch then turned to Rune. "I don't know you or anything about you. Do you have more proof that what you say is true, that you are indeed this Anna Masterson who seems so very important and consequential to the events of the world? I find it terribly convenient that you, a mere nothing of note, would appear out of nowhere, claim to be a Magi of all things, promising us the keys to the kingdom and expect us to accept it!"

"I'm not making any claims…." Rune started, her heart hammering in her ears.

"So tell us then, where *is* your husband?" Lady Verde asked, with a poisonous tone. She again didn't wait for an answer. "After six months of work, Mathus, your apprentices are nowhere near understanding what bastardized magic they have down there, maybe they should talk to the man himself?"

"I am looking for him."

Lady Verde double blinked. "Excuse me?"

Rune slid forward on her seat, planting both feet on the ground as she held her clasped hands before her. "You asked me a question. You asked me where is my husband. I am looking for him. And I can't tell you if the Masterson Files are real or how he did it. I can't tell you why I'm even in this mess. I don't know. There is a lot I don't know. I do know that Kodiak tortured me over the very information you are currently grilling me for and I don't have it, then or now. All I could do is…. I know that I survived. It happened and it can never unhappen and it is now a defining part of my life." Rune stopped herself, the thickness in her throat making it hard to talk. Anyway, her thoughts were getting off the point. "I don't need you to find him, really. It's obvious now that you know about as much as I do and here I was coming to you for help. I don't need any of you at the end of the day, do I? I will find him. I will get the answers to *my* questions. So if you want the answers to *your* questions, because they might be in the same place, then you can work with me. But do or do not and stop playing these meaningless political games with me."

The ringing silence dragged out long enough to make Rune rethink everything she just said.

"I'm with you." Maxamillion said, cutting the silence as he nodded. He turned to Lady Verde. "And it is uncanny that you should mention the Oberon, because our two pieces combined will not be enough to untangle the mess that Masterson, in his genius, created."

"Genius," Mathus scoffed.

"Yes, in a matter of minutes, he had broken up his code and transmitted it via an audio pulse system. He turned his code into sound, a tactic no one even considered as a possibility when he was taken. The *fact* that he succeeded is the only reason we can even have this conversation and the only reason the Magic Guild still exists. It's also why only our two pieces will not be enough. There are more alliances we will have to make."

"Who?" Madame Pooka asked.

"Us," a new voice answered.

Chapter 16

Sitting on the edge of Rune's couch, right next to her in fact, was the foxy Faerie from the vendor room who had repaired Rune's belt. She had her black top hat pushed back a little more to reveal her eyes, which were yellow-brown and unearthly. Her black-clad legs were crossed and she leaned her loosely clasped fingers on her knee as if she had been there the whole time. To her one side, her fox tail flicked happily, giving away her excitement at sitting there. The reaction from the members of the Inner Council to her sudden appearance was almost comical, which seemed to delight the Fae even more.

"Oh my, oh my. The itchy witches and buzzard wizards don't know what to do when someone just walks through their wards and barriers. Dear, oh dear," the Fae tsked, shaking her head slowly.

"You certainly know how to make an entrance, Lady Wilde," Maxamillion noted, switching his own crossed legs as the only sign that he was taken by surprise as well.

Lady Verde sputtered. "How did she get in here, our magics…."

"She is a lady-in-waiting of the Faerie Court. She is more than capable of penetrating our defenses…with an invitation," Madam Pooka said evenly.

"A Fae! You invited a member of the Faerie Court here in the Magic Guild!" Mathus bellowed, his face going splotchy again.

"Actually, you did that," the Fae said, lifting up her vendor badge from around her neck. "Cost me two thousand dollars, too. Hi Mathus. You're looking gross," the Fae added pleasantly.

"Lady Wilde," Mathus acknowledged with terse politeness.

"So, my proverbial ears are buzzing; you must all be

talking about me." The foxy Fae looked about the circle for acknowledgement.

"I was hoping it was your master who would be joining us?" Maxamillion cocked an eyebrow at her expectantly.

"What master?" Lady Wilde asked, innocently.

Lady Ursula exchanged a glance with the other Council members at the table. "Maxamillion, we did not discuss you bringing Fae here. Who have you invited?"

"The only person who can help us obtain the remaining pieces of the Masterson Files. Someone who now has a foot in both the corporate world and your world."

"The Faerie Court is not...." Mathus started.

"Your world adjacent then." Maxamillion looked to Lady Wilde again. "Where is he?"

"Your Ladyship," said a timid voice coming from one of the aides, who appeared behind Lady Ursula's couch. The aide leaned in and spoke softly. "There is...they told me to give you this." She dropped an emblem into Lady Ursula's open palm. The Wizardress stared at it for a long moment, before turning it around in her hand. "Yes, that's fine. Let him enter," she said, returning the emblem.

The aide scurried out and all further conversation ceased until she appeared again leading a young man and an old woman behind her. Rune recognized both.

The young man was dressed in a slate grey suit. His blonde hair was coiffed by someone who knew what they were doing and it was the most dapper she had ever seen Calvin look. She almost didn't recognize him without the ill-fitting sunglasses the wannabe gangster usually wore. Instead, he wore a circlet of twisted branches that disappeared into his hair with the sigil of Oberon in the center of it.

Even with the makeover, the hired thug-turned-Faerie King looked terrible. Like he was hung over and trying to hide it. He took in the room warily as he entered, but came to a full stop when his eyes landed on Rune.

The woman he was escorting looked back at him concerned, her long silver hair cascading down her back. She was dressed more elegantly than when Rune had seen her last. This time she wore various shades of orange kerchiefs layered over each other into the shape of a dress, instead of the strips of various orange made fabrics that had given her a homeless look. Lady Trella, also known as the Orange Lady, whispered something softly in his ear. He replied without removing his eyes from Rune and the Orange Lady turned toward her as well. While he glared, Lady Trella beamed at her so brightly Rune couldn't help beaming back. Then the aged Fae whispered something more to him. He relented his stare, shifting it down to the ground and allowed himself to be led further into the horseshoe of couches.

Lady Ursula gestured in the air and the couches slid apart, smoothly and soundlessly, making enough space in the circle to include three additional finely appointed chairs set next to Mathus' couch, each trimmed in green velvet that was pinned with old brass bolts. Lady Trella lowered Calvin into the middlemost chair before taking the one to his right. As she lowered herself, she caught Rune's eye and gave her a wink.

"Thanks for having us," Lady Trella said to Lady Ursula, her inelegant speech juxtaposed against the elegant way she was draping herself into the chair. "None of you will have met him, this is my new old man, the Oberon." She turned to the room for acknowledgement and was answered with polite nods, while Calvin stared only at the thumbs of his folded hands. Then the Orange Lady stopped, her smile freezing on her face as she noticed the other Fae. Her counterpart also offered a smile, but before anyone could do more but exchange questioning, awkward glances, the Orange Lady turned back to the room.

"We are very grateful for the invitation to meet with the illustrious Inner Council. Thank you for accepting our petition," she said in a saccharine sweet voice.

"And what is your petition?" Lady Ursula asked for the group.

Calvin continued to stare at his hands until Lady Trella bumped him hard with her elbow.

"Please…I need your help," Calvin mumbled, glancing up like a kid called to the principal's office. The Orange Lady cleared her throat and Calvin attempted to sit up a little more. "The Faerie Court needs your help."

"There is no Faerie Court anymore," Lady Ursula said, not unkindly.

"I never thought I would see the day the Oberon would beg us for help," Lady Verde mocked.

"Who are you, son?" Mathus asked.

"He is our Oberon," Lady Trella started to say at the same time as her Lord answered, "Calvin." That earned the young Faerie King another forcedly patient look from the Orange Lady, while Lady Wilde sniggered into a hand.

"I'm not a Faerie. I am a man. I'm a person. A...hominal," Calvin continued, his voice tripping over the last term as if he had only just learned it and wasn't sure he was using it right.

"More importantly you used to work...." Maxamillion cut in.

Calvin straightened a little. "Yeah. Who the hell are you?"

"Maxamillion Corinthe of the Corinthe Corporation," the CEO said, holding out his hand to be shook, which Calvin did stiffly before his eyes shifted to St. Benedict sitting next to him.

"You," Calvin said huskily.

"Yes, I understand you know my associate St. Benedict." Maxamillion said as the Saint cracked a wry smile and nodded.

"Your Kingliness," he said with his predatory smile, before turning to the Orange Lady with a more respectful tone, "My Lady."

"Hello Tall Drink of Water," she acknowledged. "Glad to see you're still alive."

"Despite my best efforts," he agreed, poignantly ignoring Calvin's glare.

"You believe that the...the Oberon can help us with the proposed endeavor," Madame Pooka interjected, tracing an invisible line in the air with the end of her pen, like she was literally making the connections in Maxamillion's plan. "But what does the Oberon want in exchange?"

"I said, I needed your help," Calvin repeated with childish exasperation.

"Yes, your Lordship, but what would the great Lord Oberon need with the Inner Council?" Mathus asked.

"Someone....something is trying to kill me," Calvin

answered in a small voice. He leaned forward and tried to run his hand through his hair, but was stopped by the crown. The Orange Lady set a hand to his back and rubbed in slow, soothing circles. "I need help. I can't keep going like this."

"Who is trying to kill you?" Lady Ursula asked.

"I don't know. It's like I'm cursed. Wherever I go, I keep having these near accidents, people who don't even know me have attacked me, it's like I'm cursed. This one person..." his hands were shaking, "...this one woman, drunk as can be, she pushed me in front of a car. They were this close from hitting me." He pinched his fingers together, but they continued to shake, making it hard to perceive the gap. Instead, he tucked them back under his arms. "I'm going to die, man. This isn't right."

"What do you expect us to do about this?" Mathus asked.

Calvin raised his head. "Well...help me. Protect me. You guys are the magic experts and I'm obviously cursed. I mean, I'm just a regular guy, I don't know anything about this stuff. I need your help, please!"

"Don't you have protection?" Madame Pooka asked, directing her question to Lady Trella.

"We don't have what it takes," she said. "Not like we used to."

"Do you plan on reviving the Faerie Court?" Lady Ursula asked.

"What? No. What?" Calvin declared so defensively it was obvious that it wasn't that simple.

Lady Trella cast her eyes down, but didn't say anything. Rune felt for her. She had been saddled with a guy like Calvin as their leader and she couldn't imagine anyone more unqualified for the job.

"I sympathize with your situation son, but you have to understand. The Faerie Court was the main rivalry of our Guild. A lot of bad blood has spilled in the streets of Chicago since the city's founding. There is no good reason, or frankly incentive, to help you," Mathus said.

"But...but you have to," Calvin started, panic reasserting itself.

"If I can have the floor a moment, I have a very good reason why the Magic Guild needs to extend its protection to the King of the Faerie Court and why it would be a very good thing to reestablish the Faerie Court as a power in this city."

All eyes turned to Maxamillion. He gestured a hand at the Faerie King. "Calvin, here, used to be an employee of the Kodiak Corporation." Unbidden, St. Benedict popped his hand open in a smooth gesture. Bursting from his palm, cold light filled the space, creating a five foot hologram of Calvin's face above the coffee table. Beside his image, a stream of bulleted text appeared, listing stats. The reactions from the room were mixed, with the Council members staring raptly, but otherwise maintaining calm demeanors in the face of something new. But it was easy to assume there was some sort of magical analog that they had seen before. The aides, on the other hand, gaped in awe at the technological marvel.

Without being asked, Lady Verde made a gesture in the air and the warmer light, that had no apparent source in the space, dimmed around them. The hologram sharpened for all to see, showing the face of a cocky young man with a sneer that tried to be a smile. The shadow seemed more alive than its originator sitting near Rune. As the image and stats rotated slowly in a circle, St. Benedict repositioned himself onto the floor, resting his arm on the large coffee table. Because of his positioning, he had to stretch out his back foot behind himself, which placed it close to Rune's own feet. She tried not to dwell on that inconsequential fact.

Madame Pooka stood and scratched down information from the hologram into her open book as quickly as she could, the pen moving eerily fast across the page. Maxamillion took up the space opposite from the Pantherwoman, slipping his hands into his dress pants pockets.

"Calvin Harrison here originally worked in a subsidiary mortgage company that was acquired by Kodiak." Maxamillion gestured to the highlighted title beside Calvin's name and St. Benedict interacted with the hologram with his glowing fingers. The title flashed and replaced Calvin with a corporate tree, showing the connections between the points as Maxamillion spoke. "They accomplished that acquisition by acquiring Mr. Harrison beforehand."

"You turned-coat," Mathus commented. Calvin, to his credit, nodded once.

"We're lucky he did, because that exposed him to the medallion that claimed him as the Faerie Court's Oberon." The tree disappeared, replaced by a video of Calvin throwing the Oberon's medallion and the erupting smoke surrounding around him. The image then shifted quickly to focus on Rune before abruptly ending.

"What is that?" Mathus demanded, pointing where Rune's face had been.

"What you just saw was a recorded memory from my agent, St. Benedict here."

There were more murmurs from the aids and again the council members exchanged glances.

"A mind Wizard aided you in removing a memory?" Lady Ursula asked, her brow pinching between her perfect eyebrows.

"No. St. Benedict here is a cybernetically-altered human. The Corinthe Corporation's technology is advanced enough to download those memories straight from his mind. What you saw was a witness account."

"Blasphemy," Lady Verde hissed softly.

"A violation of nature," Mathus agreed.

Maxamillion cocked an eyebrow at them. "You may not like it, but rest assured, every corporation with any ambition is creating technologically-altered people, advancing capabilities and our ability to interact with each other. We are entering a new era for our world." The way the Council members now looked at St. Benedict made Rune very concerned. While she wasn't as comfortable as she would like to be with his augmentations, the cool assessment from Lady Ursula was as worrisome as the open hostility from Mathus and Lady Verde. Rune could see it then, the cold civil war that had been growing the last few years, between the magical world and the development of the technology that mimicked it. Where did she stand in all of it?

The corporate tree appeared again in the hologram, this time with a smaller image of Calvin next to the words "Faerie

Court" with a line connecting them together. "What I'm proposing to the Magic Guild is quite simple. The Magic Guild will offer support and protection to the Oberon. The Corinthe Corporation will invest monetarily in re-establishing the Faerie Court in Chicago."

"Why on earth would you want to do that?" Mathus asked.

Maxamillion flashed a million dollar smile. "Votes."

"Votes?" Lady Verde echoed, voicing the same question that everyone was thinking.

"I see," Madame Pooka said, nodding her head. "This isn't simply about the Masterson Files."

"I think you get where I'm going with this. Don't get me wrong, the Masterson Files are important. They will be the vehicle for this enterprise I'm proposing, but what I want to accomplish is far, far more important to changing the course of our city."

"The City Council," Madame Pooka said as if she had simply reached a conclusion. Mathus's eyebrows shot up as he realized what Madame Pooka meant. He exchanged a look with Lady Ursula, who nodded.

"Yes. As things stand the only way to have true power in this city is for a corporation to acquire and hold Alderman seats. Out of the fifty possible seats in Chicago, most corporations have to acquire subsidiaries and partnerships to hold even one. Kodiak alone has two. They want three."

The hologram produced fifty boxes with the word "ward" and a number inside each. Beside those, the names of the corporations that controlled them were listed. Kodiak indeed appeared twice.

"If Kodiak succeeds in taking one of your seats, they will hold more than any other single corporation and others will choose to join their coalition and follow their lead. Kodiak will have what it needs to rule this city, at least for a time. If they get ahold of the Masterson Files, there will be nothing any of us can do to stop them. We will stop being a corporate democracy."

The tree changed again. "The Faerie Court coming back into power could spoil all of that. Out there are thousands of disenfranchised Faeries and Faerie Friends who would vote for a Fae candidate. Right now, no one represents them. The new Oberon could help deliver those votes." Two seats on the chart flipped to say Faerie Court beside them. "With the backing of the Corinthe Corporation, the Magic Guild could continue to hold two of their seats and the third," he paused a moment, confirming he had everyone's attention. It was pin-dropping silence. "Would go to the Corinthe Corporation."

"Like hell!" Mathus blustered, taking to his feet.

"With Corinthe on the City Council we would have a five seat coalition,"

"That is far from enough to do anything of worth with the votes," Madame Pooka stated.

"It would be half way to ten. Ten seats." Ten little boxes began to blink green. "Ten seats and we become a spoiler coalition. We become something to be reckoned with."

"Five seats are a near impossible thing and you are talking about ten?" Mathus countered, but not dismissively. He sounded like his wheels were turning hard.

"Five seats would fortify this coalition. It would be enough to make the other corporations sit up and take notice."

"And why is that?" Lady Verde sneered.

"Because when is the last time an independent corporation like Corinthe has taken an Alderman?" Maxamillion flashed a beautiful, white-toothed smile.

This part was a bit out of Rune's depth. She didn't pay much attention to politics except when it was time to vote. She knew any corporation could put up candidates to be voted on within their districts, but often the smaller corporations were marginalized by the larger oligarchs' control of the districts' subsidiaries. A small corporation winning an Aldermanic, beating out an oligarch's money and influence, that would make the nightly news, maybe even the national news.

"We fortify our five seats and then, with the Masterson Files, that coalition would double, maybe even triple as others moved to get a piece of our new magitech. Ten to fifteen seats later, with the Magic Guild and the Faerie Court firmly in the center of it, we could change how things are done in this city."

Lady Ursula pursed her lips and sighed before standing.

"What you propose sounds intriguing and I do intend to present all this to the entire Inner Council before we agree to anything, but only when such a proposal is feasible to consider."

Maxamillion didn't flinch or miss a beat, he simply shifted. "You have an objection?"

"The Faerie Court, as you say, is fractured."

"If one was to put it generously," Lady Verde said.

"Which she is," Mathus added.

"It is not a simple thing to re-establish it. I do not want to speak about Fae politics," Lady Verde said turning to the Orange Lady, "of which I am not an expert."

"Please, all of you on the Inner Council. If I have to get on my knees right here and lick your boots I will," Lady Trella declared as she slipped from her seat and knelt on the ground. For one alarming moment, Rune thought she was going to start licking shoes. "Please, protect him. Over the last two months, he has survived more than all the previous Oberons before him since our Father's betrayal. Please." Tears rolled down her wrinkled cheeks freely, and she made no move to wipe them away. "Please have mercy on our people."

The tension was heavy as no one responded to the Orange Lady's plea. Rune felt her insides twist as she watched. If it would have helped Rune would have spoken, but she had no authority with this Council. She was barely a part of the Guild at the moment. Finally, Calvin leaned from his chair, setting both of his hands on the Orange Lady's shoulders.

"Lady Trella, please," he said softly. She didn't tear her gaze away from Lady Ursula's, but she did yield to his gentle guidance back to her chair.

Laughter erupted from the other Fae. Everyone had been so caught up in Maxamillion's presentation they had all forgotten about the foxy Fae dressed in red, sitting beside Rune. Lady Wilde grabbed her sides, laughing so hard with such gleeful mocking, it sounded deranged.

"Oh. I'm sorry. I'm sorry. I could almost hold it in." She held up a hand in a gesture of apology while her other arm was wrapped around her middle like it was trying to do just that. She turned to look right at Rune. "I mean, don't you find this funny? You know this guy right? You were in the little machine man's brain-video. This piece of worthless trash is supposed to be the next Oberon?"

The hairs on the back of Rune's neck rose. This Fae was not on Calvin's side. Knowing what she did about the Fae, that could only mean….

Before Rune could finish the thought, Lady Wilde smiled a predatory grin, knowingly.

That was when St. Benedict howled.

The dark voice was back, roaring in his head.

"You are mine! You owe me everything!!"

The pain of it was overwhelming. He felt cold all the way to his soul, so cold it burned. His back arched as black, oily smoke erupted from his chest like a geyser. Everyone around him backed away, falling over the couches or chairs to clear. All except Rune. He saw her for the briefest of moments, the only thought to break through the pain. Even as he stretched a hand to her, the geyser fell back, the oily smoke swallowing him whole.

He would have likened the sensation to falling asleep, only he was aware of his mind disconnecting from his body. For a moment, there was only blackness and the feeling of thick oil shuddered through his being. When his body was gone, so too was the pain. He was morphing into something else, something not a man. He opened his eyes, seeing the smaller beings around him. All he felt was rage and hatred for them all. They were hateful creatures.

"Betrayers. Liars. Deceivers," the female voice chanted with his thoughts. As she spoke, he knew what she wanted from him, what she needed him to do, and who to. First, there was the ugly man and the younger woman that aided him, standing within easy reach. Vow breakers, both of them. It was so easy to crouch on all four legs, the claws of his paws pulling up curls on the table beneath him. The rumble in his throat sounded like a buzz saw to his own ears. He felt the conflicting urge to toss his equine head and trumpet to the stars. Instead he tucked it down, so the long wicked horn erupting from his forehead would skewer the vow breakers before him.

Just as he leapt, the ugly one threw up a shield, a wall of flickering yellow light. The horn pierced it easily enough, but it was like diving through water. It slowed his attack so the prey could escape him.

He heard shouting all around, but he didn't comprehend the words. Only her words mattered. Only her voice.

"They escaped us! Destroy them. Destroy him!" she cackled urgently. A flash of light caught the corner of his red world, something pure white that eluded his vision. He turned to chase it and was greeted instead by several crimson pops. A man he knew was firing a small gun, the bullets thudding into his world of mist around him, missing any true target completely. St. Benedict trumpeted his outrage. This man had sworn to protect him and be his ally in exchange for his soul, an unequal bargain. "*DECEIVER!*" the voice condemned. He charged, his prey ducking away at the last second.

Bereft of will, St. Benedict pivoted up on his back hooves, his lion paws clawing the air as he turned about. He could see his true target. While the world was red, the prey seemed to glow, outlined in white. He growled. The sight of the Oberon's crown was infuriating. The voice despaired at the sight of it.

"How dare he? How dare he?!" she wailed. *"Take it off him! Get it off him this minute! Take his head off!"*

St. Benedict's growl warped into a trumpeting whinny before he charged, setting the end of the horn directly at the Oberon's exposed chest. The coward was crab-crawling backward away, all tears, shrieks and blubbering. The anticipation of running him through mounted through St. Benedict with each step. Then someone stood in his way.

Like the Oberon, the redness of his gaze couldn't touch her, instead he saw gold. She was pure, clean and majestic. The sight of her hurt to look at, she was so brilliant. Blocking his way, she flung out both arms and shouted, her words sounding warped but he could still understand her.

"St. Benedict! Stop!"

He couldn't, it was too late.

Bucking his head at the last minute, he veered his horn up and over her. Instead he knocked her down as he tried to leap clear of her. A few feet away he tried to pivot and turn again, but his legs weren't working right. The oily blackness that made up his body was burning away at the places where his body had touch hers, burning until the black magic broke apart, dropping his human form back to the ground.

Staring down at his hands, it was like they had been charred in a fire. A thick layer of black still clung to him, forming talons over the ends of his fingertips. The vision before him was still of a red field. With one of his taloned hands, he touched the rack of antlers bursting from his head, as solid as any horn. His fedora was gone. A minor consideration, so why did he care? The new addition of the antlers didn't feel any stranger than suddenly having talons did. Though the dark miasma had been lessened around him, it had not released him completely. Not that he wanted release. He felt so free, guiltless and alive.

"Do not stop, my slave. Bring me justice!" Justice. Everything he did was to get justice. For her.

Empowered, St. Benedict sprung forward, incredible speed and strength infusing his whole body. But in mid-leap, vines erupted from the ground around him, lacing about his limbs, bringing him hard to the ground. Roaring in fury, he tried to stand and rip them away, but more vines snaked up to grip him tighter. A distance away was Lady Verde, her tongue stuck out the side of her mouth as she wove her fingers in the air, obviously controlling the growth.

"Encase him, hurry!" Mathus shouted.

Even as he shouted it, Lady Verde bucked, her hands going limp as her head snapped back and to the side. As she collapsed forward, she revealed Lady Wilde standing behind her, still holding a piece of broken chair.

"You idiot Wizards. Always forgetting it isn't just magic that can hurt you!" she crowed.

The vines lost their vitality as the magic seeped away from them, turning the greenery brown before withering into dust. Bursting out of the cloud of dead foliage, St. Benedict roared.

Another fool captured his attention, coming at him with some inconsequential weapon and the Saint's trained fighting instincts kicked on, ducking back so the swing missed, then bursting forward to swipe the talons at a vulnerable front. The foolish aide went down, clawing at their chest helplessly and St. Benedict stalked past, uncaring.

Not only was he scanning for his next opponent, or maybe his prey, he was also sniffing the air, which was thick with sweat, fear and blood. The battlefield of a predator.

They were there, against the tree. Only a few feet away, he saw his prey glowing white, pressing up, trying to climb the tree, while Rune, still threaded with gold, stood facing him. In one hand, she gripped her shield necklace.

"Move back!" she ordered, her voice ringing clearer than the garbled nonsense around him.

"*Kill her*," the voice menaced.

Her shield flickered up for a second, another convex bubble of yellow light, but she was weak, undisciplined, unpracticed with the ways of magic and it collapsed.

"*Kill her. She stands between you and justice, my Saint of Liars*," the voice purred.

He stalked closer, his black mist having already reached her, curling around her form like a lover. Her eyes were wide, the brown and green in her eyes warring in such a beautiful hazel. He wanted to devour them. Devour her. Already he could imagine the satisfaction of driving his talons through her. Unable to wait any longer, he raised his right arm high, preparing to sink them into her flesh.

"St. Benedict, don't!!" she screamed, terrified as he brought his hand down with all his strength and speed.

Blood erupted everywhere, red and wet as the taloned claws sunk into his own arm. While his right arm had moved to obey the dark voice, his left, his heart hand, moved to stop his right.

"St. Benedict!" Rune called again, her eyes like circles as she realized what he had done to stop himself.

He pulled the right arm across his body, his whole self aching as the two halves of himself fought each other. The effort forced him to his knees, curling around the offending arm in order to contain it. The talons of his left hand were dug into his forearm, up to the middle of his fingers. He was touching bone.

"St. Benedict," Rune's voice came again, gentler, worried.

Her hand, warm and painful, touched his shoulder heedless of the blackness coating him. He flinched away.

"Get out of here!" he growled. The sound was the deepest his voice could possibly go.

"I can't! I won't leave…."

"Get him out of here!" he shouted, directing his rage at Calvin. The voice in his head was screaming at him, demanding that he continue the attack, but he wiggled his fingers a little in his arm, forcing more pain to give him control. Killing Calvin would be easy enough, but not at the cost of Rune's life.

"I am not leaving you!" Rune shouted.

Pulling the talons out of his arm, he gripped the turf beneath him for purchase as he pulled himself into a run. He had to get away from her. Anywhere. It didn't matter where he went, only that it was away from her. As he approached the magic shimmering wall that had enclosed the meeting space, it shattered and fell before him as if someone had turned off a waterfall abruptly. Beyond, the garden was in panic, as people scrambled away from the meeting tree. He stood looking around in the open, waiting for an opponent to challenge him.

A wall of fire rushed over to oblige. Before it hit him, the miasma rose up about him, obscuring his vision. The smell of the fire trying to burn the miasma away was disgusting even to his own nose. As soon as the flames ceased the miasma fell away to reveal Abraxas a few feet away. The young Talent's face morphed from shock to determination. Both his hands were alight with fire and he clapped them together hard. The fire morphed from red and yellow to blue and white.

St. Benedict grinned.

The darkness curled around him, eating the ground into charred black and St. Benedict stalked forward with the grin on his bone-white face. Black ichor dripped from his antlers. Abraxas battled with himself to keep from taking a step back as the Saint encroached into his space. Before St. Benedict was an arm's length away, his prey spooked and began swiping at him with arcs of fire.

Training took over and the Saint began to weave left and right, letting the fists sweep past. Abraxas became more aggressive, trying to gain ground on the creature in front of him and St. Benedict let him have it. After a few passes, St. Benedict braced his back foot against the piece of wall that was a part of the Victorian sitting room and caught the young Talent's burning fist. Even with the fire burning away at the miasma, the dark sludge was like acid eating through Abraxas's clothing and skin. The fire guttered as the younger man began to scream.

"Get off him!" A huge gust of wind pounded into St. Benedict, knocking him back. He lost his grip on the young Talent as he began to slide across the turf. Standing a few feet back from her collapsed brother was Abraxas's twin sister. The slight woman gestured. Twin whirlwinds spun around St. Benedict, disrupting the protective miasma. It was all he could do to claw into the ground to stay where he was.

Then the ground opened up beneath him. While he had been distracted by the wind buffeting him, five magic users had encircled him, hands extended to each other as various colors of magic swirled together.

"St. Benedict! They're trying to banish you! Move!" Rune's voice screamed over the wind that tried to carry her words away.

"Traitor!" Abraxas yelled, but before St. Benedict could turn to look or even push off the ground to run, the ground was gone. He dropped into empty space. While it looked like his talon hands could grab the side of the hole, there was no way he could move his body fast enough to grip it. All he saw above was the churning darkness of the trees and a few dancing lights. Then even those were blocked out as a hand gripped his. Her hand. But there was too much weight; he was falling too fast and he slipped out of the hold as quickly as it had happened. All it accomplished was the person above him had been tugged enough to start to fall into the hole with him as well.

And then all was darkness.

Chapter 17

At first all Rune saw was a neon sign written in Japanese characters. She stared at it and noticed how it flickered every few moments. Slowly her eyes adjusted and she looked around. She sat squarely in the middle of a worn, cushy couch that someone had placed in one corner of the room. Another couch was in the opposite corner, framed by a shelf with a dim blue light that was almost entirely blotted out by plants and electronics equally piled together. Another figure sat in the center of the other mismatched couch, his head framed by decorative antlers on the wall.

"St. Benedict?" she asked, her voice sounding dry and crackly.

The figure's head turned a little bit and the antlers on his head shifted as well against the blue light. They weren't decorative antlers; they were attached to his head. After a moment the figure leaned forward, setting his shadowed face in his hands.

"Rune?" St. Benedict asked.

"Yeah." She stretched, her whole body aching like she had body-slammed into a truck. Looking about the rest of the room, she tried to figure where they were.

It was a standard eight by ten room, but it seemed smaller as it was jam packed with things. It looked like a computer shop's junk room had collided with a garden, as plants grew out of every available crack amongst the electronics. There was a desk with five keyboards laid out as if someone had been typing on all of them. More keyboards were piled up on top of each other waiting to be used or abused. Two cylinders came out of the back of the desk. The cylinders were filled with bubbling water and each was back lit, one a canary yellow and the other an electric blue. The bubbling gurgles from the cylinders were the only sounds in the room. It gave the place a Zen feeling that enticed Rune to think about curling back up on the couch and going back to sleep.

St. Benedict stood up, uncurling his spine like he was as stiff as she was.

"I feel hung over," he grumbled, before moving toward the equipment.

"Do you know where we...?"

"You jumped down the hole after me," he said. He wiggled his black taloned hand in front of his face. Through the darkness coating him, the light from his augmentations burned through. The blackness retreated from the tips, revealing his real fingers beneath. The act sent a chain reaction through the room. As if it was a small city waking up, tiny lights blinked to life throughout the room. It didn't change the pink and blue haze with its slash of yellow, but it did brighten it enough to see better. Now Rune could see graffiti glowing on the walls espousing anti-corporation sentiment, much she happened to agree with. More neon signs stuttered to life advertising alcohol or bars. Other signs that looked like they had been stolen off of their official poles filled in the rest of the wall space.

Moving further into the room, St. Benedict gestured again with his glowing hand and a holographic display appeared in front of him, floating over the empty space on top of the desk.

"We're in a hub room," he said.

"So you know where we are?" Rune asked, standing up to come up beside him.

"No clue," he said stiffly. He sensed her moving. "Stay away from me."

"You're bleeding onto the floor," she pointed out. The small plips of blackened red blood tried to form their own little pool on the chipped grey tile. "Let me see."

"No," he said, pulling his arm away. He stepped back and the blue holographic display disappeared.

"It's alright, you can't hurt me. I'm a virgin, remember?" she said with humor and a quirky eyebrow.

"What are you talking about?" He had backed up a few

more steps away from her, clutching his wounded arm against his chest. He could feel the oily miasma still clinging to his skin. He had seen what this shit had done to Abraxas.

Rune didn't seem concerned. With great determination, she crossed the space between them and set her hand over his. He tried to flinch away, but it was too late. Nothing happened.

"Wow, you are greasy," Rune said as she massaged the substance over his skin gently.

"Why isn't it hurting you?"

"Same reason you changed from the Poh to whatever this forestman-thing you have going on here is. Because I'm a virgin."

"No you're not." St. Benedict eyed her, wishing she would stop touching him. It burned.

"Yes, I am. I've never killed anyone," she said and he blinked as he remembered.

"The Poh?"

She gazed back at him intently. "Your eyes are red," she muttered, peering deeply into them. "Are you seeing red?"

Self-consciously he blinked. "Yes, mostly. Everything is sort of various shades of red."

"What in here isn't?"

"You."

Rune smiled and nodded. "I'm easy to see, aren't I? That's why you couldn't kill me when you had the chance; you could actually see me." She lifted up her fingers and rubbed them together, the bit of black oil rolling into a little snake between them. "Also why your miasma isn't poisoning me. You're possessed by the Oberon. Or something like the Oberon."

"How?"

"I have no clue," she shrugged. "Truthfully, I'm taking an educated guess with all this. But if it's like the last time we met the Poh, when it was manifesting through Calvin, he couldn't hurt me either, because I had never killed anybody, which is what made me a virgin in that instance."

"Betrayal." St. Benedict pressed his other palm against the pounding in his temple. "She kept saying to kill the betrayers. You've never betrayed anyone."

"Yeah, just call me Mary Sue," Rune quipped. "Okay, let's find a first aid kit or something of its ilk. Otherwise, I'm going to have to start tearing my shirt historical romance style and I like this shirt." She turned back to the room and started looking through the mess to see what was available.

"You jumped in the hole with me." St. Benedict said as he watched her move throughout the room.

"We established that. Or are you thinking I'm an illusion or something?" Rune asked, approaching the desk to pull open the drawers, or at least try to. She waved her hand over the desk like he had, but nothing happened. "Can you do your wavy thing? Turn this back on? Maybe it can tell us something about where we are," she said as she successfully tugged open the bottom most drawer and successfully failed to find a first aid kit.

"I still hear her voice."

"Who is 'her'?" Rune asked. "Titania? Are you hearing the Titania maybe?"

Her companion didn't answer, but started pacing, shaking his head in a way that reminded her of a restless buck getting ready for a fight. It was probably the antlers.

"Hey! Over here. Hand. Wavy-thing. Now," she ordered trying to distract him.

He approached as she commanded and gestured his hand open. Again the blackness ebbed from it and the blue light in his fingers ignited the hologram.

"Can you turn on your other augmentations?" Rune asked, focusing on his glowing fingers.

He turned to her, his eyes igniting the same blue. Instantly, the world around him cleared of all traces of red. Rune's face echoed his surprise as the darkness ebbed back from his head, dissolving the antlers, like someone was pulling a hood off of his head. The darkness continued to recede until it completely released his body. He looked at his hand again.

"It's not completely gone," he said out loud. "But…wait a minute." Then he snapped. The reality of the world around them rippled, rolling through every object, flashing the little lights. St. Benedict opened his hand and in the palm a light blue matrix appeared, twisting itself into a shape before solidifying into a soft grey fedora.

"How did you do that?!" Rune asked flabbergasted.

"We're in an augmented reality," the Saint pronounced as he set the hat onto his head.

"Okay, what does that mean?"

"Like the hologram room at the Praetorium."

Rune double blinked. "You mean this room is all digital?"

"Not all of it. But I'm not sure what is real and what is not simply an overlay that seems real enough to our senses. I've been in a few." He gestured again, making the hologram over the desk jump as he began to interact with it.

"You can just snap and, viola, you got a hat?"

"It's a preprogrammed shortcut for me when I'm in an AR room."

"Of course it is. So you've been in this place before?"

"Nothing this sophisticated…or realistic."

"Your bleeding is real enough," Rune commented, giving up on finding the first aid kit. For lack of any grabbable cloth, she decided she would have to try to sacrifice the bottom of her shirt after all. And yet, just before she tore, she spotted an old t-shirt lying on the ground by the desk. "Oh, here we go. Give me your arm."

"I've got it," he said, taking the shirt from her, except she didn't completely let go of it. The hologram collapsed again, disappearing into the desk's top.

"St. Benedict, let me help you," she chided gently.

"Helping me landed you here." The blue light in his eyes faded a second and the dark antlers flicked back over his head.

"Hey, is this shirt real?" Rune asked, looking down at the fabric as she won the small tug of war for it. "I mean if I use this to bind your wounds, will it actually do the job?"

He waved his hand over the shirt. Instantly it disintegrated into particles and vanished. "No, it's not real."

"Well, that's just great. This is bizarre." Rune looked about the room again. "I've been in magical realms before, but never one made out of data." She shifted another circle around the room. "There is no door."

"Someone is containing us here," St. Benedict answered. Gesturing the palm of his hand outward at part of the wall, the surface textures melted, the colors fading away, leaving only a glowing blue matrix in one corner of the room. Slowly, he began to circle, his palm outward, revealing the matrix underneath the surface. Everything, from the plants to the couches to the neon signs, vanished and was replaced by grids, only for the colors and textures to reassert themselves as soon as he passed.

"This is amazing," he breathed in awe. "I've never seen anything this sophisticated before. The whole room is artificial." That made him stop a second.

"What?" Rune asked. He didn't answer, but simply turned his hand toward her. "Are...are you checking to see if I'm real?"

"Maybe. You are," he answered, turning his hand back to the wall. Finally, he stopped partway between two standing shelves. "Found it."

"The first aid kit?"

"The way out." He gestured again, his eyes glowing an even brighter blue. When nothing happened he clasped both hands together and pulled. A circular hologram appeared between the shelves. It rotated slowly in space, a series of symbols with lines of code floating counterclockwise. Using both hands he twisted and manipulated the mandala. Then there was a tearing sound, which made him stop and turn.

"What are you doing?" he asked, but it became very evident as Rune placed the piece of torn off shirt over the still bleeding arm.

"Stop moving a second. I ruined my favorite shirt for you," she said. He yielded, letting her take his arm. This was the first time she got a good look at the wounds on his forearm, the gouged-out holes his talons had made. Very little blood was actually leaving the wounds compared to what should have been. Rune turned his arm more toward the light of the hologram so she could see, and to her shock she could see the miasma floating inside the wounds.

"I told you to leave me alone," St. Benedict said, his voice very cold, rumbling in his chest with a clear dark note of menace.

She felt the urge to pull away, but instead she jutted her chin a little, folding the makeshift bandage over the wounds. "We'll have to cleanse them later, but for now you at least won't have... to worry about them."

"Why aren't you repelled by me?" he asked. "I'm covered in darkness."

"This isn't your fault. You've been possessed by the Oberon spirit."

"I let the darkness in. I *welcomed* it, Rune."

"Yes, I know, you're very dark and sexy. I'm all aquiver. You going to open the door now?" Rune asked dryly, though she lost it to giggles when St. Benedict blinked in surprise.

A few more shifts of code in the mandala and a crude door appeared between the shelves, already partially open. St. Benedict tapped two fingers on it and the room around them disappeared.

"Uh," Rune commented as she looked around them. "That was surreal."

"It was a crude bit of coding so it didn't have an animate analog like the rest of the room," St. Benedict explained, even though Rune didn't even know enough to ask that kind of question.

For the briefest of moments, Rune thought she saw the world around them as an infinite grid going in every direction, then it was coated in blackness. A forest populated around them. Yet, even that wasn't an apt description. It was a forest but the trees glowed a dark blue, all smooth like barkless birches. Light pulsed up through the trunks, like spears of a heartbeat that branched off their literal branches. The ones that touched each other had a reverb effect as they shared energy. Beneath the two companions' feet, the ground had become a spongy turf that pulsed to its own rhythm as well, with energy arcing like puddles of water beneath each trunk of the trees. Rune backpedaled a few steps as she looked down at the ground. As her feet impacted that ground, more light burst with each step.

"What is all this?" the magic user asked in awe.

"How data streams would look if interpreted into a forest," the Saint answered. "It's beautiful."

"Yeah," she agreed. She continued to walk backward until

she crashed into a waist high bush. A bird, or something like a bird, scared out of it, taking flight as electricity snapped from its long feathered tail.

"Ow!" Rune yelped when one of the shocks bit her ear. A whole flock of the bird-like creatures erupted from the synthetic trees, chirping and buzzing like a chorus of dial-up modems. As they dispersed, another creature appeared, walking past. It looked like what an amoeba's interpretation of a unicorn would be. Though it had the long face, the nose seemed to end in a single glowing circle. It was that softened point that the creature moved, morphing like water instead of turning as any other animal would, to "see" the bird-ish disturbance. The glowing circle flashed a beam of light toward the action, passing over Rune's eyes like a headlight sweeping across. She blinked against it. The beam of light diffused further as the creature seem to spot Rune. It moved through the "foliage" with the glowing circle turning red as it pointed right at her, chirping and whirling.

St. Benedict stepped in front of Rune, raising his three glowing fingers before the creature.

It halted. Again, St. Benedict seemed to stutter, the black antlers blinking in and out in place of the fedora, the tips of his fingers claws one moment, then a hominal hand the next. The creature's light softened back to cool white and it moved on. They watched it go, holding still until it was completely out of sight.

Before Rune could finish taking in a breath to speak, St. Benedict's head snapped to the left. Alerted, she peered into the forest.

"What is it?" she whispered.

"My Lady calls me," he intoned, moving forward into the brush.

"Of course she does," Rune muttered, following. "Nothing like walking through a creepy alien woods with your knight mostly possessed by crazy Fae magic."

As they walked, the forest uncoiled itself around them, revealing more beauties. A large patch of flowers glowing soft purples, blues, and greens spread out beneath one of the trees, lazily pulsing like fireflies. St. Benedict stopped a moment and watched the rhythm of the flowers, which allowed Rune to catch up to him, coming to rest at his side.

"Do you hear it?" he asked softly.

"Hear what?"

With a gesture, a holographic circle appeared around St. Benedict's head. With one finger, he traced through the light, which in turn made the circle larger until it passed Rune's head, placing it within. Then, like a conductor, St. Benedict gestured with both hands upward. Music rose with his hands, moving up and down scales, but it was artificial. No string or drum or horn made that sound. It was like someone had taught a computer to sing. Synthetic music.

"Is that coming from the flowers?" Rune asked breathily.

"It's coming from everywhere," he replied, matching her quiet. She could see he was right, the lights of the trees and other plants moved and shifted with the repeating cascade of the music. When the birds flew past them, there was a flourish that harmonized and changed the rhythm of the sound. Everything in the forest was in harmony with each other, expressing a sadness and excitement, like it was telling a story that could be felt.

They stood there together listening for an unknown amount of time. When Rune became aware of the eyes floating in the dark around them, it was already too late. Maybe it was the music that first tipped her off to them. With each pair that appeared, a new note was added, but it had been subtle at first. Now there were more than two dozen eyes, each with slitted pupils glowing from the darkness.

"St. Benedict, we…."

"I know." He was already retracing his sound circle, making the music fade away. Once the hologram had faded, he pivoted so he was back to back with Rune. "What do we do, Rune?"

"I suppose that's the question, isn't it? Does my shield crystal work in here?" Rune squinted as a figure emerged from the forest. "Or are we even going to need it?"

At the change in her voice, St. Benedict checked over Rune's shoulder, seeing what she was seeing.

"Well met, Faerie Friends," Lady Wilde greeted with her broad fox-like smile. In this digital world, she looked more alien than the landscape. She wore the same red shirt, black leggings with knee high boots and black top hat she had on at the Con. Her foxtail flicked behind her happily while she stood with her fists on her ample hips, legs slightly apart. Just over her head, a single yellow light bounced in the air.

Behind her, Rune still felt St. Benedict completely turn around, his warmth a presence against her back. He was on edge, the darkness possessing him sending off an unpleasant tingle as it gathered once more around him, and subsequently her.

The Fae in front of them seemed to notice, because her smile diminished a bit. She dropped into a bow that seemed courtly, but also had an edge of submission from a lesser predator to a more dominate one.

"And greetings to you, Step-Father. Mother awaits you." The Fae cocked her head to the side.

Rune bit the inside of her lower lip. "So I was right. He is possessed by the spirit of the Oberon. Or at least a part of it?"

Lady Wilde inclined her head toward the Finder. "You are welcome to come as well, Faerie Friend. And yes, you are correct. Step-Father here is one of the few who has ever survived an encounter with Father. Because of that, the Oberon has left his mark in your companion's soul. A seed, if you will, that Mother has encouraged to grow."

Glancing over at St. Benedict, who had gone completely stony faced and still, Rune tried not to feel unsettled. There was no sign of the antlers, but the darkness seemed to cloak him, just on the edge of her ability to perceive it. Still, Rune couldn't shake the feeling of coldness coming off of him. He was becoming a Changeling, and once that happened there would be no turning back.

"Did you bring us here?" Rune asked, directing the question at the Fae.

"Eventually, but not at first. It was quite a trick of mine to save you before you were lost in who knows what dimension." Lady Wilde laughed. When Rune and St. Benedict didn't join in, she pursed her eyebrows a little. "You do understand that those little mages were trying to banish you to a hell dimension, never to be heard from again, right?" She turned her back to them, dropping a finger to point in Rune's direction. "And you, little Faerie Friend. You simply dropped into the hole after him." She crooked the finger in a come-hither gesture. "Now, please follow me. We shouldn't keep Mother waiting."

"By Mother, you mean the Titania, don't you?" Rune asked.

Lady Wilde flicked her tail flirtily, flashing a half smile over her shoulder before walking off into the forest. In quick succession, the eyes surrounding them floated closed. A few shadows moved in the low ambient glow of the forest.

"They're gone," St. Benedict's voice rumbled behind her.

"Do you know what they were?" Rune asked, scanning the darkness around them.

"You ever seen what an angler fish looks like?"

"With the big scary eyes and the equally scary teeth? But don't they also have that glowing thing in front to attract prey with?"

"What do you think that thing is?" St. Benedict pointed at the yellow floating lantern that was still drifting lazily over Lady Wilde's head.

The foxy Fae had stopped a few feet away, tapping her foot in impatience. "Are you coming?"

"I'm going to have nightmares about this," Rune muttered.

After a few minutes St. Benedict called, "Why are we walking?"

"Because walking is something I understand," Lady Wilde said, glancing over her shoulder, flashing uncertainty. "None of this makes me very comfortable, you understand. A world of darkness and order. It goes against everything I was created from."

"You were a hominal once, right?" Rune searched her memory for whatever she knew about Lady Wilde.

"We all must come from somewhere." Lady Wilde's tail flicked sharper now and Rune decided to not continue that obviously tender subject.

"I just thought that Changelings were rarer than that," Rune explained, hoping that ended it.

It didn't. "And are you asking how one such as me could have become a lady-in-waiting to the Titania?"

"Why did you bring us here?" St. Benedict asked, taking over entirely to Rune's relief. All she could think to say were panicked apologies, which was often a mistake when dealing with the Fae, even if one was a Faerie Friend.

The Lady Wilde immediately brightened, almost skipping with child-like glee as if the rage she had been building had never been. "Mother is most eager to see you, Step-Father."

"But why here?"

"Because this is where Titania is," Rune answered.

Lady Wilde nodded. "Indeed. I am a loyal Daughter to my Mother."

"That's why you and Lady Trella were sitting at odds in the meeting. She chose the Oberon and you chose the Titania," Rune concluded, speaking half to herself.

"You are very astute, Faerie Friend. I am sorry I did not have the opportunity to meet you prior to this day. Much has been said among our folk about what you and your former mistress did to aid us." Lady Wilde actually lifted her hat a bit in salute as she spoke.

"I remember that night," Rune said somberly. "Did you know Maddie?"

"Yes, and I have paid my debt to her as well. How is the repair job on your belt working out?"

Despite herself Rune blinked.

The Fae turned, sliding her eyes away with a satisfied smile. "Honestly, I would have been honor bound to repair it for free, but thank you all the same, Step-Father, for paying for my materials. It's hard for a Fae to get by these days."

"Maddie asked you to repair my belt?" Rune asked.

"Yes, so that when you took over as the Head of the Household, you'd be prepared. Sorry I was late." Lady Wilde looked down for a brief moment guiltily. "I kind of got hung up taking care of my Mother, but I still fulfilled my end of the bargain and that's what counts."

The Fae ducked under a branch and promptly disappeared. Rune checked her step, staring at the absolute blackness in front of her. Before she could follow, St. Benedict grabbed Rune by the arm suddenly, halting her.

"Step back," he ordered softly. His voice had the weight of someone who had spotted a predator. Rune complied without protest or demand for explanation. As she backed up, the glowing yellow light that had been floating above Lady Wilde appeared in her sight. She realized with horror how close she had come to...the presence that was at the end of that light. What little she could see of its black undulating underbelly and the hint of long sword-like teeth were plenty to drive home the point. It was all she could do, resisting the child-like urge to scurry behind St. Benedict for protection.

He brought them back at least three steps, which was out of the range of the creature, when a tinkling laugh, like a computer's idea of chimes, cascaded around them. A mass of lights zipped out of the digital forest, moving and undulating like a murmur of starlings, and surrounded them on all sides.

"What's happening?!" Rune had to shout over the rising noise from the lights, their calls almost drowning her out to her own ears completely.

"It's data, masses of data," St. Benedict called back. The living lights had brought a wind with them and Rune's hair whipped around her head. Oddly, the wind didn't touch St. Benedict. Out of the ground, crystals burst, shards of red, yellow, and blue.

"Whoa!!" was all Rune could say as she almost lost her footing on the unstable ground. Both of them wobbled on their feet, St. Benedict landing his hand on Rune's shoulder for all the good it did to help them balance.

"*Welcome!*" The voice declared joyfully. "*You've come! You've come! It is so wonderful to see you!*"

The mass of moving lights began undulating above them before vomiting itself over the crystals. As each light hit a different crystal, the shards began to reshape themselves. In a matter of moments, a room had appeared inside the clearing of strange trees.

It looked like something out of a Renaissance Faire. Carpets laid over the ground in fractal patterns while above silken cloth had been draped over poles to create a canopy. The patterns didn't follow how the cloth lay, instead there was a continuous image to St. Benedict's eyes. It was like a surrealist artist had painted the space. Field chairs and a pavilion had appeared at one end, as well as a decadent-looking, circular bed piled with pillows.

"That's very suggestive," Rune muttered, pointedly looking at the bed. For the briefest of moments, an image flashed in St. Benedict's mind involving that bed, but he snapped his attention back.

"Yes, the question is, who is the suggestion for?" St. Benedict wasn't really asking. He knew the answer.

Then, he turned his head to look at a Greek-style lounging couch that had appeared next to a table, holding a bowl of crystallized fruit. Upon the couch was the woman he had seen in the hotel. She was dressed now in a diaphanous robe that wasn't any one color, but rippled up and down the rainbow as she moved. Across her chest was a single dark, wine-red strip of cloth and equally dark balloon pants that hugged her hips well below her navel. When she shifted, it showed more skin exposed by slits on the side of her pants from the waistband to her knee. The underside of the cloth glowed an icy blue, lighting her pale skin when she moved. She smiled at St. Benedict as the remaining data-lights burst around her, falling slowly like stardust. It was a vision of a goddess.

"Welcome, Saint of Liars," the woman's voice came, but her lips did not move. Only her smile quirked a little bit more.

"Rune, can you hear her talking?" he asked softly.

The Finder followed his eyes to the lounger. "I'm guessing you see something I don't?"

"What happened to your lovely visage? I finally had you looking right and now you're back to the way you were before." The woman pouted out her lip, then gestured with an elegant hand. This time black flecks rose up from the miasma that cloaked him, swallowing St. Benedict as they did so.

He vaguely heard Rune shouting his name, but it was distant and tinny again. Instantly, his vision returned to various shades of red, except for the woman before him in white and the woman next to him who had once again turned golden.

"St. Benedict! It's alright, I'm here!" the woman in gold said and she touched his face. Her touch burned and made him angry, but instead of ripping her arm off and drinking her blood, he pressed his blackened taloned hand against the back of hers. The burning increased and gave him focus.

All at once, the pain stopped. The red abated, clearing back into a world of color. Rune's hand cupped his cheek and he wanted it to stay there forever. Instead, he let her reclaim it.

"Turn on your augmentations," Rune whispered to him. He heaved a deep breath and let his green-rimmed eyes go blue. "Better?"

"Yeah," he said, straightening again. The other woman had taken to her feet, her face reflecting Rune's concern. His companion glanced over at the beautiful woman.

"You can't keep doing that to him. He's not your creature," Rune said.

"You see her now?" he asked under his breath. Somehow knowing that she was real made him feel better. He wasn't simply going crazy as he unconsciously feared.

"Yes, I see her. She was glamouring herself so I couldn't. Part of a Fae's arsenal of tricks." Rune took a step forward and bowed slightly from her waist before saying louder, "Greetings Titania, Queen of the Faeries." It was a very formal way to address someone, but the Titania nodded her head solemnly.

"I did not intend for us to meet this way, but…." Titania shrugged one beautiful shoulder. "So much has been unintended lately. Welcome Rune, Heir of the Magdalene. Though my Daughter tells me that you have claimed your House as your own?"

"More or less," Rune agreed. "But it is still the House Magdalene for now."

"Very well then." The Titania returned to lounge on her couch and gestured to a chair that had grown on the other side of the small side table. In fact, the small side table had gotten a little bigger to include a crystal flask and a pair of goblets. "Please sit, little mageling. It has been ages since I've had visitors and I would enjoy a good gossip."

Rune slid a look at St. Benedict, who was now being ignored

by the royal Fae in front of him. It was like playing a chess game except he only had some of the pieces, forcing him to hope Rune held the others. She certainly seemed comfortable enough as she did as the Faerie Queen bid, walking over to sit in the chair by her side.

"I suppose you have several questions you want answers to. Your kind always does," the Titania said resignedly. She took up the flask and yanked the stopper.

"How are you feeling?" Rune asked. The Finder leaned forward a bit and if she was playacting concern, St. Benedict couldn't tell.

The Titania paused in her movements, the slightest hiccup in her otherwise smooth, graceful dance as she began to pour something like quicksilver or mercury from the flask.

"I feel wonderful, thank you for asking," she said, sounding rote and overly pleasant.

Boldly, Rune set her hand on the Titania's hand.

"Clarissa. I know I'm not Maddie, but I am a friend," she said softly. The Titania froze as rigid as the crystal surrounding them. They stayed that way for a long time and St. Benedict began calculating how fast he could move to pull Rune away or possibly shield her with his body from the attack he sensed building. All around them, the crystals shifted to a sick yellow, altering the sense of light. Precisely, the Titania turned her head to the little, forward magic user, pinning her with a sharp, hostile stare. Rune did not flinch nor look away.

Tears, like beads of light, welled at the bottom of the royal Fae's eyes.

"I'm dying," she whispered. With the tiny confession, the crystal's colors muted and began shifting quietly through the spectrum. The Titania resumed pouring the drink, regaining her composure. "I'd offer you some but it's not really wine," she said, plucking the cup up and sipping it. "I wouldn't want to accidentally poison you."

"That's fine," Rune agreed. "Clarissa, what's happening? What do you mean you are dying?"

"Well, I'm not dying now, obviously." She smiled, folding herself over her crossed legs in a picture of decadent beauty waiting for a close up. "That bastard thought he had gotten me, and here I sit having the last laugh."

"Except...the Oberon has been reborn," Rune said carefully.

The Titania leaned back, snorting. "Not for long. And I will guarantee this newest upstart will be the last soon."

Rune furrowed her eyebrows. "You can't keep killing the Oberons...Clarissa, that's murder."

Now the Fae was on her feet. "You dare much, mageling!"

"I am a Faerie Friend," Rune countered smoothly. It was amazing how serenely she kept her composure. "And an innocent, according to your own rules. You won't harm me."

"Then you should understand that those who met their *just* ends couldn't have done so if they had not already committed equally heinous deeds or worse."

"I'm not here to judge you. I am only trying to help you."

"I do not need your help," said the Titania, in the time honored tradition of those who indeed needed help. She turned away from Rune, finally fastening her eyes on St. Benedict, who had stood there watching with his hands in his pockets.

The obvious dismissal didn't even slow Rune down. "It's murder, Titania," Rune said, switching to the Fae's formal title.

"They were unworthy interlopers who were only pursuing easy power. The current one is no different."

Rune stood up as well, only because continuing to sit felt wrong. "You're right, Calvin is a piece of trash human, but he is the Oberon. After so many dead Oberons...." Rune's voice hitched a note. "You can't keep doing this to your children. Every time this happens, they lose another Father, they grieve just as badly, whether they knew him or not. They mourn him again and again."

"Soon, they will have a new Father and everything will be right. *I* will make it right." She began to slink across the fractal patterned floor toward St. Benedict, her robe drafting behind her majestically. "I'll give them a Father worthy of the name. A man of the hunt. One who understands duty and allegiance. A warrior. A King...."

"You don't look like you're dying."

The Titania double blinked at St. Benedict's interruption,

like it wasn't something that happened very often. She was less than a foot away from him. Her aura already reaching out to caress him and entice him. It was like playing with a pretty, volatile cat that might try to bite his face off as much as it was rubbing against him looking for affection. The whole time over her shoulder, St. Benedict could see Rune's anxious look in his periphery. She was jealous. He could tell by the panicked way her eyes kept darting between the two of them. Keeping his focus on the Titania, he hooded his eyes.

"Nothing about you says you are dying."

"Uh, when the Oberon dies his Titania perishes shortly after and vice versa," Rune explained, moving to physically intercede between them. She was fearful for him. Possession and protection. It was a fine line between the two.

He needed to do something about that. His gaze lingered on the Titania's lovely face in front of him and ignored the weight of Rune's presence next to him. There was pleading behind the haughty, powerful surface of the Fae Queen's eyes. She wanted him to like her and accept her. Things in her life had become complicated, anyone could see that based on her choices. She had compromised herself and wanted to believe that she was still what she had always been. She wasn't.

He slipped on his wicked smile.

"You look pretty *alive* to me," he said, letting his innuendo dwell. The smile that burst on the Faerie Queen's face was the definition of radiant, washed in relief. He felt Rune take a step back. A retreat. She wasn't going to fight, which was what he had come to expect of her. As much as she had grown in strength of personality and as much as he admired her for it, her pathway to being easily intimidated was still well-formed when she was on unsure ground. He had a shot at making her leave.

"Why did you bring us here?" he asked, letting his voice go more breathy, "Was it for a three-way?"

The beautiful woman in front of him was taken aback by the question, but he just waited with his smile as she processed it. Her calculation came to a conclusion and her eyes slid over to Rune.

Chapter 18

"Thank you for safe guarding my new consort," the Titania said, taking Rune's hands in her own. The shift from sexy and hostile, to friendly and warm was so fast, it was unsettling. Rune and St. Benedict shared a glance, both understanding in that moment that the Titania was crazy.

The Queen of Faeries cupped Rune's face gently, looking at her tenderly. "You are a true Faerie Friend. When everyone was trying to hurt him, you protected and defended him and then brought him to me." She leaned in even closer and whispered, "You are the guardian of destiny."

"Titania," Rune gently removed the hand from her face. What she was about to say needed to be out of eye scratching range. "When I leave here, I'm taking St. Benedict with me." Her eyes searched the Titania's face as the friendly mask went rigid again. Rune was sure she was about to get attacked and if she was, she would lose. Rune may have been a Faerie Friend and theoretically that meant the Titania wouldn't hurt her with magic, but Rune wasn't as sure those rules applied to fingernails.

"Do you make a claim on him?" the Titania asked, carefully.

Rune's eyes went wide, but she bit her lower lip, unwilling to speak.

"I see," the Titania clucked, stepping back with a newfound respect for Rune. "It was you who pulled him from me before. You have a strong enough connection." A new calculating look crossed her face. With a flourish she turned, her robe cascading behind her. Elegantly, she sat again on the lounging couch. "I will make you a bargain, little mageling."

"I'm not here to bargain, Clarissa," Rune said, invoking her true name again.

"And I am, Rune," the Titania answered. "Bring me the Oberon. If you can succeed in doing that, I will let the Saint of Liars go. If he wants to leave that is." Her sly smile clearly said that she intended to do whatever it took to convince him otherwise. She clasped her hands under her chin as she waited for a reply.

"You want me to trade one life for another?" Oh, Rune did not like where this conversation was going.

The Titania shrugged one shoulder as she said, "If you like."

"I won't be a party to murder."

Laughing out loud, the Titania readjusted her seat on her couch so she could lean back. "Oh my, she is such a goody two-shoes. You can see how much you're worth to her. She won't even kill for you," she said to St. Benedict. She waved a dismissive gesture at Rune. "Begone. You know my deal. Decide for yourself what you will or will not do."

With the gesture there was a cracking sound. Nearby an arc of lightening cut through the lifeless black over the ethereally lit trees to strike one of them less than ten feet away. Instead of splintering, like any real tree would do, the branches filled with the light, funneling the lightening's energy inward. Once the tree was at capacity it began to change. The inside seemed to shimmer at first, then deconstructed the tree from the outside, breaking the tree into pixelated cubes. The cubes collapsed down into a jumping pile before restacking themselves into a new shape. Within moments, a form appeared and the lights calmed and were replaced with color and texture. Where a tree had been, there now stood a familiar door.

"Is that the door to the Lucky Devil?" Rune asked, staring at the familiar scuffs and stains of the front door of her bar. Rune had a strong feeling of déjà vu.

"More or less," the Titania said.

"Which is it? More or less?" Rune cocked an eyebrow at her.

Blowing out an exasperated breath, the Titania sat up again, wiggling her bare feet like a little girl. "I'm doing the best I can, I'm pretty sure that door will take you to your bar, but the magic doesn't necessarily….translate."

To the surprise of both women, St. Benedict popped open his

hand and scanned the door with the beam that it emitted. Once he was finished, he flipped the same hand open, the hologram appearing in the center with computer code streaming in a circle beneath it. "It appears to be a coded exit door." He peered closer at the coding. "This doesn't make any sense. It's like...." his voice trailed off as he studied it.

"It's like the symbols in Abraxas's work room," Rune muttered softly, coming closer to get a better look. "Does that mean...?" She stopped saying what she thought it meant, now more suspicious of the Titania than she was before.

The Faerie Queen hadn't moved from where she was sitting, watching her guests as they were awed by what she had done. It made Rune wonder. St. Benedict had called this an augmented reality and Rune recognized it as a realm much like the Faerie Court. The implications were profound if what she was thinking was correct.

They had to tell someone.

"We could make a run for the door together," Rune whispered as softly as she dared.

"She's not going to let me through that door and we both know it. It's me she wants. You go."

"Look, I don't know where that door goes, and I really don't know if there even is a way to come back here. I'm also not sure this is a 'here.'"

"Rune, I want you to go through that door and don't even try to come back." St. Benedict collapsed his analysis, closing his hand into a fist.

"What?" She couldn't believe what she was hearing. "Of course I'll be back. I'll find Maxamillion and whoever else I need and we'll get you out of whatever this is."

"If Maxamillion has followed his standard modus operandi, and I have no reason to believe he hasn't, he has already disavowed me and will kill me or let me be killed, whichever is the most convenient."

Rune's eyebrows knitted together. "What are you talking about?" She graduated from a whisper to a hiss.

He leaned in, speaking with his own hiss. "I attacked him and everyone else at a very delicate meeting that he has tried to orchestrate for ages. The only hope he has to save face, and maybe that deal, is to burn me at the stake for it. There is absolutely no way he would want to recover me and would probably be very satisfied putting the bullet in me himself."

"He can't…."

"My contract says he can. Legally."

"But that's…evil."

"I would make the same call if I was him."

Rune huffed, jutting her jaw in frustration. "Well then, I'm not abandoning you. We can figure this out if we stick together."

St. Benedict sighed, looking down as he rubbed the back of his neck. "Look Rune, I've tried to be kind about this, but you are not getting that I simply do not want to be around you." He looked up then, watching as his words struck her. "I don't want to work with you. I don't want to be associated with you."

Unsurprisingly, she looked stunned. "But…we're in this… you need my help…like when you came after me…."

"Okay, Rune. I do not know how I can make this any clearer for you. Hell, I was never supposed to see you again, but I couldn't let you get hurt either. Okay? This all happened because I was trying to do the right thing. That doesn't mean I want…." Why was this so hard? His brain felt like it was buckling.

He glanced over at the Faerie Queen. She watched with calm reserve. Enjoying his rejection of what she had perceived as her rival. Taking a step closer, he lowered his voice and placed both his hands on Rune's trembling shoulders.

"I understand, okay? It's not your fault. When last I saw you, I had an agenda and seducing you was a way to achieve it. I manipulated you into having feelings for me. That's all it is. I preyed on a fat girl's insecurities."

To say she looked shocked would have been an understatement. Rune shoved his hands off her shoulders angrily. "Don't you dare say that to me." Her voice trembled and tears beaded at the bottom of her eyes. Good. She was getting angry. He needed her to hate him.

"I don't love you," he intoned, before gesturing between the two of them. "This is never going to happen."

She took another step back, no longer looking at him. Her

gaze elsewhere, slowly shaking her head no. "I...I never said that I loved you," she said.

He wanted to let it play out in her head. He had said the crucial things. But he had to be sure she finally got it.

"You didn't have to, Rune. I have that effect on everybody. You're nobody special."

Her head snapped up at that, her face flooded with rage and hurt. He clenched his jaw against it, meeting her eyes. He would not look away from this, he'd take all of it. He was the cause of it, after all. If he had any shred of honor left, let it be in this moment. For a moment, he thought she was going to hit him and there was a sense of disappointment when instead she turned and walked away.

He wanted to say he was sorry. He wanted to hedge, to say something kind, but he knew if he did, it would only hurt worse later. Let her walk away and deal with her pain without him once and for all.

"*Oh my, that was...cruel,*" the Faerie Queen said. She was sitting up, watching as Rune walked away toward the door. "*You know she won't be coming back for you now?*"

"*Yes.*"

A look of concern crossed the Faerie Queen's pretty face and she stood up quickly to follow the Finder. He checked himself from stopping her.

"Mageling," the Titania said, catching up to Rune before she opened the bar door. "One last thing." The Titania bit her lower lip a second as Rune patiently waited despite the hostility she felt. "If you would rather, and this is totally up to you, you can still bring me the Oberon and I will trade you something else for him."

"What?" Rune's voice was hostile and flat.

The Titania leaned in closer. "Justin Masterson. Your husband, correct? I know you want him, but for some reason you can't find him can you? Ironic for you, isn't it?" She smiled secretively.

"You know where he is?" Rune asked, the breath escaping her.

The Titania maintained her knowing smile in response.

"I'll trade you yours for mine."

Rune glanced at St. Benedict, who stood watching and listening. He looked alarmed at the offer, but Rune was past asking him his opinion. She could see for herself it was a weak deal, but still….

The Finder nodded as she turned the knob on her door. "I'll think about it."

"Oh thank heavens and earth, she's gone," the Titania laughed. "Don't get me wrong, I like the little mageling, but she is so *good*, it's laughably child-like. Not like us." Her appraising eyes drifted over St. Benedict again. "I think you agree with me, my Oberon."

St. Benedict cocked his head to the side. He was familiar with this game. "There already is an Oberon and he's not me."

Slip the hands in the pockets. Lean back a little while thrusting hips forward. He knew the posture was appealingly masculine. Her eyes reflected that it was working. She saw what she wanted, and was salivating for it.

"Or you can be my Oberon." Her smile turned predatory. "I can do it. I can make it happen."

"And why would I want that?"

Her eyes narrowed ever so slightly. He knew he had offended her, but she wanted too much from him to let that offense change her tactics.

"It is a fair question," he continued, lightening his voice as he strolled around the edges of the clearing. "I know very little of your world, your power. I understand it all in the vaguest of terms at best. Hardly an ideal candidate to rule."

"The only thing that makes you an ideal candidate is if I desire it so," she said imperiously. She was a queen after all.

"As a concubine sure, but you want to make me your equal, your partner."

"I could still make you my concubine," she purred.

"You're playing all your cards at once. Are you in a hurry? Usually when a woman wants to seduce me, they take their time."

The Faerie Queen laughed. "I don't need to seduce you, honey. You're already mine." She gestured with an open hand

and he gasped. The invisible fingers rolled up his spine as her hand moved. "If I wanted to, I could ignite a fire within you that would burn you to the core and make you ask for more."

He could feel it. He was sinking into her control. The Fae Queen's magic taking him by the balls and soul. And a part of him liked it. Liked giving up control and letting someone else decide for him. For so long he had kept himself tied to his rules, tied to his private code that no one else knew or understood. He was his own warden and prisoner. Yet, here was an escape from that, to let another be his master. The relief was tempting.

As soon as the talons covered his hands, he smashed his fingers into the wound on his arm again. Howling in pain, he continued to squeeze, forcing himself back into control. It made his knees buckle and he fell forward onto them, lancing more pain up his thighs. That was fine. He needed every ounce of stimulus to fight back.

"What are you doing?!" came the panicked voice of the Faerie Queen through the haze. She was by his side then, tearing his arm away from where he clasped it against his chest. His blood spilled onto the ground. "You're hurt!"

He stared down at his arm. He *was* hurt. The world in front of his eyes got brighter as he tried to focus on the red color of his blood. It was strange how dark, almost black, it could look when there was so much of it in one place. With tingling fingers, he plucked away the white bandage now torn and splattered red. He thought to discard it but he couldn't for some reason. He was supposed to keep it on. Someone would be very upset with him for not doing that. With numbing fingers he tried to put it back, but it was too hard to think. That's when he realized he was going into a too familiar sense of shock. He had lost too much blood too fast and when that happened he always became exceedingly dizzy.

"I need to…." he slurred, trying to rise to his feet. He wasn't in a safe place, but he was going to pass out regardless.

"No, stop," the Titania said urgently. She took his head and laid it against her shoulder. "Please, my future King, let me help you."

He wanted to pull his head away but he couldn't. The

darkness was taking him. The darkness smelled of gardenias.

It was darkness all around. But it was simply the airiness of darkness. There was a thickness to it, like she was floating in dense soup.

Rune was unsure how long she had been there in the infinite dark. It wasn't scary. She didn't feel afraid per se or terribly surprised that the Titania had tricked her. It was pretty obvious once she had gone through the door and found herself being taken by this space. She would have likened it to dreaming, except she was still very much aware. Wasn't she? She knew time had to be passing and yet it didn't feel like it. That didn't panic her either. She knew there was urgency, but there was enough time. Infinite time, actually.

"Maybe this is what feeling high is like?" she asked herself out loud. Now that was surprising. She heard that. It was also the first time in a while she had inhaled. There was air here if she needed but she didn't seem to need it. Where was she? And why did her heart hurt?

"I need to wake up," she said. Saying that did something. The darkness changed. Becoming less uniform and more…aware.

It was so tempting to stay there. So restful. She felt like her spirit was filling up, feasting on the darkness. The darkness gave itself willingly. It was a good darkness. A benevolent, loving darkness. A place of rest.

"But how do I get out of it? Where exactly am I?"

The darkness changed again. Responding to her spoken words, then pulling back a little, leaving Rune to feel like she was floating in a bubble instead of an ocean. Rune thought for a moment that the darkness was alive, with its own sentience, and she wondered if she had offended it. No, there was understanding here. But also no answers.

Rune rested in the darkness a while longer. With nothing else to do, she let the thoughts float in and out of her quiet brain, noting them and letting them go. Was she just a consciousness or did she still have a body? Sliding her hands down her sides confirmed that she still had a body and clothes. In fact, she still wore her belt. Looking down did little good, there was no light to see by.

"I need to find a way out of here and go home. Or maybe… Find…." As soon as that thought passed through her mind and out her mouth, the belt, Maddie's gift to her began to shine. Light coiled around the belt like fine thread and Rune was able to see herself by it. Parsing out a strand was simple too. It was her magic, delightfully easy to access. In this place she could see it for what it was. Potential. Simply give the magic an idea to cleave to and it would form to that idea. The magic was simply energy that needed her to form it into something. The only thing that dictated what that would be was herself and the limited being that she herself was.

A fire Talent would create fire from the magic, because fire was an idea they understood. The body could heal at the thought of healing. The mind could ease from the touch of another mind through magic. A Finder could Find their way home. She had the rope, all she needed was an anchor point.

Rune thought of the bar. She pictured Lucky Devil sitting in his booth, smiling at the room. She thought of the smell in the air and the kitschy devil memorabilia on the walls that wasn't really just memorabilia. She imagined the slight hum of magic that coated everything waiting to fulfill Maddie's dormant spells.

As she thought all these things, the bar appeared around her. It wasn't her actual bar though. It was made out of the darkness, faded to grays. She stood in the middle amongst the scattering of tables and chairs. The longer she stood there, the more the bar manifested to the slightest details, except for the color. Only three of the dozen light orbs floated over their sconces humming with magic, the broken ones sat instead, dark like blackened teeth. Other places throughout the bar were lacking the stardust shimmer of the magic as well. She could see the world she was currently in trying to feed magic into the empty places, but with no spell to hold it together, it wouldn't flow. She would need to learn to give it shape so it could fulfill itself, the darkness seemed to inform her. It was waiting.

Rune turned about the room, feeling the floor beneath her feet. For a moment, Rune thought the room was empty, but then Ally shifted in her seat at the bar. The kid sat there, heaved a big sigh as she flipped through her phone, bored. The fact that that bit of technology was working so well in the bar was another indication of how far the deterioration of the bar's magic had gone.

"Ally," Rune called, her voice sounding tinny to her own ears. No reaction from the kid. Next, Rune took a thread of her magic from around the belt, the tingle of the raw stuff swirling around her fingers. It had never behaved this way before. She liked it. "Retainer, I summon you." This time the tinny words warped into a voice echoing with power. It had an effect. Ally sat up a little straighter and looked around the bar. Sending the power out, Rune instantly connected to the kid, who jumped in her chair. The power slipped away.

"Ally! You need to help me!" Rune called out.

Ally stood up then, frantically looking around. "Alf! Elias!" she shouted.

"What?" Alf called back from the next room.

"Something's…I don't know…just get in here!"

With a lot of inaudible grumbling, there was a scraping sound and heavy footsteps.

"What is it?" Alf asked when he reached the door connecting the Lounge Bar to the Main Bar. Elias was close behind him and continued to move into the room, his eyes roving about as if he sensed something.

"I thought…I thought I heard…." Ally started, unsure.

Elias nailed her with his eyes. "You thought you heard Rune?"

The kid nodded, looking really freaked out.

"Rune!" Elias shouted into the void in the room. "Rune, if you're here. Summon us again."

"Elias Leveau, I summon you," Rune shouted and she sent her magic out again. Without looking at it, Elias's hand shot out into what seemed to him to be thin air and caught the magic line. Immediately, he filled in with color for Rune, power reverberating between the two of them, connecting their hearts. She could see Elias as he truly was, old. Far older than she had thought, by a lot. And as full of magic as she was.

"She's in the Dreamscape!" he shouted. His eyes still

searched the air for her but were unable to see her. Alf was immediately by his side.

"Alf FitzMagdalene, I summon you!"

Again, the power branched out and her bar manager caught it. "Damn it!" he shouted, wincing in pain, but he didn't let go as he turned to Ally. "Get over here you idiot girl. Your Lady is calling for you."

"Ally Janowski, I summon you!"

Ally flailed at the air, trying to catch the magic that she couldn't see. But it slipped.

"Ally, you're doing too much. Let it happen!" Elias called.

"I can't," Ally cried distressed. "I can't...I...." She was so worked up she began to transform, diminishing into her smaller white dog form in a pool of clothes. As she wriggled out of her shirt, the little white girl-dog's ears perked up, her still human brown eyes looking right at Rune. Wagging her tail she began to yip excitedly.

"Ally Janowski, I summon you," Rune tried one more time and this time the kid was able to catch the magic.

And then the world equalized.

The world felt like it was spinning as St. Benedict laid on his back. Whatever he was lying upon was soft so he guessed it was the bed he had noted earlier. Cracking open his eyes he stared up at a void that seemed to suck him into nothing, so he closed his eyes once more and waited for ten breaths before trying again. It was still void when he opened them, but he didn't want to vomit any more either. Next was the throbbing arm, which he lifted up in front of his vision to confirm. It was bandaged with gauze. Someone had cut away part of his sleeve to get to the wounds. It all looked very professional.

"My magic is not what it used to be. I did what I could." He creaked his head to the left to see the Faerie Queen a few feet away. She leaned against a tree, staring off across the distance with something that looked like a cigarette in her hand. Only the end glowed green as she puffed on it and there was no smoke coming from it. All the same, she blew into the air and an array of colors bloomed above her, like she was smoking the Aurora Borealis, before it swirled away upward.

"I'm still alive," he said.

"Of course you are."

"And I'm waking up." He curled up, forcing himself to sitting.

"Is that significant?" the Faerie Queen asked, irate.

"Yes. You can't wake up inside a computer. It means that I am actually here." He looked her up and down. "I'm not so sure about you."

Her eyes slid over to him briefly as she blew out another breath of light and color. "Nursing was not what I expected to be doing on that bed."

"To be fair, I wasn't expecting it either." It took a lot of effort and some pain to scoot back and rest himself against the headrest that seemed to emerge from the large tree behind him. It was totally worth it.

"Why did you do that to yourself?" she asked, once he had settled, indicating his arm.

"Why are you trying to force this on me?"

"I do what I want."

"Exactly." That got her attention and he gave her a lazy smile from where his head set back against the tree.

"I see," she said.

"I see threads, but it isn't a thread, is it? I always thought the magic came from outside of myself, but it comes from within me into a form I can understand it in," Rune said as she snatched her fourth slice of pizza. She could never in her life remember a time she was so hungry. Nodding and passing her more napkins, Elias smiled knowingly, echoing the smile of Lucky Devil, who sat next to him.

"I wonder if I'm going to have anything more to teach you if you keep simply figuring these things out on your own."

"Well, except, I kinda remember Maddie telling me a long time ago, I just didn't want to hear it then, or even try to understand it. But now…I mean, this is amazing!"

"But I don't understand where you were exactly," Ally piped in as she approached the table with a tray of fresh cold beers.

"I call it the Dreamscape, but there are many names for it," Elias explained, taking a swig from one of the beers. "Maddie called it the Dreamtime. I knew a guy who called it LSD Town. Whatever you call it, it's thought to be the source of all magic, and this place," he indicated the bar, "is one of the spots where it naturally flows into the world. Which is why the Magdalene built this House here. Like a magical river and this House is the dam. It's also why you were able to pull yourself out of it."

"What would have happened if I had stayed there?" Rune asked warily.

"You would have eventually dissolved away into it." He laughed at Rune's look of horror. "It would have been a very peaceful way to go."

"Is that what all the devils are about then?" Rune pointed at the figures on the walls that had on various occasions come to life when she needed them most.

"The devils have been bound to this place. They protect this House from anything that would want to simply come through the portals unwelcome."

"I've seen those, the black places, when the House is expanded. This room gets bigger and there's all these spaces in the wall," Rune said, marking the circuit of the room with a finger.

Elias nodded, "Yes. In exchange they get to feed off of the energy produced by the portals leaking magic into the world from the Dreamscape and nothing else gets in or out without your permission."

"Like gargoyles protecting a castle," Ally said.

"Pretty much," Elias confirmed.

"And I am the only one who can access this well-font of magic?"

"Also more or less. You can grant use of this place as is your right as Lady of this House. That often is done with retainers, but it's certainly not limited to that. You could charge other magic users to access the magic here, but there are a lot of reasons to not do that, the biggest one is if you tap it too much, this access point will run dry of magic. Think collapsing blood vein that's been overused."

"So the belt helps me access that?" Rune had unbuckled said belt to lay it on the table as they talked. She ran her fingers over it, feeling the grooves like brail, only with less comprehension.

"Oh yes," Elias touched it as well. When he did, Rune felt the power buzz out of it, reverberating back and forth between the two magic users. "Most Heads of House have some sort of talisman like this. This belt was modeled after one Maddie once had before she simply stopped needing such a thing. She had this one created for you."

"But she gave this to me three years ago."

"And that's why she locked the magic away in it. You weren't comfortable with magic then, but the time it takes to sync with a talisman is slow. She let you get used to it gradually."

"So, when Lady Wilde repaired it as per her agreement with Maddie, apparently…I now have access to all the magic." Rune twirled her finger to indicate the room on the word 'all,' letting go of the belt as she contemplated that. She then took a good, long swig of her beer.

"Now remember, this talisman isn't the only way to access the magic, but it's incredibly useful and especially powerful in its own right. It's probably what protected you from the raw magic inside the Dreamscape."

"We seriously have to come up with a better name for that. It sounds a like a 70s Hair Metal song," Rune said, smiling. "And if that's the case then the Titania wasn't trying to kill me or I guess 'dispose' of me." Rune threw up the air quotes with her fingers. "She was sincere in saying it was the best she could do."

"See that's where I'm not sure. If she was in the Faerie Court or something like it, she should have been able to send you straight to the bar," Elias finished his beer and set the glass back on Ally's tray. "Get me four more shots, will you?"

"Seriously?" Ally asked, but after a huff, went back to the bar to do just that.

"Four shots?" Rune asked, arching an eyebrow.

"They're not just for me," her cousin assured her.

"Okay, I'm not doing four shots either."

Elias laughed just as Ally called, "Four shots of what?"

"The Devil's liquor," he called back dramatically.

After a beat of silence, Ally shouted, "Okay, what the heck is that?"

"Locked shelf. Get the key from Alf," Rune instructed, pointing at the shelf above the official "top shelf" alcohol. Locked Shelf was a special designation for the really, *really* good stuff, like $100 a shot. "And what do we need the highest price liquor for?"

"What else? Get drunk and do some magic." He smiled wickedly and Rune felt a lurch in her heart. Elias seemed to note the reaction because he shifted in his seat, before lowering his voice. "Maddie?"

Rune smiled. "Always Maddie."

"Okay, change of subject. Do you want to tell me what happened to St. Benedict after you two fell into the hole or should I start guessing?"

"He's alive...as far as I know," Rune said. She stared at the table, no longer wanting to finish the pizza on her plate, but forcing herself to in order to appear unaffected by Elias's questions. "The Titania possessed him, which is why he went on that rampage. She was trying to use him to kill Calvin. How much trouble are we in now with the Magic Guild?"

"Not much actually. Maxamillion, on the other hand... Well, I don't think his alliance is going to happen any time soon."

"St. Benedict said something like that would probably happen. He thinks Maxamillion will try to kill him. Then there's the Titania holding him hostage in this...place, but it wasn't the Faerie Court. It was all techie and digital creepy. The other weird thing was, St. Benedict could interact with it. He could hear things and do things in that world that I couldn't. It was like he was the magic user and I was a hominal."

Elias blew out a breath, and shook his head slightly. "Yeah, all of that is outside of what I know about how the Faerie Court works. It's more wild magic."

"That's just it. I'm pretty confident that wasn't the Faerie Court. But it was a real place, a real physical place. As real as this!" Rune laid her hands upon the table and wiggled it a little for emphasis.

"Of course it was real. Items made directly out of magic are just as real as anything else for as long as the spell lasts. Powerful beings like the Titania or the Oberon can make things that last centuries. Hence why your Faerie-crafted belt is so powerful; the spells on that will last as long as you live. That is something the Titania can do, I think."

"And St. Benedict has been working for her this whole time?" Ally piped in, coming back into the room and setting Alf's keys on the bar.

"No. Not like that. She said he had been marked by the Oberon. Two months ago, when Calvin first became the Oberon, he attacked St. Benedict as a Poh."

"Oh, I remember when the Oberon acquired that form. Back when the Oberon was from Asia…I wish I could remember exactly where. I'm going to have to go look it up now," Elias said cryptically.

"How long do Oberons usually last?" Ally asked.

"A mortal lifetime, in most cases."

That made the young woman pause. "But then….how old *are* you?"

"Never ask a magi his age," he said, then turned back to Rune. "Getting back to what's important here, he was probably marked then if he was wounded at all by the Oberon and lived without reconciling."

"Yes, that's correct. And now, she wants him to be her new Oberon instead of Calvin."

Elias furrowed his brow harder. "Wait, wait. Which Titania? The old one or the new one?"

"Clarissa," Rune said.

Elias cursed in some language Rune didn't recognize, but had heard him say before. "The Titania is still alive?"

"Yes, and she is the reason the Oberons don't live very long."

"Okay, I think I'm getting a headache," Elias said, just as Ally started to unfold the very noisy metal step ladder behind the bar. "Tell me if I got this right. The old Titania is still alive and killing off her Oberons. But wouldn't that be the worst thing she could do?"

"Well, the Oberon betrayed her, didn't he?" Ally asked, sliding bottles above her looking for the right one. "Woman scorned."

"Oh, she's definitely trying to get revenge. Calvin came to

me two days ago. Was it only two days?

"You've been gone a whole day since we saw you bungee jump without a tether into that portal, so you tell me," Elias answered.

"Alright, a few days ago, he came asking me for help to get him out of being the Oberon."

"After which when you refused, he attacked you in the alley," Elias finished.

Rune sniffed as she remembered, "Oh, right. I already told you that part."

"Yes, and he said at the Inner Council meeting that he needed protection from something that was trying to kill him," Elias supplied.

"Yes and that something is the Titania," Rune nodded. "She keeps killing off the Oberons. But she knows it can't continue, therefore she's trying to set things up so she can choose who her next Oberon will be. She wants one she thinks she can control."

"Probably so she can't be betrayed again," Elias nodded.

"Yeah, but what does that have to do with us?" Ally asked.

"Technically, nothing." Elias thumped the table. "Which is probably why she chose to let you go, since you are a Faerie Friend and all. This whole mess is between her and Calvin."

"It does involve me. I'm more than a Faerie Friend, I'm a Faerie Protector." Rune pointed up at the ceiling where the little Fae nests hung from the rafters, all occupied with sleeping Fae having their mid-day naps. "On top of that, she's offered me something...I kind of want."

"Which is?"

Rune waved her hand. "We'll get to that. Now, the Fae need a Titania and an Oberon. I mean, the way the little Faeries up there reacted when they saw Calvin...it's really important to them."

"Whatever you want to do, I'm behind you. If you want to get involved in this, then let's get involved. We also can *not* get involved with any of this."

"You sound like you're saying you don't want to get involved."

"I am hedging my bets so hard right now." Elias smiled a too toothy smile, saved by Ally finally approaching the table with her tray of four shots. "Okay, line them up in front of Lucky Devil."

"Is this called bar magic?" Ally joked, as she did as she was told.

"Yes, re-imagined by the Queen of Cocktails herself, Maddie. Now the magic in the bar is absolutely drink based and you're going to have to learn all of the incantations and cocktails to access it…"

"Wait, wait," Rune set her hand on the table, stopping all activity around her as her retainers turned to stare at her. She didn't acknowledge them as she stared into nothing, trying to force her brain to make a connection it almost had. "The Titania isn't in a Dreamscape." Then the light clicked on and she met Elias's eyes, hers wider than saucers. "She's not in a Dreamscape."

"Okay where is she?"

"I don't know, but it's not a Dreamscape per se. St. Benedict, back at Corinthe headquarters, showed me a device that allowed him to transport his consciousness into an augmented world. The computer was creating the world like a Dreamscape but St. Benedict called it a hologram. Only…." Rune raked her fingers through her hair. "No, that doesn't make sense, because it was real. I was physically there. St. Benedict was physically there. The one in the Praetorium was made of light and when I touched it, that disrupted it."

There was silence as everyone thought about that information.

"Okay, here's a thought. The Faerie Court is a real place, made out of magic right? Maybe the Titania is doing that same mojo?" Rune offered.

"But in a digital world?" Elias double blinked at that thought.

Rune nodded. "Is that possible?"

"I'd say no, because magic and tech don't mix, but she also said she wanted to give you a piece of the Masterson Files?"

"Not exactly." It felt like cold water had been dumped down Rune's spine. "But if she's got the missing piece, maybe it is the piece that lets magic and technology work together, somehow."

Elias and Rune stared at each other as they let that sink in.

"We need to find Calvin," Rune said two seconds before Elias said the exact same thing. Seizing the shots, one in each hand, Elias slid one to Rune. "I guess we are going to the Faerie Court."

"Cool," Ally said, as she dropped into the seat next to Rune.

"Nope. No. Out little missy," Elias said, twiddling his fingers at Ally to get up. "You're underaged for this spell."

"Aw, come on! I'm the first retainer," Ally whined, getting up with a bang and a huff.

Elias gave a wink. "And I shouldn't have even let you serve, baby jail bait.

Ally made a face. "What are you talking about? I'm not selling it to you. That is what's illegal."

"Don't worry about it, Ally," Rune tried to reassure the disgruntled teen, but Rune's laughing at her wasn't helping her get that idea across.

"Now, kid, you are going to wait here," Elias interjected, meeting Ally's eye as her glare morphed into outrage. Elias hurried through his explanation, "I don't expect to get stuck but you're going to need to pull us back if we do."

Ally hopped up onto one of the barstools as loudly as possible, crossing her arms with her best scowl.

"It's like watching a baby owl be mad at you," Elias cooed.

"Yeah, sure." Rune said, cocking an eyebrow at her cousin before turning the attention to the shot. It was apple green and there seemed to be particles floating inside it. "What is this, a teleportation spell?"

"It'll allow us to open the door to the Dreamscape and once inside, open the door to the Faerie Court. Lucky Devil here is the anchor," Elias explained. Or thought he explained.

Rune decided she needed to ask more about how this worked later. "We can't go the Faerie Court. Not the official one. That's been taken over by the Kodiak Corporation."

Elias pursed his lips. "Crap. Then, how do we find Calvin?"

Rune screwed up her face as she thought. It was a great question. Sliding the belt over to herself a bit more, she opened the flap that held her business cards. Flipping through the stack quickly she finally came up with a very plain, very cheap white one that was dog-eared on two of its corners. Holding it, she pushed a little of her magic into it. At first nothing happened and then the tiniest sliver of gold thread curled out of the top like a new plant breaking from the earth.

She blew a sigh. "It'll have to do."

"What will?" Elias asked, nodding at the card. "You have a way to Find him?"

"I think so. If you can open the Dreamscape, maybe I can make a door with this."

"Interesting," Elias chuckled, then picked up his shot. "Do as I do." He saluted the shot to the Lucky Devil. "To your health, sir." The inanimate statue jerked a little, as if Lucky Devil had simply dozed off a moment. Then he let go of his artificial lowball glass and took up the shot himself.

"Whoa," Ally breathed from the bar, completely forgetting to be mad.

Lucky Devil raised his shot and saluted with Rune and Elias. Together they drank and Rune almost tossed up her shot.

"Oh, yuck. What the hell? It's awful."

"It's an elixir," Elias said, capturing her shot glass before she dropped it. "Don't throw it up, you need that in your system."

Rune blinked and looked around the room. It was still her bar, except now it was huge. "I've seen this before," she said, eyeballing the various devils on the wall that were now twitching and fidgeting instead of being inanimate kitsch. The walls of the room had expanded, creating spaces that disappeared into darkness where wall should have been. Ally had disappeared from the space.

"Open your second sight," Elias said.

"My second sight?"

"Yeah, but only for a moment." Elias smiled as he watched Rune puzzle out what he was saying.

"Why do I have a feeling you're playing a trick on me," she said, turning her head to the space.

"I'm not really, but it'll be fun to see what you think. Go ahead. You'll be fine."

Rune took a deep breath and did as he said. Immediately,

she was overwhelmed with colors making up everything in the room. The dark spaces were no longer dark spaces but infinite halls full of possibilities that would never exist. She saw them for what they were, highways to other realms. Rune spun her gaze to the room and could even see Ally again, shimmering on the stool as she was, is, would be. Double blinking, Rune turned back to say something to Elias but her gaze was arrested by the Lucky Devil. He was alive and inanimate, a devil and a man. A man she knew, sitting in Lucky Devil's spot with human colored skin and real cloth clothing instead of acrylic.

"Uncle…Uncle Lucas?" she heard her voice asked, asking, will ask.

Picking up the fourth shot, the sorrowful man nodded to Rune before shooting it down. "To your health, kiddo," he said and set his empty shot onto the table upside down.

"Okay, Rune, that's enough," Elias said, saying, will say as he touched, touching, will touch her hand.

Closing her eyes, the second sight dissipated.

"I saw Uncle Lucas," she reported, looking again at the Lucky Devil, who was still an animatronic devil-man with tabasco-red skin.

"Interesting. You have full sight then. Glad you got over your fear of it," Elias said, patting her head, before doing some busy work with the shot glasses.

"How is Uncle Lucas…. Why did I…?" Rune growled. Why couldn't she form her question?

"I don't know. It was something Maddie never explained to me. But we're not here for that right now. You're up." He nodded over Rune's shoulder and she turned to look at the front door of the bar. It was the same door it always was, but light seeped through the cracks, intense as the sun.

"What do I do?" she asked, standing up to face it.

"I have no idea, but whatever it is, you better do it." He handed her the belt and Rune buckled it on with practiced swiftness. Fingering the business card, Rune approached the door. When she was a couple feet away from it, she held out the card. Focusing on the tiny thread of magic, she tried to picture Calvin in her mind. His cheap suits. His slicked back hair. The cruel glint in his eyes. The thread wavered in front of her, then died. Images of Justin flashed into mind, breaking her concentration. Before her eyes she could see the network of red threads that didn't lead her to anywhere.

Why wasn't it working? Rune turned the card over in her hands again. The name Calvin Harrison was embossed on the front. She remembered the day he had first thrust it at her. Maddie was still alive, but she had refused, politely, to take the card. The weasel had sneered at her and thrust it instead at the apprentice standing beside her.

But that man didn't exist anymore, did he? She began to picture him the way he had appeared to her a few days ago. Disheveled. Genuinely frightened. Desperate. Setting the card before her again, Rune played the image of him in her mind of the little Fae swirling around him. The sight of him in the Oberon's branch crown. The tender way he touched Lady Trella's shoulder. Then she pushed her magic out again, through the business card. This time the gold thread emerged stronger, more accurate. As it stretched for the door, it wrapped itself around the strongest of the red threads. The two threads coiled and shot through the door frame. Immediately, the light behind it changed, pulsing gold and red. The threads disappeared as the spell completed.

"Nice," Elias breathed appreciatively, coming up behind her shoulder. Rune tucked the card away.

"Let's go," Rune said.

Chapter 19

"Do you think she will come back?" St. Benedict opened his eyes. The Faerie Queen had been so silent for so long, he had started to drift off again.

"Are you really concerned she will take me away?" he asked. The elegant woman took another drag from her never-ending cigarette then discarded it. The little stick twirled end over end into space, before flashing into a spark of light and vanishing.

"What is your relationship with her?"

"What's yours? She called you Clarissa."

"It is my name."

"Not Titania?"

She sniffed her nose at him with royal disdain. "You know very little of the Fae, don't you?"

"You seem to know very little about me, yet you want me to be your cabana boy," he countered, half-smiling wickedly.

"I know more than you think," she dismissed, drifting across the space to the side of the bed. She sat down on a stool that hadn't been there until she had sat upon it. She plucked a bowl from a table beside them, taking up the spoon. Steam seemed to roll from the top, carrying with it a hearty smell. "I know you betrayed your wife."

She held out a spoonful of soup to him, while he in turn stared murder at her. She was unfazed by it, but simply waited for him to take the spoonful.

"It's not poison," she finally said.

"What the fuck do you know about my wife?" he growled, all pretense of playing the game dropping away.

She smiled sharply. "You snap at me with your big teeth, but you are the one with your soul out for all to see." She laid the spoon, still full, back into the bowl and set the whole thing to the side. Taking one nail she touched St. Benedict's chest. The feeling of ice pierced through him and he hissed through his teeth. "You don't get big gaping holes like this without having done some pretty terrible things. Betrayals. Lies. Broken oaths. Death. They lace your soul, unhealed, open for anyone like me to simply slip in."

She withdrew her finger and the sensation stopped. "I could see it in your mind. You bury it deep. Couched inside yourself like a precious stone, that sin you carry. My husband was much like you. Charismatic would be putting it clinically." She laughed to herself. "That monster was quite the charmer. We grew up together, you know. I loved him every day of my life." Her face was a ballet of emotions, switching from joy to sadness to cruel rage and back. It was so horrifying to watch that St. Benedict forgot to pretend he wasn't afraid for a moment.

"Tell me, do you think I'm pretty?" she asked abruptly, picking up the spoon again. "I do not have to keep this appearance. I can change it to anything that you might find more attractive." Before he could respond she was enveloped by light. Within moments, her form shifted and rebuilt itself. Now, instead of a chocolate haired woman, a striking blonde sat there, still holding the bowl with its soup. She shook out the waves of her hair and opened stunning blue eyes. Now, the Queen of Faeries looked like something out of a pinup catalog, all curves and softness, with a tiny waist.

"Very nice," St. Benedict commented neutrally, tamping down his anger. Picking a fight with her in this place would not serve him. He was truly at her mercy and he needed to keep his head about him. Thankfully, she held out the spoon and beamed as if he had complimented her. "Do you really expect me to eat that?"

"What's wrong with it?" she asked, pouting her full-red, lower lip.

"It's not real," he answered, pushing the spoon away.

Fire flared in the Queen's eyes and the colors of the crystals shifted again. "How dare you refuse food from my table," she spat regally. So much for not pissing her off.

Quickly, St. Benedict grabbed the spoon from her and shoved it into his mouth. Vegetable broth slapped his tongue with flavor. His gut grumbled and he realized how hungry he really was. He double blinked. He slid the spoon out of his mouth to stare at it.

"How are you doing that?" he asked the spoon.

"What exactly?" the Faerie Queen huffed.

"Food in an augmented reality has no taste. I mean, it's simple enough to stimulate the brain to believe it is eating something once the computer is in there, but the food never tasted…" he swallowed again, "…right."

"It's real," she sniffed, snatching the spoon back.

"It can't be, I saw you digitally create it. I'm not trying to insult you here, but I understand how computer translation works. No matter what my brain says, this can't go into my body as if it is food." St. Benedict looked down at his hand resting on his thigh. Slowly, he spread his palm out and pressed into the fabric, into the meat of his leg, feeling the bone underneath. "Except I am really here, aren't I?"

"Anything in my world I want to be real, will be real." His host stood and thrust the bowl out to him. "Feed yourself." He took it and she turned away as lightening crackled through the air above them.

There was a crackle in the air as Rune passed through the door. Magic raced up and down her body as she broke the plane and it made her hair start to rise up.

"Oh that feels funky," she said as she shivered and rubbed her arms. Elias was right behind her through the door.

"Ah, a freshly connected door. I have to admit I was a bit nervous about that. I've seen Maddie connect this door to several places before but never blindly."

"So that's reusable," Rune asked, indicating the Lucky Devil door that was now standing in the middle of a plain plastered hallway wall.

"Yes, if you connect the front of Lucky Devil's door while in the Dreamscape and with Lucky Devil guarding it, you can open a door to technically anywhere, but you usually need to know where you are going and what you're connecting to or it won't work at all. One of the times I tried it, all I got was a brick wall."

"Can we go back the same way?" Rune asked, now taking in the rest of the somewhat familiar hall.

"Hmm. Maybe." She shot him an alarmed look. "Hey, you're the one making up spells. I've never seen someone use a business card to connect a door to elsewhere before."

"Okay, first problems first." Rune fished out Calvin's business card again.

"Do you know where we are, out of curiosity?" Elias asked, taking his own perusal of the hallway. "I'm guessing apartment building?"

"I think we're at Maxamillion's compound," she said. Again, she focused on Calvin and the thread popped out from the card leading to the farthest away of the three doors in the hall. "After I was attacked in the alley, St. Benedict brought me here. They let me stay the night in one of these suites. Looks like Maxamillion extended Calvin the same invitation."

Just as she concluded that, a woman waddled backward into the hall, dragging a large potted plant, or maybe it was a small tree.

"Lady Trella?" Rune asked. Immediately the Fae spun around, her telltale orange skirt with its multi-shades of her favorite color, spinning about her in a pinwheel.

"The Finder! It's you, oh thank the trees. You can help me talk him out of it."

"I'm going to take a guess and say you're meaning Calvin," Rune concluded as the Fae crossed the hallway to envelope the Talent in a very dedicated hug. Rune tried to return it but her arms were well and truly pinned. "Um, yeah."

As abruptly as the hug started, it ceased as the Fae jumped back like she had been burned. "You've seen Mother!" she declared, her usually slitted eyes wide and round with shock.

"Um, yes. I have seen the Titania," Rune said, nodding warily. "I've come to speak to Calvin."

"How is she?" Lady Trella looked down as she asked, using her toe to rub at a piece of nothing on the industrial carpet. "You must think me a piece of crap daughter."

That stopped Rune a moment. As much as the Fae had chosen sides in this conflict, none of it was easy for any of them. "She looked well, but I'm not sure how much of what I was seeing was real."

Nodding, Lady Trella looked up. "Losing Father cost her much. She was always the stronger of the two."

"They need to reconcile," Rune said.

A flicker of hope lit into Lady Trella's eye. "You have come to mediate, Wizardress?"

"I came to talk," Rune said, choosing to hedge instead of outright lie.

"Yes, yes. Come. Come this way, dearie," the ancient Faerie said, turning back to her plant to continue dragging it to the first suite door.

"Let me handle that, madam," Elias said, sweeping up the tree into his arms.

"Oh, thank you, Elias. You haven't aged a day, have you?" Lady Trella looked him up and down as he hefted the pot easily.

"I would say neither have you," he agreed.

"Ha! Flatterer," the Fae cooed and then turned to open the door.

"She really hasn't. She looks the same as the day I met her," Elias whispered to Rune as she turned to follow.

"And when was that?" Rune tried to ask, but Elias dodged the question yet again by swooshing the tree in her face.

"Watch out, arboretum coming through."

Inside the suite, it was much like Rune's had been, only now it was partially forested. Everywhere Rune could see were potted trees and ferns. Some lined the walls, but three were set on the couch and chair in the living room area as if they were at a tree party and having a conversation. Small potted flowers were in a rough circle on the kitchen counter, while a long window box of what seemed like an office herb garden was taking up two chairs at the dining room table across from Calvin.

"Trella, I don't need more trees. I can hardly breathe…" Calvin started to say, then stopped as his eyes landed on Rune. "Oh crap. You're here."

"You know that's not how trees work right? Trees make more air." Rune strode over to the table. She stopped just at the edge while her old bully eyed her warily. Then with gravity, she bowed at her mid-waist, closing her eyes as she did so. "Your majesty," she said formally.

"Don't make fun of me, Leveau," he snapped, dropping the fork he had been using onto a partially eaten plate of enchiladas.

"I'm not making fun, Calvin. This is serious." Knowing he wasn't going to give her permission, she righted herself and moved to pull out the chair on the end. It would have been better to sit across from him, but she wasn't inclined to disturb the herb garden. "I'm here to talk."

"About what?" He snarled his lip at her and Rune had to resist snapping at him. Calling him a child at that moment wasn't going to help anyone.

"You asked for my help. I apologize for not offering it before. I'm in a position now to do that."

"You sound like that Maxamillion suit." Calvin leaned back in his chair, tipping it back cockily. A little bit of that swaggering sneer crept back into his being.

"Obviously you made some sort of deal with him," Rune started.

"You did too. Obviously," he replied, snottily.

"Calvin, this is not a contest."

"Father please, she is a Faerie Friend," Lady Trella begged. She was standing in the kitchen preparing tea and a tray of cookies, probably Calvin's dessert.

Something softened in Calvin's face when she spoke, and it was the first glimmer Rune had seen that this rat of a person might have any heart at all. "I don't understand what that means," he said, gently.

"It means I am the closest thing to being a Fae without actually being one. Like an honorary Fae."

"Congratulations," he said dryly. "Why can't I be that?"

"Well, are you willing to put your life on the line for them, because I have. Also, I didn't invoke the power of the Oberon."

"I didn't know," he said to his plate. Rune recognized that haunted demeanor and understood it.

"Boy, you keep looking like that, you're going to make me kind of feel sorry for you."

He shot her a hostile look.

The tray of cookies and tea appeared on the table. With the exact professionalism of an English housekeeper, Lady Trella set two cups before both Rune and Calvin and poured tea. Without being asked, she dropped two lumps of sugar into Calvin's then slid a small jar of honey to him, complete with an authentic honey dipper.

"Thank you, Trella," Calvin said softly.

The older Fae smiled lovingly at him. "Let me know if there is anything else you need, Father." Then she turned away and went back into the kitchen, where Elias was waiting on a stool, a cookie hanging out of his mouth.

The Oberon glanced at Rune slightly abashed before focusing on the honey dipper. "She calls me 'father' and she's the one who's ancient."

"It's a term of honor."

He rolled his eyes at her. "I know, Leveau. I'm not an idiot. It's still weird." He dropped a large dollop of honey into the tea. "I hated sugar. And tea. Now I have to drink the stuff all the time."

"Have to?"

"Something to do with being..." he couldn't finish the sentence, so instead drank the tea. Rune followed suit, the jasmine flavor warming her tongue. "He offered to protect me and I was out of options. That was what you wanted to know right? What Maxamillion wants with me, though, I have no idea."

"He wants to unite..."

Calvin grimaced. "No, no. I know what he says. He says a lot of words, just like the rest of those big suits. It's all bullshit. The bottom line with people like that in this world is always 'what's in it for me.' Every act of charity, or altruism, whatever, it's all to serve some personal purpose. Usually a bank account." He took another sip, staring off into space. "I only wanted a piece of that for once, you know. A piece to call my own. I figured hey, they're going to take what they want anyway. If I can get mine then maybe that's a little more…fair. Create some balance in the world. These guys," he nodded his chin towards Lady Trella, "it's the one thing I get about them. They got shafted too. Only it's supposed to be by me, only it wasn't me. I don't know them and I shouldn't care but…" His eyes, those clear blue, crystal-colored eyes peeked up at Rune through the fringe of his blonde hair. "But I do," he whispered. Then he leaned in a little closer, his face lacking any mask to cover his naked emotion. "Am I going crazy, Leveau?"

"Why are you asking me?" Her voice matched his in softness. "You don't give a shit about me. You don't blow smoke up my ass, you never have. Even when it would have been to your benefit to suck up to me like the rest of those…those *sheep* out there." He practically spat the word with the amount of contempt he infused into it. Instead, he sobered. "So you'll tell me straight." He met her eyes again, his own reflecting the haunted, frightened little boy he maybe had always been. "Am I going crazy?"

Rune took a deep breath in, trying to think of what to say. It felt like she needed to say something poignant and wise, but all she could think about was how she felt two months ago. "Remember when you came to the bar and stole my mortgage money…"

Calvin slammed his hand on the table, partially standing up. "I should have known." He shoved the plate of cookies to the floor with a huge crash. "You resent me? Is that it? You holding a grudge or some bullshit. What you think, I haven't suffered enough…."

"I thought I was going insane," Rune said. She spoke softly, but somehow her words cut over his racket. "Everything in my life had fallen apart and I think that if I had let it, I would have split into two people, like a multiple personality disorder or something. I got confronted with my past and the person I used to be, who was also the person I rejected and, in that moment, I could have done it. I could have just let myself split and go insane."

The Oberon straightened, his whole self stunned. Rune looked up at him and smiled a gentle smile. "Don't you remember? You were there." He double blinked and sat down, actually managing to look chagrined. He curled his fingers around his cup.

"What did you do?" he asked.

"I didn't. I accepted who I was and what I had become as the same person, even though they could almost have been two different people entirely. I guess that's what you have to do."

"You mean, these memories, or visions, I guess. They're real?"

The Talent nodded. "You can embrace the Oberon consciousness and become the Oberon, or you can die. Those are the only two choices you really have, Calvin. I don't mean this unkindly; I'm telling you the truth. The third option is to do what you've been doing, which is nothing until the choice is taken from you and you die."

"But I can't do it." Calvin whispered. "I don't know how to be a king, or a Father."

"Or a husband?"

"What?" Calvin asked, taken aback.

"By virtue of being the Oberon, you are technically, automatically married to the Titania. Congratulations."

If Rune thought he looked stunned before, now he looked like his brain had taken a two week vacation and left him catatonic. Without either of them noticing, Lady Trella had sidled up beside the table and was transferring the cookies from the decimated plate onto a new one. Elias waited a few steps behind her with a broom and dustpan.

Abruptly, Calvin stood up. "No, no Trella, don't."

She flapped her hands at him as he approached and tried to help clean up the glass. "No, no, I've got this."

"I'm sorry. I'm sorry," Calvin repeated, when tears started rolling down his face, his voice choking into sobs. As it overwhelmed him, he tried to cover his ugly, crying face.

Immediately, Lady Trella wrapped her twig-like arms around him and cooed, "Hey, hey. It's alright. Yeah, yeah, you cry, just let it all out."

Rune exchanged a glance with Elias, who gave her a thumbs up. All she could do was shrug in response, not entirely sure what she had done or if it would help.

As they waited to find out, she finished her tea.

Once he finished the soup, St. Benedict felt less like a stiff breeze would knock him over. He was reluctant to stand up just yet. Stillness. There was no movement, no sounds. He sat on the bed looking at the world of dark, punctuated with glittering light. It felt like night but he knew it wasn't a true night. It was too still. He spent so much of his life on the move. The next task, the next mission, the next objective. Being still was a luxury.

But now there were no more objectives, were there? He had thrown it all away. As much as he wanted to think that it wasn't his fault, that he had been under someone else's control, he wasn't going to accept that. He had believed that kind of lie too much in the beginning of his life. No matter what choices had been taken away from him, there had always been a choice he could have made that could have altered his course in this so-called life. Lifting up his bound arm again, he stared at the bandage.

"Here was your choice right there, idiot," he said out loud to himself. If he had forced himself to stop sooner….

She flitted through his thoughts again. He couldn't see her face. Never her face. But a small scrap of memory, of her laugh. Her scent, which he was almost sure was that "passion flower" smell, both fruity and artificial, from her shampoo. Even when he criticized, she still bought it because she liked it. Even when he mocked her. Even when he made her cry…. Even when he failed her.

The old familiar ache cramped inside him. He pressed down on his thighs. The price he had to pay for the stillness, for the moment of rest, was the memories. The painful, useless memories.

"What are you going to do now, idiot?" he asked to himself.

The Faerie Queen was nowhere to be seen, but he didn't take that as proof that she was gone. Pushing himself up, he swung his feet off the bed. He was still dressed, his shoes were even still on. He raked his fingers through his hair, which was matted with sweat and blood in places. There was no sign of the fedora so he stretched out his right hand again and called it into being with a snap. Like before, the program initiated and created a replica of the fedora. Looking down at the rest of his clothes, he repeated the process, pulling the stored images of the clothes he liked to appear in when he was hologram-projecting. Over the torn and dirty, a fresh suit appeared, dark grey with a three button vest, over finely fitted trousers held up with suspenders. Just as the coat appeared, he changed his mind and sent it back. The vest would be enough.

"Hmm, nice," the Faerie Queen crooned from behind him. He was grateful he had resisted the reflex to jump in his skin. "Though I would have liked to watch you change the traditional way."

He stood and adjusted his vest. "Though it seems real, it's only an illusion. I'm still a dirty, ragged vagabond underneath." He turned and slid his hands into his pockets. "But if you would prefer, I can take it all off and try again."

The Faerie Queen stood a few feet away, still wearing the face of the pretty blonde. She was now dressed in a wine red gown that clung to everything as if it had been painted on.

"Come walk with me," she ordered more than requested. With a limp wrist, she offered her arm for him to take and he obliged. As she slipped her hand into the crook of his, she sighed, "I still prefer you with the antlers."

He refrained from commenting on that and she didn't seem to need one. They left the grove that she had set up residence in and plunged into the strange trees, their path lit by the surreal soft light. They crossed a stream of small critters all about the size of mice, streaming back and forth with their single bead of light for an eye. The Faerie Queen stepped through them heedlessly, managing to avoid trodding on a single one without breaking her stride. His steps were less elegant, but the two or three he got only screeched in metallic protest before continuing on. It made the Queen laugh.

"I hope I didn't cause permanent harm," he commented, glancing back at the stream.

"It's only random data. I'm sure someone's email was delayed and written in Portuguese." She tugged on his arm and they continued.

They seemed to crest a hill and she stopped. The forest

spread out before them, beautiful as a fully lit city. The music St. Benedict seemed to always hear amplified in that spot, the tones and screeches of the digital world orchestrated into beautiful, haunting music.

"What do you think?" she asked after a moment.

"I love all of this," he answered truthfully.

"I have always wondered. You mortals that pursue this realm of computer and technology. What is it you are seeking exactly?" She draped herself onto a log that seemed shaped for exactly that purpose, or maybe she just knew the trick of it. She made it look so natural and sensual.

"I'm not sure how to answer that."

"How about truthfully. Come on. What called you to want to leave your body behind and only be your mind?"

"There is a kind of power in it," he admitted. He sat down on the artificial grass, causing it to light then die as soon as he settled. He rested his elbows onto his knees and linked his fingers together. "To feel like a god in a way. Only a few in the real world know that feeling without augmentations, I imagine."

"Those with magic?"

He sighed. "Magic cheats. Creating a world like this levels the playing field at last."

She laughed at that. "It does not. Just because I know the rules, it isn't the same as cheating."

"Prior to this age, if you didn't have magic, you didn't have power."

She was silent for a long time and St. Benedict felt the hairs rise on the back of his neck. What was about to happen next?

"My husband was threatened by my power." she said with no preamble. "Cliché, I know, but there it is. It is what happened."

"I marvel at you choosing me to be your new consort."

She blinked once, then looked a little uncertain before covering it with a hearty laugh. "Oh really?"

"I betrayed my wife."

"Yes, but you regret it, don't you?" Her intensity was loud in the quiet space. "You've dedicated your life to atoning for it! My husband was very addicted to his power and prestige and the accolades that came with it." In a literal blink, she was sitting beside him. Or more like leaning against him. Her nails dug in through his shirt sleeve into his bandaged arm, yet he didn't flinch or show any sign of discomfort. "He hated sharing it with me, his equal. His partner in everything. He wanted to dominate me, be *my* Lord and Master."

Deftly, he ran a finger along her temple, pushing a strand of hair back behind her ear, caressing her soft skin. She shivered against the touch. It was interesting seducing a Queen.

"And you won, didn't you? He's gone and you're here," he whispered, warming his voice. He selected a piece of spiraling hair framing her face and began slowly curling around his finger. She wet her lips a little, making them glisten, tempting and red. He swallowed the knot in his throat down into his stomach, which churned sickly as he began the lean forward to kiss her. Just before their lips met, she laughed and disappeared into nothing. She was teasing him, or thought she was.

Relieved, he leaned back and waited for her to reappear, looking out over the vista. Above him, he noted that the sky was not black, but an inky shade of blue. And it was swirling. Narrowing his eyes, he stood up, staring at the sky. The swirling increased until a tail began to emerge from above, like a tornado reaching for the ground. It curled and writhed and St. Benedict started backing up and away from it.

"Hide!" The Faerie Queen appeared in front of him, looking up fearfully as the tornado stretched toward them, all the more threatening for its airless spinning.

"What is happening?" He grabbed her shoulder to turn her back to him. She said nothing, her eyes pleading and fearful. Blinking once, he let go, then ignited his hand's augmentations. With a swipe he shut all of them down and let the Oberon presence reassert itself, muting away his augmentations. Instantly, the blackness crawled up his back and the antlers shot from his head. It was so easy to do, it felt like relief as his vision went red. He could feel the darkness hiding him.

The Faerie Queen didn't see any of it, she had already turned her back to him again, squaring her shoulders into a more regal position. A beacon of light standing up to overwhelming darkness.

The tip of the whirling funnel touched down in front of her, congealing in place for a few minutes. Then it dissipated and a being stood there instead. He was an average-sized man, lean with wavy hair on the top of his head, but the sides and back were shaved close. Along both sides of his skull were strips of lights.

St. Benedict narrowed his eyes, recognizing through the red haze the newcomer's augmentations as the next upgrade after ocular implants failed. The Saint was the only person to have succeeded in having functioning oculars that hadn't killed him or driven him mad. His implants allowed him to upload himself into a computer. The part of him that was still a young, hungry computer programmer wanted to go over and look closer at what looked like an even more advanced hardware set-up than what he had seen previously. That doubled when the man adjusted what he thought to be glasses, but when the lens changed color he realized they were attached to his face. Questions like what were they for and how did they work almost blurted out of his mouth.

Instead, he crouched, flattening his hand with its talons onto the ground beneath him. The scientist didn't seem to even take note of anything unusual as he adjusted his long, white coat while he looked back up at the way he had come.

"Yes, yes," he muttered to himself and pulled something from his pocket. He approached the Faerie Queen while staring at the object.

"Recite the phrase please," he said with a bored air as he tapped at the screen of the device in his hands. When she didn't respond immediately, the scientist sighed and shot her an annoyed look.

"The quick onyx goblin jumps over the lazy dwarf," the Faerie Queen said tersely.

"Good." He pulled out a stylus from the device and tapped it, connecting it to something else, before he turned to thrust it into the Queen.

She flinched and it took everything in St. Benedict to not rush and attack the scientist. Logically, he knew he shouldn't interfere, that he didn't know what was going on and any move he made could make things worse for her and definitely for him, but the darkness inside him yowled with fury.

Her clothes changed the moment the stylus penetrated her. The image she had been projecting melted away, replaced with a slight, bony woman instead. She looked like she was in her late middle ages, made even older by the wasting away of her body. They stood like that for several minutes, the scientist oblivious to her while he focused on the device in front of him, she staring off into the middle distance, her face passive and regal while she waited for it to be over. When he was done, he yanked it out, partially turning away from her now that he was done. After a concentrated moment, he glanced up at her.

"You can put your illusion up now," he said at her as an afterthought.

Her eyes narrowed, hate dripping from them, before closing her eyes. Her form shimmered, the image of the beautiful blonde in red and gray reasserting itself over her form. The scientist smiled a self-satisfied smile. Then he casually grabbed a handful of breast. The Faerie Queen stiffened, sniffing in a rush of air, her whole body still as stone.

"Oh, don't make that face, it's not like it's your real body," the scientist chided, as he massaged a little bit. "Besides, I don't think you would make them this big if you didn't want me to touch them."

She said nothing as he pawed her, but the crystals around her began to pulse, turning red as blood. The scientist did seem to notice as he gave a lewd smile of triumph, enjoying the power he had over such a powerful being.

St. Benedict did nothing, but the darkness built up around him, in response. He continued to do nothing.

After a moment, as if bored with his toy, the scientist released her and continued to tap at his device. He turned away and walked to the edge of the drop off. Before he went, the funnel reappeared, sucking him away. "See you tomorrow, Clarissa," were his parting words.

St. Benedict stared at the whirlpool on the surface of the ceiling, his thoughts whirling with it. A way out.

"You weren't meant to see that," the Faerie Queen said. Now

that the intruder was gone, she had dropped her shoulders. Her arms wrapped around herself, making her seem small and mortal as she continued to gaze sightlessly out over the expanse of her created world.

"You did nothing to stop it."

The crystals around her sparked red, rolling a crackle of energy that erupted into the sky above.

"And what did you do?!" She spun in place, her screech reverberating through the crystals. The force of it was terrifying, but St. Benedict didn't move as it rolled over his skin, prickling like a thousand needle stabs.

"I obeyed my Queen," he said from his position crouched on the ground, looking more like a wild, noble knight kneeling before her. The furious storm above them calmed to a distant rumble. Daring a peek up, St. Benedict saw her calming with it. He dared more by rising to his feet. Her face said it all, fear mingled with self-disgust. She was ashamed and concerned by what he thought of her now. Slowly he reached out to her to take her hand, but before he could touch her, she flinched back.

"I do not care for this face any more," she said flippantly. "You were thinking of someone…someone just now." She focused on him again and the strange feeling, like fingers running through his hair, rolled over his head. "What do you think of this view?"

Before him, where the Queen had stood, was a perfect likeness of St. Rachel. Her blonde hair waved around her face, covering one eye in a perfect replica of her in her most sexy noir look. Her lips were blood red and she was dressed in a close-hugging, short, black dress with heels to match her lips.

He couldn't help it, he took a step back in alarm. She pouted her lips at him, delighted by his reaction.

"Hmm, this does please you, at least on a physical level," she said, then one of her eyebrows quirked, exactly like St. Rachel's did. "But…no, you don't desire this form." She misted herself again.

"Please, wait…." he said but again the feeling of fingers pulled through his scalp.

"How about this one? What are your feelings for the little, nosy mageling?" Before him stood the shorter form of Rune as he last saw her, down to her braided hair and knee high boots. She looked up at him eagerly, expectantly, before souring into disgust. "Oh. No. No, all…complicated feelings. Oh my, I don't like that at all. No, no thank you to that mess. No." She misted again.

This time when she reformed another woman, or girl really, stood there. She was a couple of inches shorter than Rune, staring wide-eyed, like she hadn't left childhood too long ago. Her hair was long, her figure the skinniness of a teen with the promise of blooming into hourglass womanhood. A cruel thought flitted through St. Benedict's mind, something he would have said a lifetime ago, "that one would go to fat one day." The wide-eyed kid waited, only the smug smile marring the picture of the barely-legal centerfold image. But he didn't really react. He didn't really get it. Why was she presenting him with this image?

"You…you don't know me, do you?" the girl asked, truly surprised.

"I…." St. Benedict started but he didn't know what to say. Her shock at his lack of reaction made him very uncomfortable.

"There's nothing," she said softly. "No reaction whatsoever. It's like…." Then understanding washed over her face, followed by pity. "You don't remember her, do you?"

A sick feeling slipped into St. Benedict's stomach as logic, not true memory, told him who he was looking at. "Who is she?" he asked, deadly soft.

"Your wife," she answered him with even more pity. "You don't remember what she looks like. It's not like you've forgotten. You *can't* remember. Not a whiff of involuntary recognition, even when you're looking right at her."

The pain in his chest was so tight he grabbed at it. "Stop it."

She pursed her lips together, then acquiesced, shimmering back into the image of a new Faerie Queen. This one had skin as pale as the moon and hair as black as a raven's wing with dark eyes shaped like almonds. Now it was his turn to shift away, to try to hide his pain. He felt the fingers roll through his hair again, this time gentle and slow. He batted them away, even though it did no good since they physically didn't exist.

"Stop it. Please."

"You shouldn't feel guilty," the Faerie Queen said. "It's not your fault. I can feel it. Here. The damage."

The sob choked out of him before he realized it was going to happen. "Don't do this. I can't…." It was hard, like vomit. He had to swallow it back, bite it down. He had to.

"Let it go. Let me see," her voice asked, truly asked. He tried to look up at a light but in the perpetual night of the strange digital world, there was no light to save him as his own grief forced its way out.

"I betrayed her," he said, his voice wavering. "I tried to save her." A hand drifted up to his head, to the place where the injury had once been. "They hit me…too hard…too many times. My brain swelled and I couldn't remember. That was the least I could do, right? I could remember *her*. After everything!" He swiped the black talons still covering his hands against the nearest digital tree. Light flashed and crackled from the assault and it felt good to destroy it. He was even screaming as he did it again and again, collapsing it into a pile of digital cubes. "I can remember how to program. How to reformat. How to tie my damn shoes, my first prom, my first kiss. Why can't I remember her!?!?" He collapsed to the ground, or did the ground come to meet him? All was quiet and calm. Was he alone? Was the Faerie Queen still there?

He turned.

She was, but instead of staring at him and his tantrum, she had sat herself on the edge of the drop off, her back to him. She was eloquently beautiful with her legs curled beside herself, her impossibly long skirt spread out around her like a bird's wing.

He pushed himself up onto his knees. Who was he fighting? It wasn't her, not really. He needed to focus, he needed to escape. Losing his shit here wasn't going to do it. Yet, coming to his feet was hard, like his body was weighed down with rocks. Even harder was crossing the distance to her, with her profile highlighted by the ethereal light.

"Did stripping out my shame help you feel better?" he asked.

"Yes, it did."

He huffed a chuckle, "You're a very honest woman."

"No, I have need for lies in this place, and yet no patience for them either."

He sat beside her. It seemed like the thing to do.

"It's not what you think. I didn't do it to hurt you," she admitted.

"Misery loves company,"

"It's harder when one believes they are truly alone."

"Yeah," he agreed. They sat quietly as the music of the data world rose up again. It was peaceful.

"Oh, Oberon," she said, soft as a secret regret, "how I have missed you."

He laid a finger across her chin, turning her tear-filled eyes to meet his own, now glowing blue, pushing back the darkness so she could see him as a man.

"Show it to me again. Show me your true face."

She looked at him suspiciously. "Why?"

He turned his whole body to her, vulnerable and open. "Let me see," he said gently and caressed her cheek with the back of his fingers. "Let me see the truth…my Queen."

A single tear streaked down her face. She pressed his hand against her, closing her eyes a moment. Finally, she nodded.

The space around them shifted, warping away. White, cold walls thumped in place around them, with splashes of white track lighting along the ceiling, making it seem dim and lit at the same time. A single tube, the size of a coffin, sat squarely in the middle of the room. It was banked at an angle, and beneath the glass, St. Benedict could see the single figure inside. He checked the room and saw that the Faerie Queen was gone. Or rather there was only one present.

Turning back to the tube, she stared at him from within, her eyes wide and full of shame. His heart ached for her. Back were her stick thin limbs and the thin cotton gown laying over her front. Her hair looked even more brittle against the pillow, the black having bleached away to pieces of grayish white. She was very clearly dying.

He laid his hand against the glass. She hesitated only a moment and laid her own in the opposing side, more tears rolling down her gaunt face.

"If I open this and take you out, you'll die won't you?" he asked gently.

She nodded and he echoed it before shifting to examine the rest of the tube.

"I have something like this back at my place," he said, keeping his voice casual as best he could. "Yours is more sophisticated." He pushed a few buttons on the display panel, quickly reading the information there, which were her life stats. "So, you're jacking into...." he paused considering. "Is this place real? Did you bring me to where you actually are?"

"Of course," her voice echoed as it was transmitted from inside the tube.

"But how?"

Chapter 20

"I think she's linked into a computer, like when the Saints jump their minds into the hologram thingy. Only she's making her holograms into reality." Stunned silence followed Rune's pronouncement.

Rune's plan to get to Maxamillion inside of his own building had been thwarted before she could even finish forming it. First off, not having come through the front door had tripped some sort of alarm system and security of every sort came piling in just as Rune was picking up her second cookie. Thankfully, her shield crystal actually stopped them from tackling her and dragging her away. They chose to disregard the fact that she had clearance to be there on her OmniSin, so it took Maxamillion coming down himself to resolve the standoff.

Now, Rune was sitting with him, St. Rachel, and Malachi in Maxamillion's well-appointed office. They were staring at her. Her own retainer and the two Fae under Corinthe's protection sat on dragged-in chairs that had been circled up in front of Maxamillion's desk. The CEO himself was perched on the front edge of said desk, dressed in a sand colored suit and making it look good as he leaned, his arms crossed as he listened to Rune's story up to this point. St. Rachel stood to his right behind the desk, leaning cross-armed against the wall, still haughtily beautiful as ever. Rune was starting to recognize her positioning as a product of a Saint's training. Malachi had one of the dragged in chairs to Maxamillion's left. He was the only one looking unsettled, leaning his elbows on his knees, staring as he listened.

"I know she's doing it with magic, through a computer."

"Holy crap!" Malachi abruptly said, jumping up to his feet

with a sense of eureka about him. "That's how they're doing it."

Rune and Elias exchanged looks. "Doing what?"

Maxamillion pushed off the edge of his desk. "Earlier today Kodiak announced to the world that they had succeeded in replicating Masterson's work." He went over to a touch screen mounted in the wall, brushing his hand across its surface to wake it up. Already loaded on the screen was the image of a news report bannered with words like "Stunning Breakthrough" and "Revolutionary." A woman's face, presumably the news reporter, was paused in an unflattering pose.

"We're too late," Elias said softly. Rune took a couple steps forward staring at the screen. Her husband's name was caught midway through the scroll.

"And they're using the Titania to do it?" she asked the screen.

"It's the end of all magic…." For the first time in her life, Elias sounded so resigned and defeated. Instead of that crushing her, it gave her a sense of calm. They had already failed, so now what?

"You were never going to be able to stop Masterson's breakthrough," Maxamillion cut in, "the question is now what *do* we do about it."

"I mean it's over, isn't it?" Malachi offered.

"No, not at all," St. Rachel stood up straight, looking every inch a warrior goddess. "Okay, they've cracked the Files. And they have the Faerie Queen. We've got the Faerie King," St. Rachel looked pointedly at Calvin. Everyone else followed suit.

"This isn't chess…." Rune said, shifting uncomfortably on her feet as Calvin's face went pale.

"Of course it is. And our enemy has a pretty powerful piece. Well, so do we," she crossed her arms as if that was the end of the argument.

It probably was because Maxamillion was nodding. "What are you proposing?"

"We have all the equipment they do. They're probably jacking the Faerie Queen in, let's plug his ass in and see what happens."

"Is that possible? Plug a magic being into the system?"

Maxamillion asked as if she was posing a solution for saving some money on the water cooler.

"You can't do that. He's a person, not a thing for you to exploit!" Rune took a step forward as she spoke, putting herself symbolically between the Corinthe Corporation and the Oberon. Rune couldn't help noting her life was becoming a series of stare down contests, and this one with Maxamillion was no less hard. His handsome face was impossible to read until it burst to a smile.

"Exactly," he pointed at her repeatedly as he chuckled more. "Take away anybody's rights, you take away everybody's rights."

"Sir, this is a war we are fighting...." St. Rachel tried to say, but he cut her off.

"Which is why we must hold ourselves to the line. Because if we do not stand beside the truths we fight for, they die. Then was it worth the cost in the first place? It's not a price I'm prepared to pay."

He stared down St. Rachel, but she yielded almost right away. Rune pointedly ignored the glare St. Rachel was now shooting at her. To Calvin's credit, he didn't fall to pieces, but gritted his jaw, waiting with fierce eyes. She hoped this new found grit would hold out.

"Would you want to jack in willingly?" Maxamillion asked.

"Well, now, hold on," Malachi cut in. "What we don't have are the specs on how to create a viable jack to make another Saint, never mind one adapted to the Magic cancellation phenomenon."

"But Kodiak probably does now," St. Rachel said.

"I'm not putting wires in my head," Calvin added.

"And that settles that," Maxamillion agreed, pointing at Calvin, "not that I blame you. It isn't something I want done to me either."

"What's more important is getting our people back," Rune redirected.

"*Our* people?" Maxamillion asked.

"The Titania and St. Benedict. This is the basis of your Alliance after all, isn't it? You need the Faerie Court and the

Magic Guild to build your consensus."

"Yes, it is," Maxamillion confirmed carefully. "But I don't need St. Benedict...."

"You do, if you want my help," Rune countered.

"But what she is describing is a rescue. The Faerie Queen is working for them." St. Rachel gestured at the Kodiak logo still frozen on the screen. "And St. Benedict is working for her." The Saint couldn't hide the bitterness in her tone.

"She has her agenda, but that doesn't make her the enemy," Rune tried to say in defense, but St. Rachel waved her down.

"It still doesn't stop the real problem. They've cracked the Masterson Files. Even if we take away their magic source, they can and are probably planning to get anyone else with magic to replace her. Then we're in the same situation."

"How easy do you think working magic is?" Elias asked. He didn't expect an answer.

"Actually, the fact is, we don't know that," Malachi said, "we don't know what they, Kodiak, know. Getting the Titania or Faerie Queen or whatever, would help us figure out what they know. We've been shooting in the dark. Maybe they can't replicate what they've done to her yet."

"So, it's tactically advantageous to risk our resources and exposure to get more information," Maxamillion said, his fingers steepled against his lips.

"Yeah, you know. In case you need a practical reason to do the right thing," Malachi said. St. Rachel redirected her glare at Malachi, who silently dared her back. Rune didn't want to imagine what he was daring her to do.

"And what you were saying earlier, Rune.... If the Titania can already create a real physical place out of a Dreamscape, like the Faerie Court...she could do the same to a holographic world with Faerie magic?" Maxamillion asked.

Rune nodded.

"What you are describing is...it sounds like you're saying she is a god?" Maxamillion shifted back in his seat, uncomfortably.

"Not at all," Elias said easily. "It's a power we all have if you think about it. Someone has an idea, a dream if you will. They tell other people about it, they start dreaming the same dream.

They start taking actions to make the dream a reality and then it becomes so. The Titania just does it all at once."

"The Fae are a symbiotic people. They can unite together into a single dream without needing to be convinced like you hominals, or any of the other races," Lady Trella explained.

"Then why did you fall?" St. Rachel asked, raising an eyebrow over narrowed eyes.

"Our dream split in two, between our Mother and our Father," the Fae lady said very levelly. Unbidden, Calvin laid a hand on her shoulder, which she gripped gratefully.

"War only occurs when competing ideas both try to manifest at the same time," Elias said sagely.

"Then why have two leaders if they could split you like this?" St. Rachel asked.

Lady Trella shook her head at the Saint. "The fact that you can easily ask such a question means you would not understand the answer."

"Because it's lonely," Calvin said instead. He was staring into nothing, a thoughtful weight on his shoulders. "That's why they die together, isn't it? It's because the bond between them… to lose that…." He turned to Rune. "Her heart broke."

"When a Fae is heartbroken, they die," Lady Trella confirmed.

"That's why she needs you to come for her, Calvin," Rune added.

"What? You want me to what? Make her fall in love with me again? Or for the first time." He shook his head. "She's been trying to kill me!"

"Because the Oberon did this to her and you are the Oberon."

"But it wasn't me who did this to her…." Calvin argued again, the same argument degrading every time he said it.

"Dammit, Calvin, that isn't the point. Are you the Oberon or not? Because all of this is pointless if you're not. Saving you. Saving her. Trying to stop Kodiak, and who knows who else, from destroying this city and everything it has ever stood for. It all hinges on this one question right now. Are you the Oberon?"

"Yes! Stop shouting at me." Calvin blinked as if caught off guard by the strength of his own voice. He looked down at Lady Trella, who had tears streaking freely down her face. Carefully, he cupped her cheek with his palm, which she quickly captured and kissed the back of. "Yes. I am. I am the King of the Faeries."

Rune smiled; for the first time in her life she liked Calvin. Just a little bit. "Then she needs you to come for her."

"Why?" St. Rachel interrupted, her harsh question shattering the sacred feeling in that moment. "If what you say is true, shouldn't she have the power to save herself?"

Rune took a deep breath in and prayed to Maddie for serenity and eloquence. "We don't know what they've done to her, and believe me...." she turned to meet every eye in the room, "they've hurt her. They've stripped her power, her sense of self and her reason to keep fighting. She needs us to come for her. Because she needs a reason to fight for herself."

"What is your plan?" Maxamillion asked.

"You're on board then?" St. Rachel challenged.

"Well, I am," Malachi said, raising his hand.

"Let's hear your plan," Maxamillion repeated to Rune directly.

"I use my magic to Find St. Benedict."

"How?" Malachi asked, genuinely wondering.

Rune pointed at him. "My problem to figure out, but once we do, we should find the Titania. We have to convince her to help us help her."

"If you can do that and you can get her to tell us where her body is, we can formulate a plan to extract her," St. Rachel said.

"We may have to hack her Dream-whatever," Malachi added, getting up to cross in front of his boss to stand before Rune. "I bet you they've uploaded her directly into their network like we do. We need every bit of computing power right now to comfortably upload a mind, I can't...wow. To upload a magical being.... How is that not frying the processors?" He started pacing in a tight little circle like a dog.

"But why wouldn't she be physically in this Dreamscape she's created?" Calvin asked, "Sounds over-complicated to me."

"Oh, I got it! You're right!" Malachi ran his fingers through his hair, jumping up and down. "She's the grounding conduit! Or really the transistor! Translating magic into data!!"

"Malachi!" Maxamillion barked, which seemed to calm the younger man instantly.

"Magical energy can't be contained. At least not in the way electricity can."

"Magic can be stored in a crystal," Rune said.

"Yes, but any time a computer has been connected to an enchanted crystal, pop boom. Dead computer. But a living being. We know that magical energy comes from magical beings. If this Dreamscape place is nothing but magical energy, the magic is filtering though her. The living being is the transistor. We can upload a living being into a data system, a huge leap on its own, and only possible if the living body is still functioning. Once that is done, the magic can be cast through a technological system by having that magical being in the system cast it." He stopped for a moment and glanced around. "Am I still making sense?"

There were a variety of nods, some accompanied by shrugs. It didn't stop him though; Malachi jumped again as another thought burst in his brain. "I bet, now this is just a theory, but if you put the physical being in the real world into the world they've created while their digital mind is creating it, well it'd be like an Escher painting, right? Impossible. So Rune's right. If we want to rescue, or kidnap, the Faerie Queen, we need to find her physical body."

"But what if that doesn't work? She might not help us. She hates me and still wants me dead," Calvin said. He had been looking down when he said it, unaware that he had all of the attention again. He touched a hand against his chest. "I can feel it. In here. She's suffering so much. She won't agree to this if I'm still alive." He turned to Lady Trella as the older Fae stood and circled to him, setting her gnarly old hands on his shoulders. "Is that real, what I'm feeling? Am I just making this up?" he asked her.

"No, it's right, Daddy-o," she assured, smiling sadly. "You're starting to let the Oberon in."

"Then maybe what we need to do is clear," St. Rachel said, "the simplest solution."

"You mean kill her," Calvin said. St.

Rachel nodded somberly.

"No," Rune started to say, but Lady Trella laid a hand on Rune's arm.

"Maybe...she's right. If she won't come with us willingly. If we don't stop her, it'll never end. I...I can't lose another Father." The old Fae hesitated a moment more, then she said with tears in her eyes, "Wouldn't leaving her there in that hell, a prisoner and slave, wouldn't that be worse?"

St. Rachel nodded again. "She's dying anyway, you already said. If we can't simply get her out of there, killing her is the only other option."

"He's afraid," the Faerie Queen muttered before giggling with childlike delight.

"Who?" St. Benedict asked, unsurprised at her sudden reappearance.

After seeing her in the medical tube, she had returned them to her digital world before she disappeared without a further word to him. Having nothing better to do he had explored the forest, trying to figure out how to work within its interface. While he had recognized several familiar systems, everything seemed written in code he didn't recognize. There were glyphs like those Rune had showed him at the Magic Guild. They were everywhere in the system, strange letters that didn't translate to anything he understood.

Yet, there was no harm in trying. Coding and learning new codes was something he did in his sleep. He had been at it for an indeterminate amount of time, when he felt the Faerie Queen reappear. He was sitting next to her version of a waterfall, which looked more like beads of light, tripping and trickling down to slop over stones. Small plinking sounds echoed from it, which made its own pretty, subdued music. His tinkering with the data code had enabled him to destroy and recreate one of the flowers nearby. As soon as he had reconstructed the flower, she had plucked it from his hand, pushing it to her nose as if she could smell any sort of scent from it.

"Who's afraid?" he repeated.

"The Oberon of course. I can feel him tickling in my brain. My worthless, choiceless husband." She bit off the head of the flower, then immediately spat it out. "Worthless," she proclaimed again and threw the flower away in disgust.

"Tasted bad?" St. Benedict asked.

"Tasted like metal and silicon and dust." She continued to spit, then leaned in toward his face. "Help me wash the foulness from my mouth."

Instinctively, St. Benedict pulled back to avoid her kiss. She didn't seem insulted, only smiled at him even more coyly. "You are strangely shy, Saint of Liars."

"You're strangely forward."

"Is it because we are strangers that you still resist me? I've already shown you my deepest secret." Then her face turned dark. "Or is that the reason you reject me now? Can't get the image of me disgusting and weak out of your mind?"

"It made you more beautiful to me," he answered. "But I won't betray my oath."

"Your oath?" Now she looked genuinely interested. "Which oath is that?"

"I have only one that matters." He stopped on that.

"I think you owe me more. That does not nearly match the secret I've given you," the Faerie Queen chided gently, her voice hypnotically musical.

St. Benedict looked down. "It's hard."

She laid a hand along his cheek. "I know. I'm here beloved."

He swallowed and sighed a groan that ended in a growl. "I promised to remain faithful to her for whatever remains of my life." He yanked his Saint's box into his fist, the familiar edges biting his palm. "I swore on this."

"To the wife whose face you can't even remember?"

"I failed her in so many other ways."

"And yet, I don't think you've embraced the life of a monk." He hadn't realized how close the Faerie Queen had sidled up alongside where he sat until the scent of honey wafted over him. She had snared him in the trap so subtly he was genuinely starting to not care. His eyes had gone red again, yet she remained clear to his sight. He knew antlers had to be jutting from his head as well, and in his ears the wild call was intoxicating.

"Would you like your memories restored?" she asked in a whisper.

St. Benedict felt like the air had been kicked out of him.

"Ha. What do you mean by restoring my memories?" he asked, pressing fists into his thighs to keep from attacking her in either sense of the word.

"The damage, silly. I will heal your wounds and make you whole."

"How can you do such a thing?" he asked.

"My body is dying, not my magic," she answered, her smile taking on a motherly quality. Gently, she brushed her fingers through his hair, confirming for him that indeed there were bone antlers on his head again as she shifted around them. A shudder rolled down his spine as her clever, warm fingers found the puckered scar along the side of his crown and over his ear. Those scars sometimes created a gap in his hair if he didn't brush it a certain way to cover it. "I see now why you wear a hat all the time."

He tried to capture her fingers and pull away. "Stop," he breathed.

"Secrets here. Secrets there. Secrets are simply lies. Protector of lies, Saint of lies, protector of those who utter them," she sing-songed softly as the same wayward finger hooked past his collar and drew out the Saint's box on its chain. "You hide the scraps of your lies in here too, don't you?"

"Please don't touch it," he repeated, but he didn't move to pull it from her fingers. She let it go on her own accord.

"Sounds like there is something inside. Clink, clink goes your box. Don't you remember me? Don't you want to see me again? Please let me out. Please let Clarissa make it better. Tell her what's in the box."

"If you can repair my memory then you will know soon enough what it is," he said.

"So, you agree to my offer?" she asked, perking up.

"You haven't said what you want in return." It was so hard to think again. The darkness was whispering to give in. To forget his vow.

"I give you a memory, you give me a piece of your vow."

He said nothing, pursing his lips together as he stared at the waterfall of light. Small fingers touched the underside of his chin and turned his face.

"Wouldn't you like to know who I am again?" the Faerie Queen asked, wearing *her* face, speaking with *her* voice. He couldn't breathe. Couldn't move away as the pretty visage moved closer, her hazel eyes gleaming with unshed tears and forgiveness. Her lips met his at the same time as her finger began to trace along the scar. He yielded, hungry. Her kiss eased into him and the deep ache, the deep longing rose to meet it.

"It's you," he whispered against her mouth, not caring that it wasn't true. "Please let it be you."

Chapter 21

"What Justin made is going to hurt a lot of people, isn't it?"

"Yes, but he isn't responsible for all of it." Elias leaned against the wall as he watched Rune paint on the blank concrete wall on the opposite side of the hologram projector in the Praetorium. Others in the room were working at their computer terminals, St. Rachel running about giving orders as they did their spy things. More than one of the techs had stopped to watch Elias and Rune work until St. Rachel barked them back to work. The two magic users pretty much ignored them all.

"Now two even lines through the center." Elias pointed to the circular glyph she had just created. They had been at it for a while, with her doing the work while Elias told her which glyphs to use to create the three way door to her bar with the Dreamscape in between. "The corporations would have taken over any way. They have been working on it for decades. I suppose in a way, you can look at it as the eternal struggle between what is good and what is right. The people versus the powerful. But in the flowing river of capitalism, Justin did make waves and ripples and those effects are what we are feeling now."

"Yeah, and now I have to stop it before it destroys the world," Rune said dully, as she was intensely focusing on the line she was making.

"There are lots of ways to destroy the world, Rune. You aren't responsible for fixing them all."

"I don't really see how I can anyway. This all seems so much bigger than me." She heaved a big, frustrated sigh. "Maybe Mathus has a point, taking the initiative to try to preserve what's left of us. Technology is going to leave us in the dust."

"A little hard to swallow from a man like him when he espouses himself a Traditionalist," Elias said dryly.

"He's in a tough position," Rune defended as she finished the line and wiped her brush.

"Why don't you hate him?" Elias asked, leaning in to check her work. "By all rights you should, considering."

"Mathus? Maybe it's because I can relate to him. To that kind of suffering. I went through hell like that too, except I was lucky, nothing permanent. Physically I could have been very disfigured. Had fingers removed, you know, brain damage... unfixable things."

"Well, as admirable as that is, he is hellbent to see you fail as Head of a Household." Elias nodded and tapped the last space at the bottom of the painted door. "Three triangles stacked on top of each other going down. Make them about the same size."

"I didn't say I wasn't going to try to stop him from trying to destroy me. He definitely must be stopped. But it's not required that I hate him. That is not going to happen."

"You are a better woman than most, Rune."

"Yeah, well. What has all this suffering been for, if not to be more kind?"

Elias nodded and took the paint brush from her, adding precise curly-q's to the corners of the triangles. "And we're done."

"This will open a door to the Lucky Devil for real?"

"Yes. You now have a two-way door connecting your front door to this place, which by the way, cancels out the other door you made. Now, just establish a code phrase and shoot it with magic. The runes around the door will direct the magic."

"Except we are going to stay in between the doors and open a third door to the Titania's world," Rune added.

"Like hanging from a suspension bridge. Probably just as dangerous. Code phrase. Go."

"How about 'Barkeep, two shots'?" Rune stood up from where she had been crouching, stretching her aching body from being in that position too long.

"Works for me, just say them the first time you invoke this door and it'll always open to the bar."

"And this is temporary?"

"It's just paint. Scratch it off and it won't hold any magic. You want it permanent, you'd need a more permanent anchor, which is why crystals work so well."

"Still can't believe it's that simple."

Elias shrugged. "Well, it's that simple for me. Most of my magic works best with an invocation circle of some sort. I've gotten to the point where I can make it out of anything, but I used to need special paint with ground up crystal inside or magnetic chalk, that kind of thing. Just how I'm wired. Your magic is much more flexible."

"And passive as hell," Rune griped.

"For now. From what you've told me, you've already figured out how to use it to pull objects to you and open doors like an Opener Talent."

Rune screwed up her face. "Yeah, but those were flukes. I mean, watch." She held out her hand palm out and focused on what she wanted to do. "Shield." Nothing happened. Then she plucked up the shield crystal from around her neck. "Shield," she repeated and instantly an egg of yellow magic burst into existence around her. "See, without crystals and other people's spells, I'm screwed. Just a Talent." She let the shield drop.

"Or a Magi with a complex," Elias said, cutting her off before she could ask more about what a Magi was. "When things calm down more, we'll figure out what your block is and I will explain everything in full, I promise. For now, keep that close to you." He pointed at the crystal around her neck.

The door from the suites that lead to the Praetorium opened and her partner in this endeavor emerged. Calvin was dressed in a pair of jeans with a plain, white t-shirt, but Lady Trella chased after him.

"Please Father, this will be your first meeting with Mother. You want to make a good impression! At least tuck your shirt in!"

"I'm not wearing that!" Calvin declared, snatching the shirt from the older Fae to hold out toward Rune and Elias. "She wants me to wear this! Look at it!"

"It's very…frilly," Rune said.

Even Elias made a face at it. "Fabio would be proud."

"See! I'm not wearing it."

"Come on! Please, at least comb your hair." The older Fae brandished a comb and before Calvin could stop her, she whipped it through his blonde, slightly shower-damp hair. Once she was finished, Rune burst out laughing.

"What now?!"

"You look like a backup singer for Grease," she screeched, before slipping into another fit of laughter, Elias joining her.

"Don't listen to them, you look dashing, Daddy-o!" Lady Trella declared firmly.

Growling, Calvin leaned forward and shook out his hair with his fingers, before scraping it back. The treatment actually helped, his natural wave settling into the follicles, despite Lady Trella's pout.

"Rune?" Malachi appeared, giving Calvin's antics a side-eye.

"We're ready when you are," she said, indicating the painted door.

Malachi eyed it and nodded. "Good, good."

"Does this mean we're going soon?" Elias asked.

"I don't know yet. Last I heard, St. Rachel found records of medical equipment having been bought by Kodiak at various times over the past few years under the pretense of branching out into a company-only medical facilities project, except the project never came to be." Malachi nodded over at the jack-in chair. St. Rachel was reclining in it, her eyes closed as if asleep. At least until they snapped open to look straight at Rune. As if on cue, the chair rotated to a more upright position as a light flashed in the circle of monitors. Once the transition was complete, she stretched.

"And you think that's all a cover up? The medical equipment." Rune asked, trying to ignore the hostile work environment.

"Maybe?" Malachi shrugged. "It's not unusual for companies to have their own medical facilities in-house but we can't find any paperwork on what happened to it. That's the part that's interesting. Again not unusual for bureaucracies to lose paperwork, but the fact that it's not unusual is what someone hiding something would be counting on."

Malachi eyed the painting of the door on the wall. "Is that all you need, really? Shouldn't there be candles or a chicken to sacrifice or something?"

"We can if you like," Elias said. His back was turned to them as he worked at painting the icon of the Lucky Devil on the middle of the door with a deft hand. It looked so exactly like the bar's icon, Rune realized that it was probably Elias who had originally created it.

Having finished the drawing, Elias took a step back and outstretched his palm toward it. He didn't say anything, but Rune felt the hairs on the back of her arm rise up with the feeling of magic wafting off of him. After a moment, the lines came to life, pulsing and shifting like they were alive. There was a small burst of air as the lines that made up the door frame became real in the concrete. And then the door of the Lucky Devil was simply there in the wall. Rune smiled as she walked up to it and opened it. Inside was her bar, quiet and still, only Lucky Devil sitting and smiling in his booth and Alf turning toward the opening door.

"My lady! I…." he started to say.

She shut it again and nodded at Elias. "Looks like it worked."

Unfortunately, Elias was distracted by the outcry happening behind him. The magical pulse that had come off of him had whipped through the Praetorium, shutting down all electronics in the room. The cry of outrage had rolled through the room as the techs lost their work and turned to the obvious culprits. A moment later everything booted up again.

"I guess I should have warned you all," Elias said, not nearly chagrined enough for what he had done, Rune thought.

"Geez! Dammit! Yeah, buddy, you think? What would have happened if you had done that when St. Rachel was still in the system?! You could have fried her brain!" Malachi shouted.

"We're sorry," Rune tried to cover, but it didn't do much to calm the tech down.

"I mean, do you understand what can happen in a power failure when you're in the system?!"

"Not really," Elias admitted, now looking the appropriate level of chagrined.

"We don't have time for this, Malachi," St. Rachel said coming up to the group. She wore something akin to fatigue pants only black, with an equally black, close-fitting shirt with sleeves. She had braided her hair back and pinned it into a tight bun behind her head. A belt of uniform pouches and a holster for a gun were strapped around her waist. Rune eyed the gun, but pursed her lips together and said nothing. "Are all assembled?" St. Rachel asked, surveying the faces looking at her. Her eyebrows knitted when she got to Calvin and Lady Trella.

"Are you coming too?" the Saint asked Lady Trella, pointedly.

"Damn straight," the older Fae said with a point of her finger at Rune's nose. For a brief moment, Rune thought she was going to boop it.

"I'm staying behind," Elias said, raising his hand, "in case."

"I think it's me, Calvin, Lady Trella, I guess, and St. Rachel," Rune turned to look at each person in turn for confirmation.

St. Rachel's lips were a very thin line. "Fine," she said, checking her gun in a pointed statement that made Rune finger her shield crystal. She really hated that St. Rachel was bringing the gun, but had no idea how to convince her to leave it behind. She certainly didn't have that kind of clout with the deadly woman to make it happen.

Once her inspection was done, St. Rachel waved her hand to make the Saint hologram ring appear around herself. A ghostly image of Maxamillion appeared in front of her. "We're all set to go, sir."

"Good luck, St. Rachel," Maxamillion said and his image disappeared.

"Well, that was inspirational," Elias quipped.

"That was damn eloquent for him. Usually we just get an 'okay,'" Malachi said, having calmed down from his justifiable tantrum. "Zita's on her way. She's prepared the stasis pod we've used on our Saints, in case you're able to extract the Faerie Queen...."

"The Titania," Lady Trella cut in.

"Stop wasting our time," St. Rachel barked at the Fae. "Anything else?!"

Malachi shook his head.

"Alright. Then open the door, Talent," the Saint ordered.

Rune stood there looking at her. No one else moved.

"I said, move out!" St. Rachel growled, taking a step closer.

Before she got two steps, Rune turned to Calvin. "With your majesty's permission?" She bowed at the waist to the bewildered Oberon.

"Uh, yeah. Whatever," he said, glancing at the reddening St. Rachel and Rune's unsuppressed wicked smile that she *was* trying to hide with her bent head. Not knowing what else to do, Calvin waved a regalish hand at the door. "Sally forth, good lady wizard…ugh, or whatever. I don't know." He threw his hands up in disgusted discomfort.

It was all Rune needed though. Turning to the door, she set her feet shoulder width apart and blew out a breath. Then held it.

"Take two more deep breaths, then open your second sight," Elias said just over her shoulder. Nodding, she did as he instructed, even closing her real eyes before opening them again with her secondary sight. Instantly, the world around her warped and wefted. Magic and energy flowed around her through time and space, overwhelming her senses like it always did. Doing so used to hurt, but continual use of it had started building up her tolerance for so much information. Resisting the urge to look around at everyone and see their other selves, Rune focused on the task at hand.

She forced another breath that echoed with vibrations all around her. In her mind's eye she tried to picture where she wanted go. With no business card or focus to help her, though, Rune struggled. She could see the magic strings, all colors this time, and varying strengths.

"Open," she heard her voice echo at the door. Nothing happened. Rune growled in her throat. "It's not going to work…."

"Use your hands if you need to," Elias said confidently. "Remember Rune, you are the Dreamer and there are no rules, only guidelines."

Setting her face into a determined grimace, Rune tried again, this time lifting her hands. They moved, moving, will move through the space before her. Relaxing her focus, she let the strings around the door pop out of the flood of color. Opening a door had something to do with that. No, it had something to do with worlds meeting, the doors opened in-between worlds. She could see the bubbles, the world of the Fae meeting St. Rachel and Malachi's tech world. Where those two met was before her, the energy between them electric. Rune only had to harness that energy to open a way where both those worlds existed as one.

Then out of the edge of her sight, Rune saw the red strings, the ones that had followed her everywhere, only this time she saw something else. Unsure of what it was, Rune gestured with her hands, sweeping them to the side and around in a wide full body circle. The red strings coiled themselves toward her, twisting in on themselves into a single red rope of magic. Then she heard it, the single tinkling sound of joyful laughter echoing from the past. The young Talent grasped the rope of magic, cascading her fingers one at a time perfectly coordinated as a dancer, as if she had done this all her life.

"I am the Dreamer," she whispered and screamed at the same time as she grasped the magic her precious great-aunt Maddie had left Rune to guide her to the answers she sought when she was ready. Intuitive magic, adapting as Rune needed, to bring her to the truth about Justin and herself. Understanding at last, Rune flung her hands toward the door. Immediately, the red magic flowed from her, surrounding the door that was and wasn't there, held between two worlds, before sinking in along the edges of the frame.

Rune stared at the Lucky Devil logo smiling at her from the middle of the door and for the briefest of moments, she swore she saw it wink at her. Then the door obeyed, flying open with a bang. She heard cries and gasps around her as the Dreamscape roared on the other side like a sea of stars and night sky. It began to flood in.

"Go through now!" Elias shouted over the roar of it.

Heeding him, Rune stepped forward, or maybe the Dreamscape came to meet her, she wasn't sure, but the Praetorium was gone. She floated in the sea of magic, feeling joyful as it warmly buzzed over her skin like salted water filled with tiny bubbles. It was like the magic was inviting her to play, but she knew she had a job to do.

She tried to picture Clarissa, how she looked, how she sounded, what Rune knew of her. In front of her, she could see her gold string try to coalesce into something solid, only to immediately collapse into the flow of the world again. "Come on," Rune growled.

"What's wrong, Rune?" someone asked. She could barely hear who, but she knew it wasn't someone she liked very much.

"I can't focus on her. She's…she's changed too much from when I knew her and what she is now is a lie. What she's shown me…it keeps crumbling."

A hand gripped her shoulder tightly. She glanced back at the gleaming face of Calvin. Or rather the face of the Oberon. He was brilliance personified in the darkness. It wasn't that he didn't look like himself; he was still Calvin, but his hair glowed like a corona around him, the blonde turning milky white. His eyes were shards of blue jewels and his skin sheened as if dusted with gold. Behind him was a shadow version, this one dark and sneering Calvin's mean smile, his skin dusted like ash. Another stood near the cluster, this one barely a faded shadow with antlers rising from its crown, another was a small boy, another was the Poh with its wicked horn and lion's paws, talons glistening, another was an old man, over and over again as far back and forward through time. If Rune focused on any one of the figures all occupying the same space as Calvin, she saw the entire story of that being, those who had been the Oberon before. The entirety of the Oberon laid before her.

"I am unworthy," Calvin didn't say, but she heard it all the same. This was what he saw and felt inside himself. She looked at a few of the individuals, previous Oberons as dark as he could be, less justified, truly unredeemable, others the greatest beings that had ever been, but still flawed. All flawed. All blessed.

Rune had to close her eyes against the cascade flowing through her chaotic mind.

"I am unworthy."

"No, Calvin. You're not." She forced her eyes open again

and clasped her hand over his on her shoulder. "You are fine. You're doing the best you can."

He quirked his eyebrows at her, unbelieving, but Rune could see he would come to accept it in time. He would understand it better than she ever would.

"What do you need?" he asked.

"Take us to her."

The Oberon turned then to look out into the vastness of the Dreamscape, keeping his hand on Rune's shoulder. "She's already here."

Then there was a bloodcurdling scream. Flipping around, Rune saw St. Rachel's form contorted, contorting, will contort in the Dreamscape. Her back was arched, arching, will arch so far back as to look painful, her fists clutched, clutching, will clutch hard to her head. Spikes of blue light were shattered, shattering, will shatter through her being, one through her head and several more pierced, piercing, will pierce her body. Rune realized where she had seen that before.

"Her augmentations! Get her out! We have to get her out of here!"

"We can't!" called Lady Trella, truly the Orange Lady as she glowed like the harvest sun in the magic pool. "The door has closed. She hesitated too long on the threshold."

Laughter, sinister and mocking, swirled in the space around them

"Ill met by moonlight, proud Titania," the Oberon shouted.

"Shakespeare. Really?" Rune said, as she used her magic to pull herself to St. Rachel.

"Hey, great way to meet chicks. And insult people. Only class I could stay awake for," Calvin replied.

"We need somewhere to be, the Dreamscape cannot join with her," Trella said as she took St. Rachel's opposite arm from the one Rune caught.

"The bitch is denying us entry!" the Oberon shouted again at the mocking voice. "We'll die out here."

Rune spun back to the welcoming void. It wanted them, it would lovingly consume them if they lingered much longer. "Use your hands," Rune reminded herself, and she gestured with both hands imagining ground coming from the depths of magic. As she pulled toward herself with empty palms, ground appeared. "I am the Dreamer," she murmured to herself as she gestured again. Like a shattered ruin, walls partially came into being and a sense of gravity returned to their forms, drawing everyone around her toward the floor Rune had created and Rune dropped her sight. Without meaning to, Rune realized she had created a replica of the Lucky Devil Lounge Bar floating in the Dreamscape. There were even a few tables and chairs, though they looked aged and worn. The bar L-shaped through the space, empty of glasses or alcohol. Jagged edges thrust themselves upward for walls and there was no roof. Still, feeling something solid was a relief.

"Solarus," Lady Trella said, and a tiny sun the size of a baseball appeared, floating over the Fae's hand, casting light in the miniscule world Rune had created. Gently the older Fae blew and the ball floated to the height where the ceiling would have been.

On the newly made ground, St. Rachel laid on her side, silent in unconsciousness. Lady Trella knelt quickly and brushed her hair gently, leaning over to listen. Rune rushed to join them.

"She is alright, Wizardress."

"She is not alright," Calvin commented, still keeping a look out into the darkness beyond.

"She still breathes," Lady Trella amended.

"At least now we don't have to worry about her trying to kill the Titania before we get a chance to talk to her," Rune commented, but it didn't seem like the silver-lining she was hoping it would. "We have to get her out of here."

A gale whipped around their small space, carrying laughter.

"She's here!" Calvin called, though it was pretty obvious. Crossing the space, Calvin's face had gone white as a sheet as he pushed past Rune to grab up St. Rachel's gun from her holster.

"No! Put that away," Rune hissed, as she tried to slap it back down.

"Look, Leveau. If it comes down to it, if it's her or me, then I am not facing this bitch without something in my hand!"

"My, my, my. Dear husband. Is that a gun in your hand or

are you just happy to see me?"

They all turned to see the figure of the Titania sitting on the edge of the bar. Both of her hands were braced as she leaned over her crossed legs wrapped in an impossibly long liquid metal skirt. It seemed to have a life of its own as it draped itself around and over the bar. Otherwise her midriff was bare, while two more strips of liquid cloth cupped and crossed at her chest and around her long, elegant neck.

Calvin didn't answer her question, but turned to point the shaky gun at her. She burst out laughing, her berry-red mouth gaping wide as she laughed all the way to her toes.

"What are you going to do with that, husband?"

A black taloned hand covered over the end of the gun, appearing out of nowhere so abruptly that Calvin jumped and immediately dropped it. The hand took it and lifted it up to examine as the rest of the dark Oberon coalesced in front of them all. The thing was entirely blackened, taking the form of a man with darkened antlers stretching impossibly long over its head. Deftly the shadow turned and flipped the gun, pulling it apart and checking its payload, then reassembled it.

"St. Benedict," Rune ventured, slowly starting to rise to her feet.

Without warning he pointed the gun, his body in perfect majestic line with the weapon and fired. Involuntary screams followed on the heels of the report and Calvin stumbled back as he cried in pain.

The Titania laughed.

Chapter 22

"Mother, please! No!" Lady Trella cried, dropping to her knees before the Titania, raising her arms in supplication. "Please, Mother."

The Titania blinked at the sight of the older Fae. "Trella?"

"Yes, Mother. It is I," the Fae said, very formally.

"What are you doing here?" the Titania asked.

"We're here to help you," Rune said stepping forward, keeping a death grip on her shield crystal. She had placed herself in front of Calvin, who knelt on the ground, clutching at his shoulder in pain. The Dark Oberon kept the gun trained on Calvin, which happened to be through Rune's navel. "I brought the Oberon as you requested."

The Titania waved her hand dismissively. "Yes, yes. I can settle with you later, mageling."

Rune took another step, but doing so triggered the dark entity in front of her and the gun went off. She reacted too late, but to her surprise the bullet sped past her head and not into her gut. A warning shot. The Dark Oberon seemed to grin, but since he was black on black it was really hard to tell. Only the red eyes continued to twinkle at her. Panting, Rune had to fight every urge in her body to turn and run. What she couldn't fight was the whimper that slipped out of her.

At that sound, the straight as iron arm crooked a little bit, the gun no longer pointing just over her shoulder. There were groans and grunts behind her, but she didn't dare turn around or take her eyes off the being she hoped was St. Benedict.

"I am trying to have a conversation with my Daughter here!" The Titania roared at the disruption.

"Mother, please, I beg you, don't hurt him. He's our Father."

Lady Trella was weeping and there was no other word to describe it.

"Oh my precious Childe, do not weep." The Titania slid from the counter and took up the pleading hands of the Fae before her. "I am making it right. For all of us." She gently stroked Lady Trella's cheek with the back of her knuckles as a mother would to a tenderly beloved child, before cupping the bottom of her chin to turn her toward the Dark Oberon. "Look at him, Trella. Is he not magnificent? He will be your Father, he already is in so many ways. He will help lead us all back to the Faerie Court and make things right again, by my side."

"Like hell!"

Rune jumped as a hand grabbed her pant leg. Calvin shouted another swear, lugging himself drunkenly to his feet. "Calvin, what the hell? Stay down!"

"Oh shut up, Leveau, it's not like I haven't taken a bullet before."

"Of course you have," Rune muttered. "Clarissa, stop this. We need to speak with you but nothing's going to be accomplished with violence."

"You have nothing to say that I want to hear."

"I understand the position you're in," Rune called. "I mean, this is really unfair, isn't it? Not only were you a good Titania, you had it ripped from you. And now, because of what that asshole you were forced to be married to did, you are going to die. And that's not fair."

"No, it's not. And now I'm going to fix it."

"It won't work." Rune shook her head. "Because you are doing exactly what was done to you. You're doing it through coercion and murder, so nothing you try will work for very long and you know it. None of this is going to work…."

The Titania let Lady Trella's hands go.

"Let me guess, you are the miraculous savior who is going to show me another way?"

"Let us take you out of here. There are people on the other side of….okay, side might not be the right word for it, but there are people waiting for us who want to help you. Your people want to help you."

"My people want balance and are more than willing to see me die to achieve it." The Titania looked down at Lady Trella as she said that and the older Fae hung her head in shame.

"Alright, full disclosure, yes there was talk about killing you and the gun there backs that up, but *I* wasn't going to let that happen."

The Titania laughed manically. "And how were you going to stop it, little mageling? Why would you want to if killing me is so much simpler?"

"Because I believe there is another way. There has to be. And we can find it together."

"There is, the way I am creating. I can't wait around for someone to come save me. No one ever comes."

"I've come." Rune looked past the gun that was still being pointed at them. She nodded her head at Calvin over her shoulder. "I brought him. I brought the person you need."

"I won't mate myself with a piece of trash."

"Then don't. I really don't understand why you absolutely have to. Why not give up being the Titania?"

"Impossible. What I am cannot be given away, I can only be what I am until the day I die." Again the derisive laugh. "You know nothing, little mageling. You can only pretend to be so wise, but you are not your master. The Titania must be mated to the Oberon. It is written in the very fabric of the magic itself, immutable as the sun rising or the moon waning. The stars themselves would fall from the sky the day this is not true."

"Really? Because it isn't true. You are not united with the Oberon. In fact you keep murdering him, over and over again."

"He seeks to kill me!"

"You've tried to kill me first, you bitch!" Calvin roared, pushing against Rune as if he was going to rush her. Rune kept her arm out to hold him back. "Will you look at this? I'm bleeding!" he kept shouting.

"You're not helping," Rune hissed at him.

"You see! This Oberon is unworthy."

"This Oberon has done nothing to you! He's innocent of the crimes you want to saddle on him."

"He is far from innocent!"

"That's true, he has done a lot of crap to me and to other people and he is overall a huge and embarrassing waste of space...."

"Hey!" Calvin protested, but no one heeded him.

"But. None of it is worthy of a death sentence and none of it, not one bit of it, was done to you!" Rune finished.

"I will not take him as my husband!"

"Alright fine. That's fine. I'm not an advocate for marital coercion, but then how about you just forgive him! Find a way to work together for the sake of your children!"

There was a long pregnant pause. Rune turned to Calvin and grabbed his good shoulder, making sure to keep herself between him and the Dark Oberon. "Calvin, say you're sorry."

"For what? I haven't done...."

"You wanted to kill her right? Apologize for that. For not making her feel safe. For not coming to help her sooner. I don't care what, but think of a reason."

Calvin blinked, flustered as he looked between Rune and the fierce woman glaring at him. No one said a word or took a breath. He tried to take a step forward and immediately the gun shifted to point straight at his nose. The two Oberons met eyes, but before the trigger could be pulled Rune stepped in front of the barrel.

"Two women walked into a bar," she said to the black creature in front of her.

The dark creature's eyes, which had been slits of red, opened a little bit wider, before turning the gun arm up to point the weapon skyward.

"When are you going to tell me the rest of that joke?" Rune asked.

"What are you doing?" the Titania hissed.

"He won't shoot me," Rune answered for him. She held out her hand toward the gun and waited.

"What are you doing?!" the Titania screeched, even louder. "Kill him! Take your place by my side!"

"He's already sworn his life to me, Clarissa." Rune's fingers touched the still warm surface of the weapon as she continued to hold his gaze. She wasn't sure what she read in those eyes, but it felt like they were looking deeply into her soul. "Isn't that right?" she asked him.

He let the weight of the gun shift from his hand into hers.

Rune smiled with relief. "It's alright," she said softly. "I forgive you."

The red in his eyes faded away, revealing the green-blue irises.

"Calvin," Rune said with a soft even tone. "Come forgive him."

"What?"

"For shooting you."

"No."

She kicked sideways and scored his shin.

"Do it."

"Fine, fine," the blonde idiot muttered and he came forward, flinching a little when St. Benedict's eyes shifted to him. "Um, it's alright, that you shot me, I guess." He let go of his bleeding shoulder and held his hand out for St. Benedict to take. There was a tense moment, then St. Benedict's black coated talons met the bright red bloodied ones. The moment they touched there was a rush as the blackness covering St. Benedict began to billow into a thick miasma, obscuring any view of the man beneath. Calvin almost let go, but it was too late as the darkness swirled and engulfed him as well.

For a moment both men were lost in the darkness, until St. Benedict appeared on the other side. He looked like himself again, only in tattered clothing, very pale and exhausted. As soon as the darkness had completely cleared, he collapsed to the ground, only his hand remained up, still held by Calvin.

For the true Oberon's part, the darkness seemed to sink into him, until it was completely gone. It had left him with antlers on his head, but real ones instead of illusionary ones made of shadow. Strangely enough, it looked natural on him.

He stood there blinking, a bit stunned himself. "Oh. That feels better."

The Oberon looked down at St. Benedict's hand still in his own before giving it a tug, levering the Saint up to his feet. Before she could meet the Saint's gaze, Rune looked away, turning back to the Titania.

Or she meant to.

"Where did she go?" Rune walked over to the bar, now absent of both the Titania and Lady Trella. "Did you guys see them leave?" she asked as she leaned over the bar, which was a bad idea because she realized there was nothing there except void, giving Rune a moment of vertigo. "She must have retreated."

She turned back to see St. Benedict kneeling beside St. Rachel, holding his fingers at her neck. "How is she?"

"Alive but she's not responding. We need to get her back to Zita," he answered, and held his hand out over her.

"Don't!" Rune caught his hand just in time before he ignited his augmentation. "Don't use your tech in this place. You'll end up like her. The only reason you're not a potato right now is because I made us a landing place, but I doubt I can shield you if you go all glowey-eyed."

"I'll be fine, I recalibrated my systems to the lowest settings," he replied and flipped his augmented hand open, popping up the hologram. Immediately, he winced. "Okay, maybe I'll make this quick." He fiddled with his hologram, again turning it into shapes Rune barely understood. He glanced up at her watching him and then said, "I'm recalibrating St. Rachel's settings."

"We can't lose her now," Calvin said. He was staring out into the void making it very clear which "her" he meant.

"Can we leave St. Rachel here?" St. Benedict asked.

"No. The minute I leave, this floating island will dissipate." She pointed out into the void. "They told me."

"Who?"

"The Eternal Consciousness of All-Magic. It's what I'm calling it. Starting now."

"I sense her out there, but I can't...." Calvin continued, pretty oblivious to the other conversation. Rune turned and laid a hand on him.

"She's there," Rune pointed, following the instinctive tug of her Talent. Rune blinked as it had been a long time since she had simply done that, simply letting herself know, rather than relying on the need to see strings. "Huh."

"What is it?" St. Benedict asked, having come up beside her.

"Nothing. I've simply been overcomplicating things lately."

She glanced over her shoulder at St. Rachel. "How is she?"

"She's going to be fine if nothing more happens. Probably have a wicked headache for a few days."

"Good, I'll open a way back for you both," Rune said, though she wasn't a hundred percent sure how she was going to do that yet.

"I'm going with you," St. Benedict said as if he was surprised she was suggesting anything else.

"Five minutes ago, you were her brainwashed minion. I don't think so buddy," Calvin sneered.

"I was in complete control of my actions," St. Benedict said, turning to say it more to Rune.

"And that's better? That means you're a traitor," Calvin continued.

"Look, just because I wasn't going to let you harm her, didn't mean I was intending on murdering you guys."

"Prove it."

St. Benedict smiled his predatory smile. "You're still alive, aren't you?" Calvin stared at him blankly doing his signature fish mouth. The Saint turned to Rune again, leaning in conspiratorially. "Do you think for a minute that I could miss a close-range shot?"

"No. But I could believe that you would play with your food," Rune replied, holding her ground, not letting his closeness intimidate her.

He narrowed his eyes and straightened. "Fair enough," he conceded. She could watch his brain start to switch tactics, but there wasn't time for this game.

"Also, I believe you."

"What? He shot me!" Calvin protested.

"And you came here intent on revenge-killing the Titania, after we said we were going to try really hard not to do that! Of course the Oberon would move to protect her. For all he says he wasn't under its influence, he was partly the Oberon," Rune shot back. "Any way, blame later, we need to chase after her."

"Great," St. Benedict nodded.

"But you'll still be useless to us," Rune said. It came out harsher than she meant.

"Yes, here I'm useless. This place is pure magic. But where the Faerie Queen is, is digital. Or half digital. Those glyphs that we found at the Magic Guild? They're written into all the code over there. Even more important, if what you say is true, that you want to get her out of here, then you can only do that if we can get to her physical body. We can get to where her physical body is through that digital interface that she's made real. But, I've got the code figured out and I am pretty sure I can open the door to where they're holding her body. You get me to the digital interface, then I can use this." He opened his hand, letting the display show the code writing itself in letters of light. Rune noticed how hard he was gripping his other hand in a fist to maintain it. "I had a lot of time to tinker with this and I think it'll work."

"We still can't leave St. Rachel here; one of us needs to take her back." She eyed Calvin, nibbling her lip. "I suppose we don't necessarily need you any more…"

"No way. I'm not running from this anymore," the blonde man said with a surety that Rune half-thought was actually kind of kingly. A little bit.

"And I need to go with to make sure all of you don't kill each other," Rune said.

"You think she'll go with you willingly?" St. Benedict challenged with a raised eyebrow at Rune. "You need her to leave with you by choice and I mean that. In here, she's basically god."

"Then she'd be useless to Kodiak," Calvin said. The other two blinked at him. "Well, think about it. If she's supposed to be the computer that casts magic, then you'd need a way to control her, right? Free will gets in the way of that."

"The power of the Titania at someone's command at the touch of a few buttons," Rune said softly, the implications sinking in. "All the Fae, owing allegiance to a computer."

"All the Fae becoming computers," Calvin said.

"Kodiak controlling that computer. Powerful people who only care about themselves and their delights like parasitic wannabe gods," St. Benedict nodded.

"Well, that's unsettling," said a new voice.

They all turned as one to see Lady Wilde sitting on the bar, her black leather hat slid back on her forehead so a small bit of red hair peaked out, her fox tail flicking back and forth agitatedly behind her. At the sight of all of them looking at her, she sat up a little more alert. "I came to see what the commotion was about."

"Somehow I don't believe you," Rune said.

Lady Wilde shifted as she jumped off the bar, giving Calvin a look up and down. "I see you managed to continue living. That's disappointing."

"You're one of those other Fae who tried to help murder me, aren't you?" Calvin sneered.

In response, Lady Wilde rolled her shoulders, seeming even more like an animal gearing up for a fight. "I am a loyal Daughter. Better than some piece of crap who thought he could win himself some power by putting on a necklace. What was it you hoped to accomplish again when you did that? I do hope it was your own attempted murder?"

The Oberon cocked his head slightly to the side as he regarded the angry Fae. It was a behavior that seemed out of joint with his normal character. "Your name is Jane Wilde, isn't it?"

The Fae's tail stopped flicking.

"Yes. You were mortal once, a true Faerie Friend, until…" his voice took on a dreamy quality. "You loved the little folk. You wrote books about them and about us, you advocated passionately for our rights in England in…in…." The Oberon's eyebrows shot up, "in the 1880s?" He looked over at Rune and St. Benedict before continuing. "You became ill with bronchitis and the little folk you loved so much begged the Titania to spare you. To make you one of us."

"Us?" Lady Wilde's voice cracked as tears ran freely down her face. It was amazing how one little word could alter a mind so quickly. "Do you mean that?"

Calvin, the Oberon, nodded. "Yes. Us."

"Father," she squeaked. She pressed the back of one hand against her mouth as if to hold back the sob building inside her. "No. No, you're not. You're not our Father."

He only looked unsure for a moment, before opening his arms. It was all the invitation the Fae needed. Rushing with her uncanny speed, she wrapped her arms around Calvin's waist and wailed. To his credit, the Oberon pulled the shuddering, smaller person close as tenderly as he had with Lady Trella, holding her as she cried.

Giving them a sliver of privacy while the Oberon continued to comfort the weeping Fae, Rune turned away to look out at the vastness of the ECAM.

"We keep talking about sending St. Rachel back, but how are we going to do that exactly?" St. Benedict asked, coming up too close beside Rune.

"I'm going to trial and error until I get it right," she answered, stepping away from him toward the spot where the door of her bar would be if they were actually in her bar. She continued looking at it, but she was in no way seeing it. Despite her best efforts, her mind was laser-focused on the presence of the man standing next to her and who was very distractingly staring at her.

Rune closed her eyes once, then opened them again, her normally hazel eyes wiped away with the ethereal white light tinged with gold that indicated she was using her secondary magic sight. Unabashedly, St. Benedict watched her, fascinated that he could pick out where she was looking, even without the guide of her irises.

"What?" she snapped. "Why are you smiling at me?"

"Maybe I'm just happy to see you."

She grimaced. Oh yeah, she was mad at him. "Do you mean what you said? You were really just protecting the Titania?"

"Yes. Absolutely."

"So was it because the price was right or because of the Oberon possession?"

St. Benedict resisted the urge to wipe his face, as she practically spat that at him.

"Maybe I was inspired to do that right thing," he said teasingly.

He expected her to smile despite her best efforts not to. She didn't. No effort required. "I would think having your free will ripped from you would make you enraged."

"Wasn't the first time I had my free will stolen from me. Sometimes pain makes you a monster, sometimes it just makes you kind."

Rune cocked her head at those words. Finally, an opening. "Rune, I…"

"Would you like me to escort your fallen one back for you?" They both turned back to Lady Wilde, who rubbed her eyes with the heel of her hand, Calvin's own hand sitting on her shoulder.

Rune was taken aback so much she let her secondary sight drop. "You mean St. Rachel?"

"You're trading sides very easily," St. Benedict said.

"St. Benedict," Rune chided under her breath, "there aren't sides."

"I am a good Daughter," Lady Wilde said, cutting Rune off. She puffed her chin and chest out proudly. "I have no contempt for my sisters who chose to follow the Oberon. But I could not abandon my Mother, no matter how crazy or demented she became." Then Lady Wilde deflated a little. In a smaller voice she added, "Nor can I take her from this place myself."

Suddenly, the foxy Fae crossed the space to Rune, moving faster than the Finder could follow. The other two men jumped, but it was already too late, Lady Wilde was already clasping Rune's hand. "Swear to me, Faerie Friend, that you will set my Mother free."

"I swear," Rune said before Lady Wilde had even finished asking. She clasped the back of the Fae's hand hard. "I swear, I will get your Mother out of this place."

"No, you won't. She can never leave here alive. Please…." Pain tore across Lady Wilde's face. "Please set her free. Don't let them hurt her anymore."

Rune was shocked. "Jane…"

Lady Wilde wiped her arm noisily across her nose and swallowed. "If I was really a good Daughter, I would have freed her myself. But…."

"A Fae cannot harm their Parents," the Oberon said, squeezing her gently, but firmly.

"No. No they can't, can they?" Lady Wilde said. Nodding,

the Fae's face broke into a sharp-toothed smile that was as unsettling as it was relieved. "Then I await you back at our place. I'll drop your girl off, then I will let our people know. We will await you under the tree." With that, the Fae trotted over to where St. Rachel laid and scooped her up as if she weighed nothing. "Come on, Sleeping Beauty. Let's get you out of here." Before she left however, Lady Wilde turned back to the Oberon one last time with a complicated look, apprehension coated with hope and something near hero worship. He nodded once, then shifted away in a clear sign of self-consciousness, crossing his arms. Then Lady Wilde spun away and both women were simply gone.

Rune gave a little huff.

"What is it?" St. Benedict asked.

"I should have asked her how she does that." Turning back to Calvin, Rune smiled. "How you handled that with Lady Wilde…. That was great. Now do that, only with the Titania."

"Shut up," Calvin said. "It won't be that easy, Leveau. You know it."

She sighed. She was going to be damned before she told Calvin he was right. What made it suck more is she was starting to wonder if…. Rune shoved the feelings of doubt away. "St. Benedict, can you tell me how you came here? Did Clarissa bring you or did you come yourself?"

"She brought us through. I can't return us to where she is, but I can sense it." He held out his hand, opening up the augmentation again with a wince. "The data signal is that way."

"I know. I don't need your tech to tell me that," Rune said, her voice very preoccupied.

"Right. You are the Finder, after all," St. Benedict said. She didn't respond and he felt a little let down.

"Calvin, can you feel it too?" Rune asked.

"Feel what?" the self-focused man asked with disdain.

"Her call?" That flipped the switch inside him and now Calvin the Oberon was looking out with Rune.

"Yes."

"Do you feel like you can grab it?" Rune asked, raising her hand in the direction they were both looking.

"What the...?" but Calvin stopped and cocked his head to the side. "Oh. Yes. I think so."

"Okay, do what I do." Rune indicated as she raised her other hand. Calvin followed suit.

"What are we doing?" he asked.

"We're going to pull ourselves there. The physical manifestation helps but keep focused on that feeling inside. Visualize it in your mind and then..." her voice drifted away as they both closed their fists like they were grabbing a bar, "...pull."

Chapter 23

Instantly, the ECAM was gone. It was like Rune's little island was swallowed up by the digital forest around them. St. Benedict gave a sigh of relief. The burning headache behind his eyes finally dissipated.

"It's changed," he said ominously, taking a slow measure of the space around them.

"What is this?" Calvin demanded, his eyeballs looking like they were going to pop out of their sockets.

"What an intermarriage of magic and technology looks like," St. Benedict said. "As far as I've been able to unravel, this is how Kodiak plans to recreate the Masterson Files." With a sweeping gesture St. Benedict passed his hand to the side and a holographic display appeared beneath it, creating a console of light. He fiddled with the displays again and more light passed over his body. For a moment, he was nothing but the silhouette of a man in a field of white before it dropped away.

Before, he had been a mess, his dress pants tattered at the bottom, with frays and small rends in his shirt as well as any number of bruises and small cuts over his body. Now he was clean, dressed in dark grey combat pants and a close-fitted shirt. His dress shoes with their square toes were replaced with thick combat boots laced up his calves and locked with a buckle at the top. A holster was strapped to his hip and thigh, thick black bands cutting over the grey. His hands were gloved to the first knuckle leaving the rest of his fingers unsheathed. Against his chest, winking on the field of dark, was his silver Saint's Box.

"What no fedora?" Rune asked, noting his hair was slicked down to his head.

"It'll get in the way," he said, and pulled a gun out of his holster. Rune's eyes went wide at the sight of it, but he ignored her response and checked the chamber.

"It's to defend only," he said.

"I've never understood that. It's a weapon," Rune said.

"Would it be different if it was a sword and shield?" St. Benedict asked, his teasing tone melting into his voice.

Rune didn't take the bait. "Yes, it would be. You can block with a shield; it's designed to protect. A sword can be used for both, but a gun, everything created in its design is to do one thing: attack."

"And what difference does it make any way? It's not real," Calvin sneered. "You just put a light projection all over yourself. What's the plan, hot shot? You can't trick her like that."

St. Benedict straightened his arm and fired the gun. Calvin and Rune jumped and squealed as the report echoed eerily.

"The hell!" Rune screeched, but St. Benedict was already pushing past her to kick the creature on the ground that was twisting in its own glowing ichor, its wicked-looking teeth chomping at the air.

"She's going to turn this whole place against us. She already knows we're here." He held out the gun to Calvin to take. "And it's real by the way."

"You made it out of a hologram, that's not possible..." Calvin stopped as his hand wrapped around the heated metal of the weapon.

"That's the power of what Justin Masterson created. Magic manifestation through programmable technology," St. Benedict said.

"You cast a spell?" Rune furrowed her brows.

"No, I was able to access plans and schematics for all of this stuff online once I hacked through this place. Pulling in information like that was easy, getting information out not so much, in case you were wondering why I didn't contact the Praetorium." He waved his hand again and created a new gun as he talked. "It's how the Faerie Queen created all of this. Once I cracked the encryption I uploaded the patterns into a program designed for a 3d printer and initiated 'the Titania protocol' which works nearly instantaneously compared to a machine."

The light bubbled around his hand again and when it left, a new gun exactly like Calvin was holding was in it. "Magic on demand."

"You're making this out of her magic? Without her in control of it?" Rune said. "It's worse than we thought."

He began checking the new gun too. "Imagine the entire city like this, those with augmentations able to access what they need at any time. No gun control possible then."

"All it would take is enslaving an entire race of Faeries by encasing them into permanent computer hook-ups for the rest of their lives," Rune said flatly, staring unblinking at the weapon.

St. Benedict stopped what he was doing to look up at her.

"You didn't follow your thoughts to that logical conclusion did you?" Rune accused. "You were simply eager to play with your new toys."

"It's not going to come to pass," St. Benedict said. "We're here to stop it."

"How?" Rune spat and turned away to storm out of the remaining piece of her bar into the forest, not caring if he answered the question. There really wasn't an answer any way.

The moment she stepped off the wooden planks, it devolved into the turf. The overwhelming nature of the digital jungle hit her all at once.

Rune took a steading breath.

"Hold on a moment," St. Benedict said coming up behind her. He felt her stiffen as he stopped his body inches from hers, encircling her into the space of his arms.

"What are you doing?"

"I want to try something. Hold still."

She tolerated the closeness, even as his front brushed and bumped her back as he created his holographic interface around them with his hands. The stiffness dissipated as she became more focused on what he was doing. Her hands even rose up to touch the holographic console.

"Go ahead, you can't hurt it," he said over her shoulder.

Tentatively, she pressed one of her fingers through the light. "Oh, that's weird."

"Here, press that panel right there twice," he indicated just to their right.

"How am I doing that? I thought you needed to have the augmentations in your fingers." Her own brushed his.

"There's a slight haptic feedback to the light. Anyone can touch it, but only I can create this interface. Two different processes happening here. Now hold still. The upload's complete."

She gasped a little when the light surrounded her torso. He stepped back and let his hologram drop away as they both focused on the Kevlar vest she was now wearing.

"That worked," he said approvingly. "Is it comfortable?"

"I guess," Rune said unsure.

"Do I get one?" Calvin asked.

"What? The Oberon can't protect himself?" St. Benedict said. The last thing he wanted to do was to get close to the whiney Faerie King. He also didn't want the dumbass-who-didn't-come-with-anything-for-this-operation to get killed. Oh, priorities.

A scream interrupted Calvin's retort, ripping through the air so that the hairs rose at the back of St. Benedict's neck. Then the sound changed, warping into an electronic screech before leaving a final, deafening silence in its wake.

"What the hell was that?" Calvin whispered. All three scanned around themselves, and all they could see were the eerie trees.

"The light has dimmed," St. Benedict said softly, laying a hand on Rune's shoulder to turn her toward the nearest one. He could barely see her in the dimming light.

"We need to hurry," she answered him, stepping away from his hand toward the trees.

"I can detect…" St. Benedict started to say, opening his palm, but Rune continued to walk, Calvin moving with her in sync.

"She's this way," they said at the same time. The double take they shot at each other was amusing.

St. Benedict rolled his hand closed, shutting down the hologram. "Okay then. Magic route it is." But instead of following he stopped and turned back, peering into the darkness.

"Run!" St. Benedict shouted, pushing the other two forward.

The funnel hit the ground with the force of an explosion, forcing St. Benedict to leap just as he tried to reach out to stop Rune from falling as well. Instead, he had to settle for curling around her so that they traded places in mid-air and she landed on his middle instead of planting her face into the turf. She tucked her face against his chest, while he buried his in her hair as another rush of air burst over them. Then there was a low, menacing hum. After a couple of breaths, he dared lift his head to look, Rune pushing up to do the same.

"Oh, that doesn't look friendly," he said.

The creature was shaped like a man of average build and average height, dressed in average clothes one would find at a chain outlet store: light blue button up shirt and tan khaki pants, brown, round-toed shoes. Its skin was light tan.

It didn't have a head.

Where a round human head would be was instead a series of monitor screens and tubing, like someone had taken used CCTV screens and had tried to jerry-rig them together. The front of the shirt was stained with rust, black and greenish watery streaks coming from the bottom of monitors. Each screen buzzed with grey static. The funnel remained above the thing, seemingly connected to the creature by a single, vine-thick tube.

"What is that?" Calvin shouted over the whir, the sound of his voice being shredded by the discordant noise coming from the funnel or maybe the creature itself.

"Whatever it is, it doesn't mean us well. Come on," Rune shouted, scrambling up to her feet. At the last second, she caught St. Benedict's sleeve to pull him up as well. Calvin was already running, the slighter built man leaping through the feathered filament bushes like a deer.

A screech cut through the discordant noise.

"I think it saw us!" St. Benedict said.

"And we don't even know why we're running from it!" Rune called back.

"Do you want to go back and find out what it wants?" St. Benedict asked as he shoved her a step out of the way of one of the lumbering creatures with the one-lit eye; he had to jump over it.

Rune glanced over her shoulder and the expression on her face answered him. "It's chasing us, isn't it?" He looked back and what he saw made his stomach twist. The creature was indeed coming after them, but it wasn't walking. In fact it didn't look like it had moved a muscle, still standing slightly slumped forward, facing its screens the direction they were running. He glanced away for a moment and checked on his companions. When he returned to looking back over his shoulder, the creature had come forward again, standing the same distance away, unmoving.

It stretched out one of its hands and touched the light-animal they had avoided earlier. Terrifyingly, the creature recoiled and turned a sickly green, the light inside wavering, then filling with more globes of light until the creature seemed about to burst. It began to whine right before it collapsed in on itself, the balls of light congealing into a mess like a pierced egg yolk. The poor animal dissolved into the ground, clearing the monster's way.

"Yeah, I don't want go find out what it wants," Rune stated.

"Me neither."

They took off running again.

"Where's Calvin?" St. Benedict asked.

"Just ahead," Rune confirmed and he took it as gospel.

"And the Faerie Queen?"

"The *Titania* is also just ahead."

"Perfect."

Then Rune skidded to a halt, flinging her arm out to stop him.

Standing less than ten feet in front of them was another one of the monitor-headed creatures, this one distinctly different in that it was wearing a light green button up and its skin was a caramel color. At its feet were the twitching remains of something, but was now nothing as the last bits of its life disappeared into the ground.

"Oh, I hope that wasn't Calvin," Rune muttered.

"I kinda hope it was." St. Benedict shifted gears and took another path through the trees to the right, perpendicular to the newest threat. "If I was to take a guess, those things may be what a computer virus looks like. Or maybe a security program."

"I didn't ask!" Rune called. Then one of the creatures popped out in front of her. She yelped and tried to avoid it, sliding to a halt just in front of it, which landed her on her butt. It looked down at her, tilting its monitors forward with slow menace. She tried to scramble away and St. Benedict didn't even hesitate. Drawing the gun, he was already firing before he had the conscious thought to do so. His eyes flashed blue as his augmentation came to life, creating targets only he could see for him to sight along. The bullets hit, their momentum making the creature's body jump and pop, but it didn't seem to notice nor mind as it continued to reach out for Rune's vulnerable body.

"Rune!"

A new light flashed above her, halting the creature's threat. Yellow energy crackled, smoke rising from the creature's hand as it tried to force its way through Rune's magic shield. Under the dome of light, St. Benedict saw her lying on her back, one hand wrapped around her crystal while the other projected the shield. Using the opportunity she was giving him, the Saint ran full tilt the short distance at the creature. Taking a flying leap, he pushed himself off the outside of the shield, the buzz of it jetting up his arm, to propel a powerful kick to the creature's chest. The gamble worked. The shield held his weight and the creature stumbled back several feet.

Rune let her shield drop and scrambled up again. Spinning, the Saint fell into step behind her as they retreated. Unfortunately, it was already too late.

More screen-headed beings began popping out of the trees. Dozens of them.

St. Benedict and Rune backed up a step at a time toward a large tree, trying to keep eyes on each of the encroaching threats.

"I've got three bullets left in the clip, another clip on my belt," St. Benedict said, recounting his inventory to himself.

"As if they gave a damn about your bullets," Rune said before sticking her shield crystal in her mouth. Throwing out both hands, her shield burst forth encircling them both in a complete dome connected to the tree. The closest creatures stumbled backward from the force. More of the beings pushed in, filling the spaces around them until there was nowhere to run even if they could.

"We ah en-loset on ah sides," Rune tried to say around her crystal.

"I can see that." St. Benedict started working as fast as his fingers could move. He opened his holographic console at the same time the first creature crashed into the shield. There had to be something he could do. He tore through the code, trying to think of something. Four more of the creatures hit the shield and Rune whimpered, taking a half step back as she tried to absorb the force. His eyes went wide as he watched a streak of white simply appear in her hair, twisting in and out of her frayed braid.

"Hold on Rune," he called. She didn't respond as she continued to brace her feet against the onslaught on her shield, every muscle in her body straining. He grabbed code, slammed it together, pulled something out of his own system, making it fast and dirty as he could, moving the light like it was physical reality. Rune went down to a knee. "Hold on! Hold on! Hold on!"

Two more pieces. No time to check for errors. The shield was getting smaller. Rune cried out in pain.

"I got it!" He took the code he had cobbled together in both hands and slammed it into the tree.

There was a reverberation, like a water drop on a still surface. It shuddered through everything around them. The trees around them morphed, the space between filling in with brick to form walls with only a few branches sticking out through the holes in St. Benedict's code. The creatures disappeared into the wall, completely engulfed by bricks. Rune let go of her shield, losing her focus on the spell when the reverberation hit her.

She dropped to the ground, kneeling before collapsing sideways to a sitting position, her hands palm-skyward on the end of rubber-weak arms. Her chest rose and fell, gulping air from the effort as she stared at the newly formed walls around them. The crystal was still in her mouth and in a delayed reaction, she let it go so she could pull in more air.

"Are you alright?" he asked, stooping beside her.

"What did you do?" she asked, bringing her akimbo legs forward so she could lean her elbows on her knees and breath.

"Input a video game layout. Only for this area. I don't expect it to hold them for long, but it seems to be slowing them." He hooked his hands into Rune's armpits to help her up to her feet.

"Fine. That works for me." She turned and looked around the space he had created. "Not having a way out ourselves doesn't work for me though."

"Got it covered." He knocked on the brick wall next to him. Instantly, metal rungs burst out of it going all the way up the wall. He leaned against the wall, striking a nonchalant pose. "Like magic, right?"

"You did that to look cool, didn't you?" Rune quipped back and started climbing up the rungs.

"Did it work?" he asked as she passed him. She rolled her lips together, trying to stop herself from smiling, which only made him grin harder.

The wall went up fifteen feet before it encountered what could only really be described as a cloud. "How far does this go?" Rune called down as she hesitated just inside the cool mistiness.

"It's a two story building. Think urban sprawl."

"Great. Two stories," he heard her mutter under her breath.

"Are you okay?"

"I'm fine," she replied tersely.

"Your hair says otherwise."

"Good to know." She stopped talking after that, and St. Benedict tried to focus on her fading form above him, looking for any sign that she was going to falter and fall. Gratefully, they both made it to the top, which was clear above the mist.

"Okay, which way. We've got to get to the Titania. Or Find Calvin." She turned around in a slow circle. "I...I don't sense him." Her heart began to thump hard.

"I'm sure he ran away," St. Benedict said.

Rune swallowed. "Or he could be dead."

"And then what? What was the plan in the first place?"

"Get her out of here was the plan. If we don't...." She shifted, looking out over the sea of mist and the islands of the other buildings around them.

"Kodiak wins." He concluded when she couldn't.

"I don't see a way out of this. We can't let Justin's...work... we can't let this happen." She looked down over the edge of the wall to where the screened monsters had been. "But how do we stop it?"

"We're not going to be able to remove the Faerie Queen," St. Benedict said somberly.

"We have to try."

"No, you don't understand." He grasped her arm, pulling her in closer so he could pitch his voice down. There was no way of truly knowing where the Faerie Queen might be. "She'll die outside her tube. She is completely contained inside a medical bed; that is the only thing that is keeping her alive. We can't simply open that up and pull her out."

"No, it's you who doesn't understand," Rune countered but then left that statement hanging. Instead, she turned to look out across the rolling sprawl that was this new rooftop world. Several buildings over was a billboard with a winking woman and a smile made entirely out of pink neon, except for the white neon that was her teeth. "I won't do...."

A screech interrupted Rune, both of them looking back down over the side of the misted building at the faint glows popping into existence below.

"We need to keep moving," St. Benedict said.

"Yeah," Rune agreed. They crossed to the other side of the roof, where another building was sticking out of the mist with a small gap that looked easy to jump.

"We need to go this way," Rune said, pointing in one direction toward a fire escape. "I can sense her over there."

"That's not where we need to go," St. Benedict said, before jumping the gap and offering a hand to her to follow him. She stared at him across the gap, not taking his hand and he didn't lower it. "Over here is a logout point. They're strewn all over the place in here. From there I think I can open us a way to where the Titania really is and we can take her out. I was very close to having it when...."

"You can't," she finally said, her voice dark and low, her eyes on the brink of sparking into fire.

He met them, coolly detached. "She should have died already."

"But she didn't. Against all the odds."

"And at what cost?"

"You can't."

"I can. Very easily. You know this about me."

"But I thought…." Tears began to bud at the bottoms of her eyes. "How can you? You spent time with her, you know none of this is her fault."

"That is way too simple and you know it. Or do all those Oberon's prior to Calvin not count? They lost their lives too. At the end of the day, Rune, your Faerie Queen is a psychopathic killer plugged into a machine, who sold herself to the highest bidder in order to save her own life which will lead to the enslavement of all Fae."

Rune opened her mouth then closed it. Finally, St. Benedict dropped his hand.

"It's not that I don't have sympathy for her, but it doesn't change what we have to do. As much as I would like it to not be true, we have to do this."

"No," Rune said firmly.

"Fine, then I'll do it without you." He turned his back on her.

"I'll stop you!" she shouted, crossing the gap finally to grab the back of his shirt.

"How?" he demanded, spinning back to grasp her arms.

"I'll…."

"What are you going to do Rune? Spend all your time fighting me?"

"If I…."

"While defending against those walking viruses? While Kodiak proceeds to enslave the entire Faerie people?"

"No, I…."

"While magic plunges into obscurity and people like you become hunted?" The panic slipped into his own voice too late. She had to see that this was the only way to keep her safe.

Rune stared at him wide-eyed, practically suspended in his arms. Without realizing it, he had backed her up a step, stopping short of the drop off the original side. She was breathless and wide-eyed or maybe that was him, as she grasped him back. Their grip was the only thing between her and the misty, unknown, very real fall behind her. Quickly, he backed up, pulling her with him.

"I won't...." What the hell was he saying? "I won't let that happen to you. I can end this. Destroy the Masterson Files and you will finally be safe." He let go and stepped back, putting space between them. "You don't have to do it. I will. This is what I was made for. I couldn't before. You know why."

"St. Benedict, don't kill her."

He held up his hand. "Please, stop." He looked up at the sky and swallowed. "I lied before. When I said I didn't want anything to do with you. It wasn't because of you. It was because I didn't want to see what your face would look like when I inevitably had to do something necessary like this. Like how you're looking at me right now."

"You can't kill her."

He sighed. She wasn't making this easy, but he couldn't make his feet walk away from her. "I can." He offered a smile, but it felt pained even to himself. "And you know that. It's what I am."

She blew out a hard breath. Rune fought for life, for what was right. He did what was necessary. He wasn't sure when he had started to care about that; he hadn't hidden his nature from her before. Now? The Faerie Queen had been right. His feelings for her were...complicated.

"Then we do it together."

His eyes went wide. "What?"

"I can't leave this to you alone. We do this together."

"No, Rune...."

"You're right. I get it, but I owe it to her as a Faerie Friend."

"All the more reason it shouldn't be you."

"All the more reason I should be there," she nodded resolutely, with more confidence than he even felt. "I'm already involved." She turned as she finished speaking, distracted by the squeal rising up behind. The creatures were catching up, crawling over the edge of the other building, their lights bursting from the mist.

"It's like a science fiction movie set...only more terrifying," St. Benedict said.

"Alright, where are we going?" Rune asked, grasping his sleeve as they backpedaled a step.

They turned together and raced over the close-quartered rooftops. Out of the mist, monsters appeared, bursting out with unnatural movements to come up all around them. The gaps between the roofs grew wider and wider.

It was inevitable that there would be one Rune couldn't make. She knew she couldn't make it before she jumped it, but St. Benedict was already over it when she leapt. He turned and caught her, pulling her to safety as her feet peddled air for a moment. They didn't speak, only kept moving.

It did no good, though. Too quickly, they came on a gap that neither could jump across. "It's a video game platform, right? Shouldn't there be a way off this roof?"

"There are also dead ends."

Chapter 24

"Do you really think killing me would be so easy?" Spinning around, St. Benedict saw the Titania standing a few feet away from them, hovering above the abyss of mist. Her eyes were fire and hate as she stared down at them trapped on the edge of the roof.

"This can't continue, Clarissa," St. Benedict shouted, daring to use her real name. In response, she flung out her arm. Trees erupted on either side of her from the mist, curling like tentacles to embed themselves into stone and concrete, crushing it.

Automatically, St. Benedict fired the gun at one of the nearest tree appendages, aiming for the glowing sphere encased at its tip before it landed on them. The shot did nothing to hurt it, but it did manage to redirect it enough to the side, crushing the building beside them.

"Where is he? Where is the Oberon? You are hiding him from me!"

"I guess she didn't get him yet!" he shouted to Rune over the crashing.

"Come on!" Rune jumped for the branch, sliding down it sideways into the mist. He followed, because what else could he do? Almost immediately after hitting the too-smooth surface of the tree, he lost his grip on the gun, which flew away into the chaos around them. Before he could even try to grab after it, he was tumbling across the ground.

Lifting his head, he saw one of the screen creatures reaching for him, the sickly green light highlighting its hand. He only had time to grab the monster around the wrist before it touched him.

St. Benedict's body locked. It wasn't painful, but it was

frightening as he couldn't move or pull away or even blink. His vision was filled with images, layering over each other like someone had exploded a pop-up screen bomb in his head. Maybe that was exactly what was happening. Soon, all he could hear was a high-pitched whining. The thought that maybe this was the end crossed his mind as this living virus hijacked all his augmentations. Maybe they were actually being destroyed, frying his brain in the process.

Rune didn't hesitate as she shot the gun. One of the largest screens shattered in front of him and went black. The thing reared back, its arms flailing in front of itself like a bug that had just gotten slammed with a good shot of bug spray. Rune shoved it hard in the side and it flopped over easily.

"St. Benedict! St. Benedict!!" She grabbed his frozen arms, but he didn't respond to her touch, his eyes wide and staring ahead of him. She shook him harder. Slowly his head turned toward her, his unseeing eyes looking directly at her.

"Rune," he croaked out.

"Yes, it's me. Are you alright?"

Slowly he blinked and shook his head in short tiny shakes.

"Okay then, can you move?"

A single slow nod, "Yeah," and he shifted to his side. With her help, he found his feet again.

"Come on," she said, unable to suppress the worry in her voice as she draped his arm over her shoulders. Together they moved, St. Benedict stumbling a bit at first as it took all his focus to move his legs in sequence. Moving along the side of a building under some metal scaffolding, Rune scanned up and down the street. Trees continued to burst, filling the otherwise deserted street. "I don't think she can find us. That all seems very random." She paused to check around the corner of the building, then continued to lead St. Benedict around it.

He was pretty much along for the ride, focusing hard on that repeating feet thing. More screeches echoed around them. Trouble was coming.

"Where are we going?" Rune asked. "Where are one of those exits you were talking about? I'm ready to get out of here."

"Rune, honey, I couldn't tell you," he said, breaking into

giggles. He laid a hand along his nose. He was moving fluidly now.

"What happened to you when that thing touched you?"

"God, I don't know. It's like I'm...high or something." He started giggling again. "Probably a virus in the matrix frying my brain like an egg. Woo."

"Don't you have, I don't know, anti-virus software or something?"

"Yeah, yeah," he nodded more enthusiastically than was necessary, "working on it."

"Okay, okay, big guy," Rune tugged him forward. "I know you're having fun, but we are still in a life or death situation here."

"Yeah, nice shooting by the way; that was surprising because you are such a pacifist." He threw his other arm around her and squeezed, saying with delight, "Tree hugger."

"No, still hate guns, I just like you more. Now, I want you to think about the exit, remember the exit? We need to get out of here before she kills us," she said, sing-songy, nodding her head. St. Benedict nodded in time with her.

"Yes. Yes I do."

"Okay, try to keep that thought in your mind," Rune said.

"Oh, okay. You're going to use your Finding magic now, right?"

"Yup," she said, sliding up his sleeve a little bit and resetting her grip on the skin of his wrist. Like she expected, a feeling tugged her instantly. "This way."

They continued along the length of the building. The trees had stopped bursting. There were street lamps shining pale yellow light every few feet and cars parked along the street. Rune's Finding tugged them toward a lone, beaten up phone booth. St. Benedict opened the door for them, the most helpful thing he had done in a while, and Rune stepped inside. All there seemed to be was a phone and a ragged phonebook.

"St. Benedict, what am I supposed to do?" Rune turned around in the close quarters of the booth and he kissed her.

It was forceful, a little awkward, and Rune froze in shock. But St. Benedict was all in, his eyes closed, bracing himself with both hands on either side of the booth so the world would hold still for a moment. He breathed in her scent and adjusted his pressure, turning his head ever so slightly to massage her mouth with his. And she responded, touching his jaw with a gentle hand, her tongue tasting inside his mouth. Then slowly he straightened, letting the kiss fall away. Rune stood there breathless and dazed. *Did that really just happen?*

At first St. Benedict looked satisfied, but when he saw her shocked look, his eyes went wide. "Oh. Oh no. I shouldn't have done that." He backed up a step out of the booth. "I remember now. I wasn't supposed to do that." Then he surged back in. "I'm so sorry, Rune. I should have asked. I should have not even tried. I...."

"It's fine," she cut him off, turning back toward the phone in the booth. "Let's just figure out how to open this..." the booth vanished from all around them, "...way out."

"Who are you?" a new voice asked from behind them.

Rune spun around to see a bizarre man floating in the air over the street. The slight man grasped one of his goggles in his slender hand. At first, Rune thought he was going to adjust them, but instead he telescoped it forward. Doing so puckered the skin of his face and Rune realized the goggles were a part of him. "Ah, yes. You were the animal she was playing with earlier," the man continued, pointedly examining St. Benedict. "Only you're not, are you? I missed it. You're a Saint. Then... what are you?" he asked, turning that creepy goggle on Rune. The floating man furrowed his brow at her.

"I am...."

"Ah!" The eyebrows shot up. "Anna Masterson."

St. Benedict pushed Rune behind him, placing himself very squarely in front of Rune.

"Very interesting," the floating man muttered to himself.

"And who the hell are you?" St. Benedict shouted as he slid the fresh bullet clip from his belt and took the gun Rune was still holding in the other. It didn't help that he immediately dropped the clip.

"Paint. Onion. Alysm. Titania!" the man shouted and St. Benedict dropped quickly to retrieve the clip. A bolt of lightning flashed beside the mad scientist and the Titania appeared, floating in the air next to him. But instead of the dramatically beautiful clothes she had been wearing, she was dressed simply, in a body suit that gleamed a dull silver. It was like someone base-coated her body. Only her eyes seemed alive, turning to look down her nose at the two invaders below her.

"You have been very busy, my dear," the goggles man said. "What is this about?"

"You promised me revenge," she said.

"Ah, that again. You're still trying to have your way, you little psychopath." The goggles man lifted up a device and began tapping at it. The detached attitude reminded Rune of the well-dressed woman. "And there are rends in the system. Someone has fucked up all the coding for this area and only hours before the presentation. I was hoping to get some sleep before this," he continued to grumble.

"You promised me revenge!" the Titania roared.

"Atropa Belladonna!" At the two words, the Titania's whole body clenched in pain. Instead of floating in space, she now seemed to be suspended by an umbilical cord that connected to the whirling sky above. The goggled mad scientist continued to shout while she suffered. "It's her own fault, she's trying to fight the programming, which is forcing me to use the backdoor protocols. Nothing she can do about that. Do not think for a moment we are fooled by your shenanigans, you Faerie bitch! You've brought a Saint here. For what purpose? Answer me!?"

"Stop it!" Rune shouted, unable to watch any longer. The Titania's writhing did stop as the goggled man turned his attention back to Rune. Slowly, he descended to the same level as her.

"Still." He looked down again at Rune. "Then there's you, Anna Masterson."

"Do I know you?" she asked. He regarded her a few minutes more, tapping a fingernail against his teeth.

"Hmm, let's talk some place less atmospheric." He waved his hand and the funnel above was upon them, wrapping them up in a bizarre feeling of wind with the thickness of water. The world around them wavered and dissolved away. In its place a white room surrounded them. St. Benedict recognized it as the room where they were keeping the Faerie Queen's real body.

"Oh my gods," Rune gasped. St. Benedict spun around to see the same coffin-shaped tube housing the still, diminished form of the Faerie Queen. Rune crossed to her side and laid a hand against the warmed glass. "What are they doing to her?"

"Keeping her alive mostly, she is very much on the brink of death. This life-support system is keeping her relatively in stasis," the voice of the mad scientist answered. "It's almost amusing to see your reaction to it. That tube was originally meant for you, Ms. Masterson. Would you like something to drink?"

Rune blinked for a moment. This was meant for her? Her hand curled away from it. *Why? Does that mean...?* Kodiak knew, even then, what she was? And now he wanted to offer her something to drink? "That's the most absurd thing I've heard all day," Rune stated. That got a reaction from the mad scientist, who actually paused as he looked up from a panel he was attending to on Clarissa's tube. His eyebrows looked like two starving caterpillars trying to escape his face through his slicked back, thinning hair.

"Whatever do you mean?" he asked.

"Everything you just said, as if you expect me to take any of it casually."

"Now, now, Ms. Masterson, you are getting emotional. After all, it *isn't* you in there."

"What the hell does that matter?!"

"Ms. Masterson, please. I would appreciate it if you would keep your voice down. There are sensitive experiments going on here. And frankly, I don't like being yelled at."

"If you like decorum so much, why don't you start by telling us who *you* are, buddy," St. Benedict said too loudly, or maybe it only seemed too loud to his own ears. The feedback loop from the virus program was still sending his augmentations for a spin.

"It's an interesting question, isn't it? Who am I? I remember who I used to be. Ms. Masterson here would have known me as Dr. Wade Clausen, yet since she last knew me, I have evolved several times over. How much of me is still Wade has been the subject of debate with various colleagues, but never to a satisfying conclusion. I suppose you, Saint, would have an opinion on the subject, having undergone many augmentations yourself. How much of you is still you? Do you identify yourself as the same man you were before?"

St. Benedict wavered, trying so hard to focus on the "good" Doctor, but he kept seeing too many versions of him warping in the same space to be sure which was the real-Doctor-please-stand-up.

"Is he always like that?" Dr. Clausen asked, nodding at St. Benedict.

"One of your monstrosities infected him with something," Rune said.

"Ah, I see. Interesting. We tested the effects of the Logic Bombmen on augmentations of course, but not while they were installed in a host server body. Might be worth keeping you alive longer to continue the testing."

Then, the mad scientist opened a hologram over his forearm. He pushed a few buttons and there was a flash of light. In the space appeared a small round table like one would find in a cafe, covered with a snowy white tablecloth. In the center was a teapot and a couple of stackable round cups waiting to be served. There was also a small stack of cookies under a glass dish. As soon as it appeared, Dr. Clausen stepped forward to pull out a functional metal chair beside the table. He indicated that Rune should sit.

Rune looked over at St. Benedict, but the Saint just stood there staring at nothing, his charmingly wicked half-smile stuck on his face.

"It really is quite amazing that you are here. When we lost you before, I was only partly sure that the company had not disposed of you." The mad scientist moved away from the chair to the other side of the table, not waiting for her to sit. Instead he started busying himself setting up two cups, leaving Rune to decide for herself whether to sit down or not. She decided to sit down.

"It's my own fault really," Dr. Clausen continued, "I kept

what you were close to the vest. I wasn't entirely sure myself at the time and I was young and skittish. I didn't want anyone else claiming you for their own or even worse, for me to be completely wrong." He smiled at her and slid the tea forward. She stared at it, then nodded politely. He accepted that as enough and opened something that looked like a sugar bowl, only inside the sugar was slightly green-tinged. He ladled a big spoonful of the stuff into his tea and stirred. "Oh, please drink up."

"You'll have to forgive me if I'm skittish about anything on offer from the Kodiak company," Rune said matter-of-factly. He stirred a couple of turns before he puzzled out her meaning.

"Oh! Oh, of course. You would think that, wouldn't you? No, no my dear. There are no poisons in your tea. I have no interest in you anymore."

"But if you did, you would?"

He tapped his spoon on the edge of his cup and sipped. "Yes, most likely, though it would be quite a trick right now because I wouldn't have known you were coming this minute." He then tapped the side of the green sugar bowl. "Well, I suppose I could use this stuff in a pinch. It's poisonous to you. For me, it's an unfortunate side effect of my life now. I need it to digest anything." He took a large swallow of his tea. "Tastes horrible just the same."

Rune lifted the cup to her lips and wet them. It was all she was willing to risk, but she really did want him to keep talking. Somewhere in this mess there had to be a way out for everyone. And he seemed willing to talk without any prompting at all.

"No, my dear. I have no interest in your Magi abilities now. Call it the last remnants of my humanity. Something never quite sat right in my stomach about enslaving a fellow human being. Also, you are a limited resource. There are far more Fae…yes, the Fae are the perfect material for this endeavor." He pushed up from the table. "Here, let me show you. You might find this very interesting."

He scurried over to a screen near where the Titania laid. After fiddling with the keyboard a minute, a diagram appeared, lines waving across a metric full of symbols Rune didn't understand. "The magical measure is strong enough here for the full technological conversion to be even more powerful, but unlike you Magi, who can only channel magic through yourselves, the Titania amplifies it. With every Fae added to the system, the magical output compounds."

"What do you know of the Magi?" Rune demanded, unnerved.

Dr. Clausen chuckled dryly to himself. "Much. Magi are special. They *are* magic. While most living beings have a little bit of magic attached to their life force, a Magi's *entire* life force is drawn from magic. I think it can be argued that the Magi aren't even human but there is plenty of evidence against that hypothesis. But what would you call a creature that can essentially live indefinitely as long as they have enough magic in their bodies? What I didn't know then was the limitation with Magi. They are a technically renewable resource, but just like if you drain too much blood from a body, drain too much magic and the Magi ages and dies. The Titania is the key to everything. Truly renewable."

His giddiness was horrifying but Rune continued to force calm like Maddie would have done. "And what about the Oberon?"

"Ugh, yes. Don't get me started on the Oberon. Stupid suits. Always looking for the quick answer that they throw away precious resources like that." He snapped his fingers, which made St. Benedict jump, then melt back into staring stillness. "With the Oberon, we'd be doing twice this, maybe even ten times. I have two different theories about what would happen and I would love to finally answer it. What do you think?"

He looked at Rune eagerly, and Rune couldn't shake the feeling she was on a first date. "I'm not sure."

His face fell. "Really? That's disappointing. Your predecessor was very keen about this sort of hypothetical inquiry."

"Maddie?" Rune was flabbergasted.

"Yes, the Magdalene. She was the one who even posed this idea in the first place. Granted, she was looking at it from the magical bend, but without her help...she sent me down the correct path. Oh, I could talk for hours with that woman. Closest thing I would have ever gotten to love I think. Too bad she was already married."

That wistful statement carried him back to the tea table, where he plucked up his cup and sipped. "Still, who knows."

"Are you trying to tell me that she knew about this? About what you wanted to do to me?"

"Yes. She helped design it. I'd have shared *credit* with her too if she just hadn't betrayed me. Going behind my back to that stupid suit woman, I can never remember her name. She was always well-dressed, smiled all the time, would always steal office creamers. I mean seriously, if you need that many, go buy your own box."

Rune couldn't believe what she was hearing. Maddie knew about this? Letting her eyes roam over the tube housing the Titania, Rune pictured Maddie's kind, loving face, trying to force the two ideas together. That could have been her fate. Even after all they had done to her before, there really had been a worse fate. Yet, even if it was true, Maddie also came for her. And Rune could only handle one world-changing moment at a time. So she pushed that issue into a corner of her mind to deal with later. There was something more pressing she wanted to know.

"I thought they just wanted me because of Justin." Rune's voice sounded small, the trace of the small person they had created six years ago. She was never truly gone, no matter how far Rune had come, but that was okay.

"Justin Masterson. Yes. Everyone thought it was all about him, didn't they? Which is why they traded you away. Uranium for gold. The dumbest thing I have ever witnessed. But that is what I mean, it was partly my own fault. I didn't make your value truly known. You were the missing component that made Justin's formula work. But *he* knew your value, I'm sure. It's why he made the deal he did to get you out of our hands."

She felt like someone had just slapped her with a monkey wrench.

"What deal?" St. Benedict asked finally. He was in much the same position he was in before, but his head was slightly turned toward Rune, watching her.

"I don't really know all the details," the mad scientist said disparagingly. "I didn't much care what he did to make that happen; I only cared that you were gone. My chance lost from between my fingers."

"You're lying," Rune declared, shaking her head. "You're making all that up. He didn't care about me at all." Her face was screwing up into a deep frown that was about to break her face and then the tears would come. They were already threatening. "He didn't care."

"I never said he did. I said he knew you were important. Would you like to see? There is footage. Would that be empirical proof enough for you? You know, now that you're asking these questions, I would like to know."

The mad scientist returned to the screen and started typing into the console. Rune waited at his elbow, with a clenching feeling in her throat. Some part of her brain mentioned taking deep breaths. That part got shouted out by the rest to shut up.

After an eternity that lasted several minutes, the screen morphed to the inside of a familiar cell. It clearly showed the man that Rune had once called husband. He was sitting at the familiar table with no edges, his wrists chained directly to the top. He looked haggard, his too-long, black hair falling forward into his face, which was covered with untrimmed roughage that never grew evenly. For a man who had always kept himself meticulously groomed, it was the greatest sign of how far he had fallen. The same piercing green-blue eyes stared at whatever, or rather whomever, was sitting next to the camera. They were haunted and hateful. At first he seemed like a statue or maybe the video was paused, but then he shifted in his seat, clanking the wrist restraints. That's when Rune realized his left wrist was broken, bone had perforated the skin. Blood had dried around the wound. Some was even drying on the table.

She wanted to whisper his name, but the word was lodged in her throat.

"He did that to himself," St. Benedict said. Somehow the walking zombie had floated over to stand over her shoulder. "He fought the restraints so hard, he broke his own wrist."

Justin's mouth moved on the screen, but no sound was coming from it.

"Ah, excuse me. I don't usually need the sound." A line

appeared at the bottom of the screen and the volume crescendoed slowly. It was screaming. A woman was screaming in pain that ended in the sounds of her sobbing before the next fresh scream. Now that there was sound, Rune could see Justin flinch slightly every time she started again, even as he continued to stare straight ahead, trying to lock his gaze on whatever he was focusing on.

"That's me…" Rune breathed. "That's me screaming."

"It's being transmitted," St. Benedict added. "That slightly hollow sound. They're playing it from another room."

"Well, I don't know about you but I've had enough," a cultured voice from the screen said. A manicured male hand appeared at the edge and pressed a button on a small panel. The light that had been reflecting on Justin's face went off and the beaten man dropped his gaze to his wrists.

"There, isn't that better? Gotta hate the sound of the wife's voice by now, right?" The cultured man chuckled as if what he said was a joke. Justin only continued to stare, unresponsive, at his broken wrist. The other man's mirth died. "Look, I have to say, I'm fairly disappointed in you." There was a scraping sound, presumably a chair and a sense of rising as Justin's eyes followed the point, just to the side of the camera, up.

"You were so arrogant when we brought you here, remember?" A man's body appeared on the edge of the scene, walking along the table. Justin's eyes followed him. "So cold, so unmovable. Nothing affected you. I really admired that about you. I was sure…I was hoping that after you went through the process you would be one of us. But now, after we've stripped everything away from you, you turn out to be like everyone else."

Justin said nothing. More of the man appeared on the screen but right before his head would have cleared he stopped and waited, his hands clutched behind his back.

"I mean you're still of use. You have talents and abilities, we can still use them. That's something I suppose."

The body turned away. Justin stared across the table, dark and haunted.

"What do I have to do to become one of you?" Justin's voice was a whisper of gravel.

"Nothing. There is nothing you can do, nothing you can bargain with, we have everything…"

"No, you don't and you know it," Justin said, cutting his interrogator off. He continued to stare straight ahead.

"He's made a decision," St. Benedict said. Rune wanted to tell him to shut up, but couldn't find the breath to.

"I'll give you what you want. I'll give you cybermagic." Justin's eyes went from up to down slowly as he spoke. "In exchange, you will let her go."

"What? *Her*? Really?" The figure paused at the edge of the screen and folded his arms. "You want me to believe that you want to trade your most precious secret, not to save yourself, but to save…wait a minute, I want to get this right." The figure pulled a lined notebook pad and lifted some pages. "The dumbest piece of ass you have ever known. She was a means to an end and nothing more." He let the pages drop. "Nothing more. Now I truly am convinced that you didn't do what you claimed to have done. It's a sham, isn't it? This whole concept of cybermagic, as you call it."

Justin did not look away or blink. "You wouldn't keep showing me her if you actually believed what I said or believed I didn't do what I claim. I did do it and I can recreate it. You won't have to try to piece my notes together. Or keep holding a gun to my head to make me comply. I'll give you everything willingly. You've been afraid to do more to hurt me, in case you mess up the goods, so you hurt her. Congratulations, you succeeded. I'll give you what you want."

There was a long pause as the two men stared at each other, at least as far as could be seen.

"You'll give it to me? Like that?" the interrogator asked. There was a distinct lilt in the interrogator's voice, like he was having trouble containing his excitement.

"Power dynamic reversal," said St. Benedict softly. "The interrogator's lost all control in this moment. He wants it too much. The secret. Amateur."

"You let her go free, you keep me. That's the deal. And with me you get everything I know. No more fighting, no more working against you."

"We have to kill her," the man said. "You know that is the only way for her to leave here. She's seen too much."

"She's only involved because of me. She knows nothing, I told you."

"Yes, we know she knows nothing, we've examined her thoroughly. You watched." There was a long, tense pause. "Here is what you're going to do, Justin. You will sign an agreement with me and me exclusively."

"Yes," Justin said too quickly.

"And you will divorce your wife."

Justin's eyebrows furrowed. "Why? Why would you need me to do that?"

"Do you want her set free or not? Look," the interrogator sounded agitated, "technically, your wife belongs to the company, like you do, but that does mean we're supposed to have some responsibility to her, on paper at least. If I set her free as you want, she's still going to be on our records as someone who needs things like insurance or housing benefits, and people might start asking questions, okay? You will sign and divorce her, then that's the end of it with her, or there is no deal."

The prisoner nodded. "Alright, alright. I'll sign whatever you want."

Another scrape of the chair. "Good. Then we're done here."

"How will I know?" Justin asked suddenly. "How will I know you actually let her go alive? That she's safe?"

"You won't. You're just going to have to trust me. But I have an idea of what we can do to let her go alive. Unless you have another option?"

Justin looked down at the table. There were steps and the sound of the door opening.

"Let me see her again."

"Excuse me?"

Justin nodded to the side of the camera. "The TV there. Turn it on for me. Let me see her again."

The door shut and the steps grew louder. There was a click, then the distant sound of sobbing. "She's just balling her eyes out."

"It's fine."

More steps and the door opened once more, this time shutting with a deep booming finality.

"Justin, where are you?" Anna's voice cried from the screen.

"I'm here," Justin said. With what little give he had in the chain, he reached out his hand towards her. "I'm here."

Then the screen went blank and turned off. Rune continued to stare at her vague shadowy reflection in it. Then her eyes picked out an arm at the corner. She looked down to see a living hand pressing the off button. She followed that up to the grim face of St. Benedict.

"You shouldn't have seen that," he said.

"He...."

St. Benedict met her eyes. "It does you no good to have seen that."

"Where is he?" she asked. Then she turned away to find the mad scientist pouring himself more tea. "What happened to him?"

"He's dead."

Chapter 25

"Rune, we need to leave," St. Benedict said. His thoughts were becoming clearer but it was still hard to tell when he said something out loud or only thought he had.

"What do you mean he's dead?" He heard her say. Maybe he hadn't said it.

"Rune." St. Benedict tried to lay a hand on her shoulder, but she shrugged him off. No, she heard him.

"I don't understand. Maddie saved me. Maddie mortgaged her *bar* to save me. To get me out. Not...*him*. This makes no sense."

"That's my understanding, yes. It was the deal...oh, what was his name...who remembers...? That was the deal that interrogator guy made with Maddie. Bought you right out from under my nose and he scored the compliance of Justin Masterson. Got himself a pretty promotion out of the whole thing."

"Rune," St. Benedict said gently. She looked at him with wild, mad eyes,

"They tortured us! They violated my rights! My body!"

"Yes! Yes, they did. But on paper they were still beholden to you. Divorced, no longer a part of the company, you became an asset they could sell off," St. Benedict tried to explain.

Rune covered her mouth with her hand and for a moment, St. Benedict thought she was going to be sick.

"You said Justin's dead?" Her eyes were swollen with tears and rage.

"Yes! This is what I mean by poor resource management. Masterson was an irreplaceable asset and the yahoos in charge of him squandered it trying to force this into creation." He gestured to the tubes. "Fried his brain. Dead in moments. Set all of this back. I was so furious. But now we have this creature. The Fae are fascinating by comparison. If she dies, we simply wait for the Titania to transfer to the next one then plug her back into the system. I was waiting to do the same thing to the Oberon, but again, competition for resources around here. Ridiculous."

"Say the word and he's dead, Rune," St. Benedict said.

The double blink on the mad scientist's face was comical. St. Benedict actually laughed at it.

"I think that's enough from you, Saint. I am finding your company very tedious now." Dr. Clausen raised his forearm again, activating his hologram, but at the same time St. Benedict snapped twice into the air. There was a flash of light and a fresh gun appeared in his hand. In one smooth, easy motion, St. Benedict brought it down level at the "good" Doctor.

Dr. Clausen stared at it, unmoving. It was hard to tell if the gun concerned him or not since the implanted goggles erased any emotional response that wasn't on the kabuki mask level. His voice was not so easy to mask.

"How did you do that?" he squeaked.

"You should really work on your shortcuts. Now, you better put your hands up, because I don't exactly have the best muscle control here."

Dr. Clausen complied. "This isn't possible. My system... what did you do to my system?"

"Your head has blown up to the size of a nice, big, poppable balloon. Not so god-like now outside of your little Thunderdome, are you?"

"Thunderdome is hardly an apt analogy." The gun went off, shattering a screen beside Dr. Clausen's head.

"Oops, finger slipped," St. Benedict laughed like a madman. It was getting easier to think, the anti-viral program had finally started to get the upper hand, but the high feeling wasn't abating too quickly. "Get on your knees."

"You can't kill me so easily. We are deep within Kodiak's compound. Security was already alerted the moment you fired your gun. Killing me will lose you all your leverage," Dr. Clausen said, reaching for his logic in his time of crisis.

St. Benedict shot the gun.

The mad scientist stood still as stone. Then he crumpled to the floor. St. Benedict watched dispassionately as the evil man's body continued to flop and then go still, lowering the weapon as slowly as he had raised it. Behind him, he heard the sound of retching. He turned and set the gun down on the table, going to Rune. She was bent over, her hands on her knees, emptying whatever was left in her stomach onto the ground. Gently, he laid his hand on her back and slowly rubbed.

"Focus on breathing. Nothing else," he said gently. She straightened and wiped her mouth. Tears streaked down her cheeks, let loose when she had thrown up, as the horror of what was happening settled in.

"Why did you do that?" She looked at St. Benedict then to the body on the ground. She began to shake her head. "Why did you shoot him?" she asked.

"He…." St. Benedict started, then stopped.

"Wouldn't he have been more useful to us alive…or…or as a hostage?" Rune shook her head, tucking her hands under her arms.

"No. We're not here to save this project. We're here to destroy it. Right? We're here for her." He pointed to the Titania's tube. "This isn't over yet."

"I know. I know," Rune tried to nod, but it morphed into shaking her head. She turned away, trying to hide the sobs building in her throat. Terrified that she would pull away from him, he didn't dare to cross the space between them.

"I know what we have to do. I know why." Roughly, Rune wiped hard at her face, "What's wrong with me? What's wrong with me?"

"Nothing. There is nothing wrong with you."

"There is. I'm not sad that he's dead," she said, still staring down at the corpse. "You shot him and I'm so…so…satisfied. I hate it."

They stayed that way, standing in silence for ages.

"We…we can't delay any longer," Rune finally said. Her voice was cold and it made St. Benedict shiver.

"You should leave. You don't have to watch this," he said, staring past the tube.

"No." She stepped toward the tube holding the Faerie Queen, while he couldn't seem to pull his eyes from the middle distance to her left. It was so hard to look at what he would have to do in front of Rune, so hard to see this good, innocent woman standing there being a part of it. Why couldn't she protect herself from what must be done? Let the sin fall to him.

Rune laid her hand on the glass surface of the tube. "She looks so wasted," she said regretfully. St. Benedict didn't respond and she stayed like that for several heartbeats. "We should wake her up."

"That would be cruel. Let her pass in her sleep."

"No, we need to tell her. We need to explain."

"She won't forgive us. If that's what you're hoping to get from her, you'll be wasting your breath."

"I don't care about that," Rune snapped. "But this isn't right. Wake her up."

He felt like his arms had been packed with lead. Or maybe he was made of lead or some metal that rusts and he was freezing into place like the Tin Man. He could always simply pick up the gun, open the case and fire. Over and done. Fast and clean. He had done it before.

But *she* had told him to wake the target.

By sheer will alone, St. Benedict turned and went to the opposite side of the case. Like Sleeping Beauty or Snow White, the Faerie Queen laid peacefully under the glass, exactly in the middle as if placed there, her hands laying passively at her side. Opening the side panel, St. Benedict initiated the waking protocol.

"She'll wake in a minute. They've kept her under controlled sedation. I had a chance to poke around a bit before."

"You poked around?"

"I wanted to find a way to take her out of here."

"You did?"

He met her eyes then. There was a light of hopefulness in those eyes. "She leaves this case, she dies."

Rune nodded her understanding. Then what was the hopeful look for?

The Titania stirred, letting out a small sigh. With effort she forced her eyes open. It took several blinks before she saw the two figures standing on either side of her. As she registered it, though, she recoiled as much as she could from them.

"No, no please," she whispered.

"Clarissa," Rune cooed gently. "It's alright, it's alright. We're not here to...make you suffer."

The Titania panted, her eyes flitting between the two of them, a lip snarled like an animal waiting in a trap.

"You...both of you...." She began to flail, her arms and legs scrabbling inside the tube, looking for a way out, a way to escape. "I could kill you both where you stand."

"Clarissa," St. Benedict said, his voice commanding. She locked her eyes on him, frozen with her arms bracing on either wall of the tube. "You're dying. You know this. Nothing we can do to you is going to change that fact."

"No, I will live! I will survive."

"At the cost of your children. At the cost of the world," Rune said.

"We could have ended this while you were still asleep," he added. "We didn't have to wake you up." Taking that in, Clarissa untensed her muscles, letting herself slide back into place on the bed.

"I offered you everything," she snarled.

"You couldn't make me the Oberon and you know it. And if you don't, you were deluding yourself," St. Benedict said. Rune set a hand on his arm, more a warning than a comfort.

"You can't keep running from this," Rune said.

"You! And what would you know about any of this?!"

Rune pursed her lips a moment. "You're right. I have never had to face what you're facing, but I'm not going to leave you alone with it either."

"You're going to kill me!" the Titania insisted and flailed inside her tube again. "Let me out! Let me out of here! I will tear your eyes from your skulls." But Rune and St. Benedict waited silently until she had calmed.

"Can we open the tube?" Rune asked St. Benedict.

He nodded and typed on the pad again, hitting buttons that sang little notes as he did it. There was a sound of decompression, then the glass slid to the side, opening the world to the Faerie Queen. Another whimper escaped the Fae as she looked side to side, panicking, as the glass barrier disappeared from around her.

"I don't...I don't want to die," she whimpered.

Rune was there, seizing the Titania's hand, setting it against her heart. "I don't want you to die either. I would do anything to take you from this place, Your Majesty."

There was a long moment, as Clarissa stared at Rune while the young woman held her hand. "But there isn't, is there?" she finally said. She stretched a hand to the ceiling, not really reaching for anything, simply feeling the air above. "I've been behind glass for so long." Then she curled her fingers under and tipped Rune's chin up, before gently brushing Rune's tears away. "You weep for me, Friend?"

"Of course."

"The tube is powering down," St. Benedict said.

"How long?" Clarissa asked.

"Once the system powers down, it looks like these scientists estimated that you would pass somewhere between ten minutes to an hour," he answered, reading off the screen in front of him. It sounded so pedestrian to his ears.

"Clarissa, before we do this...do you really want to exist like this?" Rune asked.

"No. No, but...." Something flickered in her eyes, and the Faerie Queen became serene, the woman Rune had always known. "Yes, I know. I understand. If I stay here, I condemn my Children to the same fate. A hell of glass and metal." She covered her face with her hands. "They must hate me. I've failed them."

"They miss you," Rune said.

"Alright, it's ready," St. Benedict said. "Once I push this button, you'll be free of the machine."

"Tell us what you want us to do, Clarissa."

St. Benedict and Clarissa blinked at Rune. She met both their eyes. "It's your choice. If you want us to try and take you from here, we could try to get you back to the Praetorium, where maybe...."

"No. No," Clarissa shook her head. "We wouldn't make it would we? No. Let me...let me go in peace."

The Titania leaned over the edge of her tube herself. St. Benedict indicated the button, a slowly blinking orange one on the panel. She pressed it herself then laid back with a sigh.

"For the sake of my Children," she said with regal finality that seemed appropriate to the moment. It was immediately shattered by the sound of a siren going off.

"We're about to have visitors," St. Benedict said, activating his holographic console and bringing up a screen that showed little red dots moving through rectangles.

"We can't leave her like this," Rune said.

The Saint nodded once and went to the table to retrieve his gun. "I'll be back in a minute," he said without looking at Rune.

"St. Benedict?" He stopped on his way out the door, his back to her. "Please try to avoid killing anyone, if you can," Rune requested.

"As you wish, my Lady," he said and exited. A few moments later there were shots and shouts, but they sounded distant.

"He would have made a good Oberon," the Titania said.

Rune offered a timid smile; she really didn't have anything to say to that.

Clarissa looked around. "Where is Dr. Clausen?"

"Behind me. He's dead. St. Benedict shot him before I could stop him."

"He's dead?" Clarissa asked, leaning back to look up at the ceiling, "Good. Do not weep for him, child."

"But all life is sacred," Rune said, struggling for what she knew to be right even as her emotions were so conflicted.

"He offered up his life to be taken freely when he took others. The rends in his soul left very little else. Removing such a creature from this world is justice."

Rune nodded, though she wasn't sure she agreed or disagreed.

"Why do you stay here?" Clarissa asked. "You've already killed me, why don't you just go?"

"We didn't come here to kill you."

"I know, I know. You've said. I've already absolved you. Just go." She waved her hand violently at Rune's face.

"What else does it mean to be a Faerie Friend, if not to attend the Titania on her deathbed?"

Clarissa sighed. Then sighed again. The sighing turned into tears and a grasping of Rune's hand, who waited for several minutes. It was hard, but Rune kept her word and held on. When St. Benedict came back, he didn't say a word either. Only set the gun back down on the table, and rubbed at the blood on his cheek from a cut that hadn't been there before. His eyes were ignited with the blue light that indicated his augmentations were on. He didn't seem to notice that he forgot to turn them off. It made him look like a blood stained angel.

"Are you alright?" Rune asked.

"I'm fine. That way is closed. There is no way out now," he said gravely. "Unless you can make us a way out?"

Rune shook her head. "Elias knew how to make doors. I can't remember all the steps."

There was a buzz somewhere in the room and a whole bank of computers shut down.

"The mainframe is off now. I deleted everything in the Titania's world. It's gone too," he looked at Rune. "I'm sorry, Rune. We're not going to make it."

She smiled at him gently. "Maybe that's only right."

"Oh, Saint of Liars," Clarissa said as he took up his spot on the other side of her. She let go of Rune's hand to take his in both of hers. "Tell me a lie, please. Tell me a little story to forget, please."

"I'm sorry. I can't. That's not what I do."

"Then what is it you do?"

"I am the Saint of Liars because I protect those until they can find their way back to the truth," he said. Gently he brushed the top of her hair, then leaned forward to kiss her forehead.

Clarissa laughed. "The Saint of Liars," she looked to Rune, "and the Finder of Truth."

Rune smiled, accepting the title. Such things were not taken lightly when bestowed by a Queen.

The dying woman looked back and forth between them. "I miss him. Oh dammit, I've been so stupid." Clarissa rubbed her face again, scrubbing at her tears. "I don't want to cry for him. After...after...."

"After everything that he did to you. But you still love him," Rune finished for her.

"Yes! Yes, dammit."

"I understand," Rune said.

"But it can never go back, can it?"

"I don't think it ever does."

The Titania squeezed her eyes shut. "I'm going to die and he wins. I'm going to die and here I am...just...just wanting to stay. I have so much life to live. And where is he? This wasn't how it was supposed to be. When I need him the most."

"I'm here."

Standing by a familiar door made of wood, was Calvin. Just behind him, Elias and Lady Trella waited within the threshold of the Lucky Devil's doorway. Rune glanced down at her belt and saw the silver threads of it glowing. Her and St. Benedict exchanged amazed looks.

Elias smiled. "We found the Finder."

"How did you do that?" Rune asked, her mouth practically hanging open.

"You created the magic," Elias said, "I just followed what you did."

Calvin stepped forward into the room, never taking his crystal blue eyes from Clarissa. Narrowing her own eyes, the Titania looked away from him. "What are you doing here? Did you come to gloat? To watch me die?" she said, mustering regal contempt even as she struggled to raise her head.

St. Benedict stepped aside so Calvin could approach, setting his bruised hands on the side of the tube. He looked so different, Rune could barely connect him to the smarmy man who shook her down for mortgage money only a few months ago.

"You know, I came all this way through hell and back to get you. The least you could do is look at me." There he is.

Actual fire flashed in the Titania's eyes and she did turn back to him. "How dare you!?"

"How dare...." he stopped himself, the metaphorical fire in his own eyes cooling as he dropped them down and forced himself to take a breath. Then he raised them again and gripped the side of the tube so hard his fingers went white.

"Hello," he said, meeting her eyes again, "my name is Calvin Jasper Harrison. It's nice to meet you."

Clarissa double blinked. "Excuse me?"

"I have been chosen as the next Oberon and I was told," he nodded at Elias, "that it would be appropriate to at least introduce myself to you, the Titania."

Her eyes lingered on the branch crown he wore on his head, before she looked between Calvin and Elias, and then to everyone else in the room. "Hello, my name is Clarissa Rhodenda Hill. I was the Titania. Soon there will be a new one and you won't have to worry about me anymore."

Calvin looked up at Rune, asking with his eyes "what does she mean?"

"We've disconnected her from Kodiak's life support. She will die soon."

A cry came up from the doorway and Elias pulled Lady Trella against his shoulder.

"Okay then," Calvin said. Then gently, he started to pick Clarissa up.

"What are you doing?!" she cried, even though she was too weak to stop it.

"I'm taking you home," he said and hefted her into his arms better. Rune stepped up and helped to lay Clarissa's strengthless hands back on her lap.

St. Benedict picked up the gun from the table and shoved it into his waistband before falling in beside Rune. Elias guided Lady Trella back through the door, followed by Calvin. When Rune stepped through she expected to see her bar and was surprised to see Ally and Alf waiting in a nebulous blackness.

"My apologies, my Lady. I broke the door in order to find you," Elias said when she came through, before closing the bar door behind her.

"Oh, it's okay," Rune said, not really sure what to think. "But what...what happened? We thought we lost Calvin in Titania's cyber world?"

"The Lady Trella guided him out when you became

separated. At the same time, Lady Wilde returned with St. Rachel to the Praetorium. Between the two Ladies, they were able to call the Court. Both sides of the conflict more or less united to accept the Oberon as their King, empowering him to use their collective might."

"That's how you opened the door?"

"That's how we opened a way," Elias smirked.

Rune looked around them and realized they were crossing through a tunnel, made from dark stone and smooth as marble."

"Where are we going?" Rune asked.

"To the Faerie Court," Elias smiled. "Not bad for an impromptu rescue attempt."

Alf stepped up and held out a black scarf to Rune. "Don't fuck this up, my Lady," he said.

"And how did you end up here?" Rune asked him, taking the scarf and laying it over her shoulders.

"The little Fae. They told us to come, so we went," Ally answered.

Alf nodded. "We went through the door already connected to the Court." The procession started moving faster and he stepped back to continue walking next to Ally, who was trying very hard to look somber while she held a standard that had the Lucky Devil's emblem on it. Calvin had stepped further into the darkness of the tunnel, when an outline of a door, cut out of light, appeared before him. He passed through it with Lady Trella right behind him, the sound of a merry violin greeting them as they walked. Alf nudged Ally, who fell in step behind him, still bearing the standard.

"Warrior, if you'll escort the Wizard," Elias said.

"What's happening?" Rune asked.

"We are attending the death of a Faerie Queen," Elias answered, sounding both happy and sad. "The Fae put something together quickly. It's amazing how they all assumed he'd succeed in bringing her home."

All around were Faeries. Many of them Rune recognized from the bar, flitting around the meadow of midnight grass, surrounded by a grove of real trees. A single broad tree stood proudly in the middle, on top of a gently rising hill. All around were Faerie lights laced through the leaves and winking in the grass. Calvin's feet found the path through them, carrying the emaciated Queen to the base of the tree. As they approached, everyone who was waiting rose to their feet, including Franklin who was festooned with flowers and little Fae. In the back Rune could pick out the monochromes, their pale faces floating in the mostly dark, but there were also other tall Fae, each dressed in flower colors. Near the tree Rune spied Lady Wilde, her hat in her hands, finally showing the two broad fox ears lying flat and sad against the sides of her head. A single satyr stood next to her, playing the violin they were all hearing, his tune sleepily merry even as tears streamed down his face. Rune and her entourage were encouraged to follow all the way up to the inner most circle of the tree, except for Ally, who went and stood next to the other banner holders to one side of the group.

When Calvin reached the tree he turned and, after a checking glance at Lady Trella, sat down, settling Clarissa on his lap. As one the entire assembly reseated as well, though it was clear to see where the divisions between the two factions still were as those groups clustered closer to each other. The Faerie Queen's face was streaked with her own tears and she looked around at all the faces.

"My Children. All of my Children." She tried to lift her hand toward Lady Wilde, who had knelt down beside her, but when she faltered, the Fae grasped it herself, bringing it to her cheek with a smile. "We've lost so much."

"But we are together again, Mother," Lady Wilde said.

The smaller Fae, full of giggles and innocence, flew above the Titania's head, dancing in the air, flashing their colors. The music changed a little to accompany them and Rune wasn't sure if it was planned or impromptu.

"This all seems like a dream," Rune whispered. St. Benedict nodded silently, unable to look away himself.

The Titania smiled at the little Fae as she watched. Calvin looked supremely uncomfortable but resolute. All those around them chatted quietly amongst themselves. It felt cozy and warm.

"This isn't right, it isn't right," Rune muttered to herself. St. Benedict leaned in.

"I have never seen something as peaceful as this ever. You made this possible," he said softly.

"It is a very romantic end," Elias said.

"Poetic," Alf agreed, nodding.

"Fuck poetic. I don't care what kind of story it would make. I want her to live." Unable to sit there any longer, Rune got up and made her very awkward way out of the crowd, barely seeing where she was going. Once she was clear, she ran, plunging herself into the night around her. She had no idea where they were, but she didn't care either. She simply ran. Ran as hard as her body could move with every fiber of her being pumping away. The ground was turf beneath her and it bounced her forward with every step. Too soon, she tripped and flew forward, landing hard on the ground, but even hitting that felt better than the pain inside.

She laid where she fell for a while, staring up at the vacant sky until it too began to cry around her. The summer sky rumbled above as rain plipped on her face. Soon, she was soaked through, but it was warm as tears and Rune couldn't care. Let it rain. Let it wash her away until she was nothing.

Unfortunately, that wasn't what happened. Instead, it was becoming hard to breath with water going directly into her nose and she had to sit up.

A figure was sitting on the ground waiting, only a few feet from her.

"Go away, St. Benedict."

"I can't do that," he said. He was leaning back on his hands, his rain-logged shirt pulling tight across his well-formed chest, the clothes created in cyberspace proving themselves to still be very real. "Glad I don't have my fedora with me, it'd get destroyed in this."

Rune looked back the way she had come. Through the pouring of rain, she could see the distant lights of the Faerie wake. An envelope of sorts seemed to be hovering over them all, so at least they were dry. Nothing more depressing than a funeral getting rained out.

"I failed. I failed in every way that Maddie used to stand for."

"Look, Rune, what Dr. Clausen said. About Justin...."

"Now's not the time."

"Excuse me?"

Rune turned on him. "A woman I was supposed to help is dying a few feet away from us. Now is not the time to talk about me and my messed up shit!" She glared at him hard as she stood up. He got up with her. "You know, you've put a lot of work in getting me to go away, why are you following me now?"

"Rune, wait."

She whirled on him and pushed into his space. "Answer me!"

The mighty, strong Saint cowed back, just a little. "Because I want to be where you are. That's the problem."

"I don't understand."

"You make me want to tell you everything. That's really bad for a Saint!"

"I never asked."

"Doesn't change how much I want to. I need to stay away from you. But I also can't leave you hurting like this."

"So, you're saying I *am* special to you? Because everyone who knows you insists I shouldn't read into it because you make every woman feel like she's special."

"You are special!"

"So, what is this? A Hollywood movie? I'm the magic one that makes you change your philandering ways?"

"No. You're my friend."

That slowed the rage, made it feel uncomfortable inside.

A cry rose up from the tree, full of shock and fear.

"Oh gods." Rune took off running. At the same time, St. Benedict snatched her hand to run beside her. Even at full, slippery speed, it seemed to take too long to cover the distance. The rain began to abate as they approached the tree. Instantly, the Fae moved aside for them, making a clear path to the tree's base. Still sitting where they had left them were Calvin and Clarissa, but she was now slumped against his shoulder. He was leaning into her, holding her tenderly. They were both glowing, sparkles of light floating up into the tree.

"Calvin! What are you doing? What's happening?" She dropped to her knees beside him.

Sleepily, the Oberon lifted his head. "Hell if I know." He

shifted, snuggling the Titania closer. "She just said she forgave me and...and thank you."

The light intensified, burning as brightly as the sun.

"Back up!" someone shouted, maybe Elias. Rune wasn't sure, truly unable to move as she stared in amazement.

It was like her secondary sight had been opened. Within the light was color and wind swirling around. Calvin's blonde hair ignited in a corona while Clarissa's black hair burned with blue fire, swirling and spinning. Two strong hands grabbed Rune under her shoulders and pulled her back. She knew it was St. Benedict without looking and that she was safe, so she kept watching. She didn't dare look away.

The two lights poured into each other, mixing and combining. When the intensity could not grow any higher, united, the light shot up into the sky above, boiling away the angry clouds to reveal the glittering stars. Then the light plunged into the earth. Thick magic infused the air around them, raising the hair up off the back of Rune's arms as the ground trembled and rolled, waving out from the tree like ripples made by a pebble dropped into still water. Finally, all went quiet.

There were gasps all around as Fae picked themselves up from where they were thrown, looking about themselves and to each other for answers. Rune was the first to approach the base of the tree.

"Calvin?" Rune whispered gently. She squatted down beside the Oberon. Slowly, he lifted his head, blinking sleepily.

"Oh, hey Leveau."

"Hey Calvin. What happened? Are you alright?"

"Yeah, I think so. Yeah, yeah, I'm alright." He looked down at the Titania in his arms. "Look, I did it."

Rune looked. The Titania was still small, diminished and wasted as she had been before, but there was something else. Her pale face was rosy. Her hair, which had been stiff and lifeless, was glowing with a deep raven luster. She took a deep breath and sighed into her sleep.

"She's going to live now," the Oberon said. Exhausted, he leaned his head back against the tree. "I just listened to him, you know, the Faerie King and he told me what to do. Oh. Hey Leveau...."

"What?"

He grunted once. "You are a true Faerie Friend," he said. He chuckled a little bit. "Fucking ironic, isn't it."

Rune heard it. The small whisper of magic dusted over her, the reaffirmation from the Oberon, King of the Fae, of her status amongst his people. The small, but important token of Calvin really, actually trying. She couldn't suppress her smile and she didn't want to.

"Thank you, Your Majesty. Actions show who someone is, words only prove who they want to be."

"Whatever you say, Wizard," he muttered.

"But Calvin, what did you do?" Rune asked. "How did you save the Titania?"

She didn't receive an answer because the Oberon had fallen back asleep and Rune couldn't help thinking how angelic he looked leaning back against the tree.

Chapter 26

St. Benedict stood outside of the Lucky Devil, staring up at the sign. Twice he had walked away and once he had walked around to the alley to retuck his shirt. He reset his fedora, a black one, that he had bought new. Then he lifted it up again and combed his hair back with his fingers, making sure the scar was covered without really thinking about it. He held the handle of the door for a good five minutes. Finally, there was only one thing left to do.

Inside the bar, it was quiet. The place was still shut down, but across the tables he could see the evidence of business. At the actual bar, Elias looked up from a large bowl he was stirring.

"Oh, look at you. I see your master didn't kill you outright then?"

"No, I got a reprieve. What I have on the inside of my head is far too valuable now." The Saint tapped his temple.

"Nice to be wanted," Elias replied and opened up a green jar, tipping it over to pour something thick and even darker green into the bowl.

Ally came in from the Main Bar, carrying a box sealed with shipping tape. "Sorry we're closed…. Oh. Hi, St. Benedict." She set the box on the bar next to Elias.

"Crystals come?" Elias pulled the box toward him and started pulling at the tape.

"Yeah."

"Great." He glanced up at St. Benedict, who didn't ask but was watching curiously all the same. "Thanks to her Ladyship's last client, we're able to afford to re-enchant the bar. Our thanks to his Lordship, Maxamillion." He balled up the tape and tossed it into the trashcan sitting in the middle of the room. He was about to miss, but at the last second the trashcan shifted itself to the right and caught the ball of tape. It then bopped in place like an eager dog and resettled in its spot on the floor. Elias nodded at it satisfactorily. "We'll have this place up and running again very soon."

"That's great," St. Benedict said, meaning it. "Is her Ladyship around?"

"Yeah, in the Back Bar." Elias jutted his thumb in the correct direction. St. Benedict nodded and turned to go that way when Elias held up his hand again. "One second, I got something for you." The young Wizard reached into a pocket and fished out an object that looked like a coin. He held it out in an open palm.

"What is it?" St. Benedict asked, looking down at the coin, but not immediately taking it.

"Got it as a bonus in a swap for some ingredients I picked up to reenchant the auto-clean crystals in the bathrooms. Slip it into the band of your hat."

Having very little choice other than to flat out refuse it, St. Benedict accepted the coin. It was slightly lavender and gold and seemed to be made out of a very light metal he didn't recognize. Plucking off his hat, St. Benedict did as he was instructed, slipping it in between the stitches of the band.

"What does it do?"

"It's a preservation spell. It'll keep your hat from being destroyed, damaged or stained. Also keep it smelling fresh," Elias smiled. St. Benedict had the distinct feeling that those things weren't all the talisman did, but he decided to worry about it later.

"Thank you," he said, nodding and replaced his hat. "You said the Back Bar?"

"Yes. And, St. Benedict…" Elias enunciated the Saint's name crisply, "would it be very cliché of me to say that if you ever, *ever* betray her again, I will finish what I started the other day?"

St. Benedict regarded the Wizard, not daring to ask which betrayal he might be referring to. In a soft voice, St. Benedict answered, "You won't have to."

Elias nodded and dumped a clearer liquid into his bowl, which immediately began to smoke, launching both the teenager and the Wizard into a coughing fit.

"Oh, man, it's like breathing mace!" Ally shouted.

St. Benedict passed into the Main Bar on his way to the glass double doors, escaping the smoke.

"What the hell are you doing here?" a gruff voice demanded right before he turned the handle. He turned to face the bar manager who was standing on the bar. "I hoped you'd be dead by now."

The actuary, Franklin, sat next to the bar, stacks of receipts and papers piled up next to him while he typed on a laptop. Unsure of what was going on, Franklin glanced between the two men, a pencil in his mouth like a bit.

"You *hoped* I would be dead by now?" St. Benedict asked, amused and intrigued.

"I don't know. Wishful thinking. Maybe you tore things up so badly at the Magic Guild, I would think you would hide your head or your master would have taken it for you."

"Is that why you don't like me? Because of what happened at the Magic Guild? Or is it maybe something else?"

Alf narrowed his eyes, enhancing his powerful glare. St. Benedict smiled even harder.

"You are nothing but trouble. Trouble my Lady doesn't need," Alf harrumphed, crossing his arms in challenge.

"Oh? Is she your Lady now? Or is she still just making you say that?" St. Benedict stepped up until he was nose to nose with the bar manager. They stayed that way for a long, tense moment of wills, one glaring, the other smiling.

"Uh, guys," Franklin started to say, rising to his hooves.

Like a shot, Alf's hand reached out and grabbed the Saint's collar, fisting it up "You do anything to ever harm my Lady, I will personally see to it that you will never...."

"You know what, little man? I agree with you," St. Benedict said. Then he backed off so suddenly Alf had to wheel a little bit to maintain his balance, releasing his hold involuntarily.

"Hi Franklin," St. Benedict acknowledged to the centaur with a tip of his hat.

"Uh, hey man," Franklin answered, lifting a hand thoughtlessly.

St. Benedict returned it and went to the door, opening it without looking back.

Inside the Back Bar, music was blasting. Rune stood in the middle of a room festooned in painting sheets, dancing. The backdoor was open to the alley, probably in an effort to take the smell of paint and magic out of the room, though it let in the late summer heat. She was dressed in a beat-up tank top, jeans, and her hair back in a tail under a kerchief. In time with the music, she climbed up the ladder and perched there, rolling paint to the top most corner of a wall. She looked like the poster girl for a paint shop.

The Saint couldn't help himself. Slipping his hands into his pockets, he leaned against the little bit of wall that jutted into the room by the door, and simply watched her. She didn't notice him as she climbed down from the ladder, singing along with the song, moving to the paint can to refill her pan, all while wiggling her hips in gyrating circles. It wasn't until she hit the chorus that she finally looked up to see him standing there. She immediately jumped, dropping the pan and splattering the paint in it across the plastic covered floor.

"Dammit!" She bent down in a hurry but there was no way she was going to be able to scrape all the paint back in. "Oh, crap."

"Sorry, I didn't mean to startle you."

"Yes, you did," Rune said dryly as she stood up and snatched a rag off the ladder with a quick snap. She didn't look at him as she scrubbed hard at her hands. "What do you want, St. Benedict?"

"Came to see how you were, tell you I'm alive."

"Great, I was so worried about that," she said annoyed instead of happy. She bent down and began tearing at the plastic around the spill, juggling the ends so she could keep the paint in the middle. "You know this stuff is expensive."

"Sorry. Do you want some help?" he offered.

That only earned him a derisive look. "In those clothes, really? Just stay back, I've got this."

She did in fact, pooling the paint back into her pan from the piece of the plastic she had torn out. As she did the paint color, which had started out as a light grey, seemed to warp as it pooled, flashing over a dozen colors.

"What kind of paint is that?" he asked. He came closer, cocking his head to the side as he studied it. He caught her glancing sideways up at him, but before he could make more out of it, she gave the plastic one last squeeze.

"Crystalline paint. We'll be able to change the walls to whatever color or pattern we want once it's applied. It's something Maddie always wanted to do." She shoved the roller into the paint, rolling it hard, which made the sand-sized crystals in it flash more colors. She went back over to her ladder and climbed back up to keep painting.

"You know, there is a technological version of something like that."

"Interesting," she said, uninterested.

He watched her attack the wall for a few more minutes, leaning against the bar patiently, admiring how her front jiggled with the force of her labors. As he expected, she could only stand the scrutiny for a few minutes. The moment her tense shoulders dropped and she began to turn around to snap something at him, he said, "I would have thought you would have thrown the money Maxamillion paid you at your mortgage instead."

That derailed whatever else she was going to say and he bit the inside of his lip to distract from the guilt he felt playing that kind of game on her. But it wouldn't serve his purpose if he let her continue to be mad at him. He stretched his smile instead.

"If the bar falls apart it doesn't matter if I keep up on the mortgage," she said. "Now, will you stop playing games with me and start telling me why you're really here. Is it another job for the illustrious resistance group masquerading as a corporation?"

He double blinked and felt his cheeks actually grow hot. So much for being a cool, smooth spy. A small voice in the back of his head informed him he liked that she saw right through him and he told that voice to get the hell back in the corner.

"I came to talk. About what happened." Her painting slowed. "I meant what I said about having lied to you about why I've been keeping my distance. I want to fix that now."

"Oh gods, this isn't high school." She rolled her eyes.

"It wasn't because of you. It's because of me."

"Bringing out all the clichés, aren't you?"

Oh, this was getting frustrating. St. Benedict straightened and tapped his foot more comfortably in his dress shoe while he tried to force a breath in to calm himself down. Yelling at her wasn't going to help. He had to do better this time.

"You know, this is getting typical, St. Benedict. I ask you a simple straightforward question and you stare at your shoes. I...."

"You make me want to tell you everything!" he shouted. He could hear himself shouting. He turned once in place as if that was going to help him maintain control. Instead, he gave a strained laugh, "That is really bad for a spy."

"I heard you the first time!"

"But I have to tell you...I have to tell you something and it's really hard and...I need you to let me get to it, okay?"

"Fine. What do you want to tell me?" She had come down from the ladder. The light made her look like a paint splattered angel.

"I don't. That's the problem. I don't want...." Okay this was getting worse. He turned his back and leaned both hands against the bar to stare at them, like it was his hands' fault. His heart was beating too fast. Her smaller hands appeared next to him, also holding the bar, supporting herself as she leaned in so she could look at his face.

"St. Benedict, I'm not going to hurt you. You're safe here." Why did she have to say that?

"I don't....I don't...." He couldn't say it.

"What?"

"I don't want you to know."

"Is this about you shooting Dr. Clausen? Because you've done something that you think I would think is unforgivable and you don't want me to see you differently than I did before?" she supplied. "Would it help for me to say that I won't?"

He chuffed a laugh. "That's not true. You do see me as.... You see me for what I am. I am...evil. A necessary evil. If you knew half of the truth...."

"Oh my gods, get over yourself, St. Ben." She shook her head. "If I can forgive Calvin for almost killing me, I think I can accept the fact that you have some darkness in your past. You either tell me about it or don't. But I got things to do, and I'm not waiting around." It sounded to him like she was going to move off and yet she stayed put, doing exactly that. Waiting.

"What Dr. Clausen said, about Masterson being dead, we don't know that he was telling the truth. He could still be alive…."

"No, he's dead," Rune said with certainty. Then she shook her head. "I hear what you're saying. I mean we have no proof one way or another, but…let him be dead. Wherever he is, he had no intention of coming back. So, let him stay there. I'm ready to move on." She said it with such certainty and confident serenity, that any other words died on St. Benedict's lips.

"That's the last thing I expected you to say."

She smiled and patted his arm. "Besides…and I don't mean I'm going to do this right away, but I think I'm ready to move on to other people, who actually care about me. Not just some phantom from my past."

When he didn't respond she asked, "Was that what you wanted to tell me?"

"We can't be together," St. Benedict started too fast, but she cut him off.

"I know that." Rune shook her head. "You're a walking heartache, St. Benedict. I don't know if you mean to be or not, but I've had plenty of heartache in my life to know what it looks like. I know what it feels like in a body. So, you're right, we can never be a thing like that, because I'm not interested in living in heartache again."

He looked down, his head heavy as lead. "I didn't intend…."

"To hurt me, I know. No one ever does." She sighed. "Alright, Saint of Liars, you want to know the truth? Is that what you're waiting for? I loved him, and I'm pretty sure I fell in love with you too. I don't know what people have to do to have that kind of feeling returned but I recognize that maybe those aren't the cards in my life."

"Don't believe that," he said shaking his head, uttering the words as if they would cut his mouth to say them, "Please don't…."

"No, you don't." She nailed him with a look. "I'm tired of being embarrassed and ashamed because I feel something like love for someone. Love is supposed to be a good thing and here I am feeling it." She slapped her hands in unison on the bar. "You know what, I don't care. I got life to live and I'm not going to wait around for it. If you're not onboard for being around me or being my friend then…."

He grabbed her hand, stopping her from walking away. She didn't understand. How could he make her understand? How could he do it and not hurt her? Not tell her the truth?

"I can't be with you, but I can't leave you alone either. I don't… reject you for loving me, that's not what this is."

"Let me go, St. Benedict. Whatever you're telling yourself…I don't care!" Tears rushed down her cheeks and she turned away. He *had* hurt her.

"No!" He shouted without meaning to. He scrambled up to grab both her arms. What was he doing? He should just let her go. "Please, Rune, you have to understand."

"I don't have to understand anything," she said. She was right. He knew she was right, that he was messing this up, but it hurt too much to stop. He engulfed her in his arms and held on. She could hit him if she wanted, fight to get away, he wished she would. He'd take all of it. It was what he deserved.

"Please, Anna."

That stopped her and they both froze. He hadn't meant to say it.

"God," he whispered into hair smelling of paint and fruity shampoo. He could feel her shuddering as she tried to force a breath. She was crying. "I can't….I can't be with you, but I am sure as hell not leaving you. I'm going to be here. I'm going to protect you and be your…your friend. I mean it. You can tell me any secret, tell me how you're feeling, tell me…tell me you've fallen in love with someone else and I will be there, smiling. Helping you, happy for you. I…."

"Why did you call me Anna?"

He couldn't catch his breath. "Because….it was…what you…."

She pushed back a little bit. "Why did you call me Anna?"

Those eyes were going to end him.

"Because that night when you told me…. It changed everything I knew about you and what that meant. I can't unsee you now."

"I don't understand."

"I didn't want you to be her."

She double blinked, something new was sinking into her mind and he watched it infect her understanding. God what was he doing?

"You mean…. Now that you know I'm Anna Masterson…I am the wife of the man you hate?"

"Yes," he said. He loosened his grip on her and let her pull back from his arms.

"The man that killed your wife?"

"Yes, in a matter of speaking, but also not. Kodiak is responsible for my wife, but I let it happen. I know that, but when I look at you…." *You make me forget,* he wanted to say.

She winced and looked away a moment, chewing on her lower lip. "You just see her?"

St. Benedict coughed and checked his shoes. "Look, Rune, here is the truth and I'm sorry, but my wife…I swore to her…." Realizing what he had decided to say, he dug at his collar, tearing the buttons of his shirt in his desperation. He had to make her understand.

Finally, he gripped the silver of the necklace and yanked it out hard, the Saint Box swinging free. "This is my secret. That's what this is, my pledge. I pledged that I would remain faithful for the rest of my life to her, to my wife, and no matter how I might otherwise feel, I will stand by this pledge."

Rune stared hard at the box, processing. When she tried to catch the box with into her fingers, he reflexively pulled it out of her reach.

"Please don't," he said, his heart pounding. He tucked it away.

"What's in it?" she asked.

He hesitated. "I'm not supposed to reveal that to anybody. There are certain conditions tied to the spell on the box that…."

"Wait, wait. Spell?"

"Yes, these things are enchanted," he confirmed. Here it

was. The truth. "Rune, I didn't become a Saint by choice. I was made this way." He took off his fedora and set it carefully on the bar. He wouldn't turn away from this. With a trembling hand, he ran his fingers through the side of his hair, pulling it away from his scar. Then he took her hand and set her fingers to it. She gasped softly, but did not pull away.

"What is that?" she whispered.

"When Kodiak was done with me, I was sold into a program for creating modified humans. Not just spies; secretaries, accountants, mistresses. I was a prime candidate. They used any means possible to…enhance us. Including magic. Kodiak isn't the only company trying to accumulate magic users and magic items for their own use. These boxes, they are designed to keep us loyal to whomever our master is.

"That's…." Rune looked appalled.

"They call it corporate serfdom, mostly for marketing reasons, if they talk about it at all. Prime candidates tend to be people who are out of other choices, like I was. In exchange, we get to be guinea pigs for the latest technological or magical enhancements."

He laughed, his throat dry around the sound. He had never told anyone this, not even Malachi. St. Rachel knew, only because she had been through the same painful process.

"I think that's why I chose the vow I did. A kind of fuck you to the powers that be. They didn't care for that, but the magic doesn't work unless it can hold something the subject really, sincerely believes is precious as collateral. So, becoming celibate, it was kind of a fuck you to myself as well."

"And Maxamillion is your master?"

He blinked. "Yes, more or less. For the sake of satisfying the spell, but it's more apt to say that he liberated St. Rachel and I. We were owned by people with less honor or cause. When he acquired us, our loyalty went to him."

He looked down at the box in his hand. "Our masters are supposed to hold the boxes. Maxamillion gave ours back to us, all according to his principle about the right of freedom. This is as close as a Saint can ever get to it. Sometimes he keeps St. Rachel's because she asks him to. She goes back and forth on that, but I wanted to wear mine. To remind me. It doesn't matter anyway. According to the spell, we have to obey our master or we suffer excruciating pain and eventually death."

"That kind of magic is illegal," Rune said, staring hard at the lump now under his shirt.

"A lot of things are illegal, and yet here I am."

"But how could Maxamillion do that?"

"It's the spell that does it. We have to have a master or the spells would kill us anyway. We tried a few times to have them broken, but the Wizardress Maxamillion consulted explained that it was unbreakable as far as she knew."

"And your vow is to remain celibate forever."

"Essentially. It's what I wanted, yes."

He could see the gears shifting in her head. "As a corporate spy?"

"It was a very tough vow to make," he conceded. "I have to toe the line a lot, but I have kept my vow as I specified."

"You kissed me." She crossed her arms and crooked an eyebrow at him.

Oh crap, I did.

"I'm not perfect. Some of the lines get…blurry."

"Like kissing?"

"Sure. Like you said being a spy comes with a degree of…'sexy requirements' and…I mean, there's a lot you can do without actually…." he gestured nonspecifically with his hands.

Rune laughed. "Oh gods, your face is so red!" She laughed some more which made him squirm even more, but that smile was infecting him as well. "But how does that amount to you keeping your vow?"

"The magic is to keep me loyal and obedient, the vow is for me."

"I can see why you hate magic so much." She stared off into the middle distance. "That's why we can't be 'just friends.'"

"Partners."

She double blinked. "What?"

St. Benedict pulled out a piece of paper from his pocket, unfolding it before handing it to her. "The Corinthe Corporation has requested that you be our magical liaison between our resistance and the coalition we are trying to build between us and the Magic Guild. Your ties to the Faerie Court are also a plus. Comes with a retainer. I would be your direct opposite, assigned to you and representing the interests of the resistance."

She looked at the paper, a formal letter written by Maxamillion stating exactly what St. Benedict had just said, but he let her have time to peruse it all the same. After she had a couple of times, she looked up at him.

"What do you say?" His heart was beating too hard.

"Hmm. I guess I'll have to let you know," she replied and set the page on the bar. Then she turned back and picked up her paint roller. "You wanna grab that one over there? It's on a long stick so if you start in the opposite corner, we might be able to meet in the middle?"

She climbed her ladder and set to painting again.

He went and grabbed the pole like she said, shifting his hat back on his head and sliding his sleeves up to the elbow.

"So, how about all those other secrets? You going to tell me those too, now that we're just friends?" she asked.

"What do you want to know?"

Meet the Author

Megan Mackie is a writer, actor, podcaster and playwright. Besides writing, Megan is currently running a satirical podcast called the Princess Peach Conspiracy, about how all of the Super Mario Bros games are really a conspiracy by Princess Peach to keep the war economy going. You can hear it on iTunes, Stitcher, or GooglePlay. She also likes to knit, play games involving dice, and getting into feverish discussions about why the live action Beauty and the Beast is better than the animated version. She lives in Chicago with her husband and children.

Curious about other Crossroad Press books?
Stop by our site:
http://store.crossroadpress.com
We offer quality writing
in digital, audio, and print formats.

Enter the code FIRSTBOOK
to get 20% off your first order from our store!
Stop by today!

Made in the USA
Lexington, KY
29 April 2019